THE PASSION OF MOLLY T.

Some find faith in love, and some in fury. Molly Turner's sure belief sprang from anger, hurt, and revenge for betrayal. She saw the world divided, not between the haves and have-nots, but between the ares and are-nots.

Her spiky temper would not permit compromise. If Ann Harding wanted to launch a political campaign for a Federal law decreeing capital punishment of all convicted rapists, Molly wanted to execute every rapist personally.

Her passion fed itself. But instead of enlarging, it imploded and condensed, becoming something hard, impervious, and without mercy.

As the Christmas season approached, Ann Harding made plans to return her family to Canton for a week. Unexpectedly, Molly Turner announced that she, too, would return home for the holidays.

'A couple of days around Christmas,' she told Ann. 'I haven't seen Mother in months.'

So the entire clan was reunited in Canton on Sunday, December 22. There was a big dinner, and later, they sat around and talked. They had drinks and coffee and idly discussed the 1992 election. Most agreed that Senator Dundee had the best chance to beat the incumbent.

'Over my dead body,' Molly Turner said.

THE PASSION OF MOLLY T.

Lawrence Sanders

NEW ENGLISH LIBRARY

First published in the USA in 1984 by G. P. Putnam's Sons.

NEL Open Market Edition 1984
Reprinted November 1984
First UK Edition January 1986

NEL Books are published by
New English Library,
Mill Road, Dunton Green,
Sevenoaks, Kent.
Editorial office: 47 Bedford Square, London WC1B 3DP

Typeset by Rowland Phototypesetting Ltd,
Bury St Edmunds, Suffolk.

Printed and bound in Great Britain by
Cox & Wyman Ltd, Reading

British Library C.I.P.

Sanders, Lawrence
    The passion of Molly T.
    I. Title
    813'.54[F]   PR3569.A5125

    ISBN 0–450–05835–2

AUTHOR'S NOTE

The following account of what has been variously described as a civil disturbance, an insurrection, a revolution, and a war of liberation has been assembled from a variety of sources, including:

– files, records, interval memoranda, and publications of the National Women's Union.

– records, news releases, files, and pertinent official documents of the US Government, including an appreciable quantity of classified material obtained under the Freedom of Information Act.

– newspaper and magazine articles of the period concerning the issues involved and events as viewed at the time they occurred.

– vidoetapes, especially those of news programs and special reports by investigative television journalists and war correspondents.

– personal interviews with members of the National Women's Union, including executives responsible for planning, operations, and administration, and rank and file individuals who served in the armed forces of the NWU.

– personal interviews with officials of state and federal governments who participated in the confrontation. They included executives, legislators, and military personnel.

No claim is made that the following represents a definitive account of events that occurred in the United States of America during the period concerned. But I hope this early record may prove of value to future historians since the memories of interviewees were still fresh and many significant documents not yet filed and forgotten.

I wish to express my appreciation to the William P. Berger Foundation for a grant making possible the research and writing of this report. I am particularly indebted to the executives of that organization without whose generosity, patience, and understanding this book would not exist.

Lawrence Sanders
NEW YORK CITY, 1993

THE PASSION OF MOLLY T.

MARCH 3, 1987

Canton West Virginia (Pop: 12,242), is an attractive town located on the Ohio River northwest of Charleston. It is primarily a farming community with some light industry including a factory that produces ponchos for the US armed forces.

In 1987, Canton had a chapter of the National Women's Union with a membership of fifty-eight. The president, and founder, was Norma Jane Laughlin, a woman of thirty-eight who worked as chief librarian in the Canton Free Public Library. She was unmarried and had moved to Canton from Lexington, Kentucky, where her family still lived.

Laughlin was a chunky, vital woman with absolute faith in the tenets of the NWU. She was an activist, and had led her organization in several successful feminist campaigns which had, incidentally, endangered her employment in the town of Canton.

For instance, the NWU had triumphed in legal proceedings that resulted in women being accepted in the police and fire departments of Canton. A brothel had been put out of business by the simple expedient of stationing NWU members outside the door to take Polaroid photos of entering customers. And an abortion clinic had been established that had withstood several court trials and the wrath of local Catholics.

But these victories had their price. Originally treated with amused contempt, the Canton chapter of the NWU was now viewed with open hostility by most of the town's citizens. Norma Jane Laughlin was proud of the fact that public scorn (expressed in newspaper editorials, anonymous letters and phone calls, and obscene insults on the street) had resulted in the resignation of only four members.

On the evening of March 3, 1987, a chapter meeting was planned, to be held in the basement of the First Canton Unitarian Church. Business to be conducted included the induction of two new members and discussion of a campaign to force the Board of Education to allow girls to play on the Canton High School basketball, baseball, and football teams.

The meeting was organized and chaired by the chapter's executive secretary, Molly Lee Turner.

Turner was thirty-two, single, employed as head teller at the Farmers and Mechanics Bank. She had been born in Canton, and lived with her mother in an ample, casual home on Hillcrest Avenue in the 'old part' of town. Her younger sister, Ann, twenty-eight, was married to Sergeant Rod Harding of the Canton Police Department.

Turner was the first member to be recruited by Norma Jane Laughlin when the local NWU chapter was organized in 1983. She had proved herself fearless and assertive. Her zeal for the feminist cause made her invaluable as second-in-command.

Molly Lee Turner and Norma Jane Laughlin were lovers.

The meeting was called to order at precisely 8:30 PM. Minutes of the last meeting were read, the treasurer reported on the current state of the chapter's finances (cash on hand: 3,479.27), and Molly Turner, speaking without notes, delivered a ten-minute account of the status of several ongoing campaigns.

The two new members were then inducted, and the meeting was temporarily adjourned while cocoa and oatmeal cookies were served.

When members reassembled, Molly Turner broached the subject of bringing legal action against the Canton Board of Education to allow girls to compete for positions on the high school athletic teams. A lengthy and spirited debate ensued.

While the proposal was generally approved, one member took the floor to question if any young girl would want to play football since it was a rough contact sport frequently resulting in serious injuries.

President Norma Laughlin then rose to speak for the first and last time that evening. She said that whether or not girls wanted to play football was of no consequence.

'It's the principle that matters,' she said. 'They must have the right of choice.'

When all who wished to speak had their say, Molly Turner brought the discussion to a close. In her energetic, sometimes profane way of speaking, jabbing a stiff forefinger at her audience, she said the NWU would be on firmer legal ground if the suit were brought on behalf of some girl who desired to play on a high school athletic team and was not allowed.

She urged members to search out such a girl, or girls, and submit their names.

'It would be damned tough to prove,' she said, 'that the NWU is suffering because of the sexist policy of the Board of Education. What we need is a bona fide victim of that policy. Let's all try to find one.'

The meeting was then adjourned. It was approximately 10:45 PM. The women chatted while they donned fur coats, caps, scarves, boots. It had snowed heavily the previous day, and many streets and sidewalks had not yet been cleared. The temperature was in the mid-20s.

Outside, most of the NWU members scurried for their parked cars, calling offers of lifts home to those without transportation. But perhaps a dozen women, including Laughlin and Turner, tarried a few moments on the lighted church portico, discussing how many would be able to attend that year's national convention.

It was a sharp, still night, the air as piercing as ether. Streetlights cast a mustard glow on the road where ice

11

sparkled. The black, pollarded trees on the church lawn wore hats of snow like chefs' toques.

While the women chatted and laughed, a dark pickup truck turned the corner at the end of the block and cruised slowly down the street. It drew to a stop in front of the church. The window on the driver's side was cranked down, an empty whiskey bottle came sailing through the air to crash into splinters on the stone steps.

The women gasped, drew back. They peered at the truck. Later, witnesses could not agree if it was occupied by one, two, or three men. But someone inside shouted obscene curses at the NWU women on the portico.

Molly Turner stepped forward.

'Go fuck yourself!' she screamed.

Almost immediately there was a gunshot. They saw the flash: orange-red. They heard the bullet strike the stone arch over the church doorway. Norma Jane Laughlin crumpled into a furred heap. Her knitted hat flopped off. The other women stood dazed, trembling.

The pickup truck roared, accelerated, sped away, bumping and slewing on the rutted street.

Molly Lee Turner went down on her knees beside the slack bundle.

'Norma Jane?' she said in a low voice. 'Darling?'

She smoothed the dark hair. Her hand came away wet and glistening.

Late in 1982, following the defeat of the Equal Rights Amendment, seventeen women assembled at the Americana Hotel in New York City. They came from all over the country, ranged in age from eighteen to fifty-six, and all were ardent feminists.

Although each was already a member of one or several women's organizations, they were bitterly dissatisfied with the strategy and tactics of those groups. They felt that by deciding to work within the existing establishment, feminist associations had been preempted by the establishment.

Further, they believed it hopeless to expect progress toward feminist goals by seeking to increase the female electorate. And as for lobbying male-dominated legislatures on the state and national levels—that was staking their future on the generosity of their enemies.

Therefore, over a period of three days, in disputatious debates that sometimes lasted until dawn, the seventeen women resolved to form a new sisterhood to be called the National Women's Union. The noun 'Union' was selected because, it was agreed, it expressed more militancy than 'Association,' 'Organization,' 'Society,' or 'League.'

A 'Declaration of Liberation' was drafted and signed that set forth the aims of the National Women's Union. These included the follo wing:

– Equal pay for comparable work

– Federally funded day-care centers

– A military draft of men and women alike

– A minimum wage for housewives

– A law mandating 50 percent of all appointive offices in local, state, and federal governments be held by women

– The legal right of lesbians to adopt

– Federally funded abortions for women on welfare

– The right of divorced women to share their ex-husbands' pension, retirement, and Social Security benefits

And several other goals of a controversial nature.

While many, or all, of these aims were included in the platforms of existing feminist organizations, the National Women's Union intended to achieve them through more forceful methods. They acknowledged themselves extremists, and planned to make use of the techniques of revolution.

For instance, they did not abjure the use of boycotts, mass demonstrations, picketing, sabotage, acts of terrorism, and physical violence. Although assassination as a way of furthering their cause was not openly discussed at the Americana meeting, several women who were present have

13

stated that it was implicitly approved.

For the first four years of its existence, the National Women's Union was chiefly involved in organizing and soliciting sufficient funds to set up national headquarters in Washington, D. C, and chapters in all the fifty states. These last, in turn, established branches in large cities and county seats in rural areas.

During this period of initial growth, a weekly newspaper, The NWU Call, came into existence, and annual state and national conventions were held. Membership grew slowly but steadily; slowly because the NWU deliberately kept its profile low until its leaders felt the Union strong enough to begin an aggressive nationwide campaign to achieve its goals.

However, from 1982 to 1986, state and local units were encouraged to initiate their own campaigns for the purpose of combat training and to gain experience in the kind of bold, daring actions the NWU espoused. ('Combat training' is typical of the military terminology frequently used in NWU internal directives and on the pages of The Call.)

The president during these formative years was Mrs Laura Templeton, a widow from San Francisco and a woman of intense revolutionary fervor. In 1982, she was forty-eight years old. Prior to devoting full time to the NWU, she had successfully operated a truck leasing service inherited from her deceased husband.

By the end of 1986, the National Women's Union had almost a hundred thousand members, a nationwide organization with several state, city, and county chapters, and adequate cash reserves.

Mrs Templeton and her staff decided the time was right to make a start on their radical program. Militant operations for the entire country were planned, to be presented to the national convention set for July 15, 1987, in Chicago.

But on March 3, 1987, Norma Jane Laughlin was killed in Canton, West Virginia.

MARCH 5, 1987

Headquarters of the National Women's Union were in a dull, brutish office building on Northwest H Street in Washington, DC. The NWU occupied the entire fifth floor. Offices of the executives were Spartan (furnishings were secondhand), and most of the space was assigned to the editorial staff of *The Call* or given over to membership files, copiers, and addressing machines.

President Laura Templeton had a corner office, although the view from her windows was not prepossessing. Furniture included a battered desk, squeaking swivel chair, wooden file cabinet, two sprung armchairs, a worn leather couch for visitors. A single philodendron struggled.

Templeton was a tiny, snappish woman who favored flowered print dresses with high lace collars. A fragile body disguised a muscular spirit and a determination almost obsessional. She was a gifted orator with a booming voice that belied her size.

At 11:00 AM, she met with Constance Underwood, the NWU executive vice-president. Underwood, flicking rapidly through a sheaf of newspaper clippings, telegrams, and telex printouts, brought the president up-to-date on the latest information available on the death of Norma Jane Laughlin.

'That's it,' she said flatly, slapping the folder shut. 'Killed by a ricochet shot from a rifle fired by person or persons unknown. I think we should send a telegram to the Canton chapter expressing condolences and offering all possible assistance, financial and otherwise.'

Templeton thought a moment. 'Yes,' she said, 'do that. What was the woman's name?'

'Norma Jane Laughlin.'

'Yes, of course. And send a copy of the telegram to West Virginia headquarters. They should be kept informed

15

on what we're doing. Find out when the funeral's going to be and send flowers. Let all the chapters know so they can send flowers, too.'

'Right.'

The two women were silent a moment, gazing at the walls.

'Connie,' Laura Templeton said finally, 'it was a stupid, senseless death. Probably some liquored-up rednecks looking for trouble, ready to pull the trigger on a spanking new hunting rifle – just to try it out, you know.'

'Probably,' Underwood said. 'Something like that.'

'It's getting good media coverage?'

'Yes. Very heavy. In the New York and Washington papers. The *Today Show* is covering it, and I heard this morning that *20/20* may run a segment.'

'Uh-huh,' Templeton said. 'I lay awake last night thinking about it. There's a way we can make that sister's death meaningful. What would you think of launching our national campaign immediately? We've got public sympathy. The things we plan will be seen as justified retaliation for a brutal murder.'

Constance Underwood hesitated an instant. 'Yes,' she said. 'We could do that.'

'A lot of work,' the president warned. 'In a short time.'

'We can do it,' Underwood assured her. 'Everyone's fired up over this.'

'Good. Let's get cracking. I think the first step should be a press conference: a strong statement of outrage from me followed by a question-and-answer session. I'll write the statement. You set up the conference.'

'I'll get on it right away,' Underwood promised.

She turned, headed for the open door to the corridor.

'Connie,' Laura Templeton called, 'what was the sister's name?'

Underwood turned back, face strained in a tight smile. 'Norma Jane Laughlin,' she said. 'Laura, that's the second time you've asked.'

16

The president stared at her a long moment. 'Close the door,' she said. 'Come back in and sit down.'

The executive VP did as commanded. She sat in one of the lumpy armchairs alongside the desk.

'It's my memory,' Templeton said angrily. 'I've covered it up by making a lot of notes. You didn't notice, did you?'

'I never did,' Underwood lied. 'Laura, we all forget occasionally. I sometimes – '

'No, it's more than just a lapse. It started about a year ago, and it's getting worse. Yesterday I couldn't remember the office telephone number. Soon I'll be forgetting your name. Then mine.'

'It can't – '

'Yes,' the little woman said with a grimace of distaste, 'it's that bad. A month ago I went to my doctor, and then to a neurologist, and then to a specialist, and then to another. Didn't you wonder why I was gone from the office so frequently?'

'Laura, I thought it was business.'

'It was – my business. There's no use in getting more opinions. Everyone agrees. It's Alzheimer's disease.'

'Oh my God.'

'No known cause,' Templeton went on relentlessly. 'No known cure. Gradual deterioration and then death. But they tell me I should be able to function for a few years before I become a vegetable. A year or two – possibly.'

Underwood was silent.

'I can do a lot in a year or two. Get us started on everything we've planned. And by God, I'm going to do it!'

'Of course you are. Laura, are you sure . . . ?'

'I'm sure. I know it's happening. But meanwhile I'm going to get this show on the road. And you can be a big help.'

'Anything. You know that. Anything!'

'I'll be depending on you more and more. First of all, this is strictly between you and me. No one else is to know.

17

Not even that nitwit you sleep with. Promise?'

'I promise.'

'And I want you to ride herd on me, Connie. Remind me when I forget. Tell me when I'm acting foolishly. Review all my statements before they're released. Shield me from situations I can't handle. I hope to God I'll have enough sense left to step down voluntarily when I can no longer hack it. But if I'm too far gone to do that, I want you to call an Executive Board meeting and kick my ass out of here. Will you do that for me?'

'Yes,' Constance Underwood said stonily, 'I'll do that.'

MARCH 6, 1987

There were several men in Canton, West Virginia who believed in the NWU and what it stood for – though none had the courage to voice their opinions publicly. But they made anonymous cash contributions and provided what private counsel and assistance they could when it was requested.

One of these men was Sergeant Rod Harding of the Canton Police Department. He was married to Ann, Molly Turner's younger sister, and was a frequent visitor at the Hillcrest Avenue home where Molly lived with her mother, Mrs Josephine Turner.

The three Turner women had dinner together on the evening of March 6. Rod Harding, off duty, arrived after they had finished. But they had kept food warm for him: a plate of hot dogs, beans, sauerkraut, pumpernickel with sweet butter, and two cans of Budweiser. The women sat around the wooden kitchen table with Harding, drinking coffee while he ate and talked.

'They're releasing the body tomorrow around noon,' he said to Molly. 'Have you made arrangements?'

'Hutchins' Funeral Home,' she said. 'They'll do the embalming. We picked out a casket today. We'll have a

18

small service here, and then Hutchins will drive the coffin over to Lexington. Her family has a plot there. Ann and I and some other women are going for the funeral.'

'Who's picking up the tab for all this?'

'The NWU,' Molly said. 'We got a telegram from national headquarters.'

'Isn't that nice!' Mrs Turner said.

'Rod,' Ann said, 'will you be able to come to Lexington with us?'

He pushed his empty plate away, lighted a cigarette, popped the tab of his second can of beer.

'Sorry, honey,' he said. 'I can't. I'm still on the investigation, and now is not the right time to take a day off.'

They knew it wasn't that, but they understood. He couldn't afford to display his sympathy.

Harding was a hefty man with craggy features and thick, sandy hair. A tangled blond mustache drooped from a long upper lip. He had small, dark eyes that squinched when he was thinking, pondering a reply.

'It was a rifle bullet,' he told them. 'At least we're almost sure it was. Thirty caliber. But it got banged up some when it ricocheted off the stone. We're sending it to the FBI to make sure, but I'm practically certain that's what it was – thirty-caliber rifle.'

'Great,' Molly said bitterly. 'That narrows it down to a million thirty-caliber rifles in Canton County.'

'Something like that,' Harding admitted. 'And the same for dark pickup trucks. Molly, wasn't there *anything* you remember that might help?'

She shook her head. 'I told you, Rod, it was dark, and the whole thing happened so fast no one had a chance to really *see* anything. Someone cursed us from the truck, I cursed back, and then *bang*!'

'Would you recognize the voice if you heard it again?'

'Probably not. It was just a man shouting.'

He sighed. 'Well, we're not giving up yet. You know, Eddie Holloway was first on the scene, and after he called

19

for assistance and an ambulance, he did something real smart for once in his life: he gathered up all the pieces of that broken bottle he could find. We sent them to Charleston to see if the lab guys there can lift some prints.'

'How is that going to help?' Ann asked.

'Well, it'll help if we can match them with some local who's been in trouble with the law. We'll have his prints on file. It's a long shot, I admit, but the only one we've got.'

They were silent then. Mrs Turner rose and began to clear the table, moving around the kitchen with little trotting steps.

She was a chirpy bird of a woman, fifty-eight, with a rosy complexion and wide, surprised eyes. She had been deserted by her husband soon after the birth of Ann, and had put both her daughters through college by working as bookkeeper at the supermarket on Rush Street and renting out rooms in her big home.

'Rod,' Ann said, 'if you had to guess who might have done it, who would you say?'

'Oh honey,' he said, putting a hand on her shoulder, 'I can't make a guess like that. There are a dozen cruds in town who are capable of it. I mean real rubbish who could kill and not lose a single night's sleep.'

'I'll make a guess,' Molly said sharply. 'I guess the Lemson brothers. They're the two biggest pigs in town.'

Sergeant Rod Harding looked at her, but said nothing. They all moved into the cavernous living room, leaving dishes stacked in the sink. They sat in a close circle for almost an hour. Harding packed and smoked a pipe while the women talked in low voices about the planned service, the casket, the funeral.

Mrs Turner volunteered to help pack up the dead woman's clothing and belongings so Molly and Ann could take everything back to Lexington. Ann said she thought they should rename their NWU group the Norma Jane Laughlin Chapter. Molly said that was an excellent idea,

20

and promised to submit it at the special meeting scheduled to elect a new president.

The Hardings left at around 10:30, and Molly and her mother cleaned up the kitchen. Then Mrs Turner kissed her daughter and said she was going to bed. She was still working at the supermarket although they could have managed on Molly's salary and the income from a few small investments.

'Don't stay up too late, dear,' she called as she stepped briskly up the carpeted stairs.

Molly went to the kitchen to make certain the back door was bolted and chained. She checked the side door leading to the wraparound porch, and the front door lighted by an outside bulb that would remain on all night.

She left one light burning in the living room, then went into a squarish chamber that had once served as her father's den. Molly now used it as an office for NWU activities. It was sparsely furnished with items discarded from other rooms in the house: rolltop desk, fringed lamp, wooden typing stand with an ancient Remington.

She kept a pint bottle of California brandy in the bottom desk drawer. She uncapped it and took a small sip. It warmed. She slouched in a worn upholstered chair and put her feet up on the desk.

After the first day, the numbness she had felt at Norma Jane's death had faded, to be replaced by an anger so corrosive that sometimes she feared she might start screaming and never be able to stop.

Curiously, this rage so infected her that it left little room for memories of Norma Jane's sweetness and strength, of the pleasures they shared in each other's body, of their laughter and their love. Her fury blotted out all that: A red curtain had come down on the past.

It seemed to her that she could not endure a life of such continuous frenzy, for surely it must consume her. Reason said that her wrath must be put to work, given a creative outlet. But, she admitted, she was beyond reason. She

21

wanted to rend, stomp, kill, pluck the sun from the sky, and bring to an end a world that ignored the evil that had been done by continuing to exist and going blithely about its business.

She tasted a little more brandy, brooding. After a few moments she rose and began to rummage through a narrow closet set into an interior wall. Originally it had held her father's gun collection, his hunting gear, odds and ends of his rackety life.

When Jason Turner had deserted his wife and infant daughters, he had left no note, made no farewells. He had simply walked away, leaving all his personal belongings – but remembering to clean out his bank accounts the morning prior to his disappearance.

The fact that the manicurist at Phil's Barber Shop had disappeared at the same time made it obvious what had happened. Josephine Turner endured the town's smirks and smarmy commiseration with a set smile. Would they have believed her if she had told them she was happy to see the last of her husband? The man was a fool and a brute.

Someone at Josephine's bridge club told her that after seven years, she could consider the absent Jason legally dead. She believed this, and in her fey way, she waited for seven years to pass, making no effort to locate her errant spouse. At the end of that period, having heard nothing from or about him, she sighed with relief and sold off all of his clothing and personal possessions.

Fortunately, the Hillcrest Avenue home was in her name. It had been her daddy's, and Josephine had been born in the upstairs front bedroom.

Jason's gun collection had been sold. His wife, now alone with two young daughters, kept back one revolver on the advice of the omnipotent bridge club. They convinced her that a single woman living with two young ones needed the protection afforded by a revolver.

'Just point it and pull the trigger, honey,' they advised her.

It was this gun that Molly Turner now sought in the den closet. She finally found it on the top shelf, tucked back into a corner, wrapped in a grease-stained towel. Handling it gingerly, she brought it back to the lighted desk.

She uncovered it carefully. It had wooden grips and a long barrel. The metal parts were rusty, and there was verdigris around the bullets in the cylinder. It looked like an antique dug from some ancient battlefield. It even smelled old.

She didn't care. It was a weapon.

MARCH 9, 1987

Constance Underwood, executive VP of the NWU, considered herself a rational woman. She was capable of cold analysis of a problem, judicious weighing of the options available, and decision unaffected by prejudice or emotion. She was, she told herself, always in control.

Still, she acknowledged, that control faltered in her relations with young Billy McCrea. He was, as Laura Templeton had said, a nitwit. But when they were naked in bed together, she felt a kind of befuddlement, and surrendered to it. That sweet, warm fog.

The press of his lips was a song remembered. The scent of his hair, breath, skin, was familiar and dear. He was habit and something more. She knew herself foolish with want.

So anger fueled her passion. She surrendered to her fury, wanting to punish herself, her suppliant flesh. Her body betrayed her, and she strained him close, and felt her tears start. That hateful need, that treacherous bliss.

God had spent six days creating him: crisp, reddish curls, face sculpted with elegance, suede skin, neck and shoulders of soft strength, carved thighs, tight calves. Even his feet were beautiful. But then, on the seventh day, scheduled for wit and sense, God had rested.

Connie dreamed of murdering him. To destroy her weakness. She could not endure shame.

She was a dark, stretched woman, skin olive, hair long and black, parted in the middle, falling about her coffin face in glossy wings. The secretaries at NWU headquarters called her 'Iago.' There was menace in her manner, scorn in her eyes. If she was not liked, or even respected, she was feared.

She finished a joint while she watched Billy McCrea dress. Everything he wore she had bought for him, either as a gift or with cash. But he didn't belong to her alone; she knew that. It was part of the shame.

He sat on the edge of the bed, took the roach from her fingers, puffed, handed it back.

'Hey,' he said, 'you're awful quiet.'

'Thinking,' she said.

'Well . . . yeah,' he said, 'that's cool. You busy – huh?' She nodded.

'That crazy union of yours?'

'I may soon be president of that "crazy union."'

'No kidding? That's super. Will you get a raise?'

She didn't bother answering. She took him as she found him, telling herself that if he had brains, he'd be dangerous. That divine physique was peril enough.

'See you,' he called brightly, waving a hand and giving her a sunshine smile.

When he was gone, she rose to bolt and chain the door. Then she went into the bathroom to wash him away.

Constance Underwood may have been the wealthiest member of the National Women's Union. A large inheritance was augmented by a generous monthly allowance from her husband. He lived on the Costa del Sol with an Italian creampuff.

She lived in a hard, sleek apartment in the Watergate Complex and kept a summer home near Plum Point. She drove a bright red 1971 Jaguar XK-E roadster and bought her clothes at designers' boutiques in Manhattan. She employed a daytime maid, and a hairdresser, manicurist, and a masseuse made weekly house calls. So did Billy McCrea.

She came out of the bathroom in a thick terry cloth robe and sat at her high-tech desk. She donned reading glasses and flipped through the file drawer until she found a roster of the current Executive Board of the National Women's Union.

The eleven members of the Board were elected for four-year terms by the entire membership of the NWU. Their constitution required that all members of the Executive Board be presidents of state chapters. The Board elected a president to serve a two-year term. The only requirement for president was membership in the NWU.

Originally, it had been intended that the Executive Board would set policy, plan operations, determine the future course of the Union. The president they elected would be, in effect, a manager, administering the Board's edicts.

But things didn't work out that way. Members of the Board were busy with the affairs of their state chapters. Gradually, the president they elected came to be chief executive, legislative, and judicial officer – with more power than anyone had anticipated.

With Laura Templeton as president, there had been few complaints. She had ruled wisely and firmly, solicitous of the Executive Board's prerogatives and couching her directives to the membership in discreet terms that made commands sound like requests.

But now Laura Templeton was dying – and even before her death might become so incapacitated that the Executive Board would be forced to relieve her of her duties. Then a new president would be elected. Constance Underwood, forty-two, and unfulfilled, saw no reason why that title and those powers should not be hers.

She studied the roster of the current Executive Board, recalling each woman, her appearance, manner, predilections, aversions. She put a tick to those names of members she was reasonably confident would support her ambition to succeed Templeton.

There were four she could count on. There were three who, from personal dislike or from past injuries (real or imagined), would never give her their vote. And there were four who were up for grabs. They would determine the outcome.

With increasing excitement, Underwood began to plan her campaign to sway those uncommitted four: personal letters, visits, phone calls, gifts – all the favors she could confer. She was no stranger to politicking. Quid pro quo was the first law of nature.

Late at night, having filled three pages of notes, she sat back and treated herself to a small Cointreau. She was amused by her own arousal. Remembering what she had felt with Billy McCrea, she wondered if there was not an element of sexuality in ambition.

She was still pondering that when she went to her bed, smelling his scent on the pillow and smiling with content.

MARCH 10, 1987

Rod Harding had served eight years in the US. Army, including two tours in Vietnam. He didn't sign on for another hitch, but came home to Canton, joined the police department, and used his army savings to buy a two-family house on Juniper Street.

Then he married Ann Turner, and they took over one-half of the house (with separate entrance) while Rod's aged parents, Luke and Cecily Harding, occupied the other half. They insisted on paying rent.

'You're going to get it all anyway when we're gone,' they told their only child. 'You might as well have some now when you can enjoy it.

The close but separate domiciles made for peaceful

coexistence. Ann got along with her in-laws as comfortably as Rod got along with his. At least once a month all the Hardings and all the Turners had dinner together, and sometimes a game of pinochle.

On the evening of March 10, following such a dinner at Ann's home, she, Molly, and Rod moved into the kitchen to do the dishes, leaving the older folks in the living room to watch Benny Hill on television.

'If we had a dishwasher,' Ann said, not for the first time, 'we could do this job one-two-three.'

'You've got a dishwasher, honey,' Sergeant Rod Harding told her, tying an apron around his waist. 'Me.'

He ran a pan of soapy water and began to scrub and rinse with quick efficiency, filling the drain rack. Molly did the drying while Ann wrapped and stored away leftover food.

'Those pieces of broken bottle we sent to Charleston,' Rod said. 'Well, they lifted two good prints and a bunch of partials that are no use to us whatsoever. A lot of guys handled that bottle.'

'What about the two good prints?' Molly demanded.

'Yeah, we matched them. One belonged to Ben Brightcastle, and the other was Sam Lemson's.'

'I told you it was him,' Molly said furiously. 'Didn't I tell you it was?'

'Well, we don't rightly know that,' Harding said mildly. 'Sure, his prints were on the bottle, but so were Ben Brightcastle's and a lot of others. According to Sam, that night of the meeting he, his brother Aaron, Ben, and a few other rednecks were drinking up a storm in the office of the Lemson Lumberyard. You know – that place down near the river. Well, Sam says they were passing bottles around, and sure, his prints would show up. He says the party broke about ten o'clock or a little later. He claims he and Aaron stayed right there because they wanted to go over their books. He says Ben Brightcastle and the others split, taking some bottles with them, which was okay because they had brought them. He swears that he and Aaron worked at the lumberyard till almost midnight, then went to bed in the apartment they got over the office. I saw their place. A real pigpen.'

'Bullshit!' Molly burst out. 'He's lying.'

'Could be,' Harding said. 'But Aaron swears to the same thing. And so does Ben Brightcastle and the other three guys who were there. Ben and the others claim that after they left the drinking party at the lumberyard, they drove out to the Stagger Inn on the Turnpike and had some drinks there. The bartender says yes, they were there that night, but he can't rightly recall just when they came in. Around ten-thirty, he guesses. Ben and the others swear they were nowhere near the Unitarian Church.'

'Honey,' Ann said, 'why don't you check to see if any of those animals owns a thirty-caliber rifle or drives a dark pickup truck.'

'Why that's a marvelous idea,' he said mockingly. 'Come on, babe, what kind of cop do you think I am? Of course I checked. The Lemsons' pickup is white. Mud-splattered but white. Ben Brightcastle owns a green job that might look dark at night. The others don't drive pickups. The Lemsons have a twenty-two rifle, a shotgun, and three handguns. Brightcastle has a little bitty pistol but no long-barrels. One of the other guys admits to owning a three-oh-eight Browning, a thirty-two carbine, and a forty-four semiautomatic Magnum. That guy could start a war by himself. But all that doesn't amount to a bucket of warm piss. Any of them could have owned a thirty-caliber rifle and hidden it or ditched it in the river after the shooting.'

'What does that mean?' Molly said angrily. 'The end of it?'

Harding dumped the soapy water, washed out the sink, then dried his hands slowly on a hand towel. He took off the apron. The women, motionless, watched him, waiting patiently for his reply.

'Well . . .' he said, 'it's still open. We'll keep digging

and trying to shake some of those alibis. But right now, the only hard evidence we've got are those two prints on broken pieces of bottle. That's not enough. We're a long way from an arrest that'll stand up.'

'Rod,' Ann asked quietly, 'do you think the Lemsons are guilty? And maybe Ben Brightcastle, too?'

'Not Ben,' he said quickly. 'He's a slimy little wimp, but he's just not the type to pull a stunt like that – firing a rifle at a bunch of women. Maybe he just went along for the ride. But yes, Sam and Aaron Lemson are capable. They've got no sense, and they've both got a mean streak and short fuses. They're always ganging up on one guy in a roadhouse brawl or running someone they don't like off the road. I'd love to put both of them away for a long, long time. But the law demands proof, and that we ain't got.'

'The law,' Molly said scornfully. 'Some law when drunken bastards like that can kill an innocent woman and go scot free.'

Harding shrugged. 'That's the way it is. Eventually they'll get what they deserve. These things have a way of working out. Meanwhile, what say we move into the living room and get a hot pinochle game going.'

'Not me,' Molly said quickly. 'I've got to get home and write some more letters of thanks. Do you know, condolence notes are still coming in from NWU members all over the country. I'm trying to answer them personally, but it's a big job.'

'I could help,' Ann offered. 'Give me a batch and I'll answer them.'

'Thanks, sweet,' Molly said, smiling and touching her sister's long, chestnut hair. 'But this is something I want to do myself. Rod, will you drive Mother home later?'

'Of course.'

'Ann, thanks for the feed. You still make the best pot roast in town. And the buttered noodles were scrumptious. I'll be talking to you.'

She made her farewells and drove back to the Hillcrest Avenue home in her little red Le Car, listening to Willie Nelson singing 'Stay a Little Longer' on the radio. The streets of Canton were deserted and still. She thought she saw a few snowflakes glistening in the halos of streetlights.

At home, she went directly to the den, got her father's ancient revolver from the closet, and unwrapped it from the greasy towel. She put the gun in her shoulder bag and left the house. She made certain the front door was locked behind her and the porch light was on.

All her actions since leaving Ann's home had been sure, almost mechanical. She had the detached feeling of an actor playing a role rehearsed many times before: no wasted movements, no need to question motivation or fear failure.

She drove along streets that still held plowed snowdrifts in the gutters. The sky was clearing, chilled by a peel of lemon moon. It didn't take long to find River Street and follow it south until she came to the Lemson Lumberyard. She went slowly past.

At the end of the block, she maneuvered the little Le Car in a U-turn and headed north past the lumberyard again. This time she noted the office, lighted behind drawn green shades. She parked two blocks away in the black shadow of a warehouse and walked back, footsteps crunching on crusted snow.

She stood across River Street, staring at that lighted office a long time, not feeling the cold. Occasionally she saw shadows passing behind the shades. Two people in there. Maybe more. It didn't matter.

She felt nothing special. No hysteria, no exaltation, no exploding resolve. Just her anger burning and a job to do. She never faltered. Her fingers dug into her shoulder bag to grasp the wooden grips of her weapon . . .

. . . As a heavy shoulder shoved into her back, knocking her off-balance. Rod Harding's hand slid down to her wrist, yanked her fingers from the shoulder bag.

30

'What the fuck do you think you're doing?' he said wrathfully.

'I was just – ' she started.

'I know what you was just,' he said, voice hard and furious. 'You come with me.'

He clamped her arm just above the elbow. Even through the sleeve of her parka she could feel the pressure. It hurt. He marched her a block south to where his five-year-old Buick Regal was parked on a side street. He thrust her in, pushed her over to the passenger seat, got in beside her.

He started the engine, lowered the window an inch, turned on the heater.

'You have no right – ' she began weakly.

'Shut up,' he said.

He snatched her shoulder bag away, pulled out the old revolver, examined it in the dash light.

'Beautiful,' he said. 'Last fired at the Battle of Bull Run. You shoot this thing off, and there goes your fingers, your hand, and maybe your face.'

'I don't care,' she said. 'I just don't care.'

'That's your balls talking, not your brain.'

'How did you know I'd be here?' she demanded.

He deliberated a moment. 'Ann's idea,' he said finally. 'She told me to follow you. She said you haven't been acting right since Norma Jane died.'

'I didn't think it showed,' Molly said bitterly.

'I didn't notice anything,' Harding told her, 'but Ann did. She's your sister, for God's sake. And boy, was she ever right.'

'I would have done it,' Molly said defiantly, 'if the two of you hadn't interfered.'

'Oh sure. And been behind bars an hour later. As an old infantry grunt, let me tell you what else you did wrong – besides packing a piece that might have blown your head off. First of all, you're driving that crazy little red car that people notice and remember. And you're wearing a bright orange parka that stands out like a sore thumb. And you

31

walk out of your house onto a lighted porch. People do look out of their windows occasionally, you know – even at this hour. Then you drive past the lumberyard twice. That was smart. And how were you going to get in the Lemsons' office? Knock on the door and say, "Hi there!" What would you have done if they hadn't unlocked? Shoot the door off its hinges?'

She was silent.

'Goddamn amateur,' he growled. 'You haven't got a clue have you?'

He bent toward her suddenly and kissed her cheek. Then he took a pack of cigarettes from the glove compartment and they both smoked awhile, staring at the blank windshield.

'It can be done,' he said reflectively, 'but it's got to be done right. We don't want to spend the rest of our lives in the clink.'

She turned to look at him. 'We?' she said. 'You said we. Does that mean you'll help?'

'Of course I'll help,' he said gruffly. 'What kind of a man do you think I am?'

MARCH 14, 1987

Lemuel K. Dundee had been a member of the United States Senate for nineteen years. For seven of those years he had been chairman or his party's ranking member of the Armed Services Committee. He was presently chairman – but that was likely to change after the election of '88.

For the past two weeks, the Committee had enlivened Washington with a rancorous debate over a bill that would appropriate almost two billion dollars for the development of the third generation of Cruise missiles. The Committee was almost evenly divided on the issue, and political pundits opined the outcome would hinge on the vote and influence of Chairman Dundee.

32

The senator had not revealed publicly how he intended to vote, though his plans were known to a few of his staff. But on March 12, a columnist of the *Washington post* had stated that Senator Dundee would support the controversial bill.

It was an accurate prediction, and Dundee was furious, having received a great deal of media attention by keeping his plans secret. There had been leaks from his office before, but none of this magnitude, and he was determined to discover the source.

So Dundee called in Thomas J. Kealy, an executive assistant who supervised the senator's staff of fifty-eight and was responsible for internal security. Kealy was assigned the immediate task of ferreting out the leaker. He reported on the morning of March 14, standing at attention before the ornate oak desk in the senator's private office in the Hart Senate Office Building.

Lemuel K. Dundee looked right at home in that high-ceilinged, richly furnished chamber. All the 'antiques' were reproductions – and so was Dundee. His thick mane of white hair, the fleshy, rubicund face, stentorian voice, and charm as thick as sludge were throwbacks to an era when senators debated gunboat wars and Indian treaties.

'All right, Tom,' Dundee boomed, 'did you find the son of a bitch who leaked?'

'Yes, sir,' Kealy said, heavy horn-rims firmly in place, black hair brushed sleekly. 'It was you.'

The senator stared at him, then leaned forward in a favored posture, palms down on the desktop.

'What?' he roared. 'The hell you say!'

'No, sir,' Kealy said. 'On March eleventh you had a late lunch with Senator Hufnagle at Le Gré, and – '

'And he gave it to the *Post*? I'll cut his balls off!'

'No, sir,' Kealy said patiently. 'Senator Hufnagle respected your confidence. It was the waiter. He was serving the onion soup when you told Hufnagle. He overheard and ran for a phone. He got paid for the tip.'

Dundee slapped the desk, then sat back and roared with laughter, shaking his leonine head, wiping streaming eyes with blunt knuckles.

'Shit,' he said finally, 'an old hand like me getting caught in a dumb stunt like that. This town is all ears and tongues. I should have known better.'

Kealy agreed, but didn't say so.

The senator took a deep breath. 'Well, what the hell, it's not going to kill me. Sit down for a minute, Tom; something I want to talk to you about.'

Kealy moved around to a leather club chair alongside the senator's desk. Dundee rose, then turned to stare at the dull scene outside his window. He stood with his hands thrust into his trouser pockets, his back to Kealy.

'You bored, Tom?' the senator asked suddenly. 'With your job?'

'Sometimes,' Kealy said.

'Me, too. More and more. Seems to me I keep doing the same things over and over, year after year. Debates, horse-trading, votes, bills passed, bills defeated. And all the bullshit with the reporters and the good folks back home. The whole thing's getting to be a chore. It's no fun anymore. I'm really not enjoying it.'

'Maybe you need a vacation, sir.'

Dundee turned slowly to face his executive assistant. 'No, Tom, I don't think that would help. I'd just have to come back to this pissmire again. I think what I need is a new job. Something to stir me up and get the sap rising again. What the hell, I'm still a relatively young man. Not ready for Social Security yet.'

'Majority leader?' Kealy suggested.

'Not a chance. I've made too many enemies, and those wetbrain northern liberals still think I'm in favor of lynching blacks and turning the country over to the oil business. What I've been thinking about is making a play for all the marbles. What do you think?'

Kealy stared at him. 'The presidency?'

34

Dundee nodded. 'The big brass ring. Not next year, of course. Too late. But in ninety-two. Think I'd have a chance?'

'Everyone has a chance,' Kealy said cautiously.

'Come on, Tom, cut the crap and tell me what you really think. You're the first one I've mentioned this to. I haven't even breathed a word of it to Martha. Look, nineteen years ago I came to the Senate, a barefoot lawyer elected on a fluke. I admit it. People didn't vote for me, they voted against my opponent. During the campaign, the shithead was stupid enough to announce his wife was suing for divorce. That finished him, and I found myself in Washington. It didn't take me long to discover that successful politicians tailor their principles to fit their ambitions. Well, I tailored mine, and I think you've got to admit I've made a damned good record. I've gone to bat for the blacks, women, old folks, Indians, labor, the gun lobby, doctors, big business, environmentalists, and every other bunch of hard-ons who swing any weight and are willing to put their money where their mouth is. I'm ready to run for president on my voting record as a senator. Sure, I've made mistakes – but no big ones.'

'No argument there, Senator, but . . .'

'But what?'

'Well, sir, you're not exactly a national figure. You're known in Washington, Congress, and the media as a hard worker, a man of influence who gets things done. But you're not known around the country. We can run a name-recognition poll if you like, but I wouldn't advise it.'

Dundee slammed a meaty hand down on the desktop. 'Tom, you're absolutely right. I've got everything a presidential candidate needs: I can speechify as good as anyone in Congress, I've got a churchgoing wife, three photogenic kids, and two lovable grandchildren – the little bastards! – my background is clean, and my voting record in the Senate is as good as anyone's. But you're right as rain – no one knows who the hell I am. Tom, I need an issue, a big issue. Something I can ride the hell out of, and get my name and picture in every newspaper and on every TV news program in the country. I need like a – like a – what's that word? Like some kind of a big reform or program?'

'A crusade?'

'Exactly!' Dundee cried, slapping the desk again. 'I need a big, fucking crusade. Something new and different. Something that'll make me famous and talked-about. Look what the organized crime hearings did for Kefauver. Tom, I know you're a clever lad. I want you to give this problem some thought and see if you can come up with a strong, original crusade for me. We've got about three years to make the name Lemuel K. Dundee known in every one of the fifty states, and maybe all over the so-called civilized world. If we can't do that, I might as well forget about the White House and stick to my knitting. Will you give it a shot?'

'Of course, Senator. I'll do my best.'

'Good boy. And I don't have to tell you, if I do decide to make a try for the jackpot, you'll have a key position in my campaign.'

'I appreciate that, sir.'

'And I know I don't have to warn you – not a word of this to anyone. And especially not to the waiter at Le Gré!'

Both men laughed heartily, and Kealy rose to leave. But he turned back at the door.

'Senator,' he said, 'I heard something the other night that may interest you. Are you familiar with the National Women's Union?'

'Of course,' Dundee said. 'They're a pain in the ass. The most persistent and obnoxious lobbyists I've ever had to deal with.'

'Uh-huh,' Kealy said, 'that's the NWU. Well, I heard the other night that they're getting a new president soon. My information comes from a reliable source. I don't know how you can use it, but they've been in the papers a lot lately with that shooting in West Virginia.'

The senator thought a moment, then shook his head. 'I don't know how I can use it either, Tom. But you never know. See if you can find out more about it – who's taking over, who her friends and enemies are, if this means a change of direction for the NWU, etcetera.'

'Will do, sir. And I'll give a lot of thought to that other problem.'

'My crusade,' Lemuel Dundee said, savoring the word. 'A sensational issue, Tom, but not *too* sensational.'

'Yes, sir,' his executive assistant said, smart enough not to smile.

Thomas J. Kealy was the son of Senator Dundee's old law partner. After Kealy had been graduated from law school but had twice failed the bar exam, his father had obtained a job for him on the senator's staff. Kealy moved to Washington, DC, and found a basement apartment in Georgetown.

He started in as a gofer for Dundee, was moved up to publicity and public relations, became an expert on polling, and was finally promoted to executive assistant. There were four other EAs, but they had specialties: legislation, constituent relations, research, campaign contributions.

Thomas Kealy had labored hard to become supervisor of the senator's staff and Dundee's closest confidant. He worked long hours without complaint, his loyalty never faltered, and he developed a sly cunning in senatorial infighting that Dundee relished and appreciated.

During this steady advancement, Kealy took time off to marry Theodora Birnbaum, only child of a retired colonel of the US. Army. Senator Dundee was highly pleased with the match, since he had been having a little trouble with the Jewish lobby after voting for reduced aid to Israel.

About two years after the marriage, Colonel and Mrs Birnbaum were killed in a plane crash in the Pyrenees. Their only child inherited everything, including almost a million dollars' worth of tax-exempt bonds and a fine house in Alexandria, where Mr and Mrs Thomas Kealy now lived, although he still kept his Georgetown apartment for nights when the press of work made sleeping over in Washington easier than the long drive home.

Kealy had married Dori because he thought she was the cutest woman he had ever met. She was only about five feet tall, with a great pair of knockers. She wore ribbons in her hair, blushed, and talked to her houseplants. Kealy thought she was delightful.

After five years of a childless marriage, Thomas found Dori's cuteness beginning to pall. She filled their Alexandria home with dogs, cats, gerbils, tropical fish, and exotic birds. A small stable was built for a spavined gelding, and the main house was so choked with plants that Kealy sometimes felt he was living in the Mato Grosso.

At about the same time that he began to realize his wife's intellectual tastes would never exceed Barbara Cartland novels and paintings by Norman Rockwell, Thomas J. Kealy made another discovery: he enjoyed the intimate companionship of men more than that of women.

His first homosexual experience followed a Georgetown party, and he blamed his 'fall' on drunkenness. Succeeding encounters were made while sober, and he came to accept his predilection without guilt or shame. He also spent more nights sleeping over in the Georgetown apartment. His wife commiserated but did not complain.

'You work tho *hard*, Tommy,' she said with the slight lisp he had once thought enchanting.

If Senator Dundee had learned to tailor his principles to fit his ambitions, Kealy learned to tailor his physical needs to fit *his*. He knew that promiscuity – cruising – would endanger his career. And he really had no desire to form a lasting emotional relationship with a bed partner. He called all this calculation 'discretion.'

He had several unsatisfactory affairs, and then he found Billy McCrea.

On the night of March 14, Kealy and Billy shared a joint and drank a bottle of Côtes du Rhône in the Georgetown apartment. Then they went to bed, and Billy earned his fee.

Later, watching the younger man dress, Thomas Kealy marveled at his own good fortune. Not only did McCrea, in his mindless way, seem content with the payment and gifts he received, but he never demanded protestations of undying affection. He treated their relationship as something akin to that of doctor and patient: friendly without being too familiar. Just the way Kealy wanted it.

And if that wasn't sufficient, McCrea's body was a work of art that was delightful just to observe. It moved Kealy in a way he could not quite comprehend. Admiration of beauty, of course, and physical desire. But something more, too.

Vaguely, Kealy thought of it as 'living warmth.' And it stirred regret in him, hinting of a dimension lacking in his life. There was heat there, growth and softness. There was feeling, and a world of blood and tenderness that Kealy might glimpse but never know.

'Billy,' he said dragging his mind away from such dismal thoughts, 'the woman you told me about – the one who's going to become president of that women's group . . . Have you seen her lately?'

'Tomorrow,' McCrea said, pulling on the cashmere cardigan Kealy had given him. 'Tomorrow's her day. She always calls in the morning, and we have a date at night.'

'Is she nice?' Kealy asked.

'Yeah, she's cool. Got a great pad. A real tough lady – you know? She's nice to me, but I don't think I'd like to work for her. I mean, she can be a driver. You can tell that.'

'She'll probably turn that office of hers upside-down when she gets to be president.'

'Probably,' McCrea said indifferently.

'Billy, I've got a reporter friend who's working on a story about the feminist movement and all the women's groups that are politically active. He pays for information.

39

If you could find out more about your, uh, client's plans, I'll bet you could pick up a nice couple of bucks.'

'No kidding?' McCrea said. 'I can always use more green. I'm buying a sterling silver tea service.'

'It's nothing that would hurt the woman,' Kealy said earnestly. 'And she'll never know where my friend got his information.'

'Okay,' McCrea said placidly. 'I'll see what I can pick up.'

'Don't ask her directly,' Kealy warned. 'Just get her talking and listen.'

'Sure, I can do that. You want to see me on Friday?'

'I'll give you a call.'

'That's cool,' Billy McCrea said.

MARCH 22, 1987

Three small incendiaries exploded simultaneously at approximately 3:30 AM. They fed serpentine trails of kerosene spilled around and onto stacks of dressed timber, sheds, sawmill, garage. Within minutes the Lemson Lumberyard was burning fiercely, flames reflected in the black river, a glow rising in an overcast sky.

Samuel and Aaron Lemson awoke from a drink-dulled sleep in their apartment above the office. They peered out the window to see a fire, fanned by gusty winds, sweeping over everything they owned. Sam grabbed up the phone; the line was dead.

Both men, wearing only long johns, plunged down the staircase to the office. They exited by the front door, Aaron leading by two steps. He hit the trip wire stretched across the outside stairs. The resulting explosion killed both Lemsons instantly, flinging their broken bodies aside.

At the time of the bombing, Molly Turner was sitting with her sister and brother-in-law in the darkened living room of Ann's home. They were too far away to hear the explosions, but, at about 3:45 AM, they heard the distant hoot of fire truck buffalo whistles and the sirens of squad cars.

'That's it,' Sergeant Rod Harding said. 'I expect that in fifteen minutes or so I'll get a call telling me to report in. They'll want every man available on this.'

'Rod,' Molly said, 'where did you get all that stuff?'

He laughed quietly. 'Most of it from the police locker in the station house. We got a chicken wire cage in the basement. All kinds of things in there – stuff seized in arrests, raids, evidence, lost-and-found, and so forth. We've got dynamite, TNT, fuses, weapons, ammo, drugs, and even some bootleg whiskey. And no lock on the door – can you believe it?'

'No inventory?' Molly asked.

'Supposed to be one, but it's not kept up. And what there is, I doctored. They'll find bits and pieces of the timers and fuses, and they'll figure out how it was done, but no one will guess it all came from the police locker. The wire and kerosene they'll never trace. Everyone's got some of that stuff. We're home free.'

'You sure, honey?' Ann asked nervously.

'I'm sure,' he said, his hand finding hers in the darkness. 'We've got nothing to worry about. Especially you and Molly. No one's going to believe women had the know-how to frag a couple of guys with a cute setup like that.'

'It's not Molly and me I'm worried about; it's you.'

'No sweat,' he said lightly. 'I made sure no one saw us going or coming. It was Nam all over again. I guess you never forget tricks like that.'

'I still wish we could have done it some other way,' Ann said.

'You're not feeling sorry for them, are you?' Molly said.

'No, but . . .'

'Look, babe,' Harding said gently, 'if it'll make you feel any better, they were guilty as hell. I leaned on Ben

41

Brightcastle, and he finally spilled. He said that on the night of the shooting, Sam and Aaron Lemson left the drinking party to buy more booze. They took one of the half-empty bottles with them, and borrowed Brightcastle's pickup 'cause theirs was low on gas. When they came back, they were all excited and told the others what had happened. Aaron was driving, and Sam did the shooting with a Springfield he had bought from a farmer over near Ravenswood. The Lemsons told the others what to say if they were questioned, and Sam said he was going to throw the Springfield in the river. Brightcastle told me all this, and I believe him.'

'Then why didn't you arrest the Lemsons?' Ann said.

'Because Ben said he would refuse to testify, and if he was forced, he'd lie his heart out and say he knew nothing about it. He said if he testified, he was afraid the Lemsons would kill him. They would have, too. Those were bad men, honey, and they deserved what they got. Now why don't you see if you can rustle us a belt of that good sour mash without turning on the light. I think we can all use it.'

They heard her fumbling around in the kitchen.

'Hey, brother-in-law,' Molly said softly in the living room. 'Was that the truth – what you said about Ben Brightcastle telling you what happened?'

'Nah,' he said, just as softly. 'I made it all up. But Ann had to know positively that the Lemsons were to blame. She's not as hard as you and me.'

'Right on,' Molly said. 'Rod, will you teach me how to handle a gun?'

'Sure. And how to make a bomb?'

She didn't hesitate. 'Yes,' she said, 'and how to make a bomb.'

The bombing of the lumberyard and the deaths of the Lemson brothers are generally acknowledged as the events that sparked the conflict. There were, of course, many other contributing factors.

In 1987, progress in the feminist movement had practically come to a standstill. As founders of the National Women's Union had predicted, women's organizations attempting to work within the establishment by legal means found themselves co-opted by the establishment. They became just another minority or special interest group, putting their trust in lobbyists and full-page ads in the New York Times.

The revolutionary fervor of young women had apparently waned; they seemed content with half a loaf. Also, economic conditions had improved following the depression of 1981 – 1983, and with jobs available, fewer women seemed willing to protest, picket, or even contribute funds to feminist campaigns.

Another factor, rarely mentioned, is that by 1987 most of the leaders active in the fight for women's equality during the 1960s and 1970s were older, their vigor diminished, their confidence blunted by many defeats. A headline in the Chicago Tribune *on December 11, 1986, told the story:* WHATEVER HAPPENED TO WOMEN'S LIB?

But discrimination against women still existed in 1987. The average female wage versus male wage was no higher than it had been ten years previously. The number of battered wives and sexual assaults against women continued to increase. The proportion of women in Federal, state, and local government offices remained ridiculously low considering the preponderance of women in the general population.

Progress had been made; no one denied that. But there was more to be done than had been done. And there were young women with resentments that ran too deep to be assuaged by 'equal pay for equal work.'

These women, while enjoying the benefits fought for and won by an older generation of feminists, were inclined to ask, 'Is this all there is?' and to scorn leaders who played politics and compromised. There was, in fact, a class of

43

young revolutionary women in 1987, many of them inarticulate, filled with vague yearnings, hoping only for a leader and a faith that might fulfill them.

The shooting of Norma Jane Laughlin was a one-day sensation that rapidly faded from public consciousness. But the murder of Samuel and Aaron Lemson revived interest. Newspaper and TV reporters freely speculated that the bombing was in retaliation for Norma Jane's death. People began talking about the NWU, and revolutionary young women sensed they had found their cause.

Analysis of the media for spring-summer of 1987 reveals a slow but unmistakable escalation of violence.

In Santa Monica, California, a group of NWU members attacked an accused rapist as he emerged from the courthouse, having been found not guilty. He was beaten so severely with sticks and clubs that he was hospitalized for three months.

In Indianapolis, Indiana, a gas station belonging to an alleged child molester was set afire and destroyed.

In Hartford, Connecticut, the owner of a bookstore selling pornography was dragged from the premises, stripped naked, and chased down a crowded thoroughfare while being pelted with garbage.

In these incidents, and many others, local NWU chapters claimed responsibility. A few arrests but no indictments resulted. In this respect, civic authorities seemed to be taking their cues from events occurring in Canton, West Virginia, where Molly Turner (elected president to succeed Norma Jane Laughlin) was leading her chapter to a new activism.

As Sergeant Rod Harding had predicted, investigation of the bombing of the Lemson Lumberyard and the deaths of the owners proved inconclusive. But if proof was insufficient to justify prosecution, the people of Canton were aware of what had happened. Like most residents of small towns, they 'knew' what was going on.

Their opinion of the increasing militancy of the local NWU chapter was confirmed when, late in April, Molly

Turner and an inflamed, shouting group of cohorts took over a meeting of the Board of Education which refused, with snickers, to consider the possibility of girls being allowed to compete for positions on Canton High School athletic teams.

Members of the Board were, in effect, held prisoner by NWU members for a period of six hours. Efforts by local community leaders to secure their release succeeded only after the Board agreed to debate the proposal at a public meeting.

Molly Turner led a large contingent of NWU members and sympathizers to that meeting. She spoke forcefully and eloquently, stirring her followers to noisy enthusiasm. At the end of the meeting, the Board of Education voted eight to seven to allow girls to compete.

Two nights later, the Hillcrest Avenue home of Molly Turner and her mother was attacked by a gang of masked men who broke windows with rocks, hurled bags of offal onto the porch, and peppered the walls of the house with birdshot.

A week later, the Stagger Inn on the Turnpike, hangout of most of the men suspected of the attack on the Turner home, was fire-bombed and burned to the ground. Three men were badly injured, and one eventually died of his wounds.

The clergymen of Canton pleaded for an end to the violence. But it did not end.

MAY 6, 1987

Virginia Terwilliger, a woodchopper of a woman, was president of the Maryland chapter and a member of the Executive Board of the National Women's Union.

She looked like the bullest of dykes, but had been happily married for fourteen years, had three children, and didn't take any shit from husband, kids, or anyone

45

else. Two hundred years previously she would have been potting Cherokees from the chinks of a log cabin.

She called Constance Underwood from her home in Baltimore, and talked in a loud voice that someone had once described as 'sounding like black gravel.'

'Connie,' she said, 'I'm coming to Washington tomorrow, and I want to see you.'

It was a command.

'Of course,' Underwood said. 'Lunch?'

'Sure,' Terwilliger said. 'Any place that makes a good martini. I'll call you when I get in. Listen, don't mention anything about this to Laura.'

'All right,' Constance said promptly'' 'I won't. See you tomorrow, Ginny.'

The executive VP of the NWU usually invited out-of-town guests to the Washington Club to impress them. But she knew Virginia Terwilliger was impervious to that kind of psyching. So she made a reservation at a new place in Chinatown that made a specialty of rare duck breast in ginger sauce.

Both women ordered the duck, but had two rounds of martinis first. And, as an appetizer, Ginny had a plate of prawns that she dipped in Chinese mustard with no discernible effect on her complexion.

'Listen,' she said, after the duck and wild rice was served, 'what's with Laura? I spoke to her the other day, and she didn't make any goddamned sense. Is she hitting the bottle?'

It was a moment, Constance Underwood later realized, that changed her life. Where did her loyalty lie – to Laura Templeton or to the NWU? Or to her own ambition, she might have added. She didn't hesitate.

'No,' she said, 'she isn't drinking. Ginny, don't breathe a word of this to anyone, but Laura is seriously ill. Alzheimer's disease.'

Terwilliger, slice of duck breast impaled on a raised fork, paused to stare at Constance.

46

'Shit,' she said. 'That's rough. How long has she got?'

'A year. Maybe two while she can function. Then it's all downhill. Her memory's already going. You noticed it. I'm doing everything I can to cover for her, but people are beginning to talk.'

Virginia Terwilliger continued eating. 'Goddamn it, I love Laura. What a kick in the ass. Well, no one's indispensable. I better tell the other members of the Board. I've *got* to. There's an election coming up in July. We may have to put poor Laura out to pasture and look for someone else.'

They spoke very little then until their plates of duck and rice had been emptied. They asked for more tea, and ordered pistachio ice cream and fortune cookies for dessert.

'You think I have a chance?' Constance Underwood asked suddenly.

Terwilliger didn't look up from her ice cream.

'For president?' she said. 'Maybe. You're not exactly Miss Congeniality with some of the Board. They think you're a cold, calculating bitch.'

'What do you think?'

'I think you're a cold, calculating bitch,' Ginny said, looking up. 'But that's all right – maybe that's just what the Union needs. You want the job?'

'Yes.'

'Then you better start doing some politicking.'

'Like what?'

Terwilliger gave her a sour grin. 'I don't think you need any advice from me. I've got an idea that you know exactly how to go about it.'

'Will you vote for me?'

Ginny pushed her empty plate away. 'You don't fuck around, do you? Well, I might vote for you – it depends. What do you think about what's going on in West Virginia? That Molly Turner in Canton. And the stuff they're pulling all over the country?'

47

'I'm all for it,' Constance Underwood said immediately. 'That's our whole reason for being in business, isn't it? To raise hell. Militant activism, even if it means physical violence.'

'Uh-huh.'

'But . . .'

'But what?' Terwilliger said sharply.

'These people are charging off in all directions. As you know, we were going to issue directives for a nationwide campaign at the Chicago Convention. Then, after the shooting in Canton, we decided to move up our schedule. Now the shit has really hit the fan.'

'It's getting us a lot of publicity.'

'Sure, it is – and not all of it good. What I'm saying is that proposed actions by local chapters should first be submitted to the Board for approval. That'll give us a chance at direction and coordination. If we don't have that, we end up with pure anarchy: every chapter running its own show.'

'Mmm, you may have something there. But local chapters have always had a great deal of independence. It's written in our constitution.'

'Certainly,' Underwood said, 'but now they're coming to the national organization for bail money. If the Board is going to pay the bills, the Board should have control of what's going on.'

'The Board?' Terwilliger said, amused. 'You mean the president, don't you?'

'The president is elected by the Board.'

'Oh my,' Ginny said with heavy humor, 'you *are* a sly one, aren't you? Want to be the NWU Hitler, do you? Well, you may have a point. I'll talk to some of the other members about it. Let's open our fortune cookies.'

The slip of paper inside Virginia's cookie read: 'You will live to see your grandchildren.' Constance was hoping hers would read: 'Your wishes will be granted,' or something like that. But her fortune read: 'Give to the Red Cross.'

Ginny said she had to get back to Baltimore. The two women parted outside the restaurant, kissing cheeks and promising to keep in touch. Underwood watched Terwilliger's cab pull away, then went back inside the restaurant and phoned Billy McCrea.

He said he couldn't make it that night, but he could manage to be at her apartment in an hour. She said that would be fine. The idea of sex in the afternoon excited her. She called the NWU office, said she had a splitting headache, and wouldn't be back for the rest of the day. Then she cabbed home to the Watergate.

'Oh wow,' Billy McCrea said later, 'you're really being the boss today, aren't you?'

'That's exactly what I am,' Constance said sternly. 'The boss. I pay the bills. You do exactly what I tell you to do.'

'Cool,' he said.

She had forgotten about passion in sunlight. At once innocent and depraved. It had the seasoning of guilt, and she had never wanted more.

His marvelous body glowed. Golden hairs burning on his thighs. Soft curves and musky hollows. Even the shadows steamed. She wanted to devour him.

'Hey,' he protested once. 'Hey!'

He was such a lovely thing. Such a hot, pulsing thing. Such shining magic. A tingling came from him to her, and she cursed him, saying all the words. She had one brief vision of their skins split, viscera mingling, blood mixing, hearts in a single pump.

Then, finished and sweated, she stared at him with glazed eyes, not seeing.

'Something happened to you today?' he said.

'Yes,' she said, pleased by his unexpected interest, 'something wonderful happened.'

She told him how she had taken the first steps toward a future that might prove so magnificent she could not imagine its limits. She said she had great plans. She said he would soon see her picture in the papers, her image on TV. She was on her way to power. Nothing could stop her.

He said nothing, but when his wine-wet mouth went down between her legs, she clutched his head to pull him closer, stared at the ceiling, and plotted how she might win the world.

MAY 21, 1987

Ronald Freed, middle-class, middle-aged, middle-brained, beat his wife for reasons he had never tried to fathom. All he knew was that striking her was a savage joy. The blows were against a world awry, doomed fortune, a desperate future.

Now his wife had gone back to her mother – again. But she would return – again. She would weep, and he would promise. But within weeks he would find some excuse – warm beer or cold coffee – and his fists would thud – again.

When the doorbell rang a little after 11:00 PM, he thought Clara had returned. But the woman standing on the porch was a stranger. She was pretty, with long chestnut hair.

'Sorry to bother you,' she said, smiling, 'but my car has stalled. I can't seem to get it started, and I wondered if . . .'

She gestured, and Freed peered beyond her to the street where a black Buick was parked, headlights on dim.

'Maybe you're out of gas,' he suggested.

'No,' the young woman said, 'I have half a tank. It just stopped. Can you help? Men are so much better at mechanical things than women.'

He couldn't resist that appeal.

'Well . . .' he said expansively, 'let's take a look.'

The woman turned, headed back to the car. Ronald

Freed followed. He had just come down the porch steps to the walk when a baseball bat smashed across his kidneys, sending him stumbling awkwardly, arms flung wide. A second blow knocked him facedown onto his newly seeded lawn.

The pain was so excruciating that he was certain he was going to die, wanted to die. But that wasn't the end of it; hard-toed shoes crunched into his ribs. The baseball bat came down again. And again.

'Ronald,' a woman's voice said, 'can you hear me? Nod your head if you can hear me.'

He tried to move his head.

'Ronald,' the voice said, 'don't beat your wife anymore. Ever. If you do, we'll come back and kill you. Do you understand that?'

His head moved.

'Kill you, Ronald. Remember that.'

He heard footsteps moving away, a car starting, accelerating. He lay there a long time, weeping, facedown on moldy earth. Finally, moaning, he got to hands and knees. He crawled up the steps, pulled himself erect by hanging on to the door jamb.

His body throbbed with pain. He realized with shame that he had wet his pants. He heard steps coming up the walk, but didn't dare look, fearing his attackers had returned. But then he heard his wife's soft, familiar voice.

'Ronald,' she said, 'I've come back. Whatever's happened to you?'

'Why Clara wants to go back to him, I'll never know,' Ann Turner said. She was driving. Molly, alongside, was lighting two cigarettes. She handed one to her sister.

'What else can she do?' she demanded. 'A woman of her age with no job skills. No money of her own. She's trapped. Worst of all, she loves that monster.'

'You think it'll stop?' Ann said. 'The beatings?'

'Oh, they'll stop,' Molly promised. 'Rod says he'll be

51

pissing blood for a month, but he'll be able to hobble around. Let the bastard suffer awhile.'

'You're so sure,' Ann said.

'Yes, I'm sure. Absolutely no doubts. Look, honey, you didn't have to help tonight. All you had to say was no. I could have found someone else.'

'I wanted to do it,' her sister said. 'It's not right that you should take all the risks.'

'Risks?' Molly scoffed. 'What risks? Rod planned it, and he hasn't steered us wrong yet. And, speaking of that hubby of yours, when the hell am I going to be an aunt?'

'Oh come on, not again. You know we've been trying. We both went to that fertility clinic in Charleston. Zip. We're both A-OK, but nothing happens.'

'I don't mean to be a nudge,' Molly said, touching her sister's arm. 'It's none of my business anyway. And it's not such a big deal.'

'I'd like kids,' Ann said wistfully. 'Two, maybe three. I better get started.'

'Whatever will make you happy, hon.' Pause. 'You know I love you, don't you?'

Ann glanced swiftly sideways.

'Of course I know.'

'Good. Sometimes I think I don't say it often enough. I didn't to Norma Jane, and it still bothers me.'

Ann drove Molly home to Hillcrest Avenue. Broken windows had been replaced, porch cleaned, outside walls patched and repainted.

Just before Molly got out of the car, Ann said, 'And I love you, too.'

Mrs Josephine Turner was in the living room, watching television and simultaneously crocheting an afghan. She looked up as Molly entered.

'Did you have a nice meeting, dear?' she asked.

'I didn't go to a meeting,' Molly said. 'If anyone asks, I've been home all night.'

'All right,' her mother said equably. 'There's Heavenly Hash ice cream and macaroons, if you'd like a snack.'

'I think I'll skip and go right to bed. I'm worn out. Will you lock up?'

'Of course, dear. Get a good night's sleep.'

Molly Turner undressed and got under a hot shower. She thought her helmet of tight blond curls smelled of smoke. So she washed her hair, then stood there, slumped, letting the water splay over bony shoulders and stream down hard flanks.

She wished Norma Jane were there, scrubbing her back. That bitch – dying on her like that. Deserting her. She knew that was an irrational, ignoble thought, but it came, it came.

She soaped her small, pointy breasts and wondered if she envied her sister. Ann was full-figured, but Molly decided she preferred her own tight frame. Ann might look like Juno, but she couldn't get pregnant. Molly had two abortions before she met Norma Jane Laughlin.

It was warm enough to sleep naked under a sheet and thin cotton blanket. Molly lay on her back, one hand behind her damp curls, smoked a cigarette, and stared at the starry sky through a half-open window. She thought of the night's events.

Walloping the kidneys of a wife beater had given her no charge. It was just something that had to be done. Do it, get it over with, and don't brood about it. The result was what counted. As Norma Jane liked to say, 'The only thing people remember is the score.'

God, how she missed her. What a strong, vibrant woman she was. Completely convinced that what they were doing was right. The only way.

'Sweetheart,' she said to Molly after a particularly wordy debate at an NWU meeting, 'all that was so much bullshit. We've got to get on with it. We can talk until we're blue in the face, but we're just preaching to the converted. Only action will get results.'

Molly Turner didn't want to read any more muzzy feminist tracts, discuss the historical position of women in society, or indulge in jargonized arguments about the psychological differences between men and women. She didn't need her consciousness raised.

She wanted to turn the world upside down, and could hear Norma Jane saying, 'You can do it, kid. But don't talk about it – *do* it!'

JUNE 7, 1987

Thomas J. Kealy had learned a lot since arriving in Washington, DC. One of his conclusions was that politics was a scurvy profession. Men and women of talent, ability, imagination went into the arts, industry, universities. Politics got the second-raters.

Look at his boss, Senator Lemuel K. Dundee. He was a venal opportunist with the label 'Mediocre' stamped all over his fat face. But that hadn't impeded his success. Why should it? In a society of lamebrains, an idiot could be king.

This cynicism (Kealy called it 'realism') didn't interfere with his working hard for his employer, respecting his shrewdness, and giving unswerving allegiance. There was his generous salary, of course, but Kealy really didn't need the money; his wife was wealthy, and he managed the family finances.

One reason for linking his future to that of a dolt like Dundee was that Kealy knew himself incapable of succeeding alone in the rough-and-tumble, backslapping, deal-making world of national politics. He could never be one of the boys.

But knowing that, he could still enjoy.the theater of politics and write his own role. He saw himself as a young éminence grise. He would be a string-puller, a puppet-master, and – if Dundee's outlandish presidential ambitions ever came to fruition – the power behind the throne.

So he took his duties and his loyalty to the senator seriously. And after hearing some interesting information from Billy McCrea, Kealy began to glimpse the outlines of a scenario that just might climax with Lemuel K. Dundee in the Oval Office and Thomas J. Kealy in a discreet cubbyhole nearby, making the world go 'round.

Sometimes Billy McCrea hurt Kealy physically, but he never objected. As a matter of fact, he loved it. One had to pay for one's joys in this world, he told himself, and the line between pleasure and pain was a very thin one indeed. More important, Billy, in his ingenuous way, had unwittingly become a source of potentially useful political intelligence.

Since early May, McCrea had been reporting on the power struggle within the National Women's Union, revealed in pillow talk with Constance Underwood. Billy was well paid for the information and, in his witless way, evinced no concern with how his tattling was to be used.

One result was a phone call from Kealy to the clipping service employed by Senator Dundee. Kealy requested newspaper and magazine clippings on all violent actions that had been linked to members of the National Women's Union.

The bundle of photocopics delivered exceeded his expectations. He was delighted with the quantity, of course, but even more amazed at what had been happening. Apparently he had stumbled, almost by accident, on something much larger and more important than anyone had yet realized.

After spending an evening reading through the clippings and typing out a three-page, single-spaced précis, he requested a conference with Dundee. He met with the senator on the morning of June 7.

As usual, Kealy wore his uniform: a three-piece suit of

navy blue worsted, white shirt with button-down collar, regimental striped tie, black wingtip shoes polished to a high (but not extreme) gloss. Hair brushed smoothly, trimmed neatly around the ears. Horn-rims in place. Breath deodorized.

He was not aware of it, but Kealy's face was an almost perfect political mask: a pleasant half-smile, candid eyes that rarely blinked, a long jaw of resolution, a mouth that was full without being loose. He had a vaguely professorial look, and possessed a laugh so hearty and infectious that no one guessed it had been rehearsed.

He handed the précis to Dundee and asked him to read it. He sat quietly and watched his mentor's lips move noiselessly. Then the senator looked up.

'Jesus Christ,' he said, startled. 'All this shit in three months?'

'Yes, sir. I had our clipping service do the research. It's possible you may be asked questions about this.'

'No sweat,' Dundee said. 'I'll give them the usual crappola. No one sympathizes more with the problems of women than I do, but at the same time I cannot approve of violence that results in the loss of life and the destruction of personal property. It is not the American Way.'

'That should do it,' Kealy said approvingly. 'But I think this thing is going to get bigger, Senator, and more serious. It may just prove to be that issue you were looking for to power a presidential campaign.'

The famous white eyebrows slowly rose. 'How do you figure that?'

'If it continues to grow in importance, and I think it will, you may find it politically profitable to come down hard on one side or the other, either for or against the NWU, before some other potential candidate picks up the ball and runs with it.'

Dundee swung slowly back and forth in his swivel chair. 'Mmm, you may be right, Tom. But it appears to me that if I jump in now, I stand a good chance of making a lot of friends and also making a lot of enemies. It looks like a no-win situation to me.'

'Not necessarily, sir,' Kealy said earnestly. 'The answer is in the numbers. That's why I'd like you to authorize a national poll on the issue. Let's find out how many voters are pro-NWU and how many are anti. When we have the bottom line, we can decide which way we go.'

'I don't know about that,' the senator said doubtfully. 'I learned a long time ago that you never pay for a poll unless you already know the outcome, or can word the questions to guarantee success. You really believe all those beatings and shootings and bombings are going to end up getting the headlines?'

'I do believe it,' Kealy said. 'It's an issue that's got everything: sex, violence, the war between men and women. All we've got to decide is which way to jump. A poll should tell us that.'

'Well, Tom, if you feel so strongly about it, I'll go along. Get your poll started. Take the money from the confidential fund. You handle it yourself, and keep my name out. The fewer people who know about it, the better.'

'Thank you, sir,' Kealy said. 'I really think this may turn out to be the crusade we're looking for. And by getting in on the ground floor, we can grab it before someone else does.'

JUNE 28, 1987

Virginia Terwilliger called on the 27th, introduced herself, and announced she was arriving the next day. On the 28th, she took a plane from Baltimore to Charleston. There she rented a car and drove over to Canton. She met Molly and Mrs Turner for the first time and happily accepted their invitation to dinner.

The three women ate in the kitchen. Molly had no

vermouth in the house, so Terwilliger had two straight gins before the meal. Then she ate enthusiastically, asking for seconds on meatloaf, new potatoes, and homemade cole slaw.

'Great food,' she told the Turners. 'Do you always eat like this?'

'Not as much,' Molly said dryly, and their visitor laughed.

'I've got a big carcass,' she said. 'It needs a lot of fuel.'

Mrs Turner insisted on cleaning up, so Molly took Virginia into the den. She brought along two small glasses and put out a new bottle of California brandy she had bought for the occasion. Without asking permission, Terwilliger took the worn upholstered chair at the desk. Molly sat on an old horsehair sofa.

The two women hoisted their glasses in a silent toast, sipped, then stared at each other curiously, inspecting.

'Well now . . .' Terwilliger said. 'You've been a busy little bee, haven't you?'

'Not busy enough,' Molly said shortly.

'I've kept up with what you've been doing through newspaper stories, but I suppose there were some things that were never reported. Were there?'

'Uh-huh,' Molly said.

'Tell me something – where did you learn all this? I mean, how to plan these actions and carry them off without a hitch?'

Molly considered a moment. She knew this woman was president of the Maryland chapter and a member of the NWU Executive Board, but she pondered if it would be wise to reveal what had been going on.

Terwilliger watched her, waiting patiently, and finally said ironically, 'Want to see my ID?'

'No,' Molly said, making up her mind. 'That's all right.'

She told the other woman everything, beginning with the shooting of Norma Jane. She related how Rod Harding had planned and assisted in the bombing of the Lemson

58

Lumberyard and the destruction of the Stagger Inn. Finally, she described the attack on Ronald Freed, the wife beater.

Virginia Terwilliger listened to this account with awed fascination. Then she rose, poured herself a full glass of brandy, began to pace heavily about the room.

'Son of a bitch!' she said, almost bitterly. 'We've been talking and talking and talking while you've been doing. Molly, this brother-in-law of yours, the cop – he couldn't be a plant, could he?'

'What the hell kind of a question is that?' Molly said angrily. 'Rod has endangered his job helping us. This is a small town, and sooner or later the word is going to get around, and he'll get fired. He knows that, but he's willing to help because he believes in what we're doing.'

'All right, all right,' Terwilliger said hastily. 'Don't get your balls in an uproar. I had to ask. There's no way you could have done all this without his advice?'

'Oh sure,' Molly said. 'We could have done it by ourselves and ended up behind bars. Not a single member of my chapter has ever been arrested, because Rod knows how to do things. He's ex-infantry, and he's loaned me a lot of army manuals. Look at this . . .'

She rose from the sofa, dug a pile of pamphlets from the closet to show Terwilliger. The booklets had titles such as *Guerrilla Warfare*, *Small Infantry Unit Tactics*, *How to Establish an Ambush*, *Street Fighting*, *Scouting and Reconnaissance*, and *Living Off the Land*.

'It's marvelous stuff,' Molly said. 'I've learned a lot. And Rod is teaching us how to shoot and how to make explosives from things you can buy in drugstores and hardware stores.'

'Wow,' her visitor said, impressed. 'He sounds like quite a guy. You say he's teaching you how to shoot. You've got guns?'

'A few. Not enough. We're planning to buy or steal more.'

'I wish you could do it without a man telling you how.'

'It's their game,' Molly said coldly. 'We've got to learn how to play it. I'll take help anywhere I can find it.'

Terwilliger made a gesture. 'I suppose so. The end justifies the means. Is that what you're saying?'

'Something like that.'

They were silent then. Molly sat stiffly, staring at Terwilliger, trying to puzzle out what she was after. This big woman hadn't come all the way from Baltimore just to chat about NWU affairs and exchange gossip.

'Are all your members involved in these actions' Virginia asked suddenly.

'No,' Molly said. 'They all take part in picketing and demonstrations and letter-writing – things like that. But when it comes to hard actions – physical violence – I figure only about ten percent are willing to take the risk. Rod says that isn't unusual. He says that in combat, officers and noncoms can depend on only about ten percent of their men. The others aren't necessarily cowards, you understand, but they hang back, they don't go forward until the ten percent take the lead, show the way, lead the charge. Then they are too ashamed to hang back. Or maybe they get caught up in the excitement and hysteria. Anyway, Rod says that if I have ten percent of my members who are brave, disciplined, and don't give a damn, then I can do anything I like.'

'Rod again. You really depend on him, don't you?'

'Yes.'

'Molly, you must know that other NWU chapters around the country have tried to emulate your exploits, and a lot of members have landed in jail. National headquarters has had to bail them out and pay for legal counsel.'

'They got caught,' Molly said. 'Bad planning. They didn't know what they were doing.'

'In other words, they didn't have a Rod Harding?'

'Yes,' Molly said with a small smile. 'Exactly.'

'Jesus,' Virginia Terwilliger said, looking at her empty

60

glass. 'I'm drinking like there's no tomorrow. I've got to get going if I expect to make my flight.'

'A small one for the road?'

'Sure. Why not?'

As Molly was pouring them short brandies, the other woman asked casually, 'Planning to go to the national convention?'

'Oh yes,' Molly said. 'I'm one of the West Virginia delegates. And four or five other members of my chapter are going, including my sister, Ann. I wish you could meet her. You'll like her.'

'I'll bet I will. You can introduce us in Chicago. Molly, are you a good speaker?'

'I do all right.'

'Are you nervous speaking before a big audience? Maybe a hostile audience?'

'Hell, no. I like to talk. I'm all mouth.'

'No,' Terwilliger said, 'not *all*. How would you like to address the convention?'

'Me? Why should they listen to me?'

'I might arrange it.'

'What would I talk about?'

'How you feel about the Union. How you've succeeded in all your campaigns in Canton. I'll send you some ideas that you can use, if you like. Putting them in your own words, of course.'

'What kind of ideas?' Molly asked suspiciously.

'Well, for instance, forming a paramilitary organization within the NWU. An armed cadre of that ten percent who are willing to risk their ass. Who will serve as role models and inspire the other ninety percent to start claiming their rights. Setting up a training system so all our chapters can learn what your brother-in-law is teaching you. Could you talk to the convention about things like that?'

'Goddamned right!' Molly Turner said hotly, springing to her feet. 'If we can get all the members feeling the way I do, there's no stopping us!'

Virginia Terwilliger drained her glass, rose, stepped forward, stroked Molly's cheek.

'"Tiger, tiger, burning bright . . . ,"' she said, almost sadly.

JULY 15-17, 1987

The historic Fifth Annual Convention of the National Women's Union was held in Chicago, Illinois. It was attended by 3,082 NWU members, of whom 937 were official (voting) delegates representing fifty state chapters, the District of Columbia, and Puerto Rico.

Conventioneers stayed at several hotels on Michigan Avenue. Formal meetings were held at the McCormick Place convention center. Activities were well covered by newspaper and magazine reporters, photographers, and feature writers. While no television station or network provided gavel-to-gavel coverage, TV crews filmed important speeches, debates, and votes.

President Laura Templeton wasn't certain she would be able to get through those three days without breaking. A fog was closing in, enveloping her. Each hour another memory, another part of her mind was lost in the mist.

The worst thing, the absolute *worst*, was to be aware of what was happening. Madness was one thing; then you were just gone and drifting, your make-believe world seemingly real and solid. But this creeping senility eroded the mind; you were victim and observer at once, watching the insidious decay inexorably reducing you to a lump.

This small, feisty woman had been a fighter all her life, first for her own independence and then for the success of the NWU. But now she was facing an enemy she could not fight, and hoped only that she might meet defeat with a rueful laugh – but not with tears. Weeping wasn't her style.

She sat erect on the dais during the opening ceremonies

and turned a bright, smiling face to a sea of excited women – most of them younger than she – and hoped she might live to see their triumph. In her purse she carried a sheaf of notes, little bits of paper on which she had jotted names of old friends, the address of the convention center, the name of her hotel, the number of her room.

And, God help her, her own name. She had scrawled it shakily, just in case: *I am Laura Templeton.*

The convention was gaveled to order at 1:14 PM, more than an hour late. It was the first slippage in a schedule that was to become increasingly inaccurate. The initial speaker, president of the Chicago chapter, delivered a welcoming speech. Then the permanent chairwoman, president of the Illinois chapter, was elected by acclamation.

Reports were read by committee members which dealt with NWU finances, membership, political activities, etc. The convention was then adjourned to 7:00 PM that evening. Virginia Terwilliger, also on the dais, grabbed Laura's arm.

'Come on,' she said, 'I'll treat you to a cab back to the hotel.'

Laura went along gratefully, but in the hotel lobby she tried to get away from Ginny.

'I have some things to go over before tonight's session,' she said. 'Maybe I'll have a sandwich sent up to my room.'

Terwilliger looked at her stonily. 'Laura,' she said, 'you and Connie Underwood are having dinner with the Executive Board in about an hour. Remember?'

'Oh. Oh yes.' Templeton said confusedly. 'Of course.'

'Come up to my room for a few minutes, have a drink, and relax. There's someone I want you to meet.'

The two women had kicked off their shoes and were sitting close to an air conditioner vent when there was a sharp knock on the door.

'That'll be her,' Ginny said, rose, and ushered in Molly Turner. She introduced her to the NWU president.

'This is Molly Turner,' she said loudly, distinctly. 'She's the firebrand who's responsible for all the commotion in West Virginia. Molly, say hello to your president, Laura Templeton.'

Ginny got the other two women seated and mixed gin and tonics. Then she pulled another chair close and sprawled her big frame, one knee hooked over the chair arm.

'Molly,' she commanded, 'tell Laura what you've been doing. Keep it short, will you; we've got a dinner to get to.'

Once again Molly went through the story of her Canton campaigns. She spoke rapidly, with assurance, occasionally jabbing a forefinger at the others for emphasis. Laura listened intently, smiling, nodding. Terwilliger concentrated on her own drink, rising once to replenish it.

'I think that's wonderful,' Templeton said warmly when Molly had finished. 'We've just been talking while you've been doing.'

'Exactly what I said,' Virginia agreed. 'Laura, we've got ourselves a Young Turk here. Molly, thanks for stopping by. I'll be in touch.'

If Turner was puzzled by this abrupt dismissal she didn't show it. She finished her drink, stood up, smiled at the older women, left the room.

'What a nice girl!' Laura Templeton said, unhooking the lace collar of her print dress. 'I liked the way she spoke – no bullshit about her.'

'What was her name?' Terwilliger said cruelly.

'Her name? Why . . . Ginny . . . you introduced us.'

'I know I did. What's her name?'

'Uh . . . Sally.'

'It's Molly. What's her last name?'

Laura Templeton tried to smile. She held out a trembling glass. Ginny refilled it, handed it back. Their fingers touched. Then Laura reached with her other hand to grasp Ginny's wrist.

'How long have you known?' she asked in a low voice.

Terwilliger pulled her wrist away. 'Months,' she said harshly. 'Connie told me. But I knew before that. You little shrimp, why didn't you tell me?'

'I thought . . .'

'I know what you thought. I know how much the Union means to you. How hard it is to let go.'

'Who else knows?' Laura said timidly.

'Probably the whole damn Exec Board. I mean, you just aren't making much sense these days. And if they didn't guess, Connie – that dear, sweet cocksucker – told them. She wants your job, honey.'

'I should have known,' Laura said slowly.

'If you had been thinking straight, you would have known. But you had other things on your mind. Anyway, Connie has been politicking like mad, kissing every ass in sight. She may be our next president.'

'Maybe it's for the best,' Laura said sadly.

'Bullshit it is!' Ginny said wrathfully. 'That conniving, two-timing bitch? Over my dead body she becomes president. And make the NWU another one of her playthings, like the Watergate pad, the red Jag, and her summer house. No way! I'm going to cut that lady off at the knees if it's the last thing I do.'

'How are you going to do that, Ginny?'

'Maybe she's got the votes,' Virginia Terwilliger said, grinning fiercely, 'but I've got the weight and the reach. You don't really want her taking over, do you?'

'No. She hasn't got – '

'I know what she hasn't got. Principles, for starters. It's all me, me, me with her. Well, I'm going to fuck her up, but good. Do you trust me?'

'Yes,' Laura said, with a small smile. 'I trust you, you monster.'

Ginny stood suddenly, moved to the other woman, bent down, kissed her softly on the lips.

'I'm sorry, kiddo,' she said huskily. 'I really am.'

The evening session of July 15 started thirty minutes late, but even then not all conventioneers were in their seats. It took continued gaveling by the chairwoman to bring the meeting to order.

The first two hours were devoted to entertainment: a female rock band, a stand-up comedienne, a chorus from Little Rock, Arkansas, and a black guitarist and singer from Selma, Alabama, who presented a program of revolutionary ballads.

This was followed by a half-hour color film produced and directed by members of the NWU chapter of San Jose, California. It dealt with the plight of women migrant workers in California, Texas, and Florida.

Constance Underwood was scheduled to deliver the keynote address at 10:00 PM, but it was almost eleven o'clock before she was able to take the microphone. She faced a restless audience who had enjoyed the evening's program but seemed in the mood for something stronger than jokes, ballads, and a movie.

The NWU executive vice president was introduced and stood composedly until the perfunctory applause died away. She wore an elegant black sheath by Halston. Her only adornment was a jeweled NWU membership pin.

She began in a low key, reporting on NWU progress during the past year. She then spoke of 'a new anger, a new resolve' that was sweeping the movement, resulting in well-publicized incidents of violence that had won new rights and made the general public aware of the NWU's militancy and activism.

Her listeners began to come alive during this recital. Sensing their growing enthusiasm, Underwood's voice rose, the pace of her words quickened, she began to emphasize with sweeping gestures.

She said the new revolutionary fervor was marvelous, but without direction and discipline. There was danger that the passion for liberation would be dissipated. What was needed, she stated, was a rigorous, well-organized national program. In this way, all NWU chapters could act as one.

Those command decisions, she insisted, could come only from the Executive Board, democratically elected by the entire NWU membership. And the decisions would be faithfully executed by the president, chosen by the Board, and those who served under her.

Her peroration was ardent, forceful, intense:

'We must,' she cried, 'learn to act as one woman, one hurt woman, one deprived woman. We must submerge personal ambitions and needs in our desire for progress. We cannot act on impulse and whim if we are to succeed. We must be willing to accept the good of all as our highest goal. If we are together, if we are one, we shall win! We shall win!! We shall win!!!'

That brought them to their feet, applauding, stamping the floor, shouting their approval. Constance Underwood stood without smiling, gripping the edges of the lectern, looking out at the inflamed crowd and seeming to express in her set features an absolute and cold determination.

Virginia Terwilliger leaned over to Laura Templeton. 'Goddamn it,' she said worriedly, 'she's not bad.'

The afternoon convention session of July 16 opened with a short speech by a Canadian woman who described the slow pace of feminism in her country and asked permission to organize a Canadian branch of the National Women's Union.

Her plea was formally proposed, seconded, and put to a floor vote. It was almost unanimously approved.

The vote was followed by speeches on rape, child abuse, wife battering, economic discrimination, the need for more equitable divorce laws, and an impassioned denunciation of pornography in books, magazines, films, and video cassettes.

The last order of business before adjournment was the introduction of an amendment to the constitution that would allow men full membership in the NWU. This amendment, which had already aroused strong pro and con opinions, was put over to the evening session for debate and final vote.

During the dinner break of July 16, the Executive Board of the National Women's Union assembled in a meeting room at the Conrad Hilton Hotel to elect a new president of the NWU.

Members of the Board, all presidents of state chapters, ranged in age from twenty-seven to fifty-three. They represented a diversity of occupations: housewives, business executives, three teachers, a television actress, a mathematician, a saleswoman of antique cars, and a circuit court judge.

The Board was deliberately unstructured, with no chairwoman and no staff other than one paid secretary who kept a formal record of their decisions. By common consent, speeches and rebuttals were limited to three minutes, with no member allowed to speak a second time until all who desired to be heard had an initial opportunity to express her views.

This informal method of conducting official NWU business worked surprisingly well. In the July 16 meeting, the names of Laura Templeton, Constance Underwood, and Grace Filene, an NWU member who had written several successful feminist novels, were suggested as candidates for the office of president.

It was then unanimously agreed that nominations be closed, and a round of short speeches began. To Virginia Terwilliger, keeping her hieroglyphic notes, it soon became apparent that Laura had four sure votes, Constance had four, Grace had three. A ballot was then taken, and Ginny's reckoning proved accurate.

The second round of statements was shorter but sharper. One of Constance Underwood's supporters rose to say:

'I happen to know that Laura Templeton is suffering from Alzheimer's disease. We all sympathize with her, I'm sure, but she is presently incapable of performing the duties of president of the NWU. We cannot allow emotional considerations to interfere with our responsibility to provide the Union with the very best leadership available. Connie Underwood has performed magnificently in her present position. She knows the job. We'd be fools not to promote her. You all heard her speech last night. She is exactly the woman we need to guide the NWU during the turbulent years ahead.'

Other Underwood advocates added to this encomium. Those members favoring the re-election of Laura Templeton took the floor to defend her record and to claim that her physical condition did not preclude her serving another two-year term.

The debate became louder and more acerbic. Another ballot was taken, revealing a shift of sentiments. There were now five votes for Templeton, five for Underwood, one for Grace Filene.

The lone dissenter, holding the swing vote, was a television actress and president of the New York chapter. Her steadfast loyalty to Filene, it was later alleged, was due to an affair she was currently enjoying with her nominee's husband. She was hopeful, it was said, of getting Grace elected and moved to Washington, DC.

Fervent appeals were made by both sides, but the New York member refused to switch her vote. The election now seemed hopelessly deadlocked. The Executive Board had not yet dined, and the start of the evening convention was not far off. Virginia Terwilliger deemed it the right time to try her ploy. She rose, towering over the others.

'Laura Templeton is a personal friend of mine,' she said in her gravelly voice. 'As she is of every damned woman in the NWU. She has served as president since the Union was formed. Now you want to toss her in the ash can with a pat on the head and a certificate of merit? What kind of bullshit is that? Are we machines without souls or do we really believe in love and kindness to our sisters? If we now reject Laura Templeton, this Board will make a mockery of everything the NWU is supposed to stand for. All right, Laura is sick. Admittedly. But kicking her out now amounts to the cruelest kind of euthanasia. I want to suggest a compromise solution that will leave Laura with a little dignity and, I think, satisfy those of you who are afraid she can't fulfill the responsibilities of president of the NWU. It would work like this . . .'

After the meeting of the Executive Board was adjourned, Virginia Terwilliger glanced at her digital wristwatch and figured she had time for a martini in the hotel cocktail lounge before rushing back to the convention center.

She sat at the bar and sipped her drink. She was not totally satisfied with what she had accomplished. But she had salvaged something from what she considered a dangerous situation. She had stalled for time – desperately needed if she were to ensure the future of the NWU she sought.

She glanced around the lounge and saw, at a corner table, Constance Underwood holding court with a circle of admirers. Today Connie was wearing a simple de la Renta frock that probably cost more than Terwilliger's husband earned in a month.

Connie saw Ginny staring at her and waggled a few fingers in greeting. Terwilliger nodded in return, then turned back to her drink, mysteriously depleted.

'You've got a hell of an evaporation rate in Chicago,' she growled at the bartender. 'Let's have a refill.'

She admitted wryly that some of her distaste for the Underwood woman was due to envy. Connie was everything Ginny was not. She had a willowy figure and crisp elegance. She moved gracefully, always well-groomed, always sleek. Ginny wished she had a little of that cool polish.

But envy was only a small part of her dislike. Connie was, she felt, a woman of such artificiality that entrusting the NWU's future to her would be tantamount to turning the Union over to some male sexist pig who would flaunt his office as just another affirmation of his sterling talents and character.

Ego. It was all ego with Constance Underwood. If she ever became president, the fortunes of the NWU would be hostage to her own voracious appetite for power, recognition, obeisance.

Not bloody likely, Virgina Terwilliger thought wrathfully, and began to refine the rough plan she had already conceived to bring about the downfall of that soignée woman now sipping a white wine at the corner table and accepting the flattery of her sycophants like a crowned queen.

The evening convention session of July 16 began with the adoption of several resolutions, the most important of which was to withhold endorsement of any political candidate in the 1988 election until he or she subscribed to 'The NWU Creed,' a document that included all the Union's beliefs and goals.

The assembly was then addressed by Margaret Afton Fuller, one of the two female members of the current US. Senate. The speech by Senator Fuller aroused little interest, being mostly a tired defense of her party's efforts in support of women's rights.

The debate was then opened on the amendment to the NWU constitution that would allow membership to men.

The argument, sometimes vituperative, lasted almost two hours and was almost competely filmed by TV cameras. Those opposed to the amendment insisted the NWU remain what it always had been: a militant union of women. Those in favor argued that support for the NWU's aims should be welcomed from any source, and members could not claim to be truly antisexist if men continued to be excluded from membership.

It was close to midnight when the chairwoman gaveled an end to the debate and called for a vote. The counting, interrupted frequently by cheers and jeers, resulted in the amendment being passed by a margin of twenty-four votes. Henceforth, men would be allowed to become full members of the National Women's Union.

The afternoon session of July 17, scheduled to be the last of the convention, was planned to begin at 1:00 PM. It would include only the announcement by the Executive Board of their choice of a new president, followed by an address to the convention by the woman selected.

On the morning of July 17, Virginia Terwilliger met with Laura Templeton in the latter's hotel room to tell her of the Board's decision. The two women shared a breakfast of orange juice, coffee, and croissants with honey. It wasn't until their second cups of coffee that the subject uppermost in their minds was broached.

'Well . . .' Laura said, smile tight, 'let's have the bad news. I got canned, didn't I?'

Terwilliger opened her shoulder bag, took out a folded sheet of paper, set it carefully aside. She then dug deeper in the enormous pouch and brought out a pack of the brown cigarillos she smoked. After offering one to Laura, who declined, she lighted up and blew a plume of smoke at the ceiling.

'No,' she said, staring at the other woman, 'you didn't get canned. But there's a price you have to pay.'

'Oh? What's that?'

Ginny poked at the folded paper. 'It's an undated letter of resignation. You sign it, you become president again. But if, at any time during your two-year term, the Executive Board in its infinite wisdom decides you are no longer capable of carrying out the duties of your office, then the letter of resignation is dated, goes into effect, and you go out the window.'

Templeton tried to laugh. 'Not exactly an overwhelming vote of confidence, is it?'

Ginny shrugged. 'It was the best I could do, honey. If you refuse to sign, the presidency goes to Constance

Underwood. That was the agreement. Is that what you want?'

'No.'

'Then sign the goddamned paper. With luck it'll give you another two years. Give us another two years. A lot can happen in that time.'

Templeton was silent.

'Laura,' the other woman pleaded, 'I worked hard to wangle this for you. I know it's not an enthusiastic endorsement, but it was the best I could do under the circumstances. Everyone knows you're sick – Connie made sure of that. They were ready to toss you to the wolves.'

'Oh, Ginny, I appreciate all you did for me. But I wonder if it's worth it. Maybe I should just fold my tent and steal away.'

'And let Underwood take over?' Terwilliger said furiously. 'And then see the NWU go down the tube? Is that what you want?'

'No.'

There was silence awhile. Terwilliger lighted another cigarillo. If she was nervous, she didn't show it.

'Laura,' she said casually, 'before you decide, I better tell you there's something else – something I want you to do for me.'

Laura signed. 'I was sure there would be. You have a taste for intrigue, Ginny.'

'Intrigue, my ass,' the other woman said angrily. 'This is just good common sense. Let me tell you what I want you to do – and why . . .'

The final session of the Fifth Annual Convention of the NWU opened with a series of announcements by the chairwoman regarding the place and date of the 1988 convention. This was followed by a few moments of confusion on the dais while several NWU officers conferred. The conventioneers stirred restlessly.

The chairwoman then stepped to the microphone. She

introduced Virginia Terwilliger, member of the Executive Board, who would announce the Board's choice to be the NWU president for the next two years.

Terwilliger was greeted with polite applause. Her announcement was brief:

'It gives me great pleasure,' she boomed, 'to tell you that your Executive Board has once again elected a woman to serve you well in the future as she has served you so magnificently in the past. Sisters, it is with pride that I introduce to you – Laura Templeton!'

They rose to their feet then, applauding and cheering the diminutive figure of their chief executive as she made her way to the lectern.

She stood there in the bright lights, wearing one of her famous print dresses with lace collar. She held up her hands in futile protest, but the ovation continued for more than five minutes, and ended only when the chairwoman returned to the lectern and gaveled for order.

Then Laura Templeton spoke:

'Sisters,' she said, reading from a typed script, 'it is a great joy to once again thank you for the honor you have bestowed upon me. I pledge to you, with all my heart, that I shall try my best to justify your faith and trust in me and in your Union. I know it is customary at this time to review the progress of the past and tell you something of our plans for the future. But I am not going to do that today. Instead, I am going to introduce a sister who, by her courage and resolution, has brought new vitality to our movement and proved that the National Women's Union is a force to be reckoned with. It gives me so much pleasure to have you meet the president of the Canton, West Virginia, chapter who has demonstrated that we mean what we say! Sisters, please give a big welcome to our newest heroine, Molly Turner!'

Their response was instantaneous. They had all heard of her, of course. They knew of her exploits – and approved. They rose to their feet cheering, laughing, stamp-

74

ing, waving state standards. The television crews turned on their cameras.

Virginia Terwilliger led Molly forward, their hands clasped. At the rostrum, Molly and Laura Templeton embraced, then faced the shouting audience, smiling and nodding. Finally Laura withdrew, leaving Molly Turner standing alone.

Applause gradually died. Conventioneers regained their seats. Turner waited patiently for quiet. Her smile had faded. 'She greeted the convention with a grim expression,' one reporter wrote later.

'Sisters,' she said in a hard voice, 'the number of rapes and sexual assaults on women increases every year. Is that what you want?'

'No!' her audience shouted.

'The number of battered wives and abused children increases every year. Is that what you want?'

'No!' they screamed.

'Women continue to be underpaid, insulted on the street, made the victims of sadistic pornography, denied their rights in the courts. Is that what you want?'

'No! No! No!' they chanted, rising to their feet again and roaring with anger.

Ginny Terwilliger leaned over to Laura Templeton. 'This kid is dynamite,' she said.

Molly Turner then launched into a short (eleven minutes, thirteen seconds), fiery oration, delivered without script or notes to an audience that remained standing throughout. They provided a constant accompaniment of cheers, cries, tears, and a prolonged rumble of approval that sometimes drowned out the speaker's words.

A speech analyst later published a recondite article dissecting the famous extempore indictment and noted that the word 'fight' had been used 23 times, 'war' 19 times, 'battle' 13 times, 'action' 11 times, 'militant' 9 times, and 'sacrifice' 6 times.

The first section of the speech was a condemnation of

the conditions under which women were forced to exist. This was followed by a short account of the measures Turner and her Canton NWU members had taken to liberate themselves from this oppression.

The last few moments of the address were those that attracted the loudest applause from the convention and most attention from the media. This section was the one generally shown on network TV news programs on the evening of July 17.

'There are those,' Molly Turner said, 'who will tell you we must work within the establishment to change the laws, to elect legislators favorable to our cause.' She shouted: 'I tell you this is not true!

'This nation was founded in violent revolution. Violence is in our blood. If we are honest, we must recognize it. A nonviolent revolution? What a stupid contradiction of terms!

'I say to you that this country, born in violence, respects only violence. This is 1987, and this is America – where men can beat their wives, abuse children, rape any one of us, pay us the minimum wage, and then desert us or take our children if a marriage breaks up. Are you willing to submit humbly to these indignities? I am not! Are you willing to believe nonviolence will solve your problems and bring you to the promised land? I am not!

'I want you to make a commitment today, now, this minute. Not just to picket, demonstrate, or sign petitions. I want you to pledge your life – oh yes, it may come to that! – in this fight against inequality and injustice. If you do not believe in what I believe, then I do not want your applause. If you want to go to the Congress, curtsy, and say, "Please, sir, could you throw me a crumb" – then I *shit* on your humility, and you are no sister of mine. But if you are willing to fight, fight, fight and, if needed, die for what you believe in, for what I believe in, then I say come to me, hold me, kiss me, for I am with you and will call you sister gladly.'

She turned from the podium, strode away. The convention floor simply exploded, women cheering, weeping, standing on chairs to shout, brandishing clenched fists.

It was pandemonium, with many NWU members storming the dais to reach for Molly Turner, try to speak to her, touch her, embrace her. The television cameras swung madly back and forth, trying to capture the spectacle. Reporters rushed to interview members, NWU officers and, if possible, the woman who had sparked the turmoil.

In the midst of this noisy madness, Virginia Terwilliger sat serenely on the dais. Then she leaned forward and stared until she caught the eye of Constance Underwood, sitting erect and unsmiling. Ginny waggled her fingers in a sardonic imitation of the greeting Connie had bestowed upon her in the hotel cocktail lounge.

She was delighted to get a glare of fury in return.

AUGUST 9, 1987

Senator Lemuel K. Dundee was not the complete dolt that Thomas J. Kealy and many others thought him. He looked like a dolt, he spoke like a dolt, occasionally he acted like a dolt. But the man had depth and wit. He was wise enough not to reveal them. Look what had happened to Adlai Stevenson!

Early in his career, shortly after entering law practice and before election to the US. Senate, he had come to a momentous decision: 'If I am to succeed, I must be something I am not.' He then began his rise, and like all maskers eventually lost the ability to distinguish reality from illusion. He *was* the man he pretended to be.

Still . . . twinges remained. An occasional dream. A love for poetry he could not cure. But these were minor pangs. Generally he played the game he had selected, with enthusiasm and skill.

And politics, Dundee believed, was a gambling game. It was an enormous crapshoot, the biggest in the world. You sometimes gambled recklessly to win, cut your losses, never cried, and always yearned for the big pot. It took nerve, resolve, and the cool smile of the professional whether you won or lost.

Certainly, by ordinary standards, he could be counted a winner. He owned a beautiful home in Spring Valley, two cars, a boat, a summer place on Chesapeake Bay. All his children had gone to college, his wife could buy as many of those crappy porcelain figurines as she wished, and he had a sweet portfolio of blue chips.

He had not done all this on a senator's salary. It had required a little help from his friends. He never took cash bribes, of course.

Campaign contributions, yes; cash, no. And there were other ways of doing things . . .

One phone call from a friend to a bank got Lemuel Dundee a special mortgage rate. Another friend could be trusted for inside tips on upcoming corporate mergers. A third, with vague under-world connections, occasionally provided sure-fire predictions on horse races and basketball games.

Yet another friend frequently entertained at stag weekends in a South Carolina hunting lodge during which they shot quail and fucked teenage prostitutes. Other friends whispered to Senator Dundee information on potential oil wells, secret advances in biomedical technology, and arcane methods of moving cash around from the Cayman Islands to Luxembourg to Liberia to Hong Kong in a crazy trail that would give the IRS such a headache they'd finally stop trying to trace it.

In other words, his friends took care of him, and he took care of them, to the limit of his influence as a prestigious senator and member of the Armed Services Committee. And he knew that if he ever decided to take the ultimate gamble of running for the presidency, he could only do it with the advice and consent of his generous, cold-eyed friends.

He met with Tom Kealy late on the afternoon of August 9. Congress wasn't in session; Dundee was at his summer place near Cove Point. But he had driven into Washington to hear the results of the poll Kealy had authorized. At 8:30 PM, they had the senator's suite of offices to themselves; the skeleton summer staff had long since departed.

It had been one of those summer days that turns the nation's capital into one big sauna. Dundee was wearing a loose knitted sport shirt and seersucker slacks, but his executive assistant was in the usual uniform. His only recognition of the heat and humidity was that his dark blue three-piece suit was now tropical worsted. The man never seemed to sweat.

Kealy got right down to business. He opened his black calfskin attaché case, withdrew two sets of documents backed with blue paper, like legal briefs.

'Selig and Conover did the poll,' he started. 'They're busy as hell with the presidential candidates, so it took them awhile to get around to our business. But the delay worked in our favor; the poll was completed in the two weeks following the convention of the National Women's Union, and all the media exposure that got, so this poll is as up-to-date as possible. It's based on telephone interviews with a sample of 1,882 people, evenly divided between men and women, all of voting age. The demographic profile of the sample used was similar to that used for presidential candidates. Three questions were asked: "Are you familiar with the National Women's Union? Are you aware of their goals and methods? If so, do you approve or disapprove of those goals and methods?"'

'All right, all right,' Dundee said impatiently. 'What have we got?'

Kealy sat back, crossed his legs, sighed. 'Senator, I don't know what the numbers mean. It may be I gave you a bum steer on this poll idea. Even Selig and Conover admit it's the weirdest canvass they've ever done. For starters, about seventy-eight percent of those polled, both men and women, knew what the NWU is. Now that's a damned high recognition factor, considering how few people are familiar with the Federal Reserve Board or the Securities and Exchange Commission. Of those who knew about the NWU, eighty-six percent of the women and sixty-one percent of the men were familiar with their goals and methods. Again, surprisingly high.'

'High?' Dundee said. 'It's unbelievable.'

'When it comes to approval or disapproval of the goals and methods, thirty-two percent of the women approved, ten percent disapproved. Twenty-seven percent of the men approved, thirteen percent disapproved. All the others had no opinion. But the pollsters say that the term "undecided" would better describe those who don't approve or disapprove of the NWU's methods.'

'And what's the percentage of the undecided?'

'Eighteen percent undecided on the NWU's goals. And a whopping sixty percent undecided on their militancy and violence. Senator, I just don't know what it means. I feel guilty about this. I was hoping we'd get a big bulge either way – approval or disapproval – and could ride the issue into the White House. But you can't count on undecideds for votes.'

'Mmm,' said Senator Dundee, reflecting that his executive assistant had not yet learned to think politically. He leaned back in his swivel chair, parked his feet on the desk, clasped his hands behind his head. 'You watch the NWU convention, Tom?'

'I saw some of it.'

'Did you see the last woman who spoke? What's her name – Molly Turner? Yes, that's it. The one who wanted to lynch every man in the country.'

'I saw her. What a rabble-rouser!'

'Rabble-rouser? I guess you could call her that. But I thought she was one of the most effective public speakers

I've ever heard – and I've heard some good ones. She's a winner. I really enjoyed her performance – as a professional, you understand.'

'What about her ideas? The things she wants to do?'

'Oh, that's all bullshit. The question we've got to decide is – is it dangerous bullshit?'

'You're not taking her seriously, are you, Senator?'

'Well . . .' Lemuel Dundee said slowly, 'no one took John Brown seriously at first. Or Hitler, for that matter. Did you read that funny guy who writes a column in the *Herald*? He called her a "female Napoleon" and said the convention was her finest period. Now *that's* funny. Leave me a copy of the poll, Tom; I want to read the whole thing and give it some thought. And don't apologize for spending the money for the poll. It may turn out to be the best investment I ever made.'

Driving back alone to Cove Point, Senator Dundee said aloud, 'President Dundee,' and liked the sound of it. 'Lemuel,' of course, was a crappy name, though it had a certain down-home flavor. But there was nothing wrong with 'Dundee.' It was hard, assertive, definite. Nothing wishy-washy about 'Dundee.'

He kept his mind resolutely away from bands playing 'Hail to the Chief,' the red carpets, twenty-one-gun salutes, Air Force One, weekend helicopter trips to Camp David, state dinners, sleeping in Lincoln's bed, traveling abroad with a retinue, rewarding his friends and punishing his foes – he hardly thought of those things at all.

The important things were what he could do for the country: reduce the national debt, bring down unemployment, balance the budget, increase US markets overseas, stop the Communists, beef up the armed forces, cut taxes, help the poor, succor the sick, feed the children, aid minorities, be kind to big business and labor, save the whales, serve the Pope hot dogs in the White House. President Dundee could do all that.

When he got home, his wife was playing backgammon

against herself in the living room. There was a tumbler of bourbon on the table.

'Martha,' he announced, 'I've been giving some thought to running for president. What do you think?'

She looked up from the board to stare at him fixedly.

'Shithead,' she said.

Research of the records of the National Women's Union indicates that in the three months following the Fith Annual Convention of July 15-17, 1987, almost 100,000 new members were added. Applications continued in subsequent months. A year after the convention, the NWU had more than doubled its membership.

In addition to revenue received in the form of dues from these recruits, the NWU also benefited from a surge in voluntary contributions from nonmembers. Cash and checks were received from women, men, associations, corporations, and foundations. The most generous gift was a bank check for $100,000 from an anonymous donor.

President Laura Templeton and the Executive Board had no doubt that the increase in membership and contributions was almost wholly due to Molly Turner's inflammatory convention speech.

Late in September, Turner was asked to come to Washington, DC, where she met with Templeton and the entire Executive Board in a lengthy and significant conference. Minutes of that meeting and testimony of participants reveal the following decisions were taken.

– A paramilitary division of, or adjunct to, the National Women's Union would be immediately organized with its own officers, staff, budget, and headquarters.

– This separate administrative structure would be assigned the militant defense of women's rights, including aggressive acts against those who sought to limit or deny those rights.

– The new division would follow traditional military

organization, with a regiment recruited from each state chapter of the NWU, consisting of battalions, companies, and platoons drawn from city, county, and rural chapters.

– Officers would hold titles of colonel, lieutenant colonel, major, etc. Those in the rank and file would be called 'sisters.'

– Whether a distinctive uniorm would be worn on active service by members of this division was left to the discretion of the commander in chief.

– Molly Turner was unanimously elected to head the cadre, given full-time employment with an annual salary of $50,000, and granted wide latitude in appointment of staff, dispensing of funds, methods of organization, and selection of a headquarters location.

– The paramilitary division would be called the Women's Defense Corps. But this was a semantic ploy for the sake of public relations. All present at the meeting at which the WDC was voted into existence recognized that a more accurate name would have been Women's Liberation Army.

OCTOBER 8, 1987

Constance Underwood did not take kindly to the creation of a new NWU division over which she had no control and little influence. She acknowledged that with the re-election of Laura Templeton as president and the appointment of Molly Turner as commander of the WDC, she had suffered a serious defeat.

Briefly – very briefly – she considered resignation from the National Women's Union. But so obsessive was her ambition, so excessive her amour propre that she – almost automatically – began plotting how she might yet find her way to power.

She had learned details of the Chicago meeting of the Executive Board. She knew that she would undoubtedly succeed to the presidency of the NWU in two years' time

– or less if Laura Templeton was unable to fulfill the duties of that office.

Keeping that possibility in mind, she began seeking ways to reduce or limit the hegemony of Molly Turner – that upstart who suddenly loomed as a rival to Underwood's preeminence in the NWU. Not only did Connie disagree. with Turner's supermacho theories of radical militancy, but she disliked the woman personally.

Constance Underwood was the kind of person made glum by the success of friends and infuriated by their happiness. Consequently, she had few confidantes. She found herself, more and more, confiding in Billy McCrea – only because he was a patient listener, never argued, and provided Connie the opportunity, in private, to vent her frustrations and spin her dreams.

'It's really two problems,' she told him. 'Yes, that's nice, Billy; don't stop. The first is the old woman. I'm certainly not going to wait two years to take over her desk. Oh my, Billy, that's nice; right *there*. And the second problem is that crude parvenue from the hills of West Virginia, with her little tin army. The woman is drunk with power, I swear it, and unless we can hold her under some kind of control, the whole Union is in trouble. Listen, there are laws against bombings, arson, physical assaults, committing a public nuisance, and all that. The next thing you know, she'll – Oh, Billy, when you do that, I want to scream. She'll be collecting guns and dynamite and God knows what else. But now, Billy, do you like this and this, and this? *Do* you?'

Later, bleary with bliss, she watched him move around the room, getting dressed. She was aware of her own body. She knew its worth: high breasts, supple waist, smooth thighs. But now, looking at Billy McCrea's proportions, she longed for a body like his.

'Billy,' she called, watching him pick up the envelope containing his fee and tucking it into his jacket pocket.

He turned to her with his vague smile.

84

'Billy,' she said, 'the things I talk about to you – the NWU and so forth – I hope you don't repeat them to anyone else.'

'Nah,' he said, 'I'm cool. I don't talk to anyone.'

'Of course not,' Connie said with a brittle laugh. 'Besides, who'd be interested?'

OCTOBER 21, 1987

Molly Turner, sharp-featured, always appeared to be in silhouette, snipped from metal with shears.

'I thought you'd be prettier,' one of her visitors blurted out, and Molly laughed.

'We seen you on TV,' the other farm woman explained.

'I was wearing makeup then,' Molly said. 'And a fancy dress. All dolled up. What can I do for you?'

The two young matrons were from Ft. Nelson, a hamlet about twelve miles northeast of Canton. It was a quiet, peaceable town, too small to have an NWU chapter and really not all that interested in the war for women's liberation.

The visitors told Molly that about six months ago it had become generally known in Ft. Nelson that drugs were being peddled from a motor home parked at night in an open space near the village dump.

'He's selling marijuana and cocaine,' one of the women said indignantly. 'And all those pills. To school kids and everyone. Two boys have already gone to the hospital.'

They told Molly they and other concerned parents had complained to the local police chief. He had promised action, but nothing had been done.

'He's getting paid off,' they said flatly. 'He must be. He knows what's going on, but just won't do anything about it.'

At this time, Turner was deeply involved in organizing the Women's Defense Corps, but she promised to see what she could do.

85

'And you and the other women of Ft. Nelson,' she told them, 'must join the NWU. Only if we all band together can we stop things like this.'

They left her a little hand-drawn map of the area. Two nights later, Sergeant Rod Harding, wearing civvies, drove over to check out the place. When he returned, he displayed a small glassine envelope to his wife and Molly.

'Yeah,' he said, 'he's pushing, and openly, too. He's got to have protection. My God, he's got a drugstore in that motor home. This is a nickel bag of shit, but he can supply grass, coke, hash, uppers, downers – you name it. I parked across the road after I made my buy, and saw five cars pull up in an hour's time. Mostly kids in jalopies and pickups. And one on a moped. It's a thriving business.'

'Thanks, Rod,' Molly said gratefully. 'How do you think we should handle it?'

He looked at her with his squinched grin. 'Hey,' he said, 'you're the commander in chief now; it's time you started planning tactics. You've been studying the books; you know how to do it. Tell you what: I'll give you all the information you need, and you work out the attack. Then I'll go over your plan and tell you what I think. Okay?'

Molly and Ann, working together, drew up a detailed scheme to burn out the drug pusher. They submitted it to Harding. He had only minor suggestions:

'Two cars filled with women look too much like a cavalcade,' he told them. 'People will notice, and people will remember. Two cars are all right, but they should take different routes and rendezvous at a specified time. And I wouldn't use Molotov cocktails if I were you. They'd do the job, but they're tricky to handle. The rag wick has got to be saturated to burn, and there's always the chance the bottle will explode before you can get rid of it. Just get the creep out of there, pour in the gasoline, and leave a trail outside for a fuse. Then light it and run like hell before the tank of the motor home goes up.'

On the night of October 21, two cars set out from Canton

86

at different times. An NWU member drove one, with Molly and two others as passengers. Ann drove the Hardings' Buick Regal with two passengers. Each car carried a gallon can of gas, a handgun, rifle, shotgun – all the weapons borrowed from members' husbands or boyfriends.

The two cars arrived at the Ft. Nelson village dump within minutes of each other. They parked in the shadows of a stand of maples across the road. They waited patiently until a customer exited from the motor home, got into a van, and roared away.

Then the women left the cars. Four, with rifles and shotguns, set up roadblocks in both directions on the access road. Molly and Ann, handguns in the pockets of their parkas, went up to the door. The seventh woman waited near the parked cars with the cans of gasoline.

Molly banged twice and the door opened a few inches. A wolfish man examined them.

'Yeah?' he said.

'A few joints?' Ann said, smiling winsomely. 'A friend told us we could score here.'

The man stared at her, up and down.

'Sure, girlie,' he said finally. 'All you want. The best Colombian. Come on in.'

He opened the door, turned his back to them to move into the interior.

'You come outside with us,' Molly said.

'What?' he said, whirling around.

His eyes lowered to the revolvers in their hands.

'What the fuck is this?' he said. 'You nuts or something? Put those things away.'

'You come outside with us,' Molly repeated. 'Now! Unless you want me to blow off your kneecaps in here.'

'What is this?' he demanded. 'A ripoff? You want my money? Here, take it.'

He thrust his hand into a side pocket, pulled out a roll of bills. He held it out to them.

'Here,' he said, waving the money. 'Take it.'

'Drop it on the floor,' Molly said. 'Then back up.'

He hesitated a moment, then did what he was told. Ann scooped up the bills while Molly kept her weapon pointing steadily.

'All right,' she said. 'Outside. Let's go.'

'You're in plenty of trouble,' the man threatened. 'I got friends around here.'

'Sure you have,' Molly said. 'The police chief for one. Tell him about it. Have me arrested. Should make a great trial. I can use the publicity. Can you?'

'Hey,' the man said, staring at her. 'I know you. I saw you on television.'

'That's right. The name is Molly Turner. Tell your friend.'

They got him out of the motor home, marched him to the parked cars, made him lie facedown on the road. Ann patted him down and took a small automatic pistol from a holster at the small of his back.

Leaving Ann to guard him, Molly and the other NWU member carried the gasoline cans toward the motor home. The man raised his head from the road and saw what they were about to do.

He began screaming obscenities at them. Molly came back and kicked him in the head. He stopped screaming.

In the motor home, the two women opened cupboard and closet doors. As Harding had said, it was a drugstore. They also found a quantity of cash in a tin box and two more handguns. They took the money and weapons. Then they spilled the gasoline onto the carpeted floor and splashed some onto the walls. The fumes were strong enough to make them gag.

They dribbled gasoline out the door to a distance of ten feet, then threw the empty cans back inside. Molly lighted the gas trail. They turned and ran.

They were at the parked cars when the motor home ignited with a *wumpf*! Flames shot up; they could feel the heat. Molly punched a car horn three times. The women on the roadblocks came running. They piled into the cars and fled, leaving the drug pusher sitting dazedly on the road.

They were a hundred yards away when they heard a second explosion, and the night sky reddened.

'That'll be the gas tank of the motor home,' Molly said.

She was driving the Buick. Ann sat beside her. The other five women were packed into the second car, taking another route back to Canton.

'Three guns and money for the cause,' Molly said, laughing. 'Not a bad night's work.'

'Molly, was it smart to tell him your name?'

'He recognized me, so it made no difference. What's he going to do – come gunning for me?'

'He might.'

'Not that slimy fink. He had a gun on him, didn't he? If he had any balls, he'd have gone for it instead of letting two women take him.'

'Aren't you ever afraid?'

'Of course. All the time. So what?'

They drove in silence awhile. Then Ann turned sideways to look at her sister.

'Honey,' she said, 'this is the last action I'm going to do with you.'

'Oh?' Molly said coldly, staring straight ahead. 'Getting a little hairy for you, is it?'

'No,' Ann said, 'you know that's not it. I still believe in what we're doing. I'm with you one hundred percent. I'm so proud of you and everything you've done. But I can't take an active part anymore. Molly, I'm pregnant.'

'What?' her sister screamed. 'Say that again!'

'I'm pregnant.'

Molly pulled off the road with a whoosh of gravel, stopped the car, turned and embraced her sister, covering her face with kisses.

'Oh Jesus, Jesus, Jesus,' she said. 'How wonderful! How

absolutely goddamned wonderful! Darling, I'm so happy for you. And for Rod. And for me and the whole fucking world! Pregnant! When did you find out?'

'Two days ago.'

Molly drew away, stared at Ann angrily. 'Two days ago? Idiot! I'd have never let you come along tonight.'

'That's why I didn't tell you. We planned this together and I wanted to do it.'

'Oh God, Molly said, and I was ready to doubt you. Please, please forgive me, honey. I should have known. Of course the baby has to come first. Does Rod know?'

'Yes – I told him.'

'And he let you come along tonight?'

'Oh, Molly, Rod doesn't let or not let me do things – you know that. Yes, he tried to talk me out of it, but when he saw it wasn't doing any good, he just said, "Do what you've got to-do, babe," and so I did. He's got his own problems. He thinks he's going to get fired.'

'Rod? Fired? Oh God. Because he's been helping us?'

'Probably. You know how people talk.'

Molly started the car and got back on the road.

'Listen,' she said. 'I'm going to talk to Rod tonight. I think he should quit before he's canned. I've got this big budget for the Women's Defense Corps, and I haven't even begun to hire a staff. I need Rod. He's done so much for the NWU already. I can get him a salary higher than he's making now. He can be chief of staff or something like that. Do you think he'll go for it?'

Ann pondered a moment. 'I think he will, Molly. He loves you; I know that. And he really is very sympathetic to what we believe in. God knows we'll need the money with the baby coming and all.'

'He may have to join the NWU,' Molly said, 'but that's no problem. Men can be full-fledged members now. Jesus, I really hope he says yes. I don't think I'll be able to do the job without him. Listen, honey, do you want a boy or a girl?'

'A girl,' Ann said promptly. 'What else?'

'Right on, sister!' Molly cried joyously, banging the car horn with her clenched fist.

NOVEMBER 14, 1987

A wet day in Washington, DC. Rain came down in steel strings. There had been no Senate rollcalls. On the floor, four comatose senators dozed to a desultory debate on a bill to license chiropractors. In the gallery, tourists from the hinterlands marveled that this was what they paid taxes for.

'Let me tell you something about politics,' Senator Lemuel K. Dundee said to Thomas J. Kealy.

All senators were entitled to a suite in one of the Senate office buildings. But only senior senators, those with clout, were also allotted a hideaway or 'escape room' in the Capitol itself. These chambers – some small and simple, some large and lavish – existed behind locked, unmarked doors in public corridors and tunnels.

Dundee's hideaway was not far from the Senate floor. He found it an excellent spot to cut a deal, refresh with a wee drop of the old nasty, entertain important constituents, or just catch a nap while a debate droned on.

The room, not large, was comfortably appointed with soft chairs, sofa, game table for poker, television set, a sideboard that contained an assortment of elixirs. There was a telephone and a bell that might rouse Dundee from slumber and summon him to the floor for a vote.

It was close to 5:30 PM, and the senator and his executive assistant had come over from Dundee's office to relax, enjoy a Happy Hour, and talk politics.

'What about that letter to the FBI?' the senator asked.

'Edith is finishing it up now, sir,' Kealy told him. 'She'll bring it over for your signature. You won't have to go back to the office.'

91

'Splendid,' Dundee said. 'Now to get back to what I was talking about . . .'

Both men were sipping bourbon. Kealy loathed the stuff, but it seemed to be *the* macho drink of American politicians, so he had learned to swallow it without a grimace.

'Law One of politics is this,' the senator said. 'Everyone votes out of self-interest. That's basic. Law Two is that there's only a cat's hair of difference between the two political parties.'

The senator was stretched out on the couch, tie loosened, collar opened, shoes off. Kealy sat alongside him in a leather wing chair, like a psychiatrist holding a session with a supine patient. He rose momentarily to pour Dundee another generous dollop of sour mash.

'Law Three,' the senator maundered on, 'is that life has become so goddamned complicated that no one, including politicians, knows what the hell is going on. There are no experts anymore; just various degrees of ignorance and confusion.'

'You paint a gloomy picture, Senator.'

'Not really,' Dundee said, laughing. 'Not half as gloomy as life would be if we knew exactly what was going to happen and how to handle it. Where's the fun there? Did you ever consider, Tom, that politics is a reactive profession? We wait for a crisis, and then we try to plug the hole in the dike. But damned few politicians have the brains or balls to look ahead and say, "Hey, this is liable to happen a few years down the pike, and we damned well better do something about it right now before it gets bad." And that, m 'lad, is why I've decided to run for the presidency by putting all my money on a campaign to stop the National Women's Union and all similar terrorist organizations that threaten the American Way of Life.'

Even knowing Dundee's penchant for dramatic, unexpected announcements, this sudden declaration left Kealy stunned. To cover his confusion, he rose and poured himself another drink with a shaking hand.

'Are you serious, Senator?' he managed to ask.

'Serious? Shit, boy, I'm *solemn*! This is a holy crusade as far as I'm concerned.'

'But that poll – '

'That poll shows a big majority of undecideds. That means they're up for grabs. I've got just as good a chance to swing them my way as the NWU has to bend them their way. I think I can beat the shit out of them. I've got the Bible, old-fashioned Americanism, motherhood, and the sanctity of the family on my side. Tom, you were right: this is an issue that's got everything – sex and violence. I'm going to pick up the ball and run with it as soon as I get the go-ahead from my friends.'

'But the women – '

'You think all women are in favor of this crazy Molly Turner? Forget it! That Turner woman is so wild she's going to turn off at least half the females. I'll get their votes. And practically all the males'.'

'I hope you're right, sir,' Kealy said, sighing. 'But you're going to make a lot of enemies.'

'Listen, Tom,' Senator Dundee said earnestly. 'No one respects the ladies more than I do. They are creatures to be cherished, protected by law, given every possible opportunity to achieve political and economic equality. I'm all for that stuff. But when it comes to shootings and bombings and burnings, it's time to draw a line.'

There was a knock on the door. Kealy got to his feet.

'That'll be Edith with the FBI letter,' he said.

He let her in. Dundee sat on the couch, read the letter swiftly, scrawled his signature.

'Thank you, dear,' he said, beaming at the young woman. 'I apologize for bringing you out in this miserable weather, but I wanted the letter in the mail tonight.'

'That's perfectly all right, sir,' she said. 'Good night, and have a pleasant evening.'

Both men watched her leave the room. The door closed behind her.

'Nice boobs,' Senator Dundee said. 'Good ass.'

DECEMBER 27, 1987

Virginia Terwilliger drove down from Baltimore almost every week to visit NWU headquarters. She wanted to check on the physical condition of Laura Templeton and keep an eye on what she termed the 'deep, dark plots' of Constance Underwood.

But in spite of this occasional surveillance, Underwood's intrigues went briskly forward. Her plan to end the reign of President Laura Templeton was simple and sadistic:

She came into Laura's office and said, 'Here's that folder you wanted.'

'What folder?'

'The one you asked for this morning.'

'I did? Now what did I want that for?'

Or:

'Did you call Molly Turner?' Connie asked.

'No, I didn't call her. Should I?'

'You asked me to remind you, Laura. You said there was something important you wanted to discuss with her.'

'I don't remember. Oh God.'

A compact was purposely mislaid, a file moved from one drawer to another, notes destroyed, messages never delivered. Templeton began to crumble under this harassment, convinced that her mental deterioration was accelerating. She depended more and more on the woman who was destroying her.

'What would I do without you, Connie?' she'd say.

And Connie would smile her thin, dissolute smile, and a few hours later the boy from the deli would deliver to Templeton a sandwich and coffee she could not recall

94

ordering. But there was her name on the check. The poor woman's desperation grew.

The manipulation of Molly Turner took a little more doing. Underwood handled it this way:

In the presence of Virginia Terwilliger, she suggested to Laura that it might be wise to assign a full-time public relations aide to the Women's Defense Corps.

'They're growing so rapidly,' she said casually, 'and Turner is so busy I don't think she has the time to even think about publicity. But the public image of the WDC is very important. I'm not sure Molly appreciates that. I'm not saying we should dictate to her, but I do think we might diplomatically urge her to take on a press secretary. It should be someone who can schedule interviews and conferences, write an official biography, distribute photographs, and make certain that Turner and the WDC get the most favorable media coverage possible.'

Both Templeton and Terwilliger thought it was an excellent idea. Underwood volunteered to screen applicants for the job.

It took her a week and nine interviews before she found the woman she wanted. Her name was Yvonne Popkin. She was in her middle forties, with stringy hair, and had been out of work for more than a year. Connie took her to lunch at Le Gré and ordered a full bottle of muscadet with their broiled trout amandine.

'Yvonne,' Underwood said, 'I should explain to you immediately that I don't have the final word on this appointment. Our president, Laura Templeton, will want to approve the woman I select. And since the press secretary will be working closely with Molly Turner, she's entitled to make her own decision. You understand that?'

Popkin nodded, busy with trout, endive salad, wine. Connie watched her, wondering how long it had been since she enjoyed a decent meal.

'You'd be willing to move to Canton – or wherever Turner decides to set up her headquarters?'

'Oh yes. That's no problem. I have no house or furniture – nothing like that.'

'You've been divorced for – how long?'

'Almost twenty years.'

'And no children?'

'No, none. So I'm free as a bird!'

'Uh-huh. Well, Yvonne, you certainly have the qualifications we're looking for. Newspapers, radio, television . . . You've changed jobs frequently, haven't you?'

'Well, uh, I wanted the experience, and for a woman, you know, so many media jobs are just dead ends. And there's a lot of discrimination against, uh, more mature women. They want the young blondes, especially on TV. So yes, I changed jobs frequently.'

Watching her gulp the wine, Underwood guessed that discrimination against older women might not be the only reason Popkin had rarely lasted more than a year with each employer.

'Well, Yvonne, I might as well tell you, I think you're the woman for the job.'

The woman looked up from the skeleton of her trout, astonished.

'Really? Thank you. Thank you so much.'

'As I told you, the final decision isn't mine to make. But I think I can say my recommendation will carry a lot of weight. In return for the recommendation, there's something I want you to do for me.'

'Of course,' Yvonne Popkin said eagerly. 'Anything.'

Constance Underwood explained carefully what services she wanted Molly Turner's press secretary to provide.

'Well . . . sure,' the other woman said slowly, gazing down sorrowfully at her empty plate. 'I guess I could do that. As long as I don't get in trouble.'

'You won't,' Underwood assured her, 'if you follow my orders exactly.'

Later that night, Constance told Billy McCrea about the luncheon with Yvonne Popkin.

'Popkin!' she said. 'What a name! Can you imagine? But she'll do. She won't be a spy. Exactly. More like a private liaison officer. She'll report directly to me, keep me informed.'

'Cool,' Billy said.

JANUARY 19, 1988

Ann Shelby Harding had been called 'Kitten' as a child, being soft, cuddly, a romper. She had long outgrown the attributes and the nickname, becoming a tall, full-figured, determined woman. She could be as assertive as her older sister, but without Molly's abrasiveness.

Now, four months with child, she displayed a new dignity and serenity. Her complexion bloomed, eyes sparkled, movements became languorous. Molly said she could pose for a huge Maillol nude titled 'Mother to Be.'

Her role in the organization of the Women's Defense Corps was necessarily limited, but she continued to serve as her sister's confidante, adviser, defender. She was present during most of the conferences, and invariably her decision was the one accepted. She brought perceptive insight and pragmatic knowledgeableness to the knottiest of problems.

For instance, the question of where to locate the headquarters of the WDC arose early on. Molly wanted it to be in Washington, DC, as close to the NWU national offices as possible. She argued that proximity to the source of power could prove useful for the fledgling army.

Ann agreed there might be advantages to such an arrangement, but cautioned that it might also endanger the independence of the WDC.

'We'll run the risk of constant interference,' she warned. '"Why are you doing that? Why don't you do this? It would be better if you did it this way."'

Rod Harding, who had resigned from the Canton Police Department and now worked full-time as Molly's chief of staff, turned to his commander.

'Ann is right,' he said. 'I know in the field we tried to stay as far away from headquarters as possible. Too much meddling and Monday morning quarterbacking. Headquarters is all chiefs and no Indians.'

'All right,' Molly agreed. 'Let's put the whole problem on the back burner. For the time being, we'll stay in Canton and work out of the Hillcrest house. We've got spare bedrooms for some of the staff. When we run out of room, we'll take office space downtown. When we outgrow that, it'll be time to think about moving to Washington.'

Another debate involved the employment of Yvonne Popkin, the woman sent by NWU headquarters with the suggestion that she be hired as press secretary.

Molly didn't see the need of one person handling only publicity and public relations. Ann and Rod thought a public affairs officer would be a real plus – but Rod had his doubts about Popkin.

'I think she's a lush,' he said flatly. 'Watch her when drinks are available. She just soaks it up.'

Ann proposed that they add Yvonne to the staff on a trial basis, keep an eye on her drinking, and see how she performed. So that's what they did; Popkin moved into the Hillcrest Avenue home to join a personal secretary, chief of operations, and chief of intelligence and planning already on duty.

Those were minor, peripheral problems. The main tasks were to establish an infrastructure for the Women's Defense Corps and plan a program for the recruitment of sisters. Harding drew on his military experience and, on the evening of January 19, suggested the following:

Each state chapter of the NWU would be allotted one colonel. The woman would be in command of all the field and junior officers in her state, and of the rank and file.

'Molly,' Rod said, 'you can't do *everything*. In an organization as big as we plan, you've got to learn to delegate authority. Pick your key people, tell them what you want, and turn them loose. If they deliver, fine. If they can't cut the mustard, kick their ass out.'

'Ann,' Molly said, 'what do you think?'

'It looks good on paper,' Ann said slowly, 'but I think you should select the state colonels yourself. Don't let the presidents of NWU state chapters pick them. Then you'll run into political patronage and favoritism, and we'll end up with a lot of dead-heads.'

'Yes, you're right – as usual. It means I'll have to do a lot of traveling, but it's got to be done. Can you come with me?'

'I don't think I better, honey. God forbid I should lose the baby; it would just kill me. But I think Rod, your personal secretary, and the Popkin woman should go along. While you're interviewing, Rod can try to line up Vietnam vets or anyone else willing to serve as military advisers.'

'Great!' Harding said enthusiastically. 'Molly will pick her own staff and I'll sign up some hard-nosed guys as combat instructors.'

'They don't *all* have to be guys,' Molly said sharply. 'A lot of women have served in the armed forces and have had military training.'

'Well, you know I'm just a sexist pig,' Harding said solemnly, 'and want the best jobs in this raggedy-assed army for men.'

'Bastard!' Molly said.

And on that note, Ann announced, 'I'm going to call it a night. You two can sweat over your tables of organization as long as you like; this little mother needs her sleep.'

They exchanged kisses and Ann went to bed. Molly and Rod continued working. It was almost two o'clock in the morning when their animated discussion flagged and they put aside their papers.

'God, I'm exhausted,' Molly said.

'Too tired to drive home?' he said. 'Take the other bed. I can sleep on the living room couch.'

'No,' Molly said, 'but thanks anyway. And thanks for letting me come over. I'm finding it harder and harder to get anything done at home. Too many people, too many interruptions.'

'Sure,' he said, 'that figures. Hey, we've got some – what the hell have we got? – not much. A little rotgut rye, I think. Would you like a jolt?'

'A small one,' Molly said. 'With a lot of water and a lot of ice.'

He returned a few minutes later with two glasses filled with mahogany-colored liquid.

'You call that a small jolt?' Molly said, holding her glass up to the light. 'It looks like straight whiskey.'

'Not quite,' he said. 'But I figured you needed it.'

'I do,' she said gratefully. 'Thanks' brother-in-law.'

'You're welcome, sister-in-law.'

They stretched out their legs, sipped their drinks, lapsed into a comfortable, reflective silence. After a while their eyes slowly rose, they stared at each other.

He saw a hard, rawboned woman wound up tighter 'n a drum. No one had ever called Molly Turner pretty, but Harding thought there was strong beauty in her face. She had lean, skin-tight features that recalled something primitive. Something of the peasant there, something close to the earth and the earth's verities.

She saw a big man with a quirky grin. His blond mustache was always scraggly, sandy hair uncombed. There was sometimes a look in his small, dark eyes that troubled her: maybe the mocking look of a soldier and cop who had seen everything and knew the final answer.

'By the way, kiddo,' he said casually, 'I think you're doing a helluva job.'

She leaned toward him. 'You really think so, Rod?'

He raised his palm. 'Scout's honor.'

'It means so much to me,' she said in a low voice. 'It's my life. My *life*, Rod! It's not just an ego thing with me; I swear it's not. I believe in this cause, with all my heart.

I've got to make it go. I'll do anything, use anyone – including you – to make it succeed. A women's army! Jesus, what an idea, what an absolutely wonderful, crazy, logical idea. It should have been done years ago. But I'm going to do it now, I know I am!'

'You're working your ass off,' he told her, 'but the idea is beginning to take shape. You're hacking it, Moll.'

She rose abruptly, leaned down, kissed him lingeringly on the lips.

'Norma Jane used to call me Moll,' she said throatily.

FEBRUARY 3, 1988

Senator Dundee did not want the conference held in the District; some nosy reporter might get wind of it. So Kealy rented a suite in a posh, secluded motel near Silver Spring, Maryland. As standard operating procedure, he had one of Jake Spencer's boys come in to sweep the place for bugs and hidden recording devices an hour before the meeting.

He drove Dundee to Silver Spring in his, Kealy's, silver-gray Continental, which had a computerized dashboard that could show miles per gallon, estimated time of arrival and, Kealy supposed, current stock quotations – if he could ever learn to operate the damned thing.

'Plenty of booze?' the senator asked.

'Plenty,' Kealy assured him. 'And if anyone gets hungry, room service is available all night.'

'You do your presentation first,' Dundee said. 'Then I'll make my pitch. But we'll all have a few drinks first to loosen up.'

'I had some charts made,' the executive assistant said. 'So they can see what those numbers in the poll look like.'

'Good. Charts are good. Make the whole thing look like an official briefing.'

'These men are important, Senator?'

'They are to me. Right up there on top of the totem

pole. I've got a lot of other friends, of course, but these are the guys with clout. If I can persuade them, all the rest will follow along. It's make-or-break time for me, Tom.'

'Nervous, sir?'

'Nah. I get up in situations like this. The heavy roll. The adrenaline pumps a little faster is all.'

Their five guests arrived within half an hour of each other, a remarkable accomplishment considering that one had flown in from the Coast and another from the Bahamas. Kealy served as bartender and made certain no one's glass was ever empty.

They were big, overfleshed men with soft smiles and hard eyes. They laughed loudly and touched each other frequently: shoulder pats, arm tugs, backslaps. They exchanged gossip and told jokes. It was all relaxed, friendly, with that special camaraderie of the lucky.

Lemuel K. Dundee was at his benevolent best, moving among them beaming, pressing the flesh, and laughing at their gibes. At no time was he subservient. If they had money and power, he was a United States senator and had shared a pizza with the President. They did not take him lightly.

By 10:00 PM, Dundee had them all seated, attentive.

'Gentlemen,' he said, smiling, 'I sincerely want to thank you for taking the time from your busy schedules to attend this little confab. You know damned well I want something from you or I wouldn't be picking up the check for all the booze you're drinking!'

Laughter.

Then the senator stopped smiling. His features became serious.

'I know you've all heard of the National Women's Union and their private army, the Women's Defense Corps. I know you are familiar with their aims and their activities. Anyone who's been reading the papers or watching TV for the last six months knows the goals of their commander, Molly Turner. Now I'd like to turn this meeting over to

102

Tom Kealy for a few minutes. He'll tell you how the American people feel about the NWU, according to a recent poll I had taken. You've all met Tom – he's my executive assistant, and I don't know what I'd do without him! – and I'm sure you're going to be interested in what he has to tell you. Tom?'

Kealy took the floor and, with the aid of large, multicolored charts, set up on a folding easel, reviewed the salient results of the poll. As he spoke, he looked directly at his audience, switching his stare from face to face.

He thought he had their attention, but their expressions revealed nothing. He had rehearsed his presentation. Five minutes; no more.

'The most important revelation of this poll,' he concluded, 'the most significant, is the enormous number of men and women who have not yet formed a firm opinion in favor of or opposed to the NWU and its military arm. Each of you gentlemen will be given a confidential copy of the poll before you leave. It will show in greater detail the breakdown by age, sex, income, and so forth. Are there any questions?'

There were no questions.

'Thank you, Tom,' Senator Dundee said, taking the floor again. 'An excellent job – as usual. And now, friends, I want you to keep in mind what Tom has just told you while I throw you a real blockbuster.'

He paused three beats for effect, then:

'I intend to run for the presidency in 1992. I am completely serious about this, completely confident, and for the sake of our friendship, I ask you to hear me out and see if what I offer doesn't make sense.

'I think all of us here tonight, regardless of political affiliation, agree that my party is going to get the shit kicked out of it in this year's election. There is little I can do to influence that sad result. But now is not too early to start looking ahead and planning for 1992.

'What I wish to propose to you is a candidate and a

103

platform that will unite the thinking patriots of *both* parties. The candidate, obviously, is me. Is there anyone in public life today who, by legislative experience, executive capabilities, and judicious temperament, is better qualified?

'You may say that I am not a national figure, not well enough known around the country. I agree! But I ask you to hold that objection in abeyance for just a moment while I dwell briefly on the program I intend to offer to make my candidacy attractive to every one of you.

'In a nutshell, I want to put the United States of America on a paying basis. I say that if this great nation can't show a profit, then we're no goddamned better than any banana republic or pipsqueak African country where everyone takes in everyone else's laundry. Gentlemen, I want to base my presidential campaign on a new idea: I call it a Bottom Line political philosophy.'

He caught them with that. There was a stirring, a leaning forward. He was talking to them like a businessman.

'I have roughed out a national program which, I fervently believe, will enable the United States to turn a profit every year. Now is not the time to go into details, but I can tell you that it includes abolition of the corporate and capital gains taxes, subsidies for foreign investment, increased import taxes, conversion of the State Department into an agency for economic expansion, and the turning over to efficient private enterprise many of the services now performed at horrendous cost by the Federal government. I say that any law passed in this country should have one and only one criterion: will it show a profit?'

He was talking their language. He had them and he knew it. His manner became looser, more confiding. He loomed over them, his voice softening so they had to crane to hear. He seemed to be whispering in each man's ear.

'Now you know and I know,' he said, 'that I can't take a platform like that to the American people. Every minority in the land, every pressure group, would dump

104

on me. No way can I get elected if I publicly exposed what I've just told you. So the problems are two . . .'

He held up two fat fingers, carefully folding them down as he ticked off his points.

'One, I am not as yet a national figure, an easily recognized media personality. I must make my name and face known over the length and breadth of this great land. Two, I must go to the good people of this country with a cause, a crusade, they can identify with. What the hell do they know or care about budget deficits, trade balances, and the International Monetary Fund? I've got to hit them in the gut with an issue they can feel deeply about.

'Now we come to Tom Kealy's presentation of the poll I had taken on the National Women's Union. *There* is the issue! The crusade that's going to put me in the White House and insure you gentlemen the program I have outlined tonight will become a reality.

'I propose that I become the main spokesman *against* the unlawful acts and illegal tactics of the Women's Defense Corps. I propose to label this revolution for what it is – a terrorist assault against everything we hold dear. You saw the proportion of undecideds in the poll. I am convinced those poor people are confused, and I intend to point them in the right direction. By God, I can swing them! And not only give me a helluva chance of winning the Oval Office but, more important, making certain that everything this nation stands for does not go down in a bloody mess of beatings, burnings, and bombings. With your help, your sympathetic understanding and financial support, I know I can do it. I *shall* do it!'

His final flourish of oratory left them stunned and silent. They drained their drinks. Kealy, moving to provide refills, was awed by the persuasiveness of his mentor. The senator had poured it on, and there was no doubt the moneymen had been impressed. They turned to each other in earnest conversation.

Lemuel K. Dundee stood at the liquor table, sipping a

105

tall drink and letting his guests confer without interruption. Finally, the man from the Bahamas came up and spoke briefly. Dundee went over to Kealy.

'Tom,' he said with a kindly smile, 'why don't you go down to the cocktail lounge and rub knees with whatever ginch is available? The boys want a little private talk. I'll make it as short as possible. I'll pick you up down there. You understand, don't you?'

'Of course, Senator,' Kealy said.

Dundee put a heavy hand on the younger man's shoulder.

'Nothing against you, Tom,' he said, 'but some things have to be said in confidence. Don't let it bother you.'

'It doesn't, sir,' Kealy said – but it did.

He sat down in an empty cocktail lounge, drinking white wine for almost an hour before the senator came down.

'All set, Tom,' he said shortly. 'You settle up. I'll wait for you in the car.'

On the drive back to Dundee's home in Spring Valley, the senator was silent, staring stonily through the windshield. Finally, Kealy couldn't endure the suspense . . .

'Well, sir?' he asked. 'How did it go?'

'They're in,' Dundee said in a cold voice. 'Those bastards drove a hard bargain. I'll be doing more traveling, stroking state chairmen and power brokers. We've got to start thinking about Sunday morning TV talk shows. Dinners and speeches. Shit like that. And then we've got to think about a campaign staff. A manager. Setting up a national organization.'

'Yes, sir,' Kealy said. 'It does sound like a lot of work.'

'But worth it,' Dundee said fiercely, 'if we're going to save the country.' And Kealy wondered if the old man had convinced himself.

They pulled into the driveway of the senator's handsome home. Dundee made no effort to get out, and after a moment, Kealy turned off the engine. Silence. Then . . .

'Tom, I want you to go to Jake Spencer – do it personally; not by phone – and ask him to do a rundown on this Molly Turner. From the day she was born. Childhood, education, family and friends. Who she's fucked. Who shc's fucking now. Does she drink? Do drugs? Everything.'

'Sure, Senator. First thing tomorrow morning.'

'We'll need all the ammunition we can get. You can trust Jake to keep his mouth shut about this.'

'I know. Senator, as I told you, I have an inside inform- ant on NWU activities. Stuff going on at their headquarters and Executive Board meetings. These are verbal reports; nothing in writing. For your own protection, I don't think you should know his name. But I've been paying him out of my own pocket. I think his information can be of increasing value as we get into this campaign, and I'd like your permission to pay him out of the Confidential Fund.'

'Of course,' Dundee said. 'By all means. Doesn't hurt to have an ace in the hole.'

'That's him all right,' Kealy said, but the senator didn't get the joke.

FEBRUARY 4, 1988

Jake Spencer had put in almost twenty years with the Federal Bureau of Investigation, most of them during the reign of J. Edgar. Spencer had never risen higher than special agent in the field. That was all right with him; he liked the work.

After Hoover died, Spencer stayed on through the hys- teria of Watergate. But then new men took over the FBI, and Jake decided it was time to move on. He had pulled one too many unauthorized black bag jobs. Also, during his career three fugitives he had been sent to apprehend had died of 'self-inflicted gunshot wounds' – a remarkable coincidence.

His resignation was accepted with alacrity. He was given

a nice going-away party and presented with a set of matched luggage. Were they trying to tell him something?

If they were, Jake Spencer didn't travel far. He rented a small, two-room office in Rosslyn, right across the Potomac, and set up Spencer Security Services – which, after it had been in business a few years, came to be known to its customers as the Three-S.

Jake had only two regular employees: a cleaning woman who came in once a week and a spinsterish secretary who gave him a blow job twice a week. When Spencer got a job – and he got a lot of them – he hired free-lancers: bodyguards, security people, researchers, PIs, muscle, thieves, prostitutes, etc. Whatever your particular problem called for, Jake Spencer could provide the personnel.

He was a mountain of a man, on the downside of fifty-five and going to suet. A lot of good beef and bourbon had contributed to his meaty nose and cheeks covered with the chicken tracks of burst capillaries. His eyes were wet stones, and most people didn't like to hear him laugh.

But he got the job done; all his customers in the nation's capital said that. And they agreed he could be trusted to keep his mouth shut.

On February 4, at 11:00 AM, Jake Spencer met with Thomas J. Kealy on a Lafayette Park bench that afforded an excellent view of the White House. It was a biting day with the raw smell of snow in the air, and both men had turned up their overcoat collars.

Kealy explained rapidly what was needed: a complete dossier on Molly Turner, commander of the Women's Defense Corps.

'Sure,' Spencer said. 'I know what you mean – the works.'

'Right.'

'You got a budget on this?'

'No,' Kealy said. 'Whatever it costs.'

'What happened?' Spencer said with his lewd laugh. 'The senator hit the Daily Double?'

'Something like that,' Kealy said, trying to hide his

distaste for this man. 'How long do you think it'll take?'

'Give me a month. Tops.'

'Fine,' Kealy said, rising. 'You've got my private number, haven't you?'

'Sure.'

Spencer watched the executive assistant stride away. A wimp. The city was filled with them. Sharp dressers with horn-rims and attaché cases. Very aware of their own importance. And, Jake Spencer knew, when you leaned on them, they wept.

He sat on the cold bench a few more minutes, wondering why the hell Senator Lemuel K. Dundee of the Armed Services Committee was interested in Molly Turner. Then he rose heavily and lumbered along for three blocks until he found a public telephone that worked.

One of Spencer's greatest assets was his phenomenal memory. He kept no notebooks, files, directories. He remembered names, addresses, telephone numbers – everything. He could even remember his army dogtag number – and how many guys his age could do that?

The phone he called rang twelve times. Spencer waited patiently; he knew it was always manned. Finally he got an answer.

'Gargan,' a man's voice said.

'Jimbo,' he said. 'Jake Spencer.'

'How's by you, Jake?'

'Can't complain.'

'What's on your mind?'

'Jimbo, has the Department any interest in that Molly Turner woman?'

Silence a brief moment. Then: 'We're aware of her activities.'

'Yeah,' Spencer said with his loose laugh, 'I'll bet you are. You got anyone close to her?'

'You know I can't tell you that, Jake.'

'Sure you can,' Spencer said genially, 'if I can give you something.'

'All right, we've got someone close to her – but I can't tell you who. What have you got?'

'I was just hired by Senator Dundee to get all the poop on that cunt.'

'Oh? That's interesting.'

'I thought you'd like it.'

'Keep in touch, Jake. Maybe we can help each other.'

'That's what I figured,' Spencer said, hanging up.

He wasn't *quite* as close-mouthed as his customers liked to think.

Examination of pertinent documents reveals that during the spring and summer of 1988, the Women's Defense Corps was organized into a functioning army, with an administrative structure, headquarters staff, divisions for planning, operations, logistics, intelligence, and public relations.

The tables of organization and chain of command were gradually fulfilled as Molly Turner traveled around the country, delivering innumerable fiery speeches and recruiting sisters from the ranks of the National Women's Union – and even many women who did not belong to any established feminist group but were inspired by her revolutionary fervor.

She was accompanied on her journeys by her chief of staff, Rod Harding; her personal secretary, Lois Campbell; her public affairs officer, Yvonne Popkin; and occasionally by other members of the headquarters staff.

During visits to state NWU chapters in this period, Rod Harding recruited a cadre of military advisers, mostly male war veterans who were willing to instruct WDC members in combat skills. These men were volunteers, who were not paid for their services.

While the infrastructure of the WDC was being developed, a number of militant actions were planned and carried out that kept Molly Turner and her army of women's liberation in the public eye and garnered an enormous

110

amount of media attention.

In Ottumwa, Iowa, a grown man accused of joining in the gang rape of a twelve-year-old girl by a group of young boys was shot dead in his home while he was out on bail.

In Phoenix, Arizona, a child molester, freed during the appeal of his conviction, was killed by a bomb wired to the ignition of his car.

In Shreveport, Louisiana, a middle-aged woman who had stabbed her husband to death, alleging many years of physical abuse, was convicted of second-degree homicide. While being transported from courthouse to jail, she was 'rescued' by a large group of furious women. Her subsequent whereabouts were never discovered.

In these three cases, and several others of a similar nature, no arrests or indictments resulted. And though it was widely suspected that they were the work of the Women's Defense Corps, no conclusive evidence to prove it was ever presented. But it should also be noted that Turner never denied responsibility for any of these acts.

It was perhaps inevitable that masculinists denounced the campaign of the WDC as dangerous to law and order and a threat against the public weal. It seems obvious that these foes were inspired and encouraged by a speech delivered on the Senate floor by Lemuel K. Dundee on April 18, 1988.

In harsh terms, he denounced the WDC as a 'terrorist organization' intent on accomplishing its aims 'by the bullet, not the ballot.' He called for stern repressive measures by local and state police and by the Federal Bureau of Investigation.

Senator Dundee was not strictly accurate in labeling the WDC a terrorist group. It was legitimately chartered as a nonprofit organization. It did not operate in a clandestine manner. Its members did not go underground; indeed, they flaunted their membership pins. WDC officers gave frequent press and TV interviews; made endless public speeches outlining their goals and how they intended to achieve them.

Still, careful perusal of the records indicates that many

111

WDC activities, especially during its formative months, were of a surreptitious nature and in many cases clearly illegal. This was particularly true of their efforts to obtain handguns, rifles, grenades, and explosives.

MARCH 19,1988

During her recruiting tour around the country, Molly Turner and female members of her entourage invariably stayed at the homes of NWU members. Rod Harding usually took a room in a local motel. The group met at least once a day, often at a late dinner, to exchange reports of progress.

On the night of March 19, they dined in the restaurant of the Starlite Motel near Independence, Missouri. In addition to Turner and Harding, Yvonne Popkin and Lois Campbell were present. Because the restaurant was crowded, they didn't discuss WDC business at dinner, but later adjourned to Harding's unit.

Molly reported on a sister she had interviewed to serve as colonel of the Missouri regiment. Harding said he had lined up a private club of a dozen Vietnam vets who expressed interest in acting as drill instructors. Popkin said she thought she could get a good human interest story on an eighty-three-year-old grandmother who insisted on joining the Missouri chapter of the WDC.

Campbell took shorthand notes of this discussion.

They then reviewed the planned itinerary for the next two weeks, which would include trips to Minnesota and Wisconsin before their return to West Virginia.

'I'd like to hang around for that Kansas thing,' Molly Turner said – and Rod Harding stood abruptly to search for pipe tobacco in his jacket pocket.

'What Kansas thing?' Yvonne Popkin asked.

'Aw, it's pie-in-the-sky,' Harding said, staring at Molly Turner.

'Is something going down?' Lois Campbell asked. 'In Kansas?'

'No,' Turner said shortly. 'It's just in the talking stage. Something for the future.'

But Campbell wouldn't give up. She was a small, plumpish woman who wore her tawny hair cut as short as a Marine recruit's. No one had ever seen her in anything but skin-tight jeans and a blue chambray workshirt. Her nails were bitten down to the quick.

'If something is going down,' she said, 'I should be keeping an official record.'

'Nothing's going down,' Harding assured her. 'It's some cockamamie scheme the Kansas sisters are considering. Nothing will come of it.'

'If anything does,' Turner promised her secretary, 'you'll know all about it beforehand.'

'And me, too,' Popkin said. 'I've got to know about these things ahead of time so I can plan how to handle press coverage.'

A little before midnight, Campbell and Popkin departed. Molly Turner was left alone with Harding.

'You think I talk too much?' she demanded.

'You did tonight,' he said sternly, taking a bottle of bourbon from his suitcase. 'Moll, you're just too damned trusting. I'm not saying Campbell and Popkin are plants, but you've got to act as if they are. I'll bet a million the FBI and God knows who else have placed people close to you. You can't trust anyone.'

'Does that include you?'

'Sure it includes me,' he said, not at all offended. 'I don't mean you should be paranoid, but for Christ's sake, watch yourself. Your people have to know some things to do their jobs. But don't talk in front of those who have no need to know. That way you limit your risks. Campbell and Popkin have no need to know about the Kansas thing until after it's over.'

'Anything else?' she said angrily. 'Any other beefs

113

you'd like to lay on me?'

'Yes,' he said promptly. 'You're working too god-damned hard. You've lost weight and you look all wound-up. Moll, you can't do everything in a week, a month, or a year. You've got to learn to pace yourself. You worry me.'

'Do I?' she said, softening. 'That's nice, Rod. I like that.'

He put his drink aside and stood behind her chair. He began to massage her neck and shoulders with his strong fingers.

'You're all knotted up,' he said. 'Relax.'

'Ooh, that feels good,' she said, sighing. 'Don't stop.'

'I called Ann tonight,' he said. 'Just before dinner. She's feeling fine. Everything's okay. She said to give you her love.'

'Did she get the check from the NWU?'

'Yep. All deposited. Memberships up. Contributions up. Money's no problem – at the moment.'

Silence while he kneaded the muscles of her upper back and arms.

'Rod, were you serious about the FBI having plants on my staff?'

'Of course. That's their job. And if that Kansas thing comes off, they'll really start taking us seriously. Another thing . . . Moll, we can buy guns and ammo legally in a dozen states. But bringing them across state lines makes us illegals if they're transported to commit a felony.'

'You have a better idea?'

'We can save a lot of money by buying from underground brokers. Miami is a good place. You can buy anything there from slingshots to tanks and missiles. They outfit most of the terrorists in Central and South America. The best thing about these guys is that they'll deliver – for extra bucks, of course. But it might be smart to let them take the risk. Should I look into it?'

'Sure, you do that, honey.' Then, when he stopped the

114

massage, reclaimed his drink, and sat on the edge of the bed: 'That's all?'

'That's all I had on my mind,' he said with a hard smile. 'Thanks for the rubdown. I feel better.'

'You've got to start eating more, Moll. You barely touched your dinner tonight. You're getting bony as a catfish.

'I know. I've got no tits at all. And my hipbones look like elbows. Jesus, Rod, this is the first time I've felt relaxed in I don't know how long.'

They stared at each other.

'It would be a kindness,' she said in a low voice. 'To me.'

'Ann –' he started.

'It's got nothing to do with Ann,' she said sharply. 'It's got nothing to do with emotion, love, or any of that bullshit. Not as far as I'm concerned. It's doing a pal a favor.'

'If you say so.'

'Well, I'm not going to beg you,' she said.

'You don't have to,' he said, standing and holding a hand out to her.

Her body was white, hard, splintery. He lay beside her, looking down, shaking his head dolefully.

'Jesus,' he said. 'Skin and bones.'

'I don't turn you on?'

'Sure you do. But start eating.'

'You?'

'You know what I mean. You're a toothpick.'

'Compared to Ann, every woman's a toothpick.'

'I guess,' he said, sighing. 'Am I going to be too heavy on you?'

'Try me,' she said.

They made love intently, staring into each other's eyes.

'Oh God,' she said. 'It's been a long time. I had almost forgotten.'

'You're tight as a fist,' he said. 'But hotter.'

She cried out, once so loudly that he put a hand over her mouth to muffle her sobs.

115

'All right, Moll,' he said soothingly. 'All *right*.'

Later, much later, they lay side by side, had another small drink, shared one cigarette between them.

'Purely physical,' she said. 'Nothing more. Right?'

'Right,' he said.

'I was all wound-up,' she said. 'Tense. Needed to get out. We'll never do it again.'

He made no reply.

MARCH 25, 1988

It now seems clear that the famous raid on the National Guard armory at Logan's Ferry, Kansas, was planned and carried out by Company A, Kansas Regiment, of the Women's Defense Corps. There is evidence (not conclusive) that Molly Turner and Rod Harding were present as observers.

Company A was headquartered in Wichita, while the armory at Logan's Ferry was close to Topeka. It was deemed wiser to have the raid executed by 'strangers' rather than by members of Company B, residents of the Topeka area who might be recognized and identified during the attack.

The approach from Wichita to Logan's Ferry was made by single cars, pickups, vans, and one truck with a stake body and canvas cover. The heavier vehicles were included to transport back to Wichita the matériel expected to be looted from the armory.

Preliminary reconnaissance had revealed that the armory was an ugly, two-story cinder block building resembling a warehouse. It was surrounded by heavy chain link fencing with a single locked gate providing access to a large parking area and the armory itself. There was no night watchman. The only security alarm was on the armory door.

The cars, vans, and trucks of Company A rendezvoused

at 11:00 PM on the graveled road running past the armory. The attacking force consisted of thirty-three sisters, two sergeants, a lieutenant, and was commanded by Captain Florence Eiley. All the women wore dark jeans and jackets or parkas. None were masked.

Most, but not all, of the raiders were armed with handguns, rifles, or shotguns. Dollies and skids had been brought along to facilitate moving booty from the armory to the raiders' trucks. It was hoped that such matériel would include weapons, ammunition, and military supplies.

It had been anticipated that the armory would be darkened and deserted at that hour. But the first arrivals from Company A found the gate wide open, private cars in the parking area, and lights burning within the armory itself. Rather than set up roadblocks immediately, as had been planned, a whispered conference was held.

Finally, Captain Eiley and Sergeant Ruth Vizzio made a personal reconnaissance. They succeeded in crossing the lighted parking area without being detected and were able to peer cautiously through the barred windows.

It became evident that the armory was occupied by a National Guard lieutenant, a noncom, and a six-man squad busily taking an inventory of supplies. It was one of those unforeseen happenings that can bedevil any combat plan.

The captain and Sergeant Vizzio returned to their troops. Florence Eiley made the final decision to go ahead with the raid despite the presence of guardsmen. She and her second in command then established roadblocks to stop traffic approaching the armory from east or west.

Eiley selected ten sisters, all armed, and led them in the assault. Entrance was simplicity itself; they merely knocked on the door, it was opened by a guardsman, and the women rushed in.

The guardsmen froze. 'What the hell . . .' one of them said aloud.

Another realized almost at once what was happening

117

and paid for his wit with his life. He grabbed for a holstered automatic pistol. One of the WDC sisters (later determined to be Ruth Vandercook of Clearwater, Kansas) aimed and fired her shotgun. The guardsman was killed instantly. Two other men standing nearby were wounded.

The sudden shooting left both sides in a state of shock. Captain Eiley recovered first, and ordered the dazed men to lie facedown on the armory floor, hands clasped behind them. Three sisters were stationed to guard them. Two other WDC members did what they could for the wounded men, using first aid supplies taken from armory lockers.

The women cut the telephone line and summoned the other members of the raiding party. The plundering of the National Guard armory continued for more than one hour.

Later, official press releases on this incident stated that a small number of M-1 rifles and handguns had been taken. Actually, the loot was much more extensive than that, consisting of a large quantity of pistols, revolvers, Thompson and Ingram submachine guns, BARs, .30 caliber carbines, M-16 rifles, three light and one heavy machine gun, boxes of ammunition, crates of fragmentation, smoke, and tear gas grenades, tools, cleaning kits, maps, and sundry other military paraphernalia.

The raiding party retired in good order after binding and gagging their captives. Not until they were home safely did Captain Florence Eiley make an anonymous phone call to the authorities telling them about the wounded men, one of whom subsequently died.

In addition to the success of this audacious raid in augmenting the armament of the WDC, it had one other important result. When the men taken prisoner were asked why they did not immediately go for their weapons, one of them said, 'My God, you can't shoot women!'

Soon after, directives were issued by the US. Army and by National and State Guards, ordering that any assaults of a similar nature were to be resisted with all means at

118

hand, regardless of the gender of the attackers. There was to be no sex discrimination.

It was a command that occasioned bitter laughter from members of the Women's Defense Corps.

APRIL 19, 1988

'Gargan? Jake Spencer here.'

'Hi, Jake. What's up?'

'Where the hell was the Department when that Kansas thing went down?'

'Shit. We knew something was going to happen but didn't know exactly where or when. The little lady is watching her mouth these days. Jake, how did the senator like the dossier you did on her?'

'Loved it. In fact, he's put me on retainer. He wants more. I've got a man following her all over the goddamned country.'

'No kidding? What's Dundee's interest?'

'Who the hell knows? He really blasted her in that speech yesterday.'

'Jake, you don't suppose he's prepping for the ninety-two election, do you?'

'Stranger things have happened. He'd make as good a president as I would the Queen of England. Hey, Jimbo, it's trade-off time – okay?'

'Sure. What have you got?'

'The Turner dame was sleeping with that Norma Jane Laughlin woman who got knocked off last year.'

'Oh hell, Jake, we've had that from the beginning. Anything else?'

'She's had two abortions – so I guess she swings both ways.'

'Two abortions? That's news. You're sure?'

'Have I ever screwed you? Sure, I'm sure. Both in Charleston at a clinic. I can supply the name if needed.

119

Now what have you got for me, Jimbo?'

'Something raw; not yet verified. She's banging her brother-in-law.'

'Ahh, that's choice. You thinking of sending an anonymous letter to the wife?'

'It's under consideration, Jake. Keep in touch.'

MAY 2, 1988

Virginia Terwilliger came down from Baltimore with increasing frequency, and the evidence of Laura Templeton's deterioration dismayed her. Ginny talked to Constance Underwood and several other staffers at NWU headquarters. They all agreed: Laura just wasn't functioning.

So, after heavy thought and a few sleepless nights, Terwilliger telephoned all the other members of the Executive Board. Because Ginny had been Templeton's most ardent advocate, they were willing to accept her recommendation: Laura's signed letter of resignation would be dated, put in effect, and Constance Underwood would serve out the remainder of her term as president of the National Women's Union.

Telling Laura Templeton was the second hardest thing Virginia Terwilliger had ever done in her life. In her bluff, crusty manner, she came on hard to keep from weeping.

'Listen, kiddo,' she said in Laura's office, 'the Exec Board has decided you better step down.'

Templeton tried to smile. 'I'm that bad?'

'Bad enough,' Terwilliger said roughly. 'Laura, Molly Turner is up to her ass in work. She's doing great, but she needs all the support we can give her. We've got to have someone in charge here who's on the ball. Sorry.'

'When?' Templeton asked.

'Now. Today. What's the sense of prolonging the agony? Laura, what are your plans? Have you thought of what's ahead for you?'

120

Mr 105

Acton Poli

29th August

but the name

any entry to

I would be gr

you examined m

provide me wi

83.

Yours sincere

[signature]

M ROSSER

Chief Inspe

6 Area (We

'Stay at home as long as I can. Until I have to go into a nursing home or hospital. Maria – she's my housekeeper; you met her – she's promised to move in with me. And her husband, Carlos. They're nice people. They'll take care of me as long as they can. Thank God I've got the money.'

'Yeah. And I'll be coming by, you know. You can still help us out. You know so much about the Union. You've had so much experience. You've been such a . . .'

The two women rose, and big, tough Virginia Terwilliger broke, just came apart. She gathered the diminutive woman into her strong arms, covered her face with teary kisses, hugged her close.

'I'm sorry,' she gasped. 'Oh, Laura. Darling. Sister. Shit, shit, and goddamn it.'

The doomed woman provided the comfort. She soothed Ginny, stroking her back, murmuring to her, trying to ease her pain.

'It's all right,' she said. 'All right. Don't let it hurt you this way. Remember the Union, honey. That's all that counts. You and I are nothing much, but the Union . . .'

The hardest thing Virginia Terwilliger had ever done in her life was to go into Constance Underwood's office and tell the bitch she was now president pro tem of the National Women's Union. Connie surprised her by standing and shedding what appeared to be a few genuine tears.

'Oh, poor Laura,' she mourned. 'I must go to her.'

'Not yet,' Terwilliger said sharply. 'First, you and I have to get a few things straight. I don't much like you, and I imagine you return the favor. But I carry a lot of weight on the Executive Board, and if you expect to get anything done, you better listen to me.'

'The president's duty is to carry out the edicts of the Board,' Underwood said primly.

'Yeah. Sure. But we give you broad directives. The way you carry them out is something else again. Let's face it, Connie: the president *runs* the Union. You know it, I know it, everyone knows it. When Laura was well, we gave her the widest latitude in the world. Because we trusted her to do what was best for the Union. With you, I'm not so sure. I think with you it's "Me first" all the way. I just want to make it perfectly clear that you'll be on a short leash; I'll be looking over your shoulder every inch of the way.'

'All I want to do,' Connie said virtuously, 'is follow Laura's policies.'

'I hope you do that. The main thing is to let Molly Turner run. That sister has done more for us in one year than anyone else since the Union was formed. Give her whatever she wants. Money, staff, anything. Don't hobble her. She's got the country's attention. Look what she's done for memberships and contributions. So let her run the Defense Corps, and don't interfere.'

'Of course,' Constance said earnestly. 'I understand that.'

It was only after Virginia Terwilliger had left that Underwood allowed herself one small, brief smile of triumph. Laura Templeton out. That was the first win.

The reports on Molly Turner phoned to Connie's private, unlisted number from Yvonne Popkin had not been too satisfactory. Some, in fact, were incoherent. Popkin was obviously a heavy, heavy drinker. Still, Underwood now had an agent close to Turner, and she counted on that, plus her new power as president of the NWU.

It was not that she had any great moral objections to what Molly was doing. It was the political wisdom of the WDC that Connie questioned. And the woman was becoming the Joan of Arc of the feminist movement. After all, Underwood told herself, the Union was too important to become a personality cult.

She rose and touched her hair. Her first job, she supposed, was to bid a tearful farewell to Laura Templeton. Her next job, she vowed, would be to redecorate that tacky president's office before she moved in.

MAY 23, 1988

Lemuel K. Dundee's speech on the Senate floor on April 18 was the first public condemnation of Molly Turner and the Women's Defense Corps by any national political figure. Most politicians had carefully avoided any comment on the subject, believing it to be a no-win situation.

Dundee and his staff – particularly Thomas J. Kealy – eagerly awaited press and public reaction to the speech. When newspaper and magazine clippings were received and the mail read, Kealy prepared a statistical analysis.

It showed press and TV comment had been almost universally favorable, although most opinions were cautiously worded. The letters from the public – more than 40,000 – were not as one-sided. At least half were obviously from members of the National Women's Union and condemned Senator Dundee for his 'masculinist views.'

The remaining letters generally approved of the senator's opinions, but many revealed the troubled minds of the writers. They recognized the wrongs women suffered, but wondered if there couldn't be a more peaceful redress.

Dundee was delighted. 'Let 'em keep killing innocent guardsmen,' he said boisterously. 'For every soldier boy they shoot, another thousand votes for me.'

Meanwhile, with the country entertained and bemused by the upcoming nominating conventions and national election of 1988, the senator began planning quietly for 1992, keeping his ambitions a secret from all but his closest advisers. But he traveled extensively, responded to every invitation to speak, worked unselfishly for his party – and hired a computer service to put on tape the names, addresses, phone numbers, and personal data of all the thousands of important people whose flesh he was pressing in his travels.

On the evening of May 23, he met in his Spring Valley

home with Ruth Blohm, one of several persons he was interviewing for the job of campaign manager. During the interview Mrs Martha Dundee sat quietly in a corner, playing backgammon against herself and sipping occasionally from a large whiskey.

'I presume,' Dundee said with a deprecatory smile, 'our mutual friend told you the purpose of this meeting.'

'He told me,' Blohm said, nodding.

'Do you think I have a chance?'

'Senator, with enough money and the right handling, the Three Stooges could be elected president.'

Dundee turned sharply to the corner of the room where his wife sat, thinking he had heard a sound suspiciously like a snort.

'Well, I've got the money,' he told Blohm. 'Enough to get started – that's for sure. Management of the campaign is the big problem, and that's why you're here. You come very highly recommended, Miss Blohm. Or is it Mrs.?'

'Miss. I've had some successes, but I've never handled a national campaign. And the last governor's race I bossed, we lost.'

'I'm aware of that,' Dundee said genially. 'The people I've spoken to seem to think it was due to lack of funds.'

'That was part of it,' Blohm admitted. 'The other part was that the candidate had principles. Do you have principles, Senator?'

'A few,' he said with a cold smile, 'but none engraved on stone.'

He stared at her, seeing a short, blocky woman made even squarer by the black gabardine suit she was wearing. Her complexion was sallow, fingers stained with nicotine, hair a stringy mess. But Dundee thought she had the sharp, defiant eyes of a fighter.

'Do you know why I'm interviewing you for the job?' he asked her.

'Well, there are good men available who have a better record than mine, more experience and more contacts. I'd

124

guess you're talking to me because you plan to base your campaign on opposition to the Women's Defense Corps, and you figure having a female manager will prove you're really not prejudiced against women.'

He looked at her admiringly. 'Your mother didn't raise you to be an idiot, did she?'

'My father raised me,' she told him, 'and he writes books on chess.'

'Well, let's get some pieces on the board, Ruth. May I call you Ruth?'

'Sure.'

'Ruth, how do you feel personally about the WDC?'

'Their problems come pretty far down on my anxiety list. To tell you the truth, I'm too busy hustling a buck to get involved.'

'Well, that's honest enough. Oh . . . I've been derelict in my duty as a host. May I offer you a drink?'

'No, thanks. But you go ahead.'

'Not at the moment. Ruth, if I decide to put you on the payroll, how would you proceed?'

'I haven't given it any thought, Senator. But off the top of my head, I'd say it's much too early to declare for 1992. If any reporter puts the direct question to you, deny, deny, and deny. Meanwhile, set up a small Draft Dundee group in your home state. Have nothing to do with it – except financing it on the QT, of course. If your anti-WDC campaign catches fire, you can use the Draft Dundee group as a nucleus for a national organization.'

'I like the way you think,' he said.

'You're sure you've got the money for this, sir?'

'I'm sure.'

'We're talking millions you know. Millions and millions.'

'I am well aware of campaign costs,' he said, somewhat frostily. 'Ruth, is there anything in your private life, in your background, that might be dug up and used to embarrass me? I'll have you checked out, of course, but I'd rather you tell me now.'

'I'm clean as a whistle,' she said cheerfully. 'All I've done all my life is work my ass off. A few one-night stands along the way, but nothing serious. I smoke up a storm, but my favorite drink is herbal tea and I'm not into drugs. But let's get one thing straight: If you hire me to run your campaign, I *run* it. No coaching from the sidelines. The issues of the campaign are your responsibility. I'll show you the polls, but try not to influence you. But I handle the nuts-and-bolts. That's what you're paying me for.'

'Well, thank you very much, Ruth,' Senator Dundee said, rising. 'I've enjoyed the opportunity to meet you and have this very frank and honest discussion. I have some other people to talk to. I'll let you know one way or the other.'

He walked her to the door. Just before she left, he laughed heartily and said, 'Were you serious – that with enough money and the right handling, the Three Stooges could be elected president?'

'Try me,' she said.

When the door closed behind her, Dundee came back into the room. He walked slowly, thoughtfully, over to his wife's backgammon table. He picked up her tumbler and drained the remainder of the bourbon.

'What do you think, Martha?' he asked.

'Hire her,' she said.

JUNE 10, 1988

Thomas J. Kealy was not happy about the appointment of Ruth Blohm as Senator Dundee's 'political liaison aide.' She was given that title rather than 'campaign manager' to keep from the media as long as possible the fact that a campaign was actually under way.

'Politics is not a world of facts,' Blohm pronounced. 'It's a world of perceptions.'

Kealy just didn't like the woman. He could not fault

her professional qualifications, but he thought her ugly, awkward, and, he told himself, she exuded an odor of burning hair, as if she had used an old-fashioned curling iron on her unruly mop.

Also, he didn't like her manner toward him. There was none of the respect he thought his position deserved. Instead, she invariably turned on him a smile tarnished with irony that said they were engaged in an indecent conspiracy, and if they were lucky they'd eventually have adjoining cells. Kealy didn't enjoy that thought.

Finally, Kealy admitted to himself, he didn't like Blohm because she represented a threat. The senator had promised him a key position in the campaign. Kealy knew he wasn't qualified to do the job Blohm was hired for, but he wondered exactly where he would be fitted into the 'holy crusade,' and he resolved to make his private counsel invaluable to the candidate.

With this aim in mind, he pondered how he might more effectively exploit his connection with Billy McCrea and reap personal advantage from the simple-minded boy's relationship with the president of the National Women's Union.

On the night of June 10, in his Georgetown apartment, Tom Kealy, bruised and sore, said, 'You don't have to leave right away, do you, Billy?'

'I guess not.'

'I've got a bottle of champagne in the fridge. How's about we share it?'

'Sure,' Billy said. 'I like that stuff. The bubbles go up my nose.'

Kealy also had some stronger stuff in the fridge that could go up Billy's nose, but he thought it wiser not to mention it. One pleasure at a time . . .

'Billy,' Kealy said, 'that woman you know with the National Women's Union, that Constance Underwood, she – '

'Hey,' McCrea said. 'I never mentioned her name. I

never say the names of my clients.'

'I know you don't,' Kealy said hastily, 'and I respect you for it. It's very commendable. But it wasn't hard for my reporter friend to find it out. She's the president of the Union now, isn't she?'

'Yeah, I guess.'

'My friend is very appreciative of the inside information you furnished, Billy. Were you satisfied with what he paid?'

'Oh sure. The money was nice.'

Kealy finally got the bottle uncorked and poured them each a glass. They hadn't yet dressed, and sat naked in facing armchairs. It was difficult for Kealy to keep his mind on business; the boy was so beautiful.

'This is great stuff,' McCrea said.

'Isn't it? Seventy dollars a bottle.'

'Wow. Now it tastes even better.'

Kealy wasn't sure if that was deliberate humor or not, so he reacted with a small laugh.

'Plenty more where that came from,' he said. 'Billy, my reporter friend got such good reactions to his articles on the feminist movement that he's decided to write a book on the subject. He tried to set up a personal interview with the Underwood woman, but she won't talk to him. I guess she read his articles and didn't like them. Maybe she thinks he's prejudiced against women or something.'

'Uh-huh,' Billy said, not much interested.

'So I told him I'd try to meet her and see if I could smooth the way for him. You know, you've never told me anything about your apartment. Is it nice?'

'It's okay. An old loft in Adams-Morgan.'

'A lot of blacks?'

'A lot of everything.'

'Do you ever have parties in your pad?'

'Oh sure. Once I had a party there, and more than fifty people came. I mean it's a big place.'

'Well, I was wondering if you'd be willing to have a

128

cocktail party and invite Constance Underwood and me and anyone else you'd like. That way I'd get a chance to meet her and see if I can persuade her to talk to my friend.'

'Why don't you just call her at her office and ask her?' McCrea said, reasonably enough.

'Oh, Billy,' Kealy said, with a laugh that sounded tinny even to him, 'that's not the way things get done in this town. She'd know I was calling because I wanted something, and be on her guard. No, the best way is to meet someone at the home of a mutual friend, get to know one another face to face. Then you can see how you can help each other. That's how Washington works.'

'I guess.'

'I'd pay for everything,' Kealy said earnestly. 'All the booze, all the food, and a nice bonus to you for the use of your place and setting it up.'

'You'll pay for it?'

'Sure – but only if the Underwood woman will be there. So the first step is to get her to come. Then you can go ahead with the party.'

'Can I invite anyone else I want?'

'Of course,' Kealy said. 'I don't mean hundreds of people, but about thirty or so would be all right. I'll pick up the tab for that.'

'Sounds cool,' Billy McCrea said. 'I owe a lot of people. I'll ask Connie if she'll come.'

'Fine. Just tell me when it's going to be, and I'll give you the money.'

'I've got a new blender,' McCrea said. 'I can make strawberry margaritas.'

They had more champagne, draining the bottle. Finally the older man could stand it no longer. He put his glass of champagne aside, rushed over to McCrea's chair.

'Hey,' Billy said. 'A double?'

'I'll pay, I'll pay!' cried Thomas J. Kealy.

They were in another bed, another motel, another city, both of them exhausted by a kaleidoscope of changing scenes.

'Moll,' Rod Harding said, 'Ann's coming down to the wire. I've got to get home to be with her.'

'Of course you do,' Molly Turner said drowsily, her head resting on his bare chest.

'She says it's all right. Stay on the trail. Fight the good fight. All that bullshit. But I know if I'm not there when the kid is born, she'll never forgive me – and I'll never forgive myself.'

'You've got to go; no two ways about it. I wish I could be there, but sister Ann will understand. Call me the moment she pops – okay?'

'Of course,' he said, tugging gently at her blond curls. 'And I'll come back as soon as I can. It shouldn't be more than a week. Two at the most.'

'Aunt Molly,' she said ruefully. 'Just think: I'll be an aunt.'

'Auntie,' he said, cupping her bare breast. 'Old Auntie Moll.'

'Oh Jesus,' she said fiercely, clutching him to her. 'I wish you didn't have to go.'

But he flew back to Canton to rejoin his wife. Ann cried a little when she saw him, and he knew he had done the right thing.

A few weeks previously, Ann had received a letter signed 'A Friend' that stated Molly and Rod were having an affair. Ordinarily mail was opened by a WDC staffer. Much of it was disgusting stuff and promptly trashed. But this letter was addressed in a feminine hand to Mrs Ann Harding, the envelope post-marked Independence, Missouri, and marked PERSONAL in big letters.

Ann read it through twice. It seemed to have been written by a literate; it was couched in rather old-fashioned phrases, but there was no mistaking its meaning: her husband and her sister were sleeping together.

Ann was not a witless woman; she knew very well the letter could be a deliberate attempt by someone, anyone, to create dissension, cause trouble for the leaders of the Women's Defense Corps. A single letter was nothing; their enemies were capable of more vicious tactics than that.

But when the second letter arrived a week later, giving the exact date and place (a motel in St Paul, Minnesota) where Molly and Rod had allegedly cohabited, Ann thought long and hard about the chance of its being true.

She had never considered the possibility of her husband being unfaithful; it seemed so out of character for him. And in reviewing their happy marriage, she could find nothing in her own conduct that might drive him to seek physical solace elsewhere; she had always been an enthusiastic bed partner.

Nor could she conceive of Molly playing the role of the 'other woman.' She had long known her sister was bisexual, but Molly was so strong, so honest, that it was impossible to believe her capable of a deceit of this nature. It would be the foulest kind of treachery. No, she told herself, if Molly was in love with Rod, she'd come to Ann and tell her; she was that kind of a woman.

Having Rod home, big and handsome, solicitous and endlessly patient, did a great deal to restore her confidence and calm her fears. Like most wives, she was convinced that if her husband was unfaithful to her, she would *know*. But there was absolutely nothing in his look or manner that even hinted of perfidy.

The first night he was home, they sat in the bedroom talking until almost 2:00 AM, exchanging chatter on what each had been doing during their separation.

Despite her pregnancy, Ann had continued to function as headquarters commander. She had a retentive memory and quoted to Rod the latest membership figures, bank balance, matériel on hand.

'We're running out of room in the Hillcrest Avenue place,' she reported. 'I've got my eye on an empty building on River Street. It used to be a warehouse – really just a big shed. But it shouldn't cost too much to partition it off into offices. It's heated, but the plumbing is kind of primitive. Will you take a look at it, Rod?'

'Sure. We'll also need a safe place for our guns, ammo, and supplies. It's a problem we're having in every state we visit. A farmhouse or barn out in the country would be best. I'll look around.'

'How are you doing, hon?'

'On recruiting guys for instructors? I'm doing fine – I think. It's a nice surprise to find so many Nam vets willing to work with us. But maybe it's not such a surprise at that. This is their chance to kick the establishment in the balls.'

'And how is Molly?'

'She's doing great!' he said enthusiastically. 'She's lining up a good officer corps, and we're gradually filling in our table of organization. Some of the state chapters are in business already.'

'Like Kansas? What happened there, Rod?'

He shrugged. 'That kid should never have been scragged. No one planned anything like that. But he went for his gun, and the sisters had no choice. Just a lousy accident; no one was happy about it.'

'Is Molly all right – personally, I mean? How does she look?'

He frowned. 'Thin as a rail,' he said. 'On the go every minute. not eating right. I've tried to get her to slow down – but you know your sister.'

'Sometimes I'm not so sure.'

'She's a powerhouse,' he said, either ignoring her comment or not hearing it. 'But she's going to burn herself out if she keeps on like this. Hopefully, in another couple of months, the worst will be over. But enough about business

132

– how are you feeling, sweetheart?'

'You know me, Rod – I'm a horse. Doc Feldman calls me a perfect baby-making machine.'

'Aches and pains?'

'Some. nothing I can't handle. Learning to sleep on my back was the toughest job. It should be within a week or so, daddy.'

'Can't come too soon for me,' he said cheerily.

They undressed, and he helped her get into her nightgown.

'Is there anything I can do?' he said anxiously. 'Massage? Rub your feet? Give you a lesson in how to nurse?'

'Nut,' she said, laughing. 'Just have the car gassed up and ready to go. My suitcase is packed. And I've got a card with Doc Feldman's number propped on the phone. I'm organized.'

'As always,' he said.

When she was in her bed, lying on her back, and he was naked, he came over to her and lifted her nightgown. He kissed her huge belly, then put his ear to her navel.

'Hello, in there,' he called. 'Can you hear me? We love you. We want you to know that.'

Ann began to cry, happily, grasped his head and pressed it into her flesh.

'And I love you,' she said, blinking her tears away. 'I want you to know that. I love you so much. I'll never give you up.'

'You better not,' he said sternly. 'Unless someday you'll want to turn me in for a newer model.'

'Never,' she vowed, moving his head up to press it into her swollen breasts. 'We're together until death do us part.'

'You better believe it,' he said. 'Hon, can I lie beside you for just a few minutes?'

'Do,' she breathed.

Like most expectant parents, they believed there would be a midnight emergency, a careening drive to the hospital, hours of agonizing labor pains. It didn't happen like that at all.

At around 8:30 AM, on the morning of June 21, Ann Harding, timing her contractions, said calmly, 'Rod, I think you better call Doc Feldman. No great rush, but *call* him. And Mother. And your folks. And headquarters. Tell them I won't be in this morning.'

The car started with no problem, Ann arrived at Canton General Hospital at 9:10 AM, and an hour later the maternity waiting room held Rod, the hopeful grandparents, five cigarette-chewing WDC staffers – and one other waiting father-to-be, who was completely bewildered by the mob scene.

At 10:35 AM, Doc Feldman, grinning, came into the waiting room and shook Rod's trembling hand.

'Beautiful,' he said. 'A handsome baby boy. Eight pounds, six ounces. Mother and child doing well. Congratulations and mazel tov.'

So Jefferson Turner Harding came into the world. A big name for a big baby.

Rod stayed in Canton for almost two weeks after the birth of his son. Ann urged him to rejoin Molly and complete the work of setting up the officers' cadres.

'The sooner you go,' she said, 'the sooner you'll be back – for good. And Molly needs you, hon, to settle her down. You know how wild and excitable she can be sometimes.'

She thought she would be depressed by his leaving. But she found such a sublime joy in the care and feeding of little Jeff that she had neither desire nor time to mourn her husband's absence.

Rod rejoined Molly Turner and the WDC entourage in Portland, Oregon. That night, in his motel room, he showed Molly color photos of Jefferson Turner Harding.

Then they went to bed and devoured each other.

The infrastructure of the Women's Defense Corps and the

*appointment of staff and line officers were generally com-
pleted in 1988. Recruitment of volunteers continued. The
goal was an army of 50,000 sisters. Half that number had
already enlisted by July 1.*

*This period also saw a refining of the functions and
responsibilities of the WDC. Turner and Constance Underwood agreed to the following:*

*The National Women's Union, alone or in conjunction
with other feminist organizations, would continue to fight
in the courts and legislatures for women's political and
economic rights. The Union would engage in lobbying,
picketing, demonstrations, and boycotts.*

*The Women's Defense Corps would limit its activities to
those situations in which women's physical well-being was
abused or threatened, their legal rights denied, or a deliberate attempt was being made to denigrate all women; for
example, pornography and sexist advertising.*

*Careful analysis of existing records shows that the WDC
engaged in thirty-nine separate actions during its formative
months in 1988. Most of these were directed against accused
and/or convicted rapists.*

*It is of some interest to sociologists and behavioral scien-
tists that the category of crimes against women that showed
the greatest growth during the 1980s was gang rape.*

JULY 17, 1988

Ruth Blohm sweated excessively. She used jacket and
dress shields, antiperspirants and deodorants – all to little
avail. In the middle of July, with most of the country
sweltering in a heat wave, she was acutely conscious of her
affliction.

But she did not let physical discomfort slow her down.
She flew to Senator Dundee's home state, bearing several
teller's checks that would get the Draft Dundee movement
started. The senator had selected the men he wanted to

135

front for him, and had called ahead to set up appointments for Ruth.

She spent three days dealing with attorneys, state legislators, judges, and district bosses. Before she left, an empty store had been rented, a staff of three people (a white, a black, an Hispanic) had been hired, posters, badges, and bumper stickers were being designed – and the grass roots Draft Dundee campaign was off and running.

On her way back to Washington, Blohm stopped off in Atlanta to visit an acquaintance who owned and managed a successful business called Legal Psychometrics, Inc. It was one of only a half-dozen similar organizations in the country which provided an unusual legal service.

Two years previously, Ruth had met Lyle C. Hayden at a seminar on behavior modification in Boston. The meeting had turned out to be a waste of time, but Hayden fascinated her.

Legal Psychometrics, Inc., provided a unique service for any defense attorney whose client could afford it. They analyzed the defendant and the crime of which he or she was accused. They then drew up a psychological profile of those jurors who would be most sympathetic to the client.

During the voir dire, the defense attorney attempted to match prospective jurors as closely as possible to the profile drawn. After the jury had been impaneled, the psychologists and behavioral scientists of Legal Psychometrics, Inc., really went to work. They investigated, poked, pried – and drew up psychological profiles of the twelve seated jurors as well as the two alternates. The profiles included such things as religiousness, prejudices, eating and drinking habits, dress, ambitions, familial relations, and sexual preferences.

The defense attorney based his or her arguments (and sometimes even his clothes and manner of speaking) on these analyses. He spoke not only to their conscious minds, but to their hidden bigotries, fears, hopes, and irrational beliefs.

The services of Legal Psychometrics, Inc., were costly –
only the wealthiest defendants could afford them – but
they had contributed to a solid series of successes: the
client found not guilty or given just a slap on the wrist.

'What it is,' Lyle C. Hayden had said, laughing, 'is
perfectly legal jury tampering.'

Ruth Blohm called him on the morning of July 17. He
seemed pleased to hear from her and readily agreed to
drive out to the airport to have lunch.

They had chicken sandwiches and Coors beer. The air
conditioning in the luncheonette fought a losing battle
against the heat generated by the mob of travelers wolfing
down cheeseburgers between planes.

'I've been thinking about Boston for the last two years,'
Blohm said, mopping her face. 'I mean, what you said
about your job, how you go about it. I'm interested because
I'm a professional campaign manager. I don't care if you're
a Democrat, Republican, Socialist, Communist, or born-
again Christian. If you're running for office, and you've
got the money, I can manage your campaign. My record
is pretty good.'

'I'm not running for office, Ruth,' he said with a mild
smile.

He was a tall, willowy man with hair, beard, and mustache so blond they appeared white against his tanned skin.

'I didn't think you were, Lyle,' Blohm said, wiping her
wet hands. 'You've got too much sense for that. But I want
your take on something. Do you think your techniques
would work in a political campaign? Not to analyze individuals, of course, but to draw up psychological profiles of
blocs of voters?'

The white eyebrows rose.

'Maybe,' he said cautiously. 'But the cost would be
prohibitive – even assuming you could recruit sufficient
qualified personnel. On a nationwide basis, it would cost
not millions, but hundreds of millions.'

'Not so,' she said, shaking her head. 'You know your

business, but I know mine. In any national election, for instance, every candidate knows there are throwaway states where he'll never win, no matter what he does or how much he spends. And there are states that are in his hip pocket, sure things, and just need a minimum of stroking. So he concentrates his time and resources on the swing states, the ones that can go either way. And within those states there are precincts that dictate which way the state's electors will go. Now we're down to a few areas. Well, maybe not a few, but at least manageable.'

Hayden began to get interested. He stopped eating.

'Wouldn't conventional polling be cheaper?' he asked.

She shook her head angrily. 'Look around you – ' She waved a hand at the horde of diners. 'Now suppose you polled all the men in this room and asked two questions: "Would you object to working for a woman?" and "Would you object if a black family moved in next door to you?" Ninety percent of them would say, "Hell no, I wouldn't object to working for a woman or living next door to blacks." Now you know and I know that's a lot of bullshit. But they don't want the pollster to know how sexist and racist they are.'

'Or maybe,' Hayden said, 'they don't realize it themselves.'

'Right!' Blohm said. 'But your techniques would reveal what the voters really care about. And if a smart candidate knew all that, he could plan his direct mail, print ads, and TV commercials to swing those voters.'

Hayden looked at her curiously. 'Ruth, are you handling a national candidate?'

'Well . . .' she said, wiping her glistening face with a paper napkin, 'let's just say I'm doing some preliminary fieldwork. Lyle, are you interested in the idea of applying your ideas to the general electorate?'

'Hell yes, I'm interested.'

'Interested enough to do some work on spec?'

'How much work?' he asked warily.

'When I get back to Washington, I'll send you all the data on, say, three political areas: a black ward in Chicago, a rural county in Iowa, and maybe a retirement town in Florida. I'll give you all the latest census and demographic stuff I can dig up. You look it over, figure out how you'd handle it, the staff you'd need, and so forth. Then send me an estimate of what it would cost. Okay?'

'Sure,' he said. 'I could do that. It's a fascinating concept. Not too far from psychoanalysis of groups. Or nations, for that matter.'

'Except we don't want to cure them,' Ruth Blohm said. 'We just want their votes.'

She got back to Dundee's office late in the afternoon, picked up her mail, and drove home to Arlington, Virginia.

Ruth and her father, Eric Blohm, lived in a small, two-bedroom home – almost a bungalow – near Waverly Hills. It was on a half-acre tract with a scrabbly front lawn and a minuscule backyard, where several tomato plants had already given up the ghost.

Eric Blohm was seated at a folding card table in the living room. As usual, he was hunched over a chessboard, working out a problem. He glanced up when Ruth walked in.

'Hey,' he said. 'You're home. Hungry?'

'Famished,' she said, coming over to peck his cheek.

'Good,' he said. 'I've got a day-old beef stew ready to heat up. It always tastes better the second day. Be ready in twenty minutes.'

'Good. That'll give me time to shower.'

During dinner in the kitchen, she told him everything she had done on her trip. She was especially elated about arousing Lyle Hayden's interest in depth-analysis of voting blocs.

'Hmm,' Eric Blohm said thoughtfully. 'Your idea?'

'Not exactly. Just an expansion of what Hayden has been doing with juries. Father, too much pepper in the stew.'

139

'I should stop smoking cigars,' he said. 'I can't taste anything anymore, so I overspice everything. You think you'll be able to talk Dundee into going along with your plans?'

'I don't know,' she confessed. 'To tell you the truth, I'm revising my estimate of Senator Lemuel K. Dundee. When I first met him, I thought, O God, another hot-air balloonist. But I've begun to realize there's something inside the balloon besides gas. A shrewd man. Very, very ambitious. Not too well educated, but intelligent. And apparently he's got all the money in the world behind him.'

'Go along for the ride,' her father advised. 'Maybe you'll get a chance to test your theories.'

'Right!' Ruth Blohm said. 'Until they're tested, that's all they are – theories. But if they work, they'll revolutionize the way people get elected in this country.'

'O brave new world,' her father said mordantly.

'What's wrong with manipulating the voters?' she asked. 'Lincoln did it with stump speeches. I want to do it with computers. What's the difference?'

'Dundee isn't Lincoln,' her father said.

AUGUST 8, 1988

'Spencer Security Services. Good morning.'

  'Mr Spencer, please.'

  'May I ask who's calling?'

  'Just tell him it's his old dumpster buddy.'

  'His old dumpster buddy?'

  'That's right.'

  'Just a moment, sir.'

  'Jimbo?'

  'Who else? Who answered the phone, Jake?'

  'My secretary. She gives great head. Interested?'

  'No. I think we should have a face-to-face, Jake.'

  'Whatever you say. When?'

'Tonight? Ten o'clock?'

'Okay. Where?'

'Remember that place where Tony M caught it?'

'Sure, I remember.'

'There. The gates will be locked so you'll have to use the back road.'

'I know, Jimbo, I *know*. But Tony M didn't.'

'See you, Jake.'

It was a small state park near Friendship Heights in Maryland. The gates to the picnic area were locked at sundown, but those in the know could follow a one-lane back road to the lake and the graveled parking area.

Jake Spencer rolled his car to a stop and doused the lights. In a few seconds, the only other car in the area blinked its lights three times. Jake got out of his car, lumbered over to the boat dock.

'Hello, Jake. How's it going?'

'Can't complain.'

'You wouldn't be wired, would you, Jake?'

Spencer turned to stare at the other man in the gloom. Gargan was as big as he was, but leaner, harder, younger. Spencer thought he could take him, but he hoped it would never be necessary to try.

He turned his back to the other man, raised his arms above his head. James Gargan stroked him down, ignoring the holstered Police Special on Spencer's hip.

'Now it's my turn,' said Jake.

Gargan raised his arms, and Jake performed the same ritual frisk.

'This is a lot of shit,' Spencer said. 'You could have a bug up your ass for all I know.'

'I don't.'

'Or a parabolic mike in the car hooked to a recorder.'

'Want to look?'

'Of course not. We're old friends, Jimbo.'

'Sure we are, Jake. You still working for Dundee?'

'Uh-huh. The guy's a fucking gold mine. I told you I'm

141

on retainer. Plus special jobs.'

'Like what?'

'Am I going to get anything out of this, Jimbo?'

'Molly Turner is definitely banging her brother-in-law. That's confirmed.'

'You send the wife a letter?'

'Sure. We're still sending them. Nothing so far.'

'Keep it up. It's like the Chinese water torture. A drop at a time. She'll break eventually.'

'Maybe. Now what's the special job you did for Dundee?'

'We ran a trace on Constance Underwood. She's president of the National Women's Union. Molly Turner's official boss.'

'I know who she is. Find anything interesting?'

'Yeah. She's balling a kid named Billy McCrea. Ever hear of him?'

'Oh sure. We've had an eye on Billy-boy for a couple of years now. The guy's a high-priced whore with a very select clientele.'

'Jimbo, what's the Department's interest in all this?'

'Remember the last time we talked, we kidded about Dundee running for president? Well, he is.'

'Son of a bitch.'

'He's setting up a Draft Dundee movement in his backyard. He's got a lot of money behind him, Jake.'

'He'll need it.'

'The Department thinks he can make it in ninety-two.'

The two big men stared at each other in the semidarkness.

'You mean,' Jake Spencer said, 'the Department *wants* him to make it in ninety-two.'

'Sure,' Gargan said. 'Why not? He's a friend. Also, the Pentagon would be happy. And a lot of other people.'

'I bet. Well, you know me, Jimbo – always ready and willing to help out any way I can.'

'You already have,' Gargan said. 'The business of the

Underwood woman and Billy McCrea might be something. Keep us in the picture, Jake.'

'Sure.'

'You got a guy following Molly Turner around the country?'

'I told you that.'

'Is he a skinny gink with pimples?'

'That's him.'

'He's not very good, Jake.'

'I know,' Spencer said with a hawk of laughter, 'but he's cheap, and Dundee and his prat boy Kealy seem satisfied.'

'Jake, something's going down with Molly Turner and her merry crew of lunatics. Something big. We don't know what it is or where. Apparently it's in the planning stages now. Will you see if you can pick up anything?'

'A shooting, a bombing, a raid – what?'

'We don't know.'

'I thought you had a plant close to Turner.'

'We do, but she's not a professional. She's got a heavy dope bust hanging over her head. Anyway, she sends us what she can, but all of a sudden the Women's Defense Corps has become very security conscious. All she hears are whispers, hints – nothing definite. Sometime later this year, she thinks. But what, where, and exactly when, she doesn't know. See what you can pick up.'

'Okay, Jimbo.'

'That's all I got. You got anything else?'

'Nope.'

'I'm carrying a jug of Jack Daniel's in the car. Want a belt?'

'I thought you'd never ask,' Jake Spencer said.

AUGUST 23, 1988

When Thomas J. Kealy got his first look at the building in which Billy McCrea lived, he was reminded of an old

143

Harper's Weekly engraving of a Civil War hospital in Washington, DC.

Then, as he tramped up the cast-iron staircase, the image changed: he was certain he would find Billy entertaining guests in the equivalent of Mimi's attic in *La Bohème*.

The reality was more astonishing than any of his fancies: McCrea's apartment was a six-page layout from *Architectural Digest*, with a delightful meld of high-tech, Swedish modern, and Victorian that gave the impression of a joyous, lived-in home.

The loft was crowded with a young, chattering mob. There were jeans and djelabas, miniskirts and burnooses, Halston shifts and Black Watch kilts.

The party was being catered; there was a buffet table with a toqued black chef serving, and a bar tended by two midgets perspiring in admirals' uniforms. Kealy had a fast vodka-rocks as he wondered how much this saturnalia was going to cost him. But then, calmed by vodka, he realized it could easily come out of Senator Dundee's confidential fund.

Looking around at these attractive, voluble people, he began to revise his opinion of Billy McCrea. Perhaps he had underestimated the idiot-boy. He recognized an under secretary, a deputy secretary, a third deputy under secretary. Plus representatives from at least three embassies. And a White House aide. Not an important aide, true, but still – the White House!

It took him almost five minutes to work his way through the crush to a corner of the enormous loft where McCrea was showing his collection of Georgian silver to a tiny, dark man wearing what appeared to be a bedsheet.

He caught Billy's eye and beckoned. McCrea excused himself and came over.

'She's at the buffet,' he said. 'The tall one with long, black hair. She's wearing a Hanae Mori sheath.'

Kealy turned to look. 'I see her. Thanks, Billy. Nice party.'

'It's cool,' McCrea acknowledged.

Kealy picked up a vodka refill and moved slowly closer to Constance Underwood. Not a beautiful woman, he thought, but striking. He seemed to be thinking in visual images that night, and she reminded him of the long-haired witch in Chas. Addams' cartoons.

He circled around and got a good look at her lean, graceful figure, which excited him. She was younger than he had expected, more intense, more vital. He thought of his wife, Dori. Short little, blond little, Dori. Probably feeding her gerbils at that very moment. He hastily turned his attention back to Constance Underwood.

It had been a long time since a woman had aroused him. But this one, he told himself, was something special. There was a hard, detached somberness that attracted him. Something cold and strong there. A formidable enemy.

The woman Underwood had been talking to eased away, and Kealy moved in quickly.

'Constance Underwood?' he asked. 'President of the National Women's Union?'

'Yes,' she said, inspecting his black horn-rims, three-piece suit, white shirt, repp tie, wingtip shoes. 'Who are you?'

'I'm afraid to tell you,' he said, showing his teeth. 'You might deck me.'

'No,' she said with a faint smile, 'I don't think I'll do that. Who *are* you?'

'Thomas J. Kealy. Executive assistant to Senator Lemuel K. Dundee.'

'Oh,' she said. Then: 'You're right – I might deck you.'

He liked her voice: deep, throaty, with good timbre.

'I hope not,' he said, still smiling. He held out his hand. 'I really am glad to meet you.'

She hesitated, briefly, then shook his hand, briefly.

'Dundee is not exactly our favorite senator,' she said.

'I know,' he said humbly. 'Sometimes he suffers from a diarrhea of words and a constipation of ideas.'

'I like that. Is it original with you?'

'Oh God, no. Someone said it years and years ago. But I thought it was apt.'

'Do you always put down your employer to strangers, Mr Kealy?'

'Never. Until now. Hey, I see your glass is empty. And so is mine. May I bring you another drink?'

'Thank you. Perrier with a slice of lime.'

'You won't go away, will you?'

'No,' she said, looking at him curiously, 'I won't go away.'

Ten minutes later they were standing on a cast-iron fire escape grating outside Billy McCrea's bedroom. It was warmer out there, but the air was fresher. Best of all, they were alone.

'Look,' Kealy said. 'I know Dundee has been giving the NWU a hard time, but you've got to realize the man is a politician. If opportunism was made a Federal crime, the entire US. Congress would be in the slammer. And that *is* original.'

'And not bad,' she said, smiling.

'You should smile more often,' he said. 'It lights up your face.' Then swiftly, he got back to business. 'He's dumping on the Women's Defense Corps because he thinks it'll mean votes. He's up for re-election as senator in ninety-two, you know. I think he's making a mistake with this anti – WDC campaign, and I've told him so. Did you ever try to change a senator's mind? Difficult. But they're pragmatic animals, and sometimes they'll trim their sails – if you don't mind my mixing figures of speech.'

'I don't mind,' she said.

'Miss Underwood – ' he began. 'Oh hell, may I call you Constance, and you call me Tom? I don't think a fire escape is the place for formality.'

'All right.'

'Constance, I – '

'Connie.'

146

'Connie, I just have a feeling that you and I could do each other some good. Even if it's only an exchange of information. I'm trying to mollify Dundee's more virulent outbreaks. That could help you. And, in my opinion, help the senator. And the NWU and WDC could benefit by having a powerful senator brought around to their side.'

She looked at him. 'Are you a feminist, Tom?'

'I could swear by my father's sword that I am, but it wouldn't be the truth. Actually, I'm not into the women's movement at all. But I want to protect Senator Dundee as best I can. And, as I said, I think we might help one another, you and I, if we could work together. Could we meet occasionally? To exchange information to our mutual benefit? What do you think?'

She dug into her tapestried evening bag for a pack of Players. Kealy was right there with his gold Dunhill lighter.

'You're a friend of Billy McCrea's?' she asked idly, staring out at the rosy glow over the nation's capital.

'Billy? Oh yes. I've known him a few years. And you?'

'Yes,' she said shortly, 'I know Billy. Let me think about this, Tom. You may be right, there may be advantages for both of us in setting up some kind of liaison.'

'I think there would be,' he said earnestly. 'At least give it some thought. Will you call me?'

'I don't think that would be wise,' she said. 'I'll give you my private unlisted number. Call me in a few days.'

'Fine.'

'Where could we meet?' she asked – and he knew he had her. 'Not in a restaurant or any other public place. It would be in the columns the next day.'

'Do you live in DC?'

'Yes,' she said. 'At the Watergate. But I wouldn't want you coming up there. Too public.'

'I have a little apartment in Georgetown,' he said. 'Not much of a place, but private.'

'Are you married, Tom?'

'Yes. My wife lives in Alexandria.'

147

'And you keep a separate apartment in Georgetown?'

'Yes.'

'Handy,' she said.

The next morning Kealy went into the office and called Dundee at his summer home on Chesapeake Bay. He was on the phone for almost a half-hour, describing his conversation with Constance Underwood in great detail. The senator listened without interrupting.

'I thought it would be smart to make personal contact,' Kealy concluded. 'First of all, it will cut out an informant who might represent a potential danger in the future. And a one-on-one relationship always yields more accurate intelligence. I really think there may be heavy benefits for us in this. I told you she's got a plant on Molly Turner's staff – the public affairs officer. Obviously Underwood sees the Turner woman as a threat. So I'm hoping she'll relay information to us – to protect her kingdom, you understand.'

'Sure,' Dundee said. 'I can appreciate the way the little lady is thinking. Good work, Tom. Go right ahead with it – and keep me informed.'

'I'll do that, sir. Have a nice day.'

'If I don't,' the senator said with heavy good humor, 'you'll be the first to know.'

The following day, James Gargan listened to a tape recording of this telephone conversation.

'Interesting,' he remarked to his assistant.

SEPTEMBER 13, 1988

By this date, Molly Turner had visited thirty-seven state chapters of the National Women's Union and selected the volunteers to serve as regimental colonels of the Women's Defense Corps. Her final recruiting stop was in Florida. The state NWU chapter was headquartered in Fort Lauderdale, and it was there that Rod Harding met Brother Nabisco.

As usual, he started at a counseling service for Vietnam veterans. They sent him to a small storefront social club where Nam vets met to play cards, shoot a game of pool, or just have a few beers and shmooze.

Harding contributed a cold six-pack and made his pitch. The men present listened to him politely, but no one volunteered.

'Man,' one of them said, 'my wife would kill me.'

It was a reaction Harding had heard before.

He stayed awhile, swapping improbable combat tales, drinking a beer. He was about to leave when one of the vets stopped him.

'Hey,' he said. 'You ought to talk to Brother Nabisco. He's nutty enough to sign up.'

'Brother Nabisco?'

'That's not his real name,' the vet said, laughing. 'We call him that because all he eats is shredded wheat. I guess he can't afford much else. No job. He's a black, and crazy as a coot.'

'Any idea where I can find him?'

'Hey, you guys,' the man said, calling to the others. 'Anyone know where Nabisco is hanging out these days?'

One of the cardplayers looked up. 'Yeah. He's in the clink. Committing a public nuisance. He pissed on a police car. He can't make bail.'

'That's Brother Nabisco,' the vet said to Rod, grinning. 'I told you he's a wild sonofabitch.'

Harding asked for directions. He drove his rented car and finally found the place. It looked more like a hacienda than a police station, but when he went inside, it smelled like every station house he had ever been in.

He showed all his identification to the sergeant on duty and asked if there was any chance of bailing out Brother Nabisco.

'Who?' the sergeant said.

'A black who peed on a police cruiser.'

'Oh, that maniac,' the sergeant said. 'Lemme talk to the lieutenant. He'll probably be happy to get rid of him.'

Harding waited patiently. Then the sergeant returned with an older man. The lieutenant was wearing sharply creased, spotless khakis. His gray hair was cut *en brosse*, and wire-rimmed spectacles were pushed halfway down his bony nose. He carried a case folder.

'Who are you?' he demanded.

Harding went through it all again, handing over his driver's license and identification cards. The lieutenant inspected them carefully.

'You still on the Canton, West Virginia, force?' he asked.

'No, sir. I resigned late last year.'

'How come?'

'Too much bullshit.'

'Yeah,' the lieutenant said tiredly, 'I know what you mean. I wish I could afford to resign, but I'm pension-whipped. What's your interest in this' – he opened the case folder and scanned it – 'this Todhunter Clark?'

'Is he the man they call Brother Nabisco?'

'Brother Nabisco?' the lieutenant said. 'That's the first time I've heard that one. But Todhunter Clark is the guy who pissed on our cruiser. Just the latest in a long series of merry pranks – all adding up to committing a public nuisance. The guy's a pain in the ass.'

'Sounds like it,' Harding agreed. 'But he's an old Vietnam buddy. I heard he was in trouble. Can I bail him out?'

The lieutenant stared at him. 'Can you afford fifty to spring him?'

'I guess – if that's what it takes.'

'Can you get him out of the county?'

'No guarantee, but I'll try.'

'You do that,' the lieutenant said. 'If I ever see that black bastard again, he's going to be chopping cane until he's ready for Medicare. Let's have your cash – no checks

150

'– and you've got to sign some papers. Sergeant, bring that nutball out here.'

Harding paid over the money, signed release papers, and sat down on a hard wooden bench against the wall. In a few moments the sergeant came back with a tall, loosely shambling black dressed in soiled jeans, old, unlaced combat boots, and a baseball cap with the bill turned to the back.

The sergeant tore open an envelope and spilled some junk onto his desk. Brother Nabisco stowed the stuff in the pockets of his denim jacket and signed a receipt. He said something to the sergeant, who gestured toward Harding. Todhunter Clark turned and stared. Then he came over. Harding got to his feet.

'I know you?' Clark asked abruptly.

'No.'

'How come you sprung me?'

'I was talking to your buddies down at the center. They told me you were here.'

'Yeah? That don't explain why you sprung me.'

'Let's get out of here,' Harding said. 'They might change their mind. I got wheels.'

'Oh yeah, let's go,' Brother Nabisco said.

They drove at a sedate speed, then faster as they got away from the police station.

'You smell ripe,' Harding said, switching the air conditioning to high.

'No shit? You spend five days in that tank, you don't come out smelling like roses. Where we going?'

'My motel.'

'Hey, man,' Brother Nabisco said suspiciously, 'you're not looking for a trip up the old chocolate road, are you?'

'No, nothing like that. I got a pint of sour mash, and you can get cleaned up. There may be a job in it for you.'

'Uh-huh,' Nabisco said. 'We'll talk about it. First the sour mash.'

But in the motel room, he asked if he could take a hot

151

shower before he touched the whiskey. Harding counted that a plus. When Clark came out of the shower, there was a drink waiting for him, and a pair of shorts, clean jeans, a white T-shirt. He was as tall as Rod but weighed about fifty pounds less. The borrowed clothes hung on him.

'Wooee,' he said, sipping the bourbon. 'This is something like. I do thank you kindly. What's your name?'

'Rod Harding.'

'Todhunter Clark is mine.'

'They call you Brother Nabisco?'

'That's just jive. Mostly I'm called Tod.'

'You hungry, Tod?'

'Not so much. I had a bowl of soup tonight. They called it stew, but it was soup. Plenty of bread though.'

'All right,' Harding said. 'Now it's talking time. I'll go first.'

He told Clark about the Women's Defense Corps, how they were organizing along military lines, what they hoped to accomplish, the weapons they were using.

'Mostly,' he said, 'these women are out to get rapists, guys who hassle them, men who put them down, employers who pay them half of what guys in the same jobs are getting.'

'Yeah,' Clark said sardonically. 'I can see why they'd be a mite upset. Being treated like niggers . . .'

Harding said he had been recruiting Nam veterans to teach combat skills to the sisters of the WDC, all the stuff recruits in the armed forces learned in basic training.

'Crazy,' Brother Nabisco said. He held up his empty glass. 'A taste more?'

'It's a job for volunteers,' Harding said, pouring the bourbon. 'We'll cover your expenses, but no paycheck.'

The other man laughed. 'You in Nam?'

'Army grunt. Two tours.'

'And you want me to *volunteer*? Man, you know better 'n that.'

152

Harding stared at Todhunter Clark. Whip-thin and razor-sharp. A tall, skinny gink with a little gray goatee. Big eyes and a head of short black hair that fitted as tightly as a felt helmet. Hands with long, spatulate fingers. A fast, smooth way of moving.

'What did you do in Nam, Tod?'

'Demo mostly. I was here, there, everywhere. They moved me around a lot. Loaned me out for special jobs – you know? Like booby traps. They want a guy taken out, I'd figure how to do it.'

'You know explosives?'

'Like mother's milk. And fuses, caps, detonators, timers. Everything.'

'Were you good?'

'Good? I was a fucking genius. I got out with the medals and letters of commendation to prove it. I hocked the medals and lost the letters. What I need that shit for? What good was it when Nam closed down?'

'Are you talking about counterespionage?' Harding said, frowning. 'Stuff like that?'

'That was part of it.' Clark pointed at the pint whiskey bottle. 'See that jug? If I had my old kit, which I don't, I could rig that bottle, you unscrew the cap, and *BLOOIE*! there goes your head.'

'What was the best job you ever pulled?'

'The best?' Brother Nabisco said, his big eyes lighting up. 'Oh God, it was so sweet. They wanted this big-shot politico taken out. So I get into his office, see, and rig his phone. Okay? Now, I'm a mile away. I call his office. His secretary answers. Nothing. I ask for him personally. I tell her I got some secret stuff for him. After a little hassle she puts him on. I make sure it's him. Then I blow a little whistle into my phone. It sets off the juice in his. They had to scrape him off the walls. Later, they refined the whole setup, but it was my idea. Now you can snuff a guy from halfway around the world. You don't have to *be* there. My idea. All my idea.'

153

As he described this assassination, he became more excited, leaning forward, gesturing, laughing in short bursts. Rod Harding recognized the type: the violence junkie. Useful but dangerous. Guys whose idea of fun was to toss a live grenade back and forth.

'Tod,' he said, 'you got a place to sleep tonight?'

'No, not really. But I'll make out.'

Harding gave him two twenties. 'Find yourself a bed. No alley or park bench. Stay out of trouble. Get some food. No shredded wheat.'

Brother Nabisco fondled the two bills. 'Ribs, I think,' he said dreamily. 'A big platter of ribs and fries. Maybe a beer or two or three.'

'I'll give you the number here,' Rod said. 'Call me in the morning.'

'I told you, man, I ain't volunteering for *nothing*.'

'This is a paying job I got in mind. I'll have to clear it with my boss. If she says yes, I'll talk to you about it.'

'Okay,' Todhunter Clark said. 'What about these borrowed duds?'

'You keep them,' Harding said. 'Now take off, will you? I'm expecting guests.'

'Sure,' Brother Nabisco said. 'I dig.' He turned at the door and they shook hands for the first time. 'Thanks, man. For getting me out of the slam and letting me clean up. That was an important thing you did. I owe you. You want someone scragged, just let me know.'

'I'll keep it in mind,' Harding said, smiling. 'By the way, do you speak Spanish?'

'A little. Enough to get by. My buddy in Nam was a crazy little spic. He taught me.'

'Oh? What happened to him?'

'You'll never believe this, but . . . He was fucking another spic's wife in the States before he was shipped out. He was all the time writing her love letters and figuring out how to get rid of her old man. One day he was trying

154

to rig a tortilla and lost a hand. They had to ship him back. Crazy – no?'

'Crazy yes. Where is he now?'

'Miami, last I heard.'

'Be sure to call me tomorrow, Tod.'

An hour later Molly Turner was in his room, slumped in a cretonned armchair.

'What the hell is that smell?' she said, nose crinkling.

'Todhunter Clark,' he said, laughing. 'He came in slightly aromatic but left squeaky clean.'

He told her all about Brother Nabisco. He said the guy wouldn't volunteer as an instructor, but Harding wanted him as second in command to the chief of staff. On salary.

'The budget can afford it,' he said, 'and I need an assistant. This thing is just getting too big for me to manage by myself.'

'He sounds like a nut case.'

'He is,' Harding said, 'but I can handle him. Moll, I know something about explosives and electronics, but this guy is an expert – if half of what he tells me is true. I mean he's a specialist, and we can use that know-how.'

'He's a black,' she said. 'Is that what you want?'

'Sure. What percentage of our membership is black?'

'Not enough.'

'Exactly. Because black women think the WDC is the white women's latest trendy fad. So we put a black man on staff, and we send a signal that the Corps is color-blind and important to *all* women.'

'Now you're talking like a politician.'

'Well, what the hell do you think *you* are?' he said hotly. 'The WDC is as much political as anything else.'

'Don't yell at me, Rod,' she said wearily, rubbing her forehead. 'I've got to get back to Canton and rest. I'm wiped out. All right. I trust your judgment. You haven't made any mistakes yet. Hire the guy. What's our next step?'

He went behind her chair and began to massage her neck and shoulders.

'You go back to Canton,' he said quietly. 'Fatten up on your mother's cooking. Sleep a lot. I'll go down to Miami with Brother Nabisco. Try to locate that buddy of his who blew off his hand trying to booby-trap a tortilla. If we find him, I'm betting he'll know where we can make a gun buy. And all the other shit we need.'

'Whatever you say,' she said drowsily, head lolling.

'Moll, you want to sleep awhile?'

'Later,' she said, eyes opening. 'I want to fuck first. Then sleep.'

In bed together, naked, she grasped him so tightly that he cried out.

'I love you,' she said fiercely.

'Hey,' he said. 'Wait a minute. This was supposed to be a physical thing. Remember? A favor between friends. Nothing emotional. That's what you agreed.'

'I lied,' she said.

OCTOBER 4, 1988

Like many well-organized women, Mrs Ann Harding tended to pooh-pooh her efficiency. 'I'm so scatter-brained,' she'd laugh. Or, 'I've got so many things to do, nothing gets done.' Friends and associates smiled sympathetically – but they knew better. Ann did get things done, in order and on time. If Molly Turner's passion fueled the Women's Defense Corps, it was Ann's managerial talents that made it work.

It was her habit each night before going to bed to make a jotted list of the next day's tasks and tick them off as they were accomplished. This reporter has come into possession of her very personal work schedule for October 4. It reads as follows:

'Jeff ped.

156

'Cop. mach.
'Booze. Pop.
'Ltr. CU
'PO
'Dep. bank.
'Hair.
'Din. Moll & Tod.'

The first notation – 'Jeff ped.' – referred to an 8:30 AM appointment with her son's pediatrician. Jefferson Turner Harding was promptly weighed, measured, thumped, flexed, peered at with lights, tickled, given one small candy, and pronounced the future heavyweight champion of the world.

Ann drove directly from the doctor's office to the new WDC headquarters in a warehouse on River Street. The big shed had been broken up into offices with plywood partitions, and there was room to spare for filing cabinets, data-processing machines, and a staff that grew larger every month.

Ann had set a padded crib next to her desk to confine the energetic Jeff. It was the perfect solution to the mothering problem during the day, because when Ann was absent, there was usually a staffer available, willing to entertain Jeff when he was awake.

Surprisingly, the most eager volunteer to dance attendance on the baby was Todhunter Clark. The black, brought back from Florida by Rod Harding, lived in a hotel on Broadway when he wasn't on assignment with Rod. While in Canton, he spent most of his days at WDC headquarters, cheerfully helping out at whatever he was asked.

He and Jefferson Turner Harding immediately formed a mutual admiration society. Ann could only wonder at the rapport between the two.

'I talk his language,' Brother Nabisco explained.

So it seemed. They spent hours together, grunting and cooing, giggling and grimacing. Seeing them play together so happily, Ann could hardly believe the stories Rod told

157

her of Clark's bloodier exploits.

'Any man who loves children can't be all bad,' she said.

'Uh-huh,' Rod said. 'Like Hitler.'

The second item on Ann's job list – 'Cop. mach.' – referred to the purchase of a newer, high-speed, high-volume photocopying machine for WDC heaquarters. This necessitated a quick trip to Canton's only typewriter and office machine retailer.

The location of WDC headquarters in Canton had initially resulted in hostility and talk of ordinances to ban the organization. But when the expanded WDC staff began to spend money with local merchants for real estate, furniture, food, and clothing, the enmity was tempered, if not eliminated. Everyone in Canton agreed the WDC was good for business.

Ann was able to inspect copiers shortly before noon. She selected the machine she wanted, arranged terms and delivery date, and left to meet Yvonne Popkin for lunch at the local McDonald's: the third note on her schedule – 'Booze. Pop.'

Over quarter-pounders, fries, and Cokes, she told Popkin bluntly that she'd have to control her drinking or face dismissal.

'I do my job,' the whey-faced woman said.

'You do it,' Ann said, staring at her, 'but not the way it should be done. Your correspondence goes out late, you screwed up that chance we had for an interview with Molly on the *Tonight Show*, and your expense account statements are ridiculous. No way am I going to okay these entertainment charges.'

'I can explain – ' the other woman started.

'If you were doing your job,' Ann said coldly, 'you wouldn't have to explain. If you were doing the job you were hired to do, I'd let you be your own boss. You agree you've got a drinking problem, don't you?'

Yvonne nodded miserably, twisting her stringy hair in nervous fingers.

'Have you tried to get help? Professional help?'

'I don't need – '

'You *do* need,' Ann said decisively. 'There's an AA chapter in town. Join it. Go to the meetings. Or pack your bags and get out of Canton. That's your choice.'

Yvonne began to weep.

'Look, honey,' Ann said in a softer tone. 'It's as much for us as it is for you. We need a bright, alert press officer. You've got the talent and ability; I know you have. But the booze is ruining your life. Will you give AA a try?'

Yvonne nodded, sniffling.

'Good,' Ann said. 'I mean really *try*. We'll all help every way we can. Now let's get back to the office. I'm so swamped, I don't know what to do next.'

But of course she did know what to do next. It was 'Ltr. CU' – a long, personal letter to Constance Underwood pointing out what Ann considered serious deficiencies in the manner in which the WDC was being treated by its parent organization, the National Women's Union.

'My resentment has been simmering for some time,' she wrote. 'I realize ours is an awkward association, but agreements were made and ground rules established when the WDC was founded. Those agreements and promises have not been adhered to – whether from carelessness, poor management, or from a deliberate attempt to sabotage the work of the WDC, I cannot say. I do know that the WDC has brought an enormous increase in membership and revenue to the NWU. Now we find our monthly remittance is invariably late (sometimes by weeks!), lists of new members are not supplied regularly – and are usually submitted in a most slipshod manner – and space promised us in *The Call* is often found to be 'Not available.'

'I must tell you frankly that if these conditions are not promptly corrected, the WDC will consider its options – including a clean break from the NWU and going our own way as an independent organization. For your information, I have discussed the subject of this letter with my sister,

159

Molly Turner, and she fully concurs with my views. Yours in sisterhood, Ann Harding.'

She typed this letter personally, kept a single copy in her personal file, and took the sealed envelope to the post office herself. The trip enabled her to tick off the fifth item on her list, 'PO,' and gave her the opportunity to inquire about the details of getting a postal metering device for WDC headquarters.

From the post office, she walked two blocks north on Broadway to the Farmers and Mechanics Bank, where Molly had once worked as head teller. At the bank, Ann met with the executive vice president and discussed terms for a mortgage loan to the WDC to purchase the warehouse on River Street they were presently leasing on an annual basis.

On her way out of the bank, Ann deposited $43,126.71, the latest (delayed) payment from the NWU. That took care of 'Dep. bank.' on her list.

She drove back to headquarters to find Todhunter Clark giving Jeff his bottle and demonstrating to the child how to make a belled rattle ring. The two of them were having a fine time.

At 5:00 PM, after working steadily all afternoon, Ann left Jeff asleep in his crib, under the watchful eye of a WDC staffer, and ran out to have her hair done at The Beachcomber on First Street. As usual, Luis tried to talk her into having her long, chestnut tresses trimmed to a short gamine cut.

'My husband likes it long,' she told him again.

'Your husband,' he scoffed. 'What does *he* know about hair styling?'

'He knows what he likes,' Ann Harding said, sighing. 'Leave it long, Luis. Just a shampoo, rinse, and a slight trim.'

'Barbarian,' Luis muttered.

Ann dashed back to headquarters from the hairdresser, and worked on correspondence and preparing financial data for the accountant until almost 7:30 PM. Then she gathered up a fretful Jeff and fled, ready for the final chore on the day's schedule: 'Din. Moll & Tod.'

Good husband Rod had mixed the salad and rolled the meatballs. When his wife and son appeared, he lighted the gas under the pot of water for spaghetti, started the sauce heating, put a low flame under the pan of garlic and chopped scallion greens, frying in oil, ready to receive the meatballs.

Ann bathed, powdered, and diapered Jeff. Then she put him down in the living room crib, propped a bottle on a towel, and watched approvingly as he immediately began to suck, gripping his jug as if it was Château Mouton-Rothschild.

Then Ann went to shower and change. Rod added dressing to the salad and tossed it, put on the meatballs, set the table. Husband and wife moved briskly around the house, never getting in each other's way, shouting news back and forth, room to room. They functioned like a team, and Ann almost forgot about those damned letters.

Molly brought a box of strawberry tarts baked by Mrs Josephine Turner, and Todhunter Clark showed up with a gallon of Gallo Hearty Burgundy. They ate in the kitchen, but their talk didn't prevent little Jeff from dropping into a deep, peaceful sleep. One moment he was gurgling; the next moment he was gone.

'A sunny kid,' Brother Nabisco said. 'And why not?'

They brought dessert, coffee, and what was left of the wine into the living room, where they could stretch out, groaning with content. Rod lighted a pipe, the others cigarettes. They watched Jeff sleep, grinning at the little burbling bubbles that rose to his lips.

'What a life,' Rod said. 'Nothing to do but eat, play, sleep, and shit. That's what I'd like.'

'I thought you had it, man,' Clark said, not without envy, and they laughed.

As usual, it was Molly who brought the conversation back to business.

'Two things . . .' she said. 'First of all, I'd like the WDC to have a motto or slogan. Something short, dramatic, easy to remember. Like the "Never again" of the Jewish Defense League. Anyone got any ideas?'

Silence.

'What about "Enough's enough"?' Rod suggested.

The others were doubtful.

'It tells the story,' Molly said, 'but it's not strong enough.'

'Too downbeat,' Ann agreed. 'Like a wail of pain. We want a brave, affirmative statement. Tod, do the blacks have a slogan?'

'Sure,' he said. '"Up yours, honky!"'

Molly glared at him. 'Don't make a joke of this,' she said sharply. 'This is serious. I want something like "Deadlier than the male." That's no good, I know, but it gives the feeling I'd like to get in a slogan – an implied threat that we're fed up with taking crap and we're going to fight back.'

'Let's think about it,' Ann said quietly. 'A revolutionary slogan is a good idea, if we can come up with something that's exactly right. What's the second thing you wanted to talk about, Molly?'

'I think we've got most of our act together. The regiments are organized and training. I want to pull some national action – the whole WDC working as a single army, hitting a single target at the same time.'

'I'm not sure we're ready for that,' Ann said cautiously. 'Are we, Rod?'

'No,' he said. 'But Molly's right – we've got to try it. If we wait for more recruits, more guns, more training, we'll wait forever. We'll have a perfect paper army with no experience.'

'Yeah,' Todhunter Clark said. 'You go ahead now, you're going to make a lot of mistakes, maybe fall on your face. But that's how you learn. I say do it. Something big. Something that'll really show we can plan and *do* it, instead of just jiving.'

162

'One thing . . . ' Rod said. 'Most important: security. Just the four of us plan it. We bring others in at the last possible moment. Nothing in writing. Phone calls only from public booths. We get our operational plan set and then we tell people who have to know and move *fast*.'

They spent almost an hour discussing various nationwide militant actions. They finally agreed on a campaign that seemed to offer a good chance of success – with minimum casualties. Then Molly and Tod left.

'She doesn't like him,' Ann said, plunking down in her husband's lap.

'Who doesn't like whom?'

'You know who. Molly doesn't like Todhunter Clark. It's not that she doesn't like him, exactly, but she thinks the WDC is a big joke to him.'

'She tell you this?'

'No, but I know Molly. Rod, the WDC is the most important thing in her life. She is absolutely sincere and completely committed. She's going to prove women can fight back, an eye for an eye. She'll use anyone who can help her, but she expects their commitment to be as total as hers. She's ready to die for this, Rod.'

'Sure,' he said, 'I know all that. You think Tod isn't ready to die? He's a black. All he wants is a cause that doesn't offend his sense of what's right. He's going to be valuable to us – you'll see.'

'You're sure you can manage him?'

'I'm sure. He did just fine in Miami when we made the gun buy.'

'Molly thinks he's laughing at her and the WDC'

'He isn't. That's just his way – to grin and pretend nothing counts.'

'Well,' Ann said, sighing, 'I admit he's a godsend with Jeff, and Mother likes him, and so do your folks. Maybe if you could just keep him away from Molly . . .'

'Sure,' he said. 'I can do that. Now let's go to bed.'

'Dishes first.'

163

'Stack 'em,' he said. 'I'll do them in the morning.'

'What would I do without you?' she said, holding his face between her palms, staring into his eyes.

He kissed her lips.

Fifteen minutes later they were lying naked in bed.

As always, their lovemaking began with laughter and ended with bliss.

After, while they were sharing a cigarette, she said, 'I think I hear Jeff. Maybe he needs a change.'

'I'll do it,' Rod said, sliding out of bed.

While he was gone, she turned to smell the pillow where his head had rested, to touch the warmth his body had left on the sheet. He had been so tender, considerate, loving, that she could not believe those dreadful letters.

Still, she now had three more, tucked under her sweaters in the bottom dresser drawer. She hadn't opened them. Why she was saving them she could not have said.

NOVEMBER 19, 1988

After it had been accomplished, officials expressed grudging respect for the first nationwide militant action carried out by the Women's Defense Corps.

Inspection of top-secret internal WDC memoranda and interviews with surviving participants in the action made it obvious that the clever planning and successful performance of the WDC derived in large part from the combat experience of Rod Harding, Todhunter Clark, and the Vietnam veterans who had volunteered to train the rank and file.

But it was Molly Turner, with the steady, faithful encouragement of her sister, Ann, who sparked the deed and whose passionate advocacy pushed it to its completion. Everyone involved credits her fervor as the single most important factor in the success of the enterprise.

Evidence indicates that these four – Harding, Clark, and

the Turner sisters – conceived and designed the project, carefully leaking disinformation to several staffers in Canton and to headquarters personnel of the National Women's Union in Washington, DC.

It was said that the proposed target was a Connecticut factory producing automatic rifles for the US Army. The action would be an armed raid – an attempt to take over the entire plant and seize existing weapons. The date of the assault was said to be November 20.

All these rumors came to the attention of the Department of Justice. An elaborate, secret plan was devised to ring the rifle factory with hidden squads of armed officers. Needless to say, the Connecticut factory was not the target, and the WDC action was not scheduled for the 20th, but for the 19th.

The object of the militant action was *Hooker* magazine, a venomously misogynistic monthly with a national circulation of more than four million.

Hooker published full-page color photographs of naked women in degrading positions, as well as cartoons of women being whipped and chained, and occasional nude photos of underage girls.

The magazine had, at this date, successfully defended several court cases, claiming immunity from prosecution under the First Amendment.

Editorial offices were located in Cleveland, Ohio, and its wholly owned printing plant was in Gary, Indiana. The magazine was distributed by wholesalers in several large cities across the country.

Chief targets of the attack were the Cleveland editorial offices and the Gary printing plant. Two assault teams were armed, equipped, and assigned to these objectives. Total destruction was the goal.

And in almost every city, town, and village in the nation, retail magazine outlets would be attacked by 'flying squads' whose mission was to seize and destroy all copies of *Hooker* on display.

The coordination of this complex operation required a high degree of sophisticated combat planning. For instance, the different time zones had to be considered in determining H-hour, and the two demolition teams had to be surreptitiously provided with the heavy explosives needed.

It now seems evident that Todhunter Clark prepared the bombs required to wreck the presses in the printing plant. He then transported them to Gary in an unmarked van, and worked closely with the colonel of the Indiana regiment for two days prior to the attack.

Molly Turner and Rod Harding, carrying a trunkload of incendiary grenades, drove to Cleveland to cooperate with the Ohio regiment. Ann Harding remained in Canton, in command of a 'combat center' that would log reports of progress or failure.

The action began at 1:00 PM, eastern time, November 19, and it soon became evident the WDC had achieved its initial goals of shock and surprise. There were no reports of organized resistance, although there were scattered incidents of physical violence as wholesalers and newsstand owners attempted to defend their property.

In Gary, the printing plant was invaded and seized by forty armed sisters. One resisting security guard was shot in the leg. All the employees were herded outside, held at gunpoint, while Brother Nabisco and two assistants disconnected fire alarms and rigged their bombs.

The presses were running with the next issue of *Hooker*, and many pallets of finished magazines were ready for shipment. These were destroyed with phosphorus grenades or by spraying with fire extinguishers found on the premises.

The presses were brought to a halt with fragmentation grenades rigged in series and with dynamite charges. All etched cylinders and artwork were ruined with incendiary grenades.

The entire operation took slightly less than thirty minutes. The attacking force then departed. Todhunter Clark was the last to leave, after setting fire to the interior of the brick building with the aid of inflammable liquids he found in a storeroom.

Things did not go as smoothly at the editorial offices in Cleveland. Disregarding Ann's and Rod Harding's objections, Molly Turner had insisted in leading this attack personally.

'I'm going,' she said decisively. 'What the hell kind of a general would I be to order the sisters to put their asses on the line while I sit home and wait for results? They've got to see that I mean everything I've been saying. I'm going to be right there in the front line with them – or they'll never listen to me again. Besides,' she said with a cold smile, 'I like action.'

Hooker editorial offices were in a two-story, Tudor-style building on Chagrin Boulevard, near Shaker Heights. The handsome structure was isolated on a five-acre lawned plot, landscaped with trees, bushes, and shrubs.

Preliminary reconnaissance had pinpointed the location of security guards, telephone trunk lines, and an alarm connected to a private security agency. These were the initial targets of the attacking force, under the nominal command of the colonel of the Ohio regiment.

The several security guards reacted to the armed invasion with surprising speed. They unholstered their revolvers and then, when that had no effect, fired indiscriminately at the advancing force. In an exchange of small arms fire, one WDC sister was shot dead and four wounded. Two security guards were killed. The others surrendered.

The attackers then cut phone and alarm systems and fanned out through the building. Frightened and hysterical employees cowered behind desks as armed women stormed into their offices. They were herded downstairs to the reception area and made to lie facedown on the carpeted floor, guarded by WDC sisters equipped with shotguns.

167

Molly Turner and Rod Harding rushed upstairs to the second-floor office of Bernard Hofstra, publisher and editor of *Hooker*. They found the door locked. Harding blasted it open with a burst from his M-16. Inside, they discovered a secretary hiding behind a desk and, in an enormous inner office, Hofstra standing erect, aiming at them with a small, nickel-plated pistol.

He was almost twenty feet away, but his single shot caught Rod Harding in the shoulder and spun him away. Molly Turner crouched, aimed, and fired twice, using a two-hand grip as Rod had taught her. Her Charter Bulldog .357 Magnum bucked, and Hofstra flopped down behind his mahogany desk.

Molly looked first to Harding, but he was still on his feet, one hand clamped tightly to his wounded shoulder. Blood leaked from between his fingers.

'I'm all right,' he said with a glassy grin. 'Let's get out of here.'

'Not yet,' she said.

She went behind Bernard Hofstra's desk and looked down. He was lying in a crumpled heap, eyes wide. He looked dead to her. Just to make sure, she leaned down and put a bullet through his brain.

'Now let's go,' she said to Harding. 'Can you make it?'

'Sure,' he said, looking at her strangely.

They got everyone outside and ignited the entire building with incendiary grenades.

Two hours later, in a motel room, Molly watched as a doctor, a WDC sister, patched up Rod's flesh wound.

'A dinky little hole,' the doctor said. 'In and out, thank God. It missed the bone. Can you lift your arm?'

'Do I have to?' Rod said, taking a belt from a pint bottle of bourbon.

'No,' the doctor said, smiling. 'Have your own doctor look at it when you get home. I've cleaned it up and dusted it. You ever been shot before?'

'Twice,' he said.

'Then you know what to expect – the shock, the weakness. But it'll pass.'

'Can I travel?'

'Not today. See how you feel tomorrow. I'll look in on you. Meanwhile, pop one of these pink beauties every three hours. And lay off the booze. I've got to run.'

'How are the others doing?' Molly asked.

'We're going to lose one. The others will pull through. But we did it, didn't we?'

Molly embraced her. 'We sure as hell did. I love you, sister.'

'And I love you, sister,' the doctor said. 'Keep up the good work. We're with you to hell and back.'

'Thank you, doc,' Rod said. 'Send me a bill.'

'On the house,' she said, grinning at him. 'See what you get fooling around with tough ladies? Have some soup, hamburger – whatever. You'll survive.'

When she had departed, Molly locked the door and came to him. She ran fingertips lightly over his bandage.

'Hurt?' she said.

'Naw,' he said. 'Feels swell.'

'Nut!' she said, laughing and kissing his cheek. 'Would you like to sleep?'

'No – but I wouldn't like to dance the fandango either. I'm sorry about the casualties, Moll.'

'We couldn't expect to get off scot-free. There'll be more, Rod, before this is over. Are you hungry?'

'Only for you.'

'It's been a long time,' she said, nodding. 'I didn't want to do anything in Canton with Ann there.'

'No,' he said, 'let's not do that. But Ann isn't here.'

'Can you do it?'

'I can try.'

'No,' she said. 'Don't try. Just lie back, relax, dream. Let me undress you and love you. Let me do everything.'

'If that's what you want.'

'Rod, I killed that bastard.'

'I know you did.'

'He deserved killing.'

'I know that too, Moll.'

'So why do I feel so depressed?'

He looked at her narrowly.

'Undress me,' he said. 'Love me.'

'Oh God, yes,' she said.

DECEMBER 11, 1988

'Senator,' James Gargan said somberly, 'they were very clever about it. These people are not wet-brained hippies.'

'I know, I know,' Dundee said testily.

'Fanatics,' the general said. 'Terrorists.'

'No, sir,' Gargan said. 'I'll have to disagree with you there. It's not an underground group. They're not threatening to over-throw the government by force. They're just trying to redress what they see as wrongs.'

'You should have known it was coming,' the senator accused. 'Haven't you infiltrated?'

'Oh yes, sir,' Gargan said mournfully. 'We're inside. But their security was top-notch. I admit they snookered us. We were set up for a Connecticut raid that never came off.'

'From a military point of view,' the general said, 'those little ladies get high marks. Their objective was to cancel *Hooker* magazine, and it's out of business. There goes my subscription,' he added, grinning, but neither of the other two men smiled.

They were seated in a corner of the elegant sitting room of the F Street Club. They were the only occupants of the elaborately furnished chamber – which suited Senator Lemuel K. Dundee just fine.

'What was it?' he asked. 'A total of six dead and twenty-two wounded?'

'Something like that,' Gargan acknowledged.

'They took their lumps,' the general said, 'but by God they got the job done. You've got to give them that.'

Dundee whirled on him. 'I hope you've beefed up security.'

'Oh yes, sir, we've done that. Strict orders: shoot to kill. It's not a joke anymore with us.'

'It better not be,' Dundee said glumly, 'or they'll be taking over the Pentagon next.' He turned back to Gargan. 'How many arrests?'

'More than fifty at the last count.'

'Are you going to press for indictments?'

Gargan shifted uncomfortably. 'Senator, I told you these are clever people. They picked a target that's hard to defend: *Hooker* magazine – a piece of shit. Do you really want the US Government going into court to prosecute women who put that abomination out of business?'

Dundee stared at him. 'No prosecutions? Was that a political decision?'

'Yes, sir,' Gargan said. 'Not mine, but at the highest levels. In all honesty, I can't fault it. Senator, the mail has been heavily in favor of what they did. Not only from women's groups but from fundamentalist churches – the Moral Majority – who are delighted to see *Hooker* off the newsstands. It's a very dicey situation.'

'So no prosecutions?' Dundee repeated.

'Not at the moment, sir. We'll continue our surveillance, of course. Sooner or later they'll go too far, and we'll mash them.'

'Can't you indict the whole outfit?' the general demanded. 'Or at least the officers?'

'I'm afraid not,' Gargan said. 'Not with all the support they've got at the moment. It just wouldn't be smart. Politically, I mean.'

'Politically . . .' Dundee said thoughtfully. 'You think the country's behind them?'

'That's not for me to say, sir; I just don't know. But our experience with groups like this shows that initial successes

171

lure them into more dangerous actions. Bank robberies, abductions, bombings, hijackings, assassinations – things like that. They keep pushing, pushing, trying bigger and bigger jobs. Eventually it all comes apart. Usually they turn on each other. A lot of egos involved there.'

'I hope you're right,' Senator Dundee said. 'As I have stated many times on the floor, I sincerely feel that while the aims of the Women's Defense Corps may be for the most part admirable, their recourse to violence in order to achieve those aims can only be deplored.'

'I concur, Senator,' the general said.

'Absolutely, sir,' Gargan said.

'Well, gentlemen,' Dundee said, glancing at his watch, 'I've got to be getting back to the Hill. I thank you for this little chat. Most illuminating.'

'If there is anything we can do . . .' the general said.

'Just give us a call,' James Gargan said.

They know I'm running, Lemuel Dundee thought at that moment, and wasn't surprised.

When he got back to his office, he tackled the stack of paper-work that had piled up in his absence; dictating rapidly to his private secretary – a stout woman with an Orphan Annie hairdo.

'Yes on this,' he said, handing her papers as he spoke. 'No on this one. Tell this guy to go fuck himself – politely, of course. I'll go to this shindig, but not this one. Tell Senator Parkins it's under consideration. This guy is a nut; don't even answer. Get a Capitol flag for this kid. Sure, I'll do this interview. On this one . . .'

He worked steadily for almost a half-hour. When he finished, his secretary said, 'Ruth Blohm is waiting to see you, Senator.'

'What's on the floor?' he asked.

'Nothing. Adjourned an hour ago.'

'Good. Tell Ruth to give me about fifteen minutes. Then I'll see her.'

When he was alone, he loosened his tie, opened his belt

172

a notch, and poured himself a small bourbon. He knew that after Ruth Blohm, he'd have to see Tom Kealy, his newly hired media adviser, a White House aide who was coming over to pressure him on a bill to increase the NASA appropriation, and finally a wealthy constituent he'd have to take to dinner.

Lemuel Dundee rubbed his forehead wearily and wondered if he was backing the wrong horse, if this anti - WDC stand would ruin his chance for the nomination. But he believed Gargan's prediction that the WDC would go on to wilder, crazier, bloodier exploits – and eventually the mood of the public would swing and the law would crack down.

If you put the thumbscrews to Lemuel K. Dundee and demanded he tell you what he really thought about women, his answer would be that he rarely thought about them at all.

There was his wife, of course – a cantankerous women well on her way to becoming a first-class lush. And there were those young professionals he banged at the South Carolina hunting lodge. And there were female reporters, female secretaries, aides, waitresses, nurses. There were even two female senators.

But generally, women were an abstraction to Senator Dundee. They were not a political reality – and politics was his life. He had never heard or read Freud's, 'What do women *want*?' or the Arabian proverb, 'Women want toasted ice,' but he probably would have sympathized with both of them.

When Ruth Blohm came in, he thought again what an exceedingly plain female she was. But then, he told himself, she thinks like a man – the highest accolade he could pay any woman.

'I know how busy you are, Senator,' she said, 'so I'll make it short. It concerns a new method of polling or sampling that could prove very valuable as we get into the campaign.'

173

Speaking rapidly, she told him about Lyle Hayden and his indepth analysis of juries. She said she believed the same technique could be used to probe the collective psyche of key districts to determine the issues that would move them to the desired lever in the voting booth.

Senator Dundee listened closely, but all this talk of computerized polling and demographic samples made him uneasy. He tried to keep up with the new hi-tech world – but it was moving so fast! Sometimes he feared it was getting away from him.

The previous week he had attended a Pentagon briefing at which a bright young colonel had spoken enthusiastically about laser-beam technology and magnetic force field interceptors. Dundee hadn't understood a word of it – but his grandchildren were using computers in *grade* school!

'You're talking about psychoanalysis of a whole voting district?' he asked Blohm.

'Something like that, Senator.'

'What will it cost?'

'Nothing,' she said, 'at the moment. I want to send Hayden demographic profiles of three districts. He'll make an estimate of the cost on spec.'

'Does he know who it's for?'

'No, sir; I didn't mention your candidacy to him.'

'Well . . .' Dundee said, 'if we're not contracting for anything, go ahead. See what he comes up with.'

'Thank you, Senator.'

The meeting with Tom Kealy was brief. The executive assistant just wanted to report that after several calls to Constance Underwood, the president of the National Women's Union had agreed to a private meeting with Kealy in his Georgetown apartment.'

'Good boy,' Dundee said approvingly. 'Keep me informed.'

The new media adviser didn't take long either. He left a smartly bound fifty-page memo with Dundee, outlining what he felt the senator could do to improve his public image – including a new hairdo, more youth-oriented clothing, shorter sentences in his speeches and – for God's sake – stop drumming his fingers during TV interviews.

The White House political liaison aide took a little longer, but the dinner with the wealthy constituent turned out to be unexpectedly pleasant. Dundee took him to Le Gré, where they had quail and wild rice and drank more chablis grand cru than was good for either of them.

By the time Senator Dundee got home to Spring Valley, the weariness and doubts of the day had floated away. He was certain he was destined for great things. He was on a roll, and had only to stay the course.

His wife was already in bed, but awoke when he stumbled into the bedroom and turned on the overhead light.

'I'm going to make it, Martha,' he told her confidently. 'I really think I'm going to make it.'

She was silent, looking at him blearily.

'What's the matter?' he said. 'Don't you think I can be president?'

'Anyone who wants the job,' she said, 'isn't qualified for it.'

'What the hell's that supposed to mean?' he demanded.

But she turned onto her side and began snoring.

To historians, the period 1988–1989 in the growth of the Women's Defense Corps is particularly interesting for its increased militarism.

As we shall see, a uniform was approved for the Corps. A decoration – the Women's Liberation Medal – was created for those sisters who participated in direct physical actions. Regimental flags were designed, and guidons issued to smaller units.

There is no doubt that these outward symbols of militarism – although treated with amusement in some quarters, and the target of many contemporary cartoons – was watched with apprehension by law enforcement agencies.

The regiments of the WDC were careful to obey the gun laws of their respective states, but few people doubted that all members were armed, whether or not their weapons were displayed publicly. By mid-1989, it seems evident that all WDC sisters were equipped with a handgun, rifle, or shotgun.

In addition, there is much evidence to indicate that many regiments had at their disposal grenades, machine guns, and handheld rocket launchers. There were rumors – reported in the press at the time – that some WDC units were also equipped with mortars, flamethrowers, and small-caliber artillery. This writer has been unable to confirm or deny those reports.

JANUARY 8, 1989

Thomas J. Kealy had thought of calling in Jake Spencer to install a hidden tape recorder in his Georgetown apartment prior to his private meeting with Constance Underwood. But after careful consideration, he rejected the idea.

First of all, it was none of Jake's business that he, Kealy, was meeting secretly with the president of the National Women's Union. And Kealy feared that if Underwood ever discovered the device, or learned it had been implanted, that would be the end of her cooperation.

He prepared for the meeting with some care. He had the apartment cleaned, windows washed, curtains changed. He bought fresh flowers, and two bottles of Korbel brut he was prepared to defend against many higher priced French champagnes.

He couldn't have made a more fortunate choice. Constance Underwood had had a difficult and vexatious day, and needed badly to unwind.

She had spent an infuriating morning with Virginia Terwilliger, who had come down from Baltimore to poke and pry and generally make herself obnoxious. Ginny was singing the same tune: the NWU wasn't doing all it could or should to support the Women's Defense Corps.

Connie made the mistake of showing her that insulting letter from Ann Harding, and Terwilliger blew her stack.

'Goddamn it, girl,' she raged, 'can't you get it through your skull that the tail is wagging the dog? The WDC has almost doubled our membership, and all you have to do is look at our bank statements to know how much money they've brought in. You should be kissing their ass instead of treating them like poor relations. They're *doing* things. Taking out *Hooker* magazine was brilliant. Brilliant! It gave a lift to every woman in the country, and got a lot of favorable media attention. If you force the WDC to disassociate and go their own way, the National Women's Union is finished. And another thing . . .'

The chewing-out went on and on, reducing Constance Underwood to a white-faced coldly furious termagant. After Ginny left, she stormed through the NWU offices, screaming at her staff, driving secretaries to tears, and piling impossible workloads on everyone.

Then, in the afternoon, came a catastrophic letter from Molly Turner. In her hard, abrupt way, Turner stated that she had decided the Women's Defense Corps would open an office in Washington, DC, for 'closer liaison with the National Women's Union and proximity to Congress, the media, and other feminist groups' headquartered in the nation's capital.

If space could not be made available in the NWU offices, Molly wrote, the WDC would rent its own suite in some suitable location. That's all Connie needed!

So Constance Underwood was in a somewhat vicious mood when she cabbed to Tom Kealy's Georgetown apartment, arriving a little before 6:30 PM, in a mini-blizzard of wet snow and freezing rain that didn't improve her disposition.

But Kealy's small, rather charming apartment was warm,

dry, and after two glasses of champagne, Connie began to relax and enjoy herself.

They chatted easily about the miserable weather, the high cost of living in Washington, the coming inauguration, and what effects the new President might have on national and foreign policies.

'Have you seen Billy McCrea lately?' Kealy asked casually, his back turned as he slid another split log into the fireplace.

'About a week ago,' Underwood said just as casually. 'Have you seen him?'

'Not too long ago,' the executive assistant said, coming over to refill Connie's glass. 'He's a beautiful boy, isn't he?'

'Not too great in the brains department,' she said, 'but yes, he's beautiful.' She thought that was enough about Billy McCrea, so she said, 'Tom, what did your senator think of the election?'

'Well, he was sorry to see his party lose, of course, but he expected it. It didn't seem to upset him too much. His theory is that it really doesn't matter which party is in power.'

'I expect he's right – although a strong chief executive can make a difference. And what did he think about the raid on *Hooker* magazine?'

'Well . . . he's delighted to see it out of business, of course. But I know he has some reservations about how it was done. All those people killed and wounded . . .'

'Yes,' she said, nodding. 'I have some reservations about that myself.'

'Connie, have you met Molly Turner?'

'Oh yes, I've met her. Several times.'

'What kind of a woman is she?'

'Very strong-willed, very intense, very ambitious. She's not inclined to compromise – about anything. Not a very cultured woman, but she's become a charismatic figure and seems able to inspire absolute loyalty.'

178

'That can be frightening,' he said solemnly. 'Look at those poor women who were killed. Was putting *Hooker* out of business worth it?'

Underwood leaned over to pour herself more Korbel.

'No,' she said decisively. 'That piece of trash wasn't worth one woman's life.'

'Couldn't you have stopped it?' he asked softly. 'The raid, I mean?'

'You've got to understand, Tom, that the WDC is a semi-independent organization. We fund them, true, but we have no control over their administration or activities.'

'Did you know the *Hooker* thing was going down?'

'No,' she said shortly and, once again in her mind, cursed that drunken, incompetent Yvonne Popkin.

They were silent for a moment. He was seated in an armchair, facing her. It was, in fact, the same armchair in which Billy McCrea sometimes sat while Kealy serviced him. Now he leaned forward, forearms on his knees. He regarded her gravely.

'Connie,' he said, 'I'm going to ask you a question. You don't have to answer it, but I hope you will. Do you consider Molly Turner a dangerous woman?'

She returned his stare. Then, apparently making up her mind, she drew a deep breath.

'Yes,' she said, 'she's a dangerous woman. Dangerous to the hysterics who follow her and dangerous to the feminist cause. Quite frankly, the woman scares me. There's something demoniac about her. I don't question her sincerity or her talents, but she lacks balanced judgment. Tom, she's a primitive. I'm afraid she can do a lot of damage.'

'Already has,' he said. 'And will probably do more. Connie, I don't think you and Senator Dundee are so far apart in your thinking. He wants what you want: all the things women have been fighting for and deserve – but achieved legally through the courts and the legislative process. Do you agree with that?'

'Yes.'

'Well then, can't we work together?'

She looked at him. 'Spell it out,' she said sharply.

'Quite frankly, the senator would like to see the defeat of Molly Turner and the Women's Defense Corps. He sees the whole movement as a threat to traditional American values.'

'He's right,' she said. 'But you still haven't spelled out how we can help each other.'

'All right,' he said, 'here's one way you can help us: pass along advance notice of anything you can learn about proposed actions by the WDC. We'll see it gets into the right hands.'

'Difficult,' she said thoughtfully. 'I told you I knew nothing about the *Hooker* job before it happened.'

'It doesn't have to be only advance notice of planned operations. It can be changes in personnel, unusual expenditures, travel plans – anything and everything. It will all help.'

'Mmm. And what do I get for this, ah, cooperation?'

He had hoped it would come to this eventually, and he had planned his reply carefully. He knew they couldn't offer much, but he was counting on her fear and envy of Molly Turner.

'In return,' he said earnestly, 'Senator Dundee will make every possible effort to disassociate the National Women's Union from the Women's Defense Corps. All his denunciations will be of Molly Turner and the WDC. If he mentions you and the NWU at all, it will be to praise you as a model of what a women's organization should be.'

Constance Underwood turned her head to stare at the little flickering blue flames in the fireplace.

'I'll think about it,' she said finally. 'I'll let you know. The fire is going out. Do you have any more wood?'

'I'm afraid not. But I have another bottle of champagne.'

She was wearing her long hair up, coiled and swirled into a crown. She lifted her arms lazily and pulled out pins. She shook her head, and hair tumbled down to her shoulders: sleek, black wings about her coffin face. He watched, fascinated.

'More champagne would be nice,' she said throatily.

Later, when he saw her naked, he ached with envy, for he dreamed her body to be his. When he touched her, he closed his eyes and caressed his own hot and pliant flesh.

'Do this,' she commanded. 'Do that.'

FEBRUARY 21, 1989

Only a year previously, Lyle Hayden had read an article in the *Atlanta Constitution* and discovered what he was. The article was entitled 'The Nature of Joylessness,' and described a mental disorder called anhedonia. It was not depression, but simply an inability to have fun, be happy, enjoy.

The typical anhedonic, the article stated, displayed 'insensibility to pleasure.' He derived no joy from food, drink, sex, art, or a pleasant spring morning. While able to function normally, life seemed to him juiceless, without delight.

This numbness to felicity, the article went on, could be due to a deep psychic trauma (the death of a loved one, for instance), to a chemical imbalance in the brain's hippo-campus, or to genetic predisposition.

Hayden, diagnosing himself, decided his anhedonia sprang from the last of these causes. His parents had been silent, dour people; he could not recall laughter or gaiety in his home while growing up. Now a forty-two-year-old bachelor, he was not unsociable, but found no joy in personal relationships or any of those things that everyone else seemed to relish.

Even his work, which had proved unexpectedly profitable, gave him no particular pleasure. So when Ruth Blohm sent him the demographic profiles of three voting districts, he took them home and read them through with no special curiosity or even interest.

He saw at once that the idea of in-depth analysis of entire blocs of voters was impossible. The Chicago ward, for instance, had more than 8000 registered voters. It would take years to analyze a group of that size.

Hayden tossed the profiles aside and decided to return them the next day, telling Blohm that her idea was completely impractical. After his lunch with her at the airport in July, he had called a friend in Washington and learned she was working for Senator Lemuel K. Dundee. Well, her plan to help him just wouldn't work.

He was standing, one hand resting on his personal computer, when the idea came to him. Maybe Blohm's brainstorm could be made to work.

He had a good working knowledge of polling techniques. He knew that a properly weighted sample of 1500 to 2000 persons could give a reasonably accurate canvass of the entire nation, with a possible error of three percentage points, plus or minus.

If a sample of 2000 could accurately indicate what the whole country was thinking, what size sample would be needed for a Chicago ward of 8000 registered voters? Hayden sat down at his computer and punched in some numbers.

He didn't know the exact total of registered voters in the US, so his calculations were based on estimates. But using the same percentages, the computer showed that he could determine the subconscious biases of that 8000-voter ward by in-depth analysis of two-tenths of one person.

He stared at that. Analyzing two-tenths of one person was ridiculous, of course, but that didn't invalidate the concept of combining polling techniques with in-depth analysis.

He began jotting notes of what would be needed. First of all, he'd have to refine the number of interviewees required to give an accurate canvass of an entire voting

182

bloc. Second, he'd have to determine how they would be weighted – age, sex, race, education, income, etc. But all that was standard polling procedure.

The trick would be to select, say, ten people at random from that ward, subject them to the in-depth analysis he did on jurors, weigh their responses, and interpret them as percentages for the whole voting district.

He thought he could do it.

MARCH 13, 1989

'She don't like me much,' Todhunter Clark said.

'Who doesn't like you much?' Rod Harding asked.

'You know who,' Brother Nabisco said. 'That Molly Turner. She cuts me up with her eyes.'

'You're imagining things,' Harding said.

'I don't think so,' Clark said. 'She just don't like me. I don't know why – I never did nothing to hurt her.'

They were sitting on blanketed cots in what they called the 'safe house.' Harding had found it: an abandoned farm about eight miles south of Canton, on the river. The house – a shack, really – was set on a twenty-acre plot that had been neglected so long it was practically a jungle.

The property was purchased in the name of Mrs Josephine Turner, and Harding and Clark worked hard to make it usable. They cleared the one-lane entry road. Then, knowing the possible need of an escape route, they hacked a rear path leading to bluffs overlooking the river.

They patched up and furnished the house as best they could, bringing in cots, a cast-off table, a few rickety chairs. And a kerosene heater. There was an outdoor privy that smelled something awful, and a backyard pump they finally got working, although the water it coughed up was rusty and tasted metallic.

The best thing about the safe house was that it had a small root cellar, reached by a trapdoor from the kitchen.

Now it held weapons, explosives, and a lot of other illegal matériel.

Only a half-dozen people knew about the farm. They were under strict orders to check their rearview mirrors before making the turnoff from the graveled access road. The safe house was hard to find – which was the way they wanted it.

The kerosene heater was glowing, but the two men were wearing quilted down jackets, and Brother Nabisco even had the earflaps of his hunting cap snugging his head. They were cleaning a new shipment of guns from Miami and demolishing a six-pack of Coors as they worked.

'Look at this one,' Harding said, holding up a pistol. 'Colt 1911. A forty-five. It looks like it went through World War One. Good condition though. I wonder how many guys it snuffed.'

'We'll never know,' Clark said. 'I packed one of those things in Nam. You got to hang on tight, or the damned thing will buck right out of your fist. Want another beer?'

'Sure, pop me one.'

'You ever consider,' Clark said, bringing both of them beers, 'that your name is Rod, and people call me Tod. Rod and Tod. Sounds like a lawyer firm, don't it?'

'Or a couple of country singers.'

'That, too,' Clark said, beginning to strip an M-16. 'You know, I never have thanked you rightly for getting me out of that Florida slammer.'

'I didn't do it for you,' Harding said gruffly. 'I did it for me. For us, I mean.'

'Yeah,' the black man said. 'I know, but still . . . You know, being around here has been a real high for me.'

'Where you from, Tod? Originally, I mean.'

'Mississippi. I never did know who my daddy was. I was what they called a "midnight baby." And then my momma took off for parts unknown, and I was kind of shipped around the family. Whoever had enough food that year took me in. The army was the first home I ever had.'

'I believe it.'

'Well, they fed me good and gave me the first pair of new shoes I ever owned. That was something. And they taught me a trade – if you can call it that.'

Harding grunted, sighted at the broken window stuffed with rags, and squeezed the trigger of the pistol. There was a satisfying click.

'Then,' Clark went on, 'after Nam they didn't want me anymore, and to tell you the truth, I didn't want them. So I was just floating when you picked me up.'

'How did you live?' Harding asked.

'This and that,' Brother Nabisco said vaguely. 'Some small arson jobs for businessmen looking for insurance bucks. I got by – just. What I'm trying to say is that I never did know what a *real* home was like till I came up here. I mean, you folks been treating me fine. I got me a regular salary, hot food every day, money in my pocket. That's *something*.'

'I can imagine.'

'No, you can't,' Clark said, 'unless you've gone without. You're a lucky man.'

'I know.'

'Got yourself your own house, a beautiful wife, and that little Jeff – he's so sweet I could eat him up. He's going to be king of the world, that kid. You got it all.'

The white man raised his head slowly and stared at Todhunter Clark. But Brother Nabisco's head was lowered as he reassembled the M-16.

'Are you trying to tell me something, Tod?' Harding asked.

'No,' Clark said, 'not really. Except that you got the prettiest, kindest wife in the world and a little baby that almost makes me cry every time I see him, he's so great. You'd be some kind of a goddamned fool to give all that up.'

'What the hell are you talking about? I have no intention of giving it up.'

185

'Uh-huh,' Brother Nabisco said, raising his head to return Harding's stare. 'I hope you really mean that. I hope you wouldn't do anything that might hurt that wonderful wife of yours and that wonderful baby.'

Harding looked at him a brief moment longer.

'Mind your own fucking business,' he said harshly.

MARCH 13, 1989

At almost the same time Harding and Clark were talking in the safe house in West Virginia, James Gargan and Jake Spencer were meeting in the small state park near Friendship Heights, Maryland.

The two men, huddled in overcoats, sat on opposite sides of a wooden picnic table. Gargan had brought along a quart thermos of hot black coffee laced with brandy. He had even remembered plastic cups.

Jake Spencer picked up the thermos and hefted it.

'I used one of these once,' he said. 'The tape recorder was in the false bottom.'

'Jesus, you're a suspicious bastard,' Gargan said.

'Sure, I'm suspicious, Jimbo,' Spencer said with his ghastly smile. 'And I'm alive. The two go together.'

'What's new with Dundee?' Gargan asked, pouring them coffee. 'Any developments?'

'Well, I'm off the payroll,' the other man said. 'No more retainer. So I called in the field guy who was tailing Molly Turner. The job's finished as far as I'm concerned.'

'You got any idea why he pulled you off?'

Spencer shrugged. 'I admit we weren't getting much. Maybe he got tired of paying for nothing. Or maybe he found a better source.'

'More likely,' Gargan said. 'Remember the last time we were out here – you tipped me that Constance Underwood was balling a kid named Billy McCrea?'

'Sure, I remember.'

'Well, just for the fun of it, I put a couple of guys on him. He's a very busy little boy. According to my guys, he fucks everything – women, men, fox terriers, knotholes – you name it. All for money, of course. It would be hilarious except that some of his clients are very important people. If this lad ever decides to get into blackmail, you'll see one grand exodus from Embassy Row and from Congress and a few departments I could mention but won't.'

'He's that active, is he?'

'You wouldn't believe. His little black book must look like the District telephone directory. Want to guess who's one of his best customers?'

'How many guesses do I get?'

'One.'

'Man or woman?'

'Man.'

'Okay,' Spencer said. 'I guess Tom Kealy, Senator Dundee's prat boy.'

'You son of a bitch,' Gargan said admiringly, 'you're right on. Why did you pick him?'

'He just looks like a guy who plays the skin flute.'

'Well, he's been playing Billy McCrea's – which creates something of a problem. I told you Dundee plans to run in ninety-two. He's got a lot of very heavy financing: guys whose names you never see in the papers. And we're very sympathetic, of course.'

'Of course. And the soldier boys. And the guys who sell toilet paper to the Marine Corps.'

'Right. Well, if it ever comes out that Dundee's top aide is a butterfly, it's not going to do his candidacy any good.'

'My God, Jimbo, go to the senator and tell him! He'll can Kealy and that'll be the end of it. It's three years before the election.'

'Well, Jake,' Gargan said earnestly, hunching across the table, 'we hate to do that. We've done a lot of soul-searching on this, and – '

'Soul-searching?' Spencer cried. 'That's a hot one!

How do you frisk a soul?'

'– and we hate to ruin Kealy's career,' Gargan went on, ignoring the interruption. 'Kealy is a valuable aide to Dundee. He can help put him in the White House. So we'd really feel bad about blowing the whistle on him.'

Jake Spencer stared at the other man. Then he reached slowly into an inner pocket, pulled out a cigar. He stripped the cellophane away, bit off a half-inch of tobacco, and spat it out. He lighted the cigar with a wooden kitchen match he ignited with his thumbnail.

'Jimbo,' he said, blowing a plume of smoke to one side, 'you've got more shit than a Christmas goose. The scenario goes like this: The Department wants Dundee in the White House – he's such a good pal. You think he has a good chance of making it. Now you learn his number one coolie has been gobbling ze goo. Should you tell the senator to fire the guy? No. Why not? Because if Dundee makes it to the Oval Office, the Department wants to have his chief aide in their hip pocket because then they can lean on him. Is that about it'

Gargan nodded mournfully. 'I told them I couldn't con you, Jake, but they wanted me to try.'

'That's perfectly all right,' Spencer said grandly, waving his cigar. 'I'm not insulted.'

'Which only leaves us one option,' Gargan said. 'I think we better take out Billy McCrea. He represents a clear and present danger.'

'Oh, Jimbo, you know I don't do wet work.'

'I know that, Jake. But you've got contacts. We want no part of this – which is why we want you to be our cut-out. Can you get a good man to handle it? It's got to look like an accident.'

Spencer regarded the burning end of his cigar. 'What kind of money are we talking?'

'Five grand tops, no haggling. That goes to you. What you keep is your business. What you pay the caveman is also your business.'

'What's the time frame?'

'Oh . . . let's say three months. Jake, it's not only the Kealy connection. This kid is a walking time bomb. If he ever decides to talk, he could make Watergate look like a fixed spelling bee. The guy is dangerous, believe me.'

James Gargan, who had the reputation with his associates of being a sly and devious operative, had another reason for wanting Billy McCrea out of the picture – a reason he had no intention of revealing to Jake Spencer.

For the past four months, the Department had been bugging Thomas J. Kealy's Georgetown apartment, and Gargan was well aware of Kealy's burgeoning affair with Constance Underwood. That suited Gargan just fine, since he reckoned it could further Senator Dundee's political ambitions.

Putting down Billy McCrea would have the added advantage of getting rid of sexual competition.

'I'll look around, Jimbo,' Spencer promised, 'and see if I can find a professional willing to do the job.'

Which was, Gargan knew, a crock of shit. But he didn't care, as long as the deed was done.

APRIL 2, 1989

On the night of August 14, 1988, Mrs Carolyn B attended a meeting of the Madison, Wisconsin, chapter of the National Women's Union, of which she was a member. The meeting broke up about 11:00 PM. Mrs B then started her drive home to Verona.

She was a young matron of thirty-eight, with three children. Her husband owned a small hardware store in Verona. Mrs B was driving alone in her own car, a Toyota. A few miles from her home, the car lost power. Mrs B coasted onto the verge of the road and stopped.

(It was later determined that the gas tank of the Toyota was empty.)

189

Mrs B then left the car and stood at the edge of the road, hoping to flag down a passing motorist and ask for assistance. Three cars sped by without stopping. The fourth passed, then braked and backed up to where Mrs B was standing.

The car was occupied by four young men, ranging in age from eighteen to twenty-six. It was later proved that all four had been drinking heavily for several hours and were in varying degrees of intoxication.

They dragged Mrs B into a wooded area alongside the road, where all four repeatedly raped, sodomized, and sexually abused her for more than two hours. The men then drove away, leaving their victim naked, bloody, bruised.

Mrs B managed to drag herself onto the road, where she lay in a semiconscious condition. The next car to come along swerved to avoid her, but didn't stop. However, the driver did call the police from the first available phone. Mrs B was found and rushed to the nearest hospital.

After emergency care, she was able to tell police officers what had happened. She provided descriptions of her attackers and their car. She also recalled the first two digits of their license plate.

Within forty-eight hours, the police arrested four men, all residents of St Charles, a small town south of Paoli, and charged them with several offenses, including rape and felonious assault. Mrs B identified all four in a lineup as her assailants.

The youngest of the four, an eighteen-year-old high school student, cooperated with the prosecution in an effort to obtain a lighter sentence. His confession substantiated Mrs B's statement in all major respects.

The four men were brought to trial in January 1989, at St Charles. The attack on Mrs B had aroused a great deal of public indignation, and the courtroom was crowded, mostly by NWU and WDC members, who frequently had to be cautioned by the presiding judge to mute their hostility against the accused.

On March 17, 1989, the men were found guilty on all counts as charged. They were remanded to the St Charles jail to await sentencing.

On March 31, the sentences were handed down. The eighteen-year-old who had turned state's evidence was given six months and three years of probation. One of the others was sentenced to eighteen months, and the other two got three years, with the possibility of parole in one-third that time. The judge stated that none of these 'boys' had criminal records and had acted 'foolishly' while 'liquored up.'

While the trial had dragged on, the Wisconsin regiment of the Women's Defense Corps had planned its own retribution. There is some evidence that Molly Turner aided in the planning, but there is nothing to indicate she took an active role in what followed.

Shortly before midnight on April 2, a platoon of WDC sisters invaded the St Charles jail, disarming and binding the two jailers on duty. It is worth noting that none of the women was masked, but since they were all recruited from Wisconsin cities far from the Paoli–St Charles area, the jailers recognized none of them.

The four rapists, who were scheduled to be transferred to a state prison the following day, were dragged screaming from their cells. They were taken to the exact spot where the attack on Mrs B had occurred, and all four were hanged from the branches of trees.

Anonymous calls to the news media in Madison alerted authorities to the lynching. One of the first photographers on the scene took the shot that was later published all over the world: four trussed bodies, necks stretched and heads awry, hanging limp and lifeless.

The execution of the four convicted rapists caused an international sensation. Foreign journalists flooded the WDC headquarters in Canton with requests for interviews with Molly Turner.

191

APRIL 16, 1989

'What the hell is this?' Molly Turner asked, coming into the living room of her Hillcrest Avenue home. 'A hen party?'

It looked like it. Ann was there, and Mrs Josephine Turner, Mrs Cecily Harding, Yvonne Popkin, Lois Campbell, and three or four other staffers. They were examining drawings of a proposed WDC uniform, designed by a sister who worked for a Manhattan couturier.

Mrs Turner passed around coffee and homemade oatmeal cookies while the others clustered around the colored sketches, debating their merits and deficiencies.

The uniform selected was to be made of khaki denim. It resembled a rancher's outfit, with pleated jeans and an Eisenhower jacket of the same material with breast pockets and snap closures.

It would be worn with a white shirt, a black ascot at the open neck. Headgear would be a black beret trimmed with a narrow edging of red leather and bearing a brass WDC badge.

'Very sharp,' Molly said approvingly. 'And the jacket is short enough so you can wear a gun belt. Yvonne, why don't you have copies made of this sketch and send out a release on the new WDC uniform. After what happened in Wisconsin, I think we'll get good coverage.'

'Will the uniform be required of all members?' Popkin asked.

Molly turned to her sister. 'Ann?'

'I don't think that would be wise,' she said. 'Some of our sisters have to watch their pennies. Let's make it optional – for the time being, at least.'

Mrs Cecily Harding then brought in little Jefferson, who immediately became the center of attention. He demon-

192

strated how rapidly he could crawl, and even stood erect for a few teetering seconds, hanging on to his grandmother's legs.

Molly drew her sister into the den and closed the door against the noise and laughter in the living room.

'Sit down for a minute,' she said to Ann. 'You and I never seem to get a chance to talk anymore. I've been so damned busy with those stupid interviews – it was a reporter from a West German magazine today. God, I'm sick of saying the same things over and over.'

'It's doing a lot of good, Molly. We're getting clippings from all over the world.'

'No kidding? Maybe we should go international. Do you think so?'

'Not yet,' Ann said. 'Maybe in the future. I think we better consolidate what we have before we think of expanding.'

'I suppose you're right. I don't know what I'd do without you, hon. I go flying off in all directions, I know, but I depend on you to keep bringing me back to earth.' She paused, looked at Ann closely. 'Is everything all right, sweetie? I mean between you and me?'

'Of course. Why shouldn't it be?'

'No reason. But lately I sense something. The way you look at me, a certain – oh, I don't know – like a coolness or a distance between us. If something is bugging you, for God's sake, tell me.'

'No, really, Molly. Nothing has changed.'

'It wasn't that lynching, was it?'

'Yes,' Ann said immediately. 'That's what it was. I admit it shook me up. That's probably why I've been acting differently.'

'It had to be done,' Molly said decisively. 'After what they did to that poor woman – and then to get a few months in jail! A few more lynchings, and you'll see rape becoming a vanishing crime – mark my words.'

'I hope you're right.'

The sisters were silent then, staring at the worn carpet reflectively.

'We've come a long way in a short time,' Molly said somberly. 'I wish Norma Jane was here to see it. She'd be proud.'

'Molly . . .' Ann said hesitantly, 'where do we go from here? Don't you think we've made our point with the lynchings and putting *Hooker* out of business?'

'Are you kidding?' Molly Turner said indignantly. 'This country is full of targets. We're only getting started.'

'I'm just worried that we may be going too far too fast. I wouldn't want to see us keep trying to top what we've already done by rushing into dangerous situations that may get a lot of sisters killed.'

'They knew they were running that risk when they signed up. Jesus, don't start talking like Constance Underwood! She thinks she can solve all our problems by getting laws passed. Fat chance! Ann, I'm going to stick to direct action – and if it's violent and bloody, so be it. I want to give that fat-ass Senator Dundee something to think about. That bastard is making a career out of putting me down.'

'He's got a lot of followers, Molly.'

'Screw him! Let him keep trying to defend *Hooker* magazine and convicted rapists. He's on the wrong side – as he'll learn one of these days. Well . . . maybe we better get back to the hen party. How's Yvonne doing with the booze?'

'Better. She joined AA and she's really shaping up. At least she shows up for work sober. Oh, another thing . . . I had a phone call from Constance Underwood today, and – '

'That woman hates my guts,' Molly said.

'Well, she claims they have no room for us in the NWU offices. Probably doesn't want us to get too close to their files and records. But she says she's got a list of three or four places she thinks might suit us. Molly, I think you better go to Washington and pick an office you'll like.

You'll be spending a lot of time there.'

'Sure, I can do that. Maybe Rod could come along and help me.

'If you feel it's necessary,' Ann said.

That night, while her husband and son slept, Ann Harding slid the anonymous letters (there were now five of them) from under her sweaters in the bottom dresser drawer. She took them into the bathroom, opened them all, and read them. They were explicit as to times, dates, places. And she knew Molly and Rod had been together at those times, on those dates, in those places.

She was a good wife, mother, manager – she knew that. But this was something beyond her experience. She knew confrontation could be counterproductive. But she sensed that this problem would not go away by itself. It was a threat that made her nauseated because betrayal by the two people she loved most was so unfair, so unjustified.

Knowing Molly and knowing Rod (better than either of them guessed), she reckoned that their intimacy had been created by circumstance. But recognizing all that did not soften their offense. She herself could never be capable of such perfidy. And they were playing her for a fool.

It was at that moment, perhaps, with the anonymous letters dangling from cold fingers, that the worm of revenge began to gnaw.

MAY 20, 1989

Rod Harding, like most people, rarely failed to read the obituary page of any newspaper he bought. It was interesting: the name, age, cause of death, career, survived by . . . Sometimes a photograph of the deceased – taken ten years previously.

Some years ago he had become conscious that an inordinate number of men and women engaged in cancer research were dying of cancer. Harding knew that was irrational. Cancer was not a communicable disease. But still, the thought persisted.

It persisted because he feared he might be suffering from a similar phenomenon. In the army, with the police force, he had been exposed to all kinds of human corruption. He thought some of the dirt had rubbed off; he had 'caught' the corruption.

There were no physical symptoms; it was a malaise of the soul. He had done a good job of hiding it from parents, wife, friends – but *he* knew it was there: a despair so corrosive that nothing in life had flavor but pleasure, and madness was the law of the land.

He was lying naked on a cot in the safe house, idly stroking Molly Turner's taut body, thinking what a shit he was and wondering without guilt why it didn't bother him.

'We weren't going to do this,' she said. 'In Canton.'

'I know,' he said. 'Good intentions . . .'

'I'm moving to Washington,' she said. 'Next week. The office is ready, and I took an apartment near the convention center. You can come visit me. WDC business.'

'Sure,' he said.

'You'll have to come often,' she said, holding his face between her palms and staring into his eyes. 'We'll have a lot of official business to discuss. But I don't think it'll be smart if you stay overnight. Just go for the day, then come back to Ann. We can have a matinee.'

'Yes, boss,' he said. 'Of course, boss. Absolutely, boss.'

She punched his shoulder. 'Does it bother you that I'm boss?'

'Nothing about you bothers me, lover,' he said. 'You want another brew?'

'No, I'm fine. How did you get this scar?'

'A snake bit me.'

'Nut. Is your shoulder all right now?'

'Sure. All I got is a dimple to show for it. Do I get a Women's Liberation Medal?'

'It's only for women,' she said firmly. 'I'll give you a Fucking Medal if you like.'

He turned onto his side and put his cunning tongue to her neck, armpits, nipples.

'Jesus!' she gasped. 'What are you doing?'

'I'm a colonel now. I'm bucking for brigadier.'

She clutched him to her. 'You're five-star as far as I'm concerned. I need you, Rod. I'm scared. I guess you know that.'

'I know.'

'I'm all front: the loud, brassy, macho lady wearing a gun belt. And I'm ready to wet my pants.'

'Bullshit. You've got more balls than any man I know. Sure, you're scared. In combat, everyone in scared. That's no disgrace. But you function: that's the only thing that counts.'

'One of these days I'm going to get my ass shot off.'

'Probably,' he said cheerfully.

'Rat!' she said, kissing him. 'My own sweet, delicious rat What really bothers me is all those sisters who believe in me They'll follow me to hell if I tell them to.'

'The responsibility of command,' he said. 'If you can't hack it, bug out.'

'You know I can't do that.'

'Then stop complaining and do what you have to do.'

'You're *sooo* sympathetic, *sooo* understanding.'

'That's why you love me: I never jive you.'

'That's true,' she agreed. 'You never do. Am I a better lay than Ann?'

'Shut up.'

'She's got bigger tits than I have.'

'Shut up.'

'Right,' she said. 'Sorry.'

He rolled over and rubbed her back. Her spine was like a string of stones.

'You've got to eat,' he told her.

'I just did.'

'You know what I mean. Moll, you're just driving your-self too hard.'

'Got to,' she murmured, face buried in his neck and shoulder. 'Lots to do. Going to die young. I know it.'

'You and Norma Jane were lovers,' he said.

She raised her head to stare at him.

'Sure,' she said challengingly. 'So?'

'Nothing.'

'You ever had a guy?'

'No.'

'Want to?'

'Not particularly. You're my guy.'

'Yes,' she said contentedly, nestling down into him. 'That's what I want to be – your guy. How long is this going to last?'

'What? The WDC? This afternoon?'

'You and me.'

'Oh,' he said. 'That. I don't know, Moll. Do you?'

'We'll take it a day at a time.'

He rolled her away. They lay side by side, staring at the muted sunlight coming through the dirty window choked with a blue rag.

'I'm happy,' Molly said. 'This moment. But something awful is happening. I think I'm falling in love with you.'

'Shit,' he said.

She nodded. 'I know. I didn't plan it, Rod. Honest to God, I didn't.'

He was silent. Then: 'Maybe it'll pass.'

'Maybe. I don't think so. Not for a while.'

'Look,' he said. 'Just cool it – okay? You know I'll never give up Ann and Jeff. You know that, don't you?'

'Yes.'

'A man can love two women at the same time, and a woman can love two men at the same time. That's not impossible, is it?'

'No.'

'Different kinds of love,' he said, 'but similar.'

198

'Still . . .' she said, 'I'd like you for myself.'

'Take what you can get,' he advised. 'I do. Now?'

'Oh God, yes,' she breathed.

He didn't tell her that he suspected Todhunter Clark knew of their intimacy. She didn't tell him that she suspected Ann knew. Neither wanted to say anything to mar their bliss.

JUNE 25, 1989

Jake Spencer had learned a long time ago that there were wheels within wheels, and if you tried to figure them out, you ended up with a king-sized migraine.

In fact, Jake often thought, there was probably little rhyme or reason to any of his assignments, either as an agent of the FBI or, after his resignation, as a private investigator. Jake thought all of his employers were insane.

So Jimbo Gargan wanted Billy McCrea taken out, but wouldn't tell Jake his real reasons. That was okay with Jake; he'd snuff McCrea; five grand was a nice piece of change, and he couldn't waste time wondering *why*.

After he started tailing McCrea, he became aware that there were two other men doing exactly the same thing. One was a guy in a floppy fedora, and the other was a little gink with a toothbrush mustache. He looked like a Latino to Jake.

He called Gargan from a public phone.

'Jimbo,' he said, 'about that assignment . . . Call off your dogs. We're walking up each other's heels.'

'Okay,' Gargan said.

The next day the fedora was gone, but the Latino was still there, dogging Billy McCrea's footsteps.

What the hell, Jake Spencer said to himself, and dropped McCrea for a day while he followed the guy with the mustache. He tailed him, in fact, right into the fancy, white marble embassy of a Central American banana republic.

199

So he called Jimbo again and explained the situation.

'Jesus Christ!' Gargan said disgustedly. 'This is getting to be a Marx Brothers movie. McCrea is playing footsie with the ambassador's wife, and they're probably planning to pop him. All right, Jake, I'll see what I can do. I've got a pal in the State Department. Maybe he can drop a hint to the embassy that the situation is under control.'

Two days later the mustache disappeared, and Spencer had Billy McCrea all to himself.

As Jimbo had said, he was a busy little boy: here, there, and everywhere – with some very heavy clients. Spencer figured he was pulling down at least fifty big ones a year – all tax-free, of course. Jake was jealous, but acknowledged he was a little long in the tooth for that line of work.

He stuck with the kid for almost two months, because this had to be done *right*, and McCrea never once tumbled to the fact that wherever he went, there was this big, hunched guy trundling after him.

Spencer got Billy McCrea's pattern down cold. And, because of his phenomenal memory, he never had to make a written note.

McCrea had a full schedule during the week, servicing clients in the morning, afternoon, evening. But on the seventh day, like God, Billy boy rested. He spent the Sabbath holed up in his apartment. He came out early in the morning to buy the Sunday papers and a buttered bagel.

Then he went back to his apartment and didn't emerge again until 7:00 PM, when he went to a nearby Chinese restaurant, where he always ordered shrimp with lobster sauce and fried rice. He returned to his apartment and didn't come out again until Monday morning. He never had visitors on Sunday.

Jake Spencer liked that.

He went back to his Rosslyn office, put his feet up on the desk, lighted a cigar, and planned long and carefully how he was going to waste Billy McCrea.

Gargan wanted it to look like an accident. That was okay when you could fake a car crash, a boat fire, a plane explosion – something like that. But an 'accident' was difficult to pull off in the mark's own apartment. What were you going to do – try to make it look like he had slipped in the bathtub and hit his head?

Over the years, Jake Spencer had accumulated what he called a 'handy-dandy nirvana kit.' It was a collection of weapons, drugs (some of them exotic), police badges, and items that provided a temporary disguise.

Pawing through this stuff, kept locked in the bottom drawer of his desk, Spencer began to create a scenario and select the equipment he'd need to trash McCrea.

On the evening of June 25, a Sunday, Jake Spencer was waiting for McCrea when he came out of the Chinese restaurant. Spencer was wearing a dark three-piece suit, a homburg, and carrying a calfskin attaché case. That last was a nice touch, he thought. Who suspected a guy carrying an attaché case?

'Mr McCrea?' he said pleasantly.

The young boy stopped and looked at him. 'Who are you?'

'Lathrop Gilmore, sir,' Spencer said. 'From the State Department.' He displayed identification of a man who had been dead for thirty years.

'The State Department?' McCrea said, grinning. 'That's cool. What's the State Department want with me?'

'Well, ah, it's a matter of some delicacy,' Spencer said with an embarrassed smile. 'It concerns the wife of an ambassador. We have received a complaint from the embassy, and I have been assigned to investigate. Mr McCrea, I hate to discuss these things on the street. Is there anyplace we could go to have a confidential chat?'

'Sure,' McCrea said, laughing. 'My apartment is only a block away. We can go there.'

'Thank you, sir,' Spencer said gratefully. And he *was* grateful. Getting invited back to McCrea's place had been

201

a gamble – and the key to the whole thing. Now Jake knew it would go as smooth as silk.

He followed Billy up the six flights of iron staircase and waited behind him as he unlocked the door. When it was open, Spencer hit McCrea behind the right ear with a leather-covered sap, knocking him forward and down. It was a blow applied with the skill of long practice. It rendered McCrea unconscious but didn't break the skin.

Spencer gripped the boy under the arms, dragged him clear of the threshold, then bolted the door. One lamp was burning in the apartment. Spencer made a rapid tour to make certain no one else was present.

When he came back into the living room, McCrea was beginning to stir. So Jake gave him another little tap.

He stood looking down at his victim. 'Pretty boy,' he said aloud.

Then Spencer took off his homburg, jacket, and vest. He opened the attaché case, pulled out a pair of gray silk gloves, put those on, and went to work.

He put a wide strip of adhesive tape across McCrea's mouth, making certain his nostrils weren't blocked. Then he hand-cuffed his hands behind his back, first protecting his wrists with sweat bands with Velcro closures so there would be no abrasions on the boy's skin. He did the same thing with McCrea's ankles, using larger gyves. All this equipment came from the attaché case.

After Billy was gagged and bound, Spencer slid the wallet from his pocket. It held more than five hundred dollars in fifties and small bills. Jake took four hundred of that and slipped it into his pocket. The remainder went back onto McCrea's hip.

Then Spencer began a leisurely search of the apartment, after making certain he could not be observed through any of the windows. The first thing he found, in the bedroom bureau, was Billy's little black book: names, addresses, phone numbers, and how much each client paid. That went into Spencer's attaché case for later study.

He also found almost three thousand in cash under a stack of silk underwear, and grinned. Jimbo Gargan had put him onto a nice thing. Spencer pocketed twenty-five hundred and left the remainder where he found it.

McCrea had some great jewelry – chunky gold stuff – and Spencer was tempted. But he left it all there. He did take an unopened jar of caviar from the kitchen refrigerator, figuring that could never be traced. Not if he ate it that night, it couldn't.

That's all he took from McCrea's apartment: the money, the little black book, the caviar. He went back into the living room and dug a heroin kit from his case. He had never shot shit himself, but he knew how it was done.

He had taken a dime bag off a doper several years ago. He had no idea if the stuff lost its potency with age, but he figured it still had enough pizzazz to show up in McCrea's blood during the autopsy.

He melted down all the smack in a tablespoon taken from a set of fine Georgian silver in the kitchen. He used the stub of a candle set on the back of one of McCrea's bone china dinner plates to heat the spoon.

When he had the hypodermic needle half-filled, he tightened a length of rubber tubing around Billy's bare arm. He watched, fascinated, as a blue vein swelled. He jabbed the needle in and pushed the plunger home. He took off the rubber tubing and remembered to press McCrea's fingertips onto tablespoon, plate, and hypodermic needle. He blew out the candle and left all the drug paraphernalia right there on the floor. He removed McCrea's gag and manacles, and put all the stuff back in his attaché case.

He closed the case, set it near the outside door. He put on vest, jacket, homburg. Still wearing his silk gloves, he lifted McCrea to his feet, grunting with the effort and, stooping slightly, let the slack body fall over his shoulder. He carried Billy into the bedroom. The boy was breathing in wheezy gasps.

During his search, Spencer had noted an open bedroom

window with a fire escape outside overlooking a concrete courtyard. With much pulling and hauling, he got Billy McCrea out onto the landing. He toppled his body over the railing. It thudded onto the concrete six stories below.

Moving quickly now, Jake came back to the living room and took a final look around. He picked up his attaché case and left the apartment, closing the door softly behind him. He stripped off his gloves and jammed them into a side pocket.

He was home in an hour. The caviar was excellent.

Social historians studying the phenomenon of the Women's Defense Corps as it existed in the late 1980s and early 1990s will find a treasure trove of raw research in a thick file of WDC correspondence dealing with that organization's relations with other minority groups: blacks, Indians, Chicanos, Hispanics, etc.

The letters are mostly requests for assistance from associations lacking the financial resources of the WDC. Some ask advice on organization and administration. Others plead for funds. Many suggest joint militant actions that would prove beneficial to both parties.

Early on, Molly Turner adamantly refused to cooperate with any underground organization that adopted violence as its raison d'être. These groups, usually small and short-lived, frequently engaged in wanton and senseless bombings, assassinations, and kidnappings. They were anarchic in every sense of the word.

Her refusal to aid such secret terrorist associations made her the target of their vilification. She was accused of being a tool of the establishment, a running dog of the capitalist imperialists, a dupe of the power structure, used to confuse and mislead the proletariat as to the 'real problems' of class, race, and the inequitable distribution of wealth in the US.

The most malignant of these (unsigned) letters came from a small terrorist organization calling itself the Frantz Fanon

Urban Guerrilla Group. It was charged by the FBI with being responsible for several bombings, bank robberies, and the attempted poisoning of the water supply of Terre Haute, Indiana.

Their vituperative and frightening letters to Molly Turner betray an almost hysterical irrationality. They also reveal an envy of her public reputation, organizational skills, and the success she was achieving while operating 'above ground' and winning heavy coverage in the news media.

An accusation had been made in the Marxist press that these letters were in fact forgeries prepared by Federal law enforcement agencies in an effort to panic Molly Turner and the WDC into close collaboration with an illegal organization. This writer has not been able to find even the slightest evidence to support such a charge.

JULY 4, 1989

'That goddamn woman is fucking me,' Senator Dundee said. 'Politically, I mean,' he added hastily. 'She's doing everything right, and I can't believe she's that smart. Luck – that's all it is: dumb luck.'

He was complaining to Simon Christie, his chief speechwriter. Christie was a paunchy, balding ex-newspaperman who had the senator's oratorical style down pat. 'Like wading through molasses in hip boots,' he confided to a friend.

They were sitting in Dundee's hideaway in the Capitol, door locked, air conditioner whirring. The Senate had just adjourned for the summer recess, and the two men had met to plan Dundee's speech schedule for the next three months.

'Senator,' Christie said, 'you're going to have to walk a mighty thin line. You can't cut her up for putting *Hooker* out of business, and a lot of people in this country think those four rapists got just what they deserved.'

'Tell me about it,' Dundee said bitterly. 'As I see it, the only tack I can take is to say, yes, they may have been worthwhile ends, but the means employed were contrary to everything this country stands for.'

'Right,' Christie said, a little bemused now by his third bourbon.

'I can make a case on those lynchings,' Dundee said bravely. 'All right, they were rapists, but they were *convicted* rapists. The law had worked.'

'Stupid sentences,' Christie muttered.

'Sure, they were stupid, but the system *worked* – that's the important thing. What the hell would happen to this great country if everyone started taking the law into his own hands? It'd be as bad as Godless Communism. That's the angle I want you to hit in the Fourth of July speech.'

'You're sure you want to go to Madison?'

'Absolutely. Practically at the scene of the crime. It'll get good press coverage. Listen, Chris, everyone tells me I'm riding this thing to oblivion, but by God I've got the courage of my convictions. I'm going to stick to it, sink or swim.'

'It's your funeral,' Simon Christie wanted to say, but didn't.

'Actually,' Dundee went on, 'I think I made the right move in taking on Molly Turner and the WDC. The whole point was to get my name known nationwide. And it's working. Have you seen the latest name and photo recognition polls? Up, up, up. Now people know who I am and what I stand for. Listen, Chris, we'll go with the set speeches most of the summer, with some local references added, but for the Fourth of July speech, I want you to pull out all the stops. Write me a real blockbuster.'

'Will do,' Christie said, reaching for the bourbon bottle.

Dundee spent most of May and June on the road. He went first to his home state – 'just to howdy around,' as he put it. He visited the Draft Dundee headquarters, shook hands, and passed out ball-point pens.

He spoke at a high school graduation and a college commencement. He lunched with judges, dined with the governor, and breakfasted with the Cardinal. He visited cities, towns, villages. He attended picnics, dances, marriages, funerals, testimonial dinners, and rubber-chicken banquets. He stood as godfather to a grandchild of a real godfather.

He mended fences, touched all bases, pressed the flesh. Local reporters, photographers, and TV camera crews trailed after him. His PR staff ground out releases every hour on the hour – or so it seemed. He didn't forget to have a haircut in his old barbershop or to visit his grade school teacher in her nursing home.

The public image he projected was that of a genial, handsome, energetic man ready to listen to his constituents' complaints and anxious to provide whatever aid he could. He ate Mexican enchiladas, Polish sausage, and Italian meatballs. He kissed babies and women of all ages.

In private, he had several conversations with the men who actually ran the state: bankers, attorneys, contractors, real estate developers, and two brothers whose hidden holdings included adult bookstores, massage parlors, a racetrack, and the state's largest policy ring.

The results of all these discussions were satisfactory. Pledges were made, funds were promised. Much encouraged, Dundee moved on to speaking engagements in other states. He worked hard, listened solemnly to what people told him, and smiled modestly when they said, 'We need you in the White House, Senator.'

He made no gaffes, ruffled no feathers. He praised his friends and placated his enemies. And, at press conferences, when an impertinent reporter demanded, 'What are you running for, Senator?' he replied, 'The bathroom,' and dashed away, leaving the journalists laughing and jotting in their notebooks: 'Gd sns hmr.'

At no time in his speeches, press conferences, and interviews during this period did Senator Dundee denounce – or even mention – the National Women's Union and its president, Constance Underwood. But he never ceased censuring Molly Turner and the Women's Defense Corps.

Everything went swimmingly until, on the Fourth of July, he came to Madison, Wisconsin.

It was not, he admitted, 'Dundee country.' Madison was a university town, and the political philosophy of the majority of voters was far to the left of Dundee's. In fact, the first thing he saw, near the assembly hall where he was to speak, was a banner: WELCOME, MASTODON DUNDEE.

In addition, the lynchings of the rapists at nearby St Charles had polarized the city, and a fierce debate still raged. The senator had been invited to speak by the local chapter of a national organization of young conservatives with the suggestion that he devote his speech to the evils of vigilante justice.

There was a group of perhaps twenty protestors outside the hall when Dundee and his entourage arrived in a limousine provided by his hosts. The pickets, mostly women, were carrying signs identifying them as WDC members.

But they seemed a reasonably peaceable group. Other than boos, jeers, and catcalls, no attempt was made to block Dundee's entry into the hall. The demonstrators were being watched by five uniformed police officers.

It was not a public gathering; attendance was by invitation only, and those entering had to surrender tickets. Dundee, with a practiced eye, estimated the audience at 300. A small crowd, he acknowledged, but he was gratified to note the presence of several reporters and a TV camera crew.

Despite the precautions taken to screen the listeners, it immediately became apparent that not all were in sympathy with Dundee's views or had any desire to hear what he had to say. When he was introduced and strode to the podium, several in the audience rose to their feet and turned their backs to him. They remained standing in that position throughout his address.

Also, his opening remarks were interrupted and drowned out by yells and shouts from the rear of the hall. A banner, DUNDEE HATES WOMEN, was unfurled and held aloft. A fistfight erupted, and a man and two women were dragged kicking and screaming from the hall by security guards.

When things had calmed down, the senator was able to continue. He said he was happy to note that he would be able to speak, no matter how unpopular his views might be with some listeners.

'The right of free speech,' he said, 'is a tradition we all cherish and must continue to protect if we value our liberty.'

He spoke of the Bill of Rights, how revolutionary those ten amendments were when first passed, and how, over the years, they had become an important part of the nation's laws.

'For this must ever be a nation of law,' he said. 'Law is the steel umbrella that protects us all. Without law, we are savages condemned to a swamp of violence, blood, and sudden death.'

He was interrupted by applause.

The recent events 'not too far from where we now meet,' he went on, were an example of what happens when people – even well-intentioned people – took justice into their own hands and ignored the majesty of the law.

'But violence begets violence,' he thundered, 'and those who live by the sword shall die by the sword!'

Applause.

He then tore into Molly Turner and the Women's Defense Corps, mentioning both by name.

'What they espouse,' he said sternly, 'is nothing more or less than anarchy. Raw anarchy! Naked anarchy! I do not doubt the sincerity of members of the Women's Defense Corps and that dictator who leads them, Molly

209

Turner. I acknowledge that their grievances are real, and the road to the equality they seek is sometimes a rocky one, with progress measured in inches. But I say to them that the bloody path they have chosen is infinitely worse. For, just as those in this audience who have turned their backs on me, Molly Turner and the WDC have turned their backs on this nation's finest traditions and the ideals which true patriots have fought and died for.'

He continued in this vein for another ten minutes, interrupted several times by enthusiastic applause. He concluded by saying earnestly:

'I warn women – all women, everywhere – that you will not find liberation at the muzzle of a revolver. Instead, you will arouse the enmity and disgust of all right-thinking Americans, and by so doing, you will endanger the achievement of the goals you seek. End your violence now before the righteous men and women of this great nation rise up in their wrath and demand their government with its enormous resources put an end to the shootings, the bombings, the lynchings.

'I say to you tonight as strongly as I can: the war you have started is a war you cannot and will not win!'

He finished his address to tumultuous applause. Many rushed to the rostrum to shake his hand and ask for autographs. Thomas Kealy, Simon Christie, and other staffers surrounded him, and the group moved slowly down the packed aisle to the exit.

Outside, the crowd of protestors had grown to at least fifty, but the number of policemen had not been increased. They were unable to control the unruly demonstrators, whose mood had turned ugly.

When Dundee appeared, the mob surged forward, screaming obscene curses and brandishing picket signs. Eggs flew through the air; one hit Dundee's shoulder and splattered across his chest. The cops fought their way to Dundee's side.

He was finally pushed and yanked into the waiting

limousine. Other staffers piled in after him. Doors were slammed and locked; the car started slowly through the crush. Sticks and fists beat on the roof, and even after they were clear, they were pelted with rocks and bottles.

A white-faced Senator Dundee glanced briefly through the rear window.

'Did the photographers get that?' he demanded. 'Were the TV cameras there?'

He flew directly back to Washington, DC. On July 5, he met with Jake Spencer in his office. He described what had happened.

'I never felt I needed a personal bodyguard,' he said tensely. 'I do now. I want a man to be with me at all times. An armed man. And maybe one or two more when I give a speech. I want a guy who knows the business and can cooperate with local security people and make sure they're doing their job. You know a good man who can handle that?'

'Sure, Senator,' Spencer said promptly. 'Me.'

So Jake became Senator Lemuel K. Dundee's personal bodyguard. Not that the salary was so great, but Jake had gone through Billy McCrea's little black book and found the names of Thomas J. Kealy and Constance Underwood, and what they had been paying for their jollies.

Spencer wanted to stay as close as he could get to Dundee's presidential campaign. He smelled big money.

AUGUST 17, 1989

'Is your boss Senator Dundee?' asked Lyle Hayden with his sweet smile.

Ruth Blohm nodded.

'Is he running for president?'

'He's considering it,' she said cautiously.

Hayden smoothed his blond beard and mustache with a knuckle. 'He thinks he's going to get elected by dumping

211

on Molly Turner?'

'He had to get his name known,' she said, bridling. 'And it's working. You object?'

'I don't object to his strategy,' Hayden said. 'His tactics worry me. The level of rhetoric seems to be rising. In that Madison speech, he practically declared war on the WDC.'

'It's not the rhetoric that bothers me,' she told him, 'it's the violence. In Madison he was pelted with eggs. Next time it may be bombs.'

Hayden had flown up from Atlanta with a thick briefcase of notes, documents, estimates, analyses. Blohm met him at the airport in her battered Toyota and drove him to her home in Arlington. Now they sat with a cocktail table between them, laden with glasses and a pitcher of iced lemonade. A cranky air conditioner banged and wheezed.

As usual, Eric Blohm sat at a card table, working endless chess games. If he was listening to their conversation, he gave no sign.

'Well . . .' Hayden said, opening his briefcase, 'it's an interesting problem you dropped in my lap. I got excited by it – I admit it. First of all, I think it's feasible.'

'It's just an extension of the work you've been doing with juries.'

'Right. With one added gimmick. It represents an opportunity to expand my business – I mean *really* expand it – if I can prove it out. There are problems, Ruth – as you probably anticipated. For one thing, there is no way to analyze an entire voting bloc, be it neighborhood, ward, district, precinct, or whatever. Too many people. Take too long. Cost too much. Now here's where my gimmick comes in.'

He paused. She waited.

'A randomly selected, viable sample of the bloc, properly weighted, should give us the answers for the entire bloc, plus or minus three percentage points.'

'A weighted sample,' she breathed. 'Lyle, you're a genius.'

'I concur,' he said seriously. 'So here's what we've got: The candidate picks the key or swing districts. I go in, and by a process of randomization, come up with a sample to be analyzed in depth. I estimate it'll run between ten and twenty units.'

Eric Blohm raised his head from his chessboard. 'Units?' he asked.

'People, sir,' Hayden said. 'Individuals. After the sample of registered voters has been picked at random, it gets tricky. Because the units have to be weighted. Age, sex, race, income, education, and a zillion other factors. Only a computer can handle it. I've written an experimental software program that looks good. Ruth, I think it can be done.'

'I knew it could!' she cried. 'My God, this could really be something big.'

'If it works,' he cautioned. 'Remember, we're talking about an experimental technique. The big problem will be persuading some politician to take the gamble. I can tell you right now, it will be an expensive program. Do you think Dundee will go for it?'

She was silent.

'Look,' he said. 'I'm going to leave you some cost estimates. I'm willing to pick up the tab for training the interviewers – that's how much confidence I have in this thing. And the software program will be on me, too. But someone's going to have to pay for the computer time, the interviewers' salaries, my work, and a modest profit margin.'

'Can you leave me the whole presentation, Lyle? Let me study the numbers and see where we go from here.'

'Of course,' he said. 'I didn't expect an instant decision.'

He began to lay out papers, printouts, and folders of notes on the cocktail table. She poured him another glass of lemonade.

'Young man,' Eric Blohm called.

Hayden turned toward him. 'Sir?'

'Do you play chess?'

'Yes, I do.'

'Are you good?'

Hayden smoothed his blond hair with a palm, smiling at the older man. 'Yes, sir, I am.'

Blohm beckoned him toward the chessboard. 'We'll see,' he said. 'We'll see.'

Their first game ended two hours and fourteen minutes later. Lyle Hayden had been telling the truth: he was good. But he lost.

In the evening, Ruth served a dinner of cold salmon, salad, and a bottle of chilled chablis. She listened amusedly while the two men fought their chess game all over again. 'If you had done this . . .' 'If I had moved to . . .' They obviously had a liking for each other, which made her happy.

She drove Hayden to the airport and they spent the entire time discovering how many important things they had in common: both loved chili, hated cats, and were indifferent to electronic music.

Just before he got out of the Toyota, he said, 'Thank you for a lovely day, Ruth. I really enjoyed it.'

'Come again,' she said, 'and stay longer.'

He swooped suddenly and kissed her cheek – which was nice.

On the drive home, alone, she pondered the problem of how to persuade Senator Dundee to finance Lyle Hayden's plan. She had almost reached her home before she came up with an idea she thought had a chance of success.

Dundee was senior senator from his state. The junior senator, also of Dundee's party, was up for re-election in 1990. Maybe, just maybe, she could convince the two politicians to share the expense of analyzing a single important ward, to test Lyle's scheme.

If the new technique didn't work – well, back to the drawing board. But if it succeeded, it just might put Lemuel Dundee in the Oval Office and make Ruth Blohm the girl genius of political engineering.

No, not Ruth Blohm. Mrs Ruth Hayden. She laughed aloud at that.

'What are you smiling about?' her father asked when she came into the house.

'Nothing in particular.'

'Did he get off okay?'

'I guess so. I dropped him outside the airport. What did you think of him?'

'He's all right,' Eric Blohm said grudgingly.

'Is he a good chess player?'

'Not very,' her father said. 'Too emotional.'

She never knew when he was kidding her.

SEPTEMBER 15, 1989

The Kentucky regiment, headquartered in Lexington, was generally recognized as having the most proficient drill team in the WDC. Every Friday evening they practiced, paraded, and put on an eye-catching display.

These military shows were held in a lighted public park, with a permit issued by the city. The snappy maneuvers were watched and enjoyed by a large number of spectators who sat in bleachers bordering a softball field.

Late in July, the colonel of the Kentucky regiment, a young black woman named Lucille Jackson, drove over to Canton to report a problem. She met with Molly, Ann, Rod Harding, and Todhunter Clark at the Hillcrest Avenue home.

'For the last three or four Fridays,' she said, 'we've been getting more and more roughnecks at our drills. These guys are real louts. There're some bikers – you know, the black leather morons – and the rest are just rednecks and clowns cutting loose on a Friday night.'

'How many of them?' Molly asked.

'Last Friday, about twenty. They don't sit in the bleach-

215

ers like the rest of the crowd, but hunker down close to the drill field. Most of them are beered-up when they get there, but they bring along six-packs and keep slopping during the drill. They think it's a joke to roll their empties under the sisters' feet. They yell obscene commands at the troops. Sometimes they stagger out onto the field just to mess up a formation.'

'The bastards!' Molly said wrathfully.

'How old are they?' Rod asked.

'Oh . . . anywhere from sixteen to thirty,' Lucille said. 'I've got enough sisters to take them out with no trouble. Break a few heads – you know? But there are too many witnesses in the bleachers, and I figure it's not worth a single sister getting arrested just to teach that trash a lesson.'

'You're right,' Ann said. 'There should be a better way of handling it.'

'Lookee here,' Brother Nabisco said, staring at Colonel Jackson with frank admiration. 'Your sisters might be recognized, but how about sending over a contingent from West Virginia? No one's going to recognize them in Lexington. They can wipe out the punks, hop in their cars, and be back here in Canton before anyone can think about charges and arrests.'

'I was hoping for something like that,' Lucille said, glancing at him gratefully.

'Then we'll do it,' Molly said determinedly. 'We'll organize a combat team. Rod, you and Clark drive over next Friday for the drill and scout the scene. Draw a map so we can figure out our tactics and maybe rehearse the attack.'

Harding and Brother Nabisco did as they were ordered. They came back with a hand-drawn map showing routes to the park, the location of the drill field, placement of the bleachers, and the area where the drunken hecklers congregated.

'Lucille wasn't exaggerating,' Harding reported. 'Those

216

are mean boys just spoiling to have a little fun. One of these nights they'll charge the drill team on their cycles.'

'The scummiest of the scum,' Clark agreed, nodding. 'No doubt about that.'

'How many sisters will we need?' Molly asked.

'I reckon forty should do it,' Rod said. 'Give you an almost two-to-one advantage. Moll, you won't need guns for this. Baseball bats, tire irons, and ax handles should do the trick.'

'You're sure?'

'I'm sure,' he said firmly. 'No guns.'

Molly asked for volunteers from the West Virginia regiment, and had no problem getting forty sisters willing to take part. They were divided into four teams, headed by two lieutenants and two sergeants. Molly insisted on commanding the combat group herself.

'You'll be recognized,' Ann warned.

'So I'll be recognized,' her sister said, shrugging. 'I can't ask the sisters to do something I won't do myself.'

Ann got busy with the logistics of the raid: lining up transportation, gathering weapons and first aid kits, and working out a time schedule that would bring the task force to the Lexington park shortly after the Friday-night drill started.

Meanwhile, Molly, with the aid of Harding and Clark, began training her troops. Copies of the map were made, and every sister familiarized herself with the approach, the battle site, and possible escape routes. Nothing, they thought, was left to chance.

'I'm going with you, Moll,' Harding said.

'You think I can't handle it?' she said angrily.

'You can handle it,' he assured her. 'I just want to see how well you do. I'm not going to interfere; I'll just be an observer.'

'Well . . . okay,' she said finally. 'As long as you sit on the sidelines. Tell Clark to stay home with Ann that evening. She gets a little antsy when big sister goes off to the wars. We'll phone them as soon as it's over.'

By September 15, everything was in readiness. Molly Turner insisted that she and Harding start from Canton at noon.

'Why so early?' he protested. 'We'll have hours to kill.'

But she was adamant, so they left before everyone else, Rod driving his Buick Regal. They stopped once for a hamburger and a Coke, and arrived in Lexington a little after 4:00 PM. Molly insisted they drive around until they found a florist shop.

While Harding double-parked, she went in and bought a small bouquet of yellow tea roses. She came back to the car and showed the flowers to Harding.

'These were her favorites,' she said.

Then he understood. 'Okay, Moll,' he said. 'Do you know how to get to the cemetery?'

She directed him, and when they arrived, made him stay in the car. She found the grave, marked with a small granite stone inscribed: NORMA JANE LAUGHLIN, 1949 – 1987.

The National Women's Union had paid for that stone, and many had wanted it engraved with a poetic tribute – but Molly Turner would have none of it.

'This was a no-bullshit lady,' she said sternly. 'Anything sentimental would embarrass her. Just leave it plain.'

She went down onto her knees alongside the grave. She tidied it up, pulling weeds, throwing away the crisp, withered remains of a few daisies that someone had left. Then she placed her own bouquet carefully, leaning it against the headstone, protected from the wind.

She remained on her knees, head bowed. She had forgotten how to pray – if she ever knew. So she thought of her time with Norma Jane, and what a hard, rigorous happiness that had been. Norma Jane had been a magnifying mirror, showing Molly Turner how she might grow and what she might be.

Finally, she rose to her feet and went back to the car.

Rod Harding was slumped relaxedly, smoking a pipe.

'All set?' he asked.

She nodded.

'Hungry?'

'No,' she said. 'We can eat later, before we drive back.'

'Then let's get over to the park. I want you to study the lay of the land. A map's fine, but nothing beats a personal reconnaissance.'

'You've told me that before,' she said crossly.

'So I did,' he said lightly, and put her mood down to precombat jitters.

The drill field was actually a large outfield shared by four softball diamonds. There were two banks of low wooden bleachers along the first and third base lines of the main diamond. Behind the first base bleachers, the ground rose to a low hill topped with a copse of scraggly pines. The spectators at the Friday-night drills usually sat in the first base bleachers.

On the third base side, the ground was level behind the bleachers, then sloped gently down to an access road. There hadn't been a good rain for some time, and the earth was hard, the summer grass yellowed and thinning.

The rednecks usually gathered at the outfield edge of the third base bleachers, leaving their bikes and vans and pickups on the access road.

The plan called for three combat teams to attack from the access road, with the fourth held in reserve. The three teams would advance on line in a concave curve, the two wings closing in while the center, moving more slowly, would prevent any escape from the flank assaults.

It was recognized that the hecklers might flee forward, across the playing fields, but it was expected that after an initial panic they would fight back.

'Oh, they'll fight,' Molly Turner said. 'Those guys are all on a macho kick. They're afraid to run away.'

The WDC sisters from the West Virginia regiment parked their cars and trucks at widely divergent spots around the drill field. Singly, or in twos and threes, they drifted idly across the park, their weapons held down alongside their legs.

Molly Turner had seemingly wandered up behind the third base bleachers, placing herself in a position to direct the attack. Rod Harding was on the knoll behind the first base bleachers, sitting on the ground with his back against one of the trees in the pine copse. He had a good view of the players drifting onto the stage.

Spectators gathered in the first base bleachers. The drill team took the field, all the sisters wearing the official WDC uniform. Their officers shouted commands, the team divided into three platoons and began performing their precise movements.

Meanwhile, the rowdies had arrived with yells, shouts, and raucous laughter. Some lay on the ground along the third base foul line; others stood and shouted obscenities at the parading women.

Harding glanced at his watch. Two more minutes. He rose to get a better look.

Suddenly he was surrounded by police. A double line of at least thirty helmeted officers, wearing plastic face shields, carrying nightsticks, moved forward purposefully through the trees. They ignored Harding, but marched down to take up positions at the rear of the beer-drinking toughs, facing back toward the access road.

Harding, shocked, knew immediately what had happened. He saw the West Virginia attack group moving forward. But then they discovered the waiting police. The line came to a wavering halt. The two forces stood in silence, confronting each other.

'Jesus!' Harding said aloud, and began running frantically down the hill. He hoped Molly Turner could control her temper and had enough sense to get her troops the hell out of there.

Back in Canton, while all this was going on, Todhunter

Clark had gone over to the Hardings' home for dinner and to stay with Ann and little Jeff until the others returned from Lexington.

They sat in the kitchen. Ann worked at the range, preparing meatloaf with tomato sauce, mashed potatoes, creamed peas. A bibbed Jeff sat at the table in his highchair while Tod spooned applesauce into his mouth.

'Come on, kiddy,' he said. 'Eat all the nice mush. You know, Miz Ann, I was thinking the other day – I never heard this fellow cry. Have you?'

'Once,' she said, smiling. 'He fell down and bumped his head. That was the only time, and it didn't last long. He never even cried when he was teething.'

'He's some kind of hero,' Clark marveled. 'And he sure likes to pack away the grub. He's finished everything.'

'Here,' Ann said, 'give him a cookie and let him gnaw on it. And that's all for him.'

Brother Nabisco sat back and watched the child attack the cookie.

'I figure he's going to be a football player,' he said. 'His daddy is big.'

'And I'm not exactly a shadow,' Ann said. 'The doctor says he's enormous for fifteen months.'

'Probably a linebacker,' Clark said, nodding. 'That's what he's going to be.'

Ann brought food to the table and put out cans of Schlitz for both of them. They filled their plates. Tod sampled the meatloaf and rolled his eyes.

'Oh my,' he said. 'That's real fine. Now I know why Jeff weighs more than average; he digs your cooking as much as I do.'

'Thank you, but Jeff gets his food mostly from jars. I feel guilty about that. I'd like to make all his food fresh, but I just haven't got the time.'

'Doesn't seem to be hurting him none.'

'Did you call her, Tod?' Ann asked, head down, busy with her food.

221

'Call who, Miz Ann?'

'You know who. That Lucille Jackson.'

'Now why should I call Lucille Jackson?'

Ann raised merry eyes and stared at him. 'I saw the way you looked at her and the way she looked at you. Don't tell me there wasn't something there.'

He gave a short snort of laughter. 'You don't miss much, do you, Miz Ann. Well, I do admit I admire Colonel Jackson greatly. I think she's a fine woman.'

'She's beautiful.'

'But how she regarded me, I can't say.'

'I happen to know,' Ann said, 'that she likes you. And she's not married, engaged, or going steady. She's even got a good job; she's a schoolteacher.'

'Now how would you happen to know all that?'

'I asked her,' Ann said, giggling.

'You think I should call her?'

'I really think you might. Nothing ventured, nothing gained.'

'I could tell her I have to be in Lex on WDC business, and it would be nice if we could have a drink together.'

'No,' Ann said, 'don't tell her that. No woman likes to hear that she's an addition to a business meeting. Come right out and tell her: you'd like to take her out to dinner, and you'd be happy to come over to Lexington to see her again.'

'You know,' he said, slapping his palms together, 'I do believe I'll do it!'

After dinner they washed the dishes, cleaned up the kitchen, and moved into the living room. Clark sat on the floor, building houses of toy blocks with Jeff. Ann stayed near the telephone, glancing at her watch every few minutes.

'Don't fret yourself,' Brother Nabisco said easily. 'They're all right. They'll call as soon as they can.'

'It's getting late. They should have called before this. I hope nothing went wrong.'

222

'That hubby of yours,' Tod said, 'he's the most put-together man I've ever met. He knows just what he's doing.'

'I hope you're right.'

After a while, Clark put Jeff inside his crib. He was asleep in two minutes. Ann went into the kitchen, came back with glasses and the bottle of California brandy she kept in the house for Molly. They sipped slowly, staring at the silent phone. They waited.

'Now I know something's wrong,' Ann said finally.

Clark sighed. 'I wouldn't kid you, Miz Ann. If everything went down as planned, we should have heard from them by now.'

'You think I should phone Lucille Jackson?'

'Yeah, give her a call.'

Ann phoned. No answer. So they waited again, watching Jefferson Turner Harding sleep and wishing they had his worries.

Finally, close to 11:00 PM, the phone shrilled and Ann pounced on it.

'Hello? Rod? What happened? We've been . . . When? . . . Oh God! . . . Yes . . . Yes . . . Any casualties? . . . Thank the Lord for that . . . How is Molly taking it? . . . Sure . . . Yes, hon . . . Have you eaten? . . . Plenty for both of you . . . All right . . . Come right back . . .'

'Let me talk to him, please, Miz Ann,' Clark said.

'Just a minute, Rod – don't hang up. Tod wants to talk to you.'

She handed the phone to Clark.

'Rod? What went down? . . . Shee-it! . . . Right on schedule? . . . Uh-huh . . . You know what that means, don't you? . . . You better believe it . . . Oh man, we got work to do . . . I'll hang around till you get back . . . Yeah, well, that's a plus . . . Take it easy, old buddy.'

He hung up, looked at Ann.

'We got snookered,' he said. 'Someone ratted and tipped off the cops. Son of a bitch! Excuse the language, Miz Ann.'

'I've heard worse,' she said wanly. 'But at least it had one good result. Rod says they had a big shouting match at the police station and finally got a promise that cops would be stationed at the drill field from now on. No charges, no arrests, and no one hurt. So it all came out all right.'

'Yeah,' he said, 'except that someone snitched. That's *not* all right. We've got to find out who or we're in the soup.'

'How do we do that, Tod?'

'Well, it's complicated. You make a list of all the people who knew the details of the drill field action and then you go through the list one by one and whisper the details about a fake action to them. You watch to see if the cops respond. If they don't, the suspect is clean. But if the cops are there waiting, you know you've found your rat.'

'My God, Tod, that'll take forever!'

'Not really. We had the same situation in Nam a couple of times. We found it saved time to divide the suspects into groups of three or four. Each group was fed a phony combat plan. One group leaked. Then we narrowed it down to the one guy in that group who had turned.'

'What did you do to him?'

He stared at her and she dropped her eyes.

'I hate it,' she said in a low voice. '*Hate* it. Now the police have promised to protect the sisters on the drill field. Maybe that's what we should have done in the first place – gone to the police instead of automatically planning violence.'

'Maybe,' he said. 'And maybe they wouldn't have moved on it without the threat of violence.'

'There's got to be a better way.'

'If you feel like that, how come you're doing what you're doing? Practically running the whole shebang?'

'It's what Molly wants,' she said shortly. 'She's been the leader – all my life. She leads; I follow.'

Todhunter Clark didn't comment. They each had another brandy and gradually relaxed, stretching their legs. Jeff roused from his nap, yawned, rolled over, got onto his hands and knees. He pulled himself erect, gripping the bars of his crib, and stood swaying, grinning at them.

'Miz Ann,' Brother Nabisco said, staring somberly at the child, 'anything I can do for you and little Jeff, ever, you just ask me and I'll do it.'

'Thank you, Tod,' she said quietly. 'Someday I may take you up on that.'

'Whatever you want me to do . . .' he said.

Ann Harding cleared her throat, then went over to pluck Jeff from his crib.

'Tod,' she said, nuzzling her son, 'do you think we should get him a dog?'

'No,' he said. 'I'll be his dog.'

OCTOBER 7, 1989

Thomas J. Kealy was in the bedroom of his Alexandria home, packing a small overnight bag.

'Oh, Dori,' he said sorrowfully to his wife, 'I feel so guilty about leaving you alone for the weekend.'

'Tommy,' she said, shaking her head sadly, 'you work *tho* hard.'

'That's true,' he said. 'But the senator's campaign is just getting started, and we've all got to buckle down. He's invited four or five of the most important staffers to his place on Chesapeake Bay. We hope to get a lot of work done.'

'When will you be home, Tommy?'

'Sunday night. If it's too late, I'll sleep over in Georgetown, but I'll call and let you know.'

It was early Saturday morning, and Theodora Kealy was

still wearing her light blue babydoll pajamas with the little rosebuds around the neck. The batiste was so sheer that he could easily see the breasts, still large and firm, that had enticed him into marriage.

He realized, with a small pang of regret, that what had once seemed to him human perfection now seemed grossly animal. His tastes had changed; he admitted it. Become more subtle, he told himself, more refined. Like the high, hard, small glands of Constance Underwood. Now *there* was understated elegance.

'Do you thtill love me, Tommy?' his wife asked, going up on tiptoes to entwine her arms around his neck.

'Of course I love you, Dori,' he said, embracing her. He felt her warmth, smelled the sweet scent of sleep that still clung to her. For a moment he was tempted. But he said: 'You're going to the Burkes' party tonight, aren't you?'

'I thuppose tho.'

'Give Eddie my regrets. Tell him it's politics. He'll understand.'

'Politics,' she cried. 'Thcrew politics!'

'Dori!' he cried, scandalized.

He drove into Washington and parked his car in the Georgetown garage. He took his overnight bag to the apartment and waited, peering out the window. Constance Underwood showed up in her bright red 1971 Jaguar XK-E roadster, only twenty minutes late.

'Why is it,' she said, inspecting him, 'you always dress like a mortician? We're going to the *country*, for God's sake.'

'I have a sport jacket and slacks in my bag,' he said nervously 'I'm all set for the country.'

'You can start by taking off your horn-rims,' she said scornfully.

He vowed to make her pay for her nastiness. He was always vowing that.

He was an intelligent man with no more self-delusion than most of us. But he could not, simply could *not*

226

understand his infatuation for this cruel, imperious woman. In a dim way he sensed she had taken over the role Billy McCrea had played in his life.

They had discussed McCrea's death with a certain amount of sorrow.

'I didn't know he was on drugs,' Kealy said. 'Did you?'

'No,' Underwood said. 'But that's what the papers said: an accidental or deliberate suicide following a heavy injection of heroin.'

'I thought he was too smart for that.'

'Billy smart?' she said with her brittle laugh. 'That boy didn't have a single brain in his beautiful head.'

That was the last time they mentioned the deceased.

'Do you always drive this fast?' Kealy asked as they crossed at the Patuxent and turned south, heading for her summer home near Plum Point.

'Always,' she said. 'I don't like to dawdle. Does my driving frighten you?'

'Of course not,' he said stiffly – but it did.

Her house was an A-frame redwood cabin, glassed front and rear, with a sundeck and a small swimming pool now drained and littered with dead leaves. The five-acre plot was off a dirt road, artfully concealed by an ivy-covered chainlink fence and a fine stand of pine, maple, a few elms, and one magnificent oak.

The interior was decorated in an open, minimal style, with low furniture accenting the soaring cathedral ceiling. Everything was blond wood, white sailcloth, a few touches of color in abstract graphics. There was one bedroom, a large bathroom with sauna and bidet.

'*Fan*-tastic,' Kealy said, looking around. 'Heated?'

'Just the one fireplace,' Constance said. 'This is the latest in the year I've been out here. I've got a man down the road who looks after it for me. I called him a few days ago and told him to bring in some firewood. And he filled the refrigerator – so we won't go hungry. Want a drink?'

'Sure,' he said. 'Whatever you're having.'

227

While she was digging out glasses, a bottle of Finlandia vodka, ice cubes, and a lime, he took his bag into the bedroom. He changed rapidly into open-necked plaid flannel shirt, khaki jeans, tweed sport jacket, and LL. Bean moccasins on his bare feet.

'That's more like it,' she said approvingly when he came back into the enormous living room-dining room-sitting room area. 'Now you look like a country squire.'

She was wearing a loose, white rough-knit Perry Ellis sweater with tight tartan slacks that looked like Scottish trews and fitted like skin. Her long, attenuated feet were bare. He loved her feet.

'We could sit out on the sundeck,' she offered, 'but that wind has an edge.'

'This is fine,' he said, hoisting his glass. 'Cheers.'

They sipped, smiled, sipped. They were both slouched down in white canvas armchairs. Through the triangle of glass panes at the front of the house they could see browning trees bending in the gusty wind.

'Beautiful place,' he said, looking around. 'Peaceful.'

'And private,' she said. 'In the summer, with all the foliage out, you can't see it from the road. I swim naked in the pool and tan on the sundeck.'

He gulped his drink. The image of her long body lying naked on the wooden sundeck set off pinwheels in his mind.

'Let's talk business first,' she said, 'and get it over with. Okay?'

'Sure.'

'Help yourself to more vodka whenever you like. Let's start with Dundee. He's going to make a run in ninety-two – right?'

'The official line is that he's considering it, that he's "testing the waters." But yes, just between you and me, he's going to run.'

'Has he got the money?' she asked sharply.

'He's got seed money to get the thing rolling. After he

228

declares – and assuming he gets nominated – he's going to have to raise about a hundred million. That's what it'll cost to get elected in ninety-two.'

'A hundred million?' she repeated, stunned.

'That's right,' Kealy said, nodding. 'The presidency is big business.'

'Can he raise that kind of money, Tom?'

'It depends. If all goes well, and he looks like he's got the best chance of winning, yes, he can raise it.'

'He's going to keep slamming Molly Turner and the WDC?'

'Well, it's worked so far. A year ago he was just another senator. His name and photo recognition ratings were zilch. Now everyone in the country knows who he is – the guy who's against Molly Turner. By the way, I hope you've noticed that he never denounces you or the NWU.'

'I've noticed, and I appreciate it. You kept your bargain. And I kept mine. You handled that business at the Lexington drill field very well.'

'I didn't handle it at all. Just passed the tip along.'

'To whom?'

He was silent.

'Tom,' she said, 'if we're going to work closely together – and I'm sure you want to – we've got to be absolutely open and honest with each other. Or the whole deal is off.'

'James Gargan,' he said. 'He's with Justice. I told him, and he tipped the Lexington cops. He figured it would be better to let the locals handle it.'

'He figured right.'

'Have you heard of anything new in the works, Connie?'

'Nothing at the moment. But I will. She can't stop now. She's got to keep topping herself. Eventually it'll backfire.'

'That's what Gargan says.'

'Sounds like a bright man. I'd like to meet him.'

'Well, uh, he's hard to pin down. Likes to keep a low profile – you know?'

'Set it up, Tom. You can do it.'

'All right,' he agreed, not happy about it.

'Jesus,' she said, hugging her elbows, 'I'm getting a chill. Should we light the fire?'

'Whatever you say.'

'Tell you what,' she said. 'Let's mix another drink and take it into the sauna with us and sweat a little. Then we'll come out, light the fire, and fix dinner. How does that sound?'

'I'm game,' he said bravely.

They sat naked on a planked bench. Hot steam hissed from a vent and fogged the little room, no larger than a cell.

'Listen,' Constance Underwood said. 'Tell me the truth. What do you hope to get out of it? Dundee's candidacy, I mean.'

Kealy made an effort to straighten up.

'He promised me a key position in his campaign. I trust him. He's never gone back on his word – not to me he hasn't.'

'And that's all you want – a big job in his campaign?'

'Well . . .' he said, 'if he gets elected, it may lead to something more.'

'Personal aide? Chief of staff?'

'Something like that,' he admitted.

'Power behind the throne?' she persisted.

He looked at her, but she wasn't jeering. She was serious and interested.

'You never know.'

'That's right,' she agreed, 'you never do. Washington is the biggest casino in the world. What you're hoping for is within the bounds of possibility. But you'll have to play your cards right.'

'I know that.'

'Choose your enemies more carefully than you choose your friends. You're getting into a big-stakes game.'

He nodded.

'Maybe I can help.'

230

He looked at her.

'The gender gap could slaughter Dundee,' she said. 'He's not the American woman's favorite hero.'

'He's one hundred percent in favor of women's rights,' Kealy said defensively.

'You know that and I know that, and it may even be true. But politics isn't a world of facts, Tom; it's a world of perceptions. And right now your senator is perceived as being antifeminist. I can help change that.'

'What do you get out of it?' he asked her, moving closer.

'I have plans,' she said. 'A new federation of all the women's organizations and groups in the country. With as much political clout as organized labor. You think I'm blowing smoke?'

'No. I think it's possible.'

'Those *were* my plans,' she said, turning to stare at him without expression. 'But your ambitions make mine seem like very small potatoes indeed.'

He had an uneasy feeling that she was weighing him, beginning to reckon how she might manipulate him. He feared it would be to her profit and his loss.

'Let's talk about this more,' she said. 'We have the whole weekend.'

'Sure.'

'Lost enough weight?' she said. 'Let's take showers. I'll go first.'

He stayed in the shower a long time, hoping his body was becoming hydrated again. When his knees stopped trembling, he got out and dried off with a towel as big as a sheet. He wrapped it about himself and wandered into the main room.

She had started a fire that was crackling merrily in the grate. She was working in the open kitchen, smearing two sirloins with a mustard sauce. She looked up as he came in.

She was wearing a voluminous robe of yellow cashmere with a rope belt. Her long black hair hung damply about her face. She wore no makeup; her olive skin was shiny, features sharp, lips thin. He thought, briefly, that she had the look of a predatory bird.

'No use getting dressed again,' she said. 'Did you bring a robe?'

'I'm afraid not.'

'I have an extra. It's a big kimono, hanging in my closet. You should be able to get into it.'

It was a light blue silk embroidered with fiery dragons. He put it on and closed it with a wide sash. The silk touched his bare skin like a kiss. He sniffed at the fabric. The kimono was scented with her perfume, with the intimate odor of her body.

He had never been happier.

DECEMBER 21, 1989

The Women's Defense Corps leased a small suite of offices less than two blocks from the National Women's Union headquarters on Northwest H Street. The WDC offices were initially occupied only by Molly Turner, her personal secretary Lois Campbell, public affairs officer Yvonne Popkin, and a secretary-receptionist.

It was decided to keep the administrative headquarters in Canton for the time being, under the command of Ann Harding. The purposes of the Washington office were to establish a presence in the nation's capital and facilitate relations with the news media. Also, as Molly said grimly, 'to keep a close eye on those fuckups at NWU.'

She rented a small furnished studio in Chinatown, an area that was undergoing a renaissance since the opening of the convention center. It wasn't much of an apartment: one small room with kitchenette and bath. The furniture looked like Salvation Army discards.

The furnishings of the WDC offices were no more prepossessing, having been purchased at a government auction. Inside the center drawer of Molly's desk were found the scrawled employment dates and names of bureaucrats who had used the desk. The first served during the administration of President Harry Truman.

Molly Turner who, by all accounts, had little interest in the perks and trappings of power, was seemingly satisfied with her extremely modest Washington office and apartment. But she was rarely in residence, traveling frequently for regimental reviews and conferences with her colonels.

She was on the phone to Ann almost every day, and at least once a month drove home to spend a long weekend in Canton. She had traded in her Le Car for a black Volkswagen Rabbit, and Lois Campbell and Yvonne Popkin usually accompanied her on these trips.

On December 21, a Thursday, the three women headed west, intending to spend Christmas week in Canton and attend a holiday party planned by staffers at WDC headquarters. It had snowed the previous day, followed by a freezing rain. Roads were open but reported to be in hazardous condition.

They left Washington a little before noon, planning to take Highway 211 westward to Harrisonburg. They would then turn onto Highway 33, which led directly to Canton. Molly Turner drove the first half. At Harrisonburg, Lois Campbell got behind the wheel. Yvonne was in the passenger's seat. Molly curled up in the back to take a nap.

At approximately 4:45 PM, the Volkswagen was ten miles west of Elkins, West Virginia, on Highway 33. Molly Turner was now awake, chatting with the other two women. It was a gloomy, overcast day, but the roads were beginning to dry. The car was traveling at about 50 miles an hour.

A white Chevy pickup truck, rusted and slush-spattered, pulled up on the driver's side, apparently intending to pass. But instead, it adjusted its speed to the Volkswagen's. The two vehicles, side by side, raced down the highway.

Molly Turner glanced to her left at the pickup. She saw

the window lowered, the barrel of a shotgun thrust out. It was, she later stated, seemingly aimed directly at her. She started to scream at Lois Campbell, to tell her to speed up.

At almost the same moment, Campbell apparently saw the weapon and reacted by taking her foot off the gas pedal. A split-second later, the shotgun was fired. The load of buckshot blasted the driver's window and blew away most of Lois Campbell's face and half her skull. The Chevy then accelerated and sped off.

Campbell, dead, was knocked sideways onto Yvonne Popkin, who was splattered with the other woman's blood and brains. In addition, she had received several minor wounds from flying shards of the shattered window.

Molly Turner, leaning forward over the driver's seat, steered the Volkswagen off the road and into a snowbank. When the car came to a halt, she piled out, yanked open Popkin's door, and pulled the hysterical woman clear. She then armed herself with the handgun carried in the glove compartment: her Charter .357 Magnum.

But the Chevy pickup was long gone. None of the other cars on the highway were willing to stop and give aid. So, leaving Yvonne Popkin weeping in the snowbank, Turner tugged the body of Lois Campbell from behind the wheel and propped the corpse in the passenger's seat.

Then, by kicking, slapping, and cursing, she got Popkin into the back seat. She slid behind the steering wheel, ignoring the blood and glass splinters. It took her almost five minutes to back the car onto the highway before she could head west for Buckhannon.

The phone call to the Hardings' home in Canton was made at approximately 7:20 PM. It was answered by Ann, who listened in silence to Molly's account, her face whitening as she heard of Campbell's death.

She handed the phone wordlessly to her husband. He spoke to Molly for several minutes and then, after learning she was calling from the police station, asked to speak to the officer in charge. He identified himself as an ex-sergeant of the Canton police, and got more details on the attack.

He hung up and turned to his wife.

'Molly's okay,' he said flatly. 'A little shook, but no wounds. Popkin has cuts from the broken window glass, but she can travel. The cops are impounding Molly's car for the time being. That's standard operating procedure. They've issued a five-state APB, and the FBI has been notified. Ann, Tod is over in Lexington romancing Lucille Jackson, so I think I better drive to Buckhannon myself and bring Molly and Yvonne back.'

'I'll go with you,' she said.

'No,' he said. 'You stay here. The newspapers are already onto it, and you'll probably be getting a lot of calls. Tell them what you know – but no more. If they try to get you to say who you think did it, just tell them you don't know. Don't accuse anyone.'

'I know how to handle it, Rod.'

'Sure you do, hon,' he said, smiling and touching her cheek. 'I'll call you just before we start back. You want someone to stay with you?'

'That's not necessary, Rod.'

He thought a moment. 'Yes, it is,' he said. 'Just to play it safe, I'm going to get a few sisters over here. With guns. If the nuts are on a rampage tonight, you can't tell what might happen. Try to get hold of Brother Nabisco in Lex. Tell him to get back as fast as he can. Put him to guarding Jeff, and order him to stick like glue. Where's your pistol?'

'In the bedroom.'

'Get it,' he commanded, 'and keep it handy.'

At almost the same time, on the evening of December 21, James Gargan was still in his office, working, when his aide entered with a brief message ripped from the teleprinter. Gargan read the staccato facts about the shooting on

Highway 33. He never doubted for a moment that it was a bungled assassination attempt, and the target had been Molly Turner.

He said nothing for a few moments, putting his priorities in proper sequence. His aide fidgeted.

'All right,' Gargan said finally. 'We'll want to go all-out on this before Senator Dundee takes the rap. Pull in as many men as you think you'll need. A rusty white Chevy pickup shouldn't be all that hard to find. Crack the whip.'

'Will do,' the aide said.

'And order me up a roast beef on white with mayo,' Gargan said. 'Black coffee. I've got a feeling it's going to be a long night.'

When the aide left his office, Gargan phoned special agents who worked under his personal command. He ordered an immediate search of Lois Campbell's Washington, DC, apartment and the hotel room she rented by the month in Canton.

Campbell had been the Department's plant in the WDC – and who knew what embarrassing or incriminating evidence that spaced-out lady might have left lying around?

Then Gargan called Senator Dundee, who was in Fargo, North Dakota, speaking at a fund-raiser for the governor. The senator wasn't happy to get the news.

'Son of a bitch!' he said bitterly. 'I'll get blamed for it.'

'I don't think so, sir,' Gargan said soothingly. 'We hope to have it cleared up by midnight.'

'You better,' Dundee said, and slammed down the phone.

Gargan's next call was to his superior, who was on the dais at a banquet for an international conference of police chiefs. It took five minutes to get the deputy director to the phone. Gargan waited patiently. He was good at that.

He related what had happened, what he had done, whom he had called.

'You want me to come in?' the man said.

'No, sir, I don't think that's necessary at the moment.

If there's any action, I'll let you know.'

His aide came back with the roast beef sandwich and a hot black coffee. He also had a map with an overlay showing where roadblocks had been set up in West Virginia, Ohio, Kentucky, Virginia, and Pennsylvania. Gargan made a few minor suggestions, but generally he left the pursuit to professionals who knew the drill.

'In the morning,' he said, 'if the Chevy hasn't been spotted and the weather's good, we'll put the copters up. Better alert them.'

His aide left again, and Gargan settled down with his sandwich and coffee.

He had learned to remain calm when there was action in the field over which he had little control. You did everything you could, then sat back, waited, and hoped luck would see you through. James Gargan believed he was a lucky man. He also loved his job. He derived an intense, almost sexual, pleasure from solving problems that required convoluted machinations and manipulations. He had a number of such productions running concurrently, but the one that interested him most was the Senator Dundee – Molly Turner imbroglio. An entertaining diversion. And what a cast of characters!

The Department's interest was clear: it wanted to help Dundee get elected. Having a firm friend in the Oval Office was the hope of every Washington bureaucracy. And should the 'firm friend' fail to show proper gratitude for past favors, having his executive assistant in your hip pocket was just prudent insurance.

A month previously, that assistant, Tom Kealy, had invited Gargan to a private dinner at Kealy's Georgetown apartment to meet Constance Underwood. Gargan had happily accepted, amused by the fact that the apartment was still bugged, and on the following day he would be able to hear a rerun of the dinner conversation – including his own brilliant remarks.

He thought Underwood was a striking woman – but

a real barracuda. He began to understand better those previous tapes he had listened to that detailed the Kealy–Underwood relationship. Gargan thought this woman could chew Kealy up and spit him over the left field fence. And probably would.

Still, she was no dummy. Cold, yes. Fiercely ambitious, sure. Power-hungry, no doubt about it. But that evening he decided he'd rather have her for a friend than an enemy.

That was a month ago. Now he had another decision to make. Someone had tried to knock off Molly Turner and in the process had trashed Gargan's snitch in the WDC.

He knew very well that Constance Underwood had a plant close to Turner. He had to decide whether to try infiltrating another informer into WDC headquarters or to depend on Underwood's contact and cooperation. He thought about it a long time, then picked up the phone and called her.

'Miss Underwood?'

'Yes.'

'James Gargan here.'

'Mr Gargan! How nice!'

'Miss Underwood, there's been a development in the last few hours I think you should know about . . .'

He told her what had happened on Highway 33, and how a search for the killer was in progress.

'How awful,' Underwood said when he had finished. 'But Molly Turner is unhurt?'

'That's correct. According to my information.'

'But that poor girl is dead. What a shame. Lois Campbell . . . I met her only a few times, but she seemed nice enough. Mr Gargan, remember what we talked about at dinner – how violence begets violence. I think this is a perfect example of that.'

'I wouldn't be a bit surprised. Well, Miss Underwood, I just wanted you to know . . .'

'Thank you so much for calling. It was very kind of you to be concerned, and I do hope I see you again soon.'

238

'I'd like that, too,' Gargan said. 'Good night.'

He hung up grinning. His instinct was to cut Kealy out as a middleman and to connive to have Underwood forward her tips directly to him. He thought he had made a good beginning.

His aide came in with the first solid report of a sighting. The white Chevy pickup had stopped at a gas station on Highway 50 near Chillicothe, Ohio. The attendant said there were two young men in the cab.

'The truck's got Wisconsin plates,' the aide said, looking at his chief.

'Oh-ho,' Gargan said. 'Revenge for the lynchings?'

Could be. Not much physical description of the two guys, but we've put what we've got on the wire. You want to call off the alert in the other states?'

'No, not yet. But patch me through to Columbus, and alert Indianapolis and Chicago. If those guys are high-tailing it back to Wisconsin, we'll cut 'em off at the pass.'

After he talked to Ohio, he ordered up another sandwich – bologna on rye this time, with mustard – and another coffee. He sat at his desk, plugging away at paperwork, and looking up only when someone came in to plunk a bulletin on his desk.

The sightings came in regularly, usually an hour or so after the quarry had been spotted: Washington Court House and Dayton in Ohio, Batesville and Shelbyville in Indiana. But then reports came faster, and special agents from the Indianapolis field office set up a heavy block on Highway 74 at Pleasant View.

At 3:37 AM, the rusted and splattered white Chevy pickup came right into their lap. There was a firefight. Two agents were wounded. Both men in the pickup were killed. Gargan woke up his chief and reported.

It was almost four o'clock before he learned the identity of the slain fugitives. One of them was the brother of the eighteen-year-old rapist who had been lynched in St

239

Charles, Wisconsin.

'That'll get Senator Dundee off the hook,' Gargan's aide remarked.

'And give him another speech,' Gargan added. 'Violence begets violence. Seems to me I've heard that song before.'

James Gargan didn't bother going home. He was a bachelor and had lived in the same hotel for twenty years. Instead, he slept in the small dormitory the Department maintained for late-night workers. He stripped to his underwear and hoped sleep would come quickly.

But it didn't. He found himself thinking about Jake Spencer, and a possible problem. He wasn't exactly happy about Jake taking the job as bodyguard for Senator Dundee, but Gargan couldn't see how he could have prevented it.

Spencer was a gross and greedy man; Gargan knew it. That was all right; sometimes you had to use men like that. The trick was to keep them on a tight leash.

What bothered Gargan was that he knew, he *knew*, Jake Spencer had doused Billy McCrea's lights. The money was too good; Jake would never farm out a profitable contract like that. And he had done a bang-up job; Gargan couldn't deny it.

But now a murderer was working as personal bodyguard for a presidential candidate in whose future the Department had a vital interest. If some reporter ever got on to the Spencer – McCrea connection – there went Dundee's chances to hear 'Hail to the Chief.'

Somewhere down the road, Gargan mused just before he fell asleep, it might become necessary to slip Jake Spencer the black pill.

The novel and frequently awkward relationship between the National Women's Union and the Women's Defense Corps underwent a significant change from mid-1989

240

to mid-1990 – a change that was to have vital conse-
quences for both organizations.

Originally the WDC had been constituted as the military
section or 'fighting arm' of the NWU. Members of the NWU
could, if they wished, volunteer for service in the WDC,
and the Corps was financed by the NWU from its general
fund.

Although the agreement between the NWU and the WDC
forbade the latter from recruiting women who were not
members of the NWU and accepting annual dues from those
women, there was nothing forbidding the WDC to solicit or
accept contributions from outside sources.

It was Ann Harding who first spotted this loophole, and
she immediately brought it to Molly Turner's attention.
After the WDC was organized and functioning, the two
sisters launched an aggressive campaign to attract grants,
bequests, and contributions.

In this effort, Ann conquered an innate shyness and
became an effective public speaker. She could never hope
to match Molly's fiery rhetoric, but audiences were impressed and convinced by her solid reasoning, quiet sincerity, and intense fervor.

The sisters made a popular team. They were invited to
speak before feminist groups and civic organizations. They
delivered addresses in churches and colleges. They appeared
on TV and radio talk shows and granted interviews whenever requested. In all these public relations efforts, they
made a strong plea for independent funding of the WDC.
The results were impressive.

Analysis of the financial records of the NWU and WDC
during the period July 1989 to July 1990 reveals that as
voluntary contributions, bequests, and grants to the WDC
more than doubled, the income of the NWU from similar
sources was nearly halved.

One of the first to become aware of this development was
Virginia Terwilliger. She was also the first to recognize that
the militant activism of the WDC was exactly what the

241

National Women's Union had promised in its original 'Declaration of Liberation,' but had failed to deliver.

Terwilliger went to visit Laura Templeton in a nursing home. The former president of the NWU was in a terribly debilitated condition, with only occasional periods of lucidity. But she was able to grasp what she was told and gave fervent approval to Ginny's plan.

The plan was simply this: to allow the gradual 'withering away' of the National Women's Union and to merge its membership, financial resources, functions, and activities with the WDC. The single organization that resulted would be called the Women's Defense Corps, with Molly Turner as president.

Terwilliger, who had a love of and gift for politicking, immediately began to implement her plan by contacting other members of the Executive Board. She used current figures on income from voluntary contributions to prove that the WDC was becoming stronger as the NWU weakened, and a complete merger would be in the best interests of both organizations.

In one letter made available to this reporter, Terwilliger writes: 'There is no doubt in my mind that the success of the WDC is almost wholly due to the energy and exorts of Molly Turner. Her implacable zeal and confrontational style have galvanized women all over the world. At last we have found the strong, charismatic leader we have sought for so many years!'

Inevitably, Terwilliger's activities were reported to Constance Underwood and only served to intensify her enmity toward Molly Turner. Underwood realized that not only was her job threatened, but her power would be diminished if not eliminated if the WDC triumphed.

JANUARY 14, 1990

The following is a transcript of a tape-recorded interview

with Molly Turner made on the above date by Susan H. Ward, who was then an associate editor of *The NWU Call*. Since the original tape recording cannot be located, it is not known if this transcript represents the entire interview or is an edited version.

'Molly, if you had to describe yourself in one word, what would it be?'

'Angry.'

'Why angry?'

'Because that's the way I feel. I'm angry about the second-class status of women in this country. I'm angry about the exploitation of women in a million debasing and disgusting ways. Rape. Wife battering. Pornography. God knows there's enough for women to be angry about.'

'A lot of women are as angry as you about those things, but they don't take the direct action you do. What is your motivation?'

'My motivation? Just to change things. They can be changed. They will be changed.'

'Apparently there was an attempt to assassinate you. And some of the militant actions you have planned, directed, and led were life-threatening situations. Aren't you ever afraid?'

'Goddamned right I'm afraid. I'd be a fool not to be. But if our cause demands personal sacrifice, so be it. All the WDC sisters feel the same way.'

'What exactly do you hope to accomplish?'

'Total acceptance of women as thinking, feeling, striving individuals entitled to all the rights men take for granted.'

'You've been called a man-hater. Do you think that's –'

'That's bullshit! To hate all men is the rankest kind of sexism. I only hate the men – and some women, too – who consider females a kind of slave class. You know – people who pat you on the head and say, "There, there, pretty one, you'll get along if you know your place." '

'Where do you think a woman's place is?'

'No higher and no lower than a man's. What we're

243

demanding is total equality. Is that so much to ask?'

'Molly, several WDC sisters have been killed or wounded in your struggle. So have men. Do you think your cause is worth the casualties?'

'If a million were killed, it would still be worth it. If you're going to count casualties, you should never start a war in the first place.'

'It's been written that your war started with the death of Norma Jane Laughlin. Is that correct?'

'Yes.'

'It's also been said that you and Norma Jane were lovers. Is that correct?'

'Yes.'

'How long do you intend to continue your war?'

'Until there is no need for the WDC.'

'Molly, what are some of the targets on your list for future direct actions in this country?'

'I'd be an idiot to tell you that, wouldn't I? But I can say we're becoming more concerned about the economic exploitation of women. I'd like to concentrate on industries that don't pay women a living wage, or don't provide safe and healthy working conditions, or discriminate when it comes to job advancement.'

'How would you handle a situation like that?'

'Send them a polite letter. Ask for a conference at which we could present our point of view.'

'And if they refuse to mend their ways?'

'Bomb the fuckers out of existence!'

'But if you destroy, say, a factory or a knitting mill, that means all the women who work there will lose their jobs.'

'That's right. There'll be hardship and dislocation at first. But after a few factories are burned to the ground, the word will get around and owners will start treating their female employees in a fair and equitable manner.'

'Molly, when the idea of a WDC was first suggested, at the NWU convention in 1987, you said, or implied, that women will never be respected until they turn to violence to achieve their goals. Do you still believe that?'

'Absolutely. This is a violent country. We worship the sixgun – John Wayne eager and willing to blast the bad guys. Those methods might not work in, say, England or Sweden. But violence is the only road to reform in America.'

'Senator Dundee says your philosophy of militant activism is un-American and completely contrary to all our traditions and ideals. How do you answer criticism like that?'

'Senator Lemuel K. Dundee is one of the great turd-brains of all time. He wants to be President so bad he can taste it – everyone knows that. And he thinks he can march into the White House over the backs of American women. Hasn't he ever heard of the gender gap? Any woman who votes for Dundee should be made to resign from the female sex.'

'Molly, he says he's sympathetic to your goals, but only objects to your methods. He says if you work through legislatures and the courts, you'll achieve everything you want without violence.'

'Oh, Susan, that's just so much crap! It's been tried for twenty-five years, and it hasn't worked. Maybe we've won a little bit here, a little bit there, but we're not much better off than we were in 1965. Women are still getting raped – and the rapists are walking out of the courts laughing. The disparity between the incomes of men and women is growing. Look at the statistics. We're still an underclass, and all the courts and legislatures in the land – predominantly male, of course – aren't going to change the situation.'

'Do you have any political ambitions yourself?'

'Of course not. All politicians are marionettes. I want to make the women of this country so strong, so dangerous, that we'll end up pulling the strings. Then we'll get what we want.'

The transcript of the interview ends here. Apparently it was set in type but never published in *The NWU Call*. At

245

the last minute it was canceled on the personal intervention of Constance Underwood, who termed it 'inflammatory and counterproductive.'

FEBRUARY 22, 1990

Ruth Blohm was playing backgammon with Martha Dundee in the senator's Spring Valley home.

'Have another drink, dear,' the older woman said.

'Is that how you expect to win?' Blohm asked. 'Get me potted?'

The senator's wife smiled. She reached out, patted Ruth's hand. 'I like you,' she said. 'You're people. If you're not going to have one, you can fix me another.'

'Of course.' Blohm rose, took Martha's glass to the marble-topped sideboard. 'Bourbon?'

'On two ice cubes, please.'

'Any mix?'

'More bourbon.'

On her way back, Blohm paused to draw aside a heavy drape, peer out at the night. Snow was still falling.

'Stop fretting,' Mrs Dundee said. 'If the plane crashed, we'd have heard by now. They'll be along.'

She was a flushed, fleshy woman in need of a good corsetiere. Her purple-tinted white hair was spun up into a beehive Blohm had only seen in old film clips, but her blue eyes were snappy and cynical, and she couldn't endure unction.

'You think that guy of mine has a chance?' she asked casually, looking down at the board and rattling the dice cup.

'Of course he has a chance,' Blohm said. 'Who's his competition? A bunch of deadheads.'

'Holy Christ,' Martha Dundee said. 'Me in the White House – can you believe it? Little Marty Seidsnicker from Willoughby Falls. It took me ten years to

246

learn to use a salad fork.'

Ruth laughed. 'You'll do great. The country will love you. You're everybody's favorite aunt.'

'Thanks a lot.'

'You know what I mean. Are you going to campaign with him?'

'Oh, no! I've done enough of that. Let him take the kids on the trail to prove what a fine, upstanding husband and father he is. Bess Truman was my favorite First Lady. She went her own way and didn't take any crap from anyone – including Harry.'

They heard the sounds of cars pulling onto the graveled driveway.

'Thank God,' Ruth Blohm said, rising and going to the door. 'They're here. Should I put on some coffee?'

'Screw the coffee,' Mrs Dundee said. 'Open the bottles.'

The men came in, stamping their feet and shaking themselves like wet dogs. Senator Dundee, Tom Kealy, speechwriter Simon Christie, bodyguard Jake Spencer, and Orrin Fischbein, who had been the media consultant but was now on the payroll as a fulltime employee. They all took off their overcoats and headed for the sideboard.

'How did it go?' Blohm asked eagerly.

'All right,' Dundee said. 'It went all right. No one took a shot at me.'

The senator had flown up to New York to address a dinner of the League of Women Voters. Christie had worked on the speech a long time, and everyone had chipped in – to strike just the right tone of stern virtue and soft reasonableness.

'It went beautiful,' Fischbein said. 'Very nice applause at the end. All the nets were there, and good local coverage.'

'Lem, did they feed you?' Martha Dundee asked.

'Of course they fed us. What do you think? Tom, what was in that cordon bleu – veal?'

'I suspect it was white meat of turkey, Senator.'

'Well, it wasn't bad if you put enough ketchup on it.'

'Any demonstrators?' Ruth Blohm asked.

'A handful,' Jake Spencer said. 'No problem. The snowstorm wet them down. Hotel security was first-rate. All ex-cops.'

'I've got to admit,' Christie said, 'I was hoping for a more, uh, active response from the audience. Senator, some of your best lines went right over their heads.'

'Look,' Fischbein said, 'like I keep saying, there's no sense preaching only to the converted; that's a waste of time. This wasn't exactly a hostile audience; let's just call them uncommitted. Under the circumstances, I think it was a success. It proved you're willing to stick your neck out. People will admire your courage.'

Dundee stared at him. 'Does that translate into votes?'

No one answered. The men fixed their second drinks, found chairs to slump in wearily. Ruth Blohm brought a fresh drink to Martha Dundee. Then, hesitating briefly, she poured herself a vodka on the rocks and took a gulp.

'Senator,' she said, 'there's something I wanted to talk to you about, but you've had a long, hard day. It can go over to tomorrow if you say so.'

'The committee meeting on the new aircraft carrier is scheduled for tomorrow,' he said dully. 'I'll be tied up all day. You better speak your piece now.'

'Okay,' she said nervously, taking another swallow of her drink. 'Here goes . . .'

Rapidly, and mostly for the benefit of Tom Kealy and Orrin Fischbein, she recapped what she had already told the senator about Lyle Hayden and his technique for in-depth analysis of jury panels.

'Lawyers buying Hayden's service have scored heavily,' she mentioned.

She said she saw no reason why the same technique could not be used for analysis of voting blocs, and Hayden concurred. Not *all* blocs, of course, because the cost and personnel requirements would be prohibitive. Only those key districts, precincts, and neighborhoods that could mean the difference between winning and losing.

'How do you pick the swing districts?' Fischbein asked, getting interested.

Blohm said it could be done by computer analysis of voting patterns of, say, the past thirty years, looking for districts that split closely but invariably ended up going with the winner.

'It'll be tricky,' she admitted. 'Writing a software program for that will be murder. And it'll require close collaboration with the local pols. But I'm convinced it can be done.'

She then said she had sent demographic profiles of three voting areas to Hayden, so he could estimate the cost and number of interviewers required to do the job. Hayden had reported that in-depth analysis of every registered voter in a bloc would be impossible, but had suggested instead the random selection of a sample that could then be weighted to give an accurate appraisal of the entire voting bloc.

'Hey, hey,' Fischbein said. 'That's a cute gimmick.'

Blohm said the whole idea was new and she certainly didn't want the senator sinking megabucks in an untried technique.

'But your junior senator is up for re-election this fall, sir,' she said, addressing Dundee. 'I was hoping there might be some way for the two of you to share expenses on a trial run of this thing. If it flops, then nothing is lost but Hayden's fee. If it proves out, you've got a secret weapon for ninety-two.'

'Not the junior senator,' Dundee said at once, massaging his forehead tiredly. 'I wouldn't give that son of a bitch the time of day. He's shafted me more than once. Tom, what do you think of all this?'

'I think it'd be a waste of time and money, sir,' Kealy said promptly. 'Ruth talks about "political engineering." Senator, you've told me more than once that politics is more of an art than a science.'

249

'It might have been an art,' Blohm said boldly, 'years ago. Like pilots flying by the seat of their pants. But not anymore. What I'm suggesting is just another logical step along the road that began with polls, computerized voting lists, and TV election night projections.'

'Orrin?' Dundee asked, turning to his media director. 'What's your opinion?'

'I'll have to go along with Ruth on this, Senator. I think she's right about what's happening in politics. My God, how could you write your constituents those personal letters without your office computer? This new technique is worth a try. Psychoanalysis of voters, Ruth?'

'Something like that, Orrin. Deep enough to uncover their subconscious or unconscious desires, needs, and prejudices. Then you extrapolate the sample's feelings to the whole voting bloc, and the candidate tailors his pitch to those results.'

'It was a lot simpler,' Jake Spencer said, 'when an alderman gave a family a turkey for Thanksgiving and knew he had their votes in his pocket.'

'Sure it was simpler,' Ruth Blohm agreed. 'But those days are gone forever. You can't buy a vote with a turkey these days, but you can buy it with promises. This technique is designed to let the candidate know exactly what promises will pay off in votes.'

'I still don't like it,' Kealy said loudly. 'A lot of mumbojumbo. A poll could end up with the same results for less money.'

They all looked to where Senator Lemuel K. Dundee sat sprawled in a club chair. He held out an empty glass to Simon Christie, and the speechwriter immediately rose to bring the boss a refill.

'I'll think about it,' the senator said finally. 'Maybe we should give it a try. But not with the junior senator. The governor is up for re-election this year . . . Well . . . I'll think about it.'

The conversation switched to other undeclared candi-

250

dates who might challenge the senator for the 1992 nomination. Everyone agreed that at this early moment Dundee
was the front-runner, but should make every effort not to
appear so.

'Front-runners have a habit of finishing last,' Christie
observed.

'It's too early to pour it on,' Fischbein agreed. 'Senator,
you've got name and face recognition now; maybe it's time
to start broadening your appeal. Get into other areas:
foreign affairs, defense, the economy, the environment.
Slowly, but forcefully, spell out your entire philosophy.'

Dundee smiled. He called to his wife, who sat in the
corner playing backgammon against herself.

'Martha,' he said humorously, 'what *is* my philosophy?'

'I've got it upstairs,' she said. 'Engraved on the head of
a pin.'

Everyone laughed, but the senator wasn't amused.

MARCH 7, 1990

Constance Underwood had met James Gargan only once
– at Kealy's apartment – but she figured him for a meat-
and-potatoes man. So when he accepted her invitation to
dinner, she instructed her catering service to prepare a
crabmeat cocktail, rare chateaubriand with béarnaise,
baked potato with sour cream and chives, ratatouille, and
fresh strawberries doused with Cointreau for dessert.

The caterer provided chef and serving maid. Underwood
provided a bottle of '62 Château Lafite and hoped Gargan
had the palate to appreciate it; it cost about ten dollars a
sip.

She had misjudged him – as so many people did. They
thought him a bluff, hearty 'black Irishman.' He was, in
fact, of Irish heritage, but more Italianate in nature. He
much preferred tripe, sweetbreads, or brains to steak, and
had an atavistic loathing of potatoes in any form.

A middle-aged bachelor living in a gloomy hotel – did that not categorize him? It did not. He was as subtle as a bishop, and wore rough Irish tweeds as a costume. Who would guess that he was an astute womanizer? He succeeded by saying, 'I love you' sincerely – and sometimes he meant it.

He showed up at Constance Underwood's Watergate apartment bearing a bottle of Bushmills Black Label, and had the grace not to mention how rare it was. She had a pitcher of Beefeater martinis waiting, and he accepted that drink with every evidence of pleasure, though he preferred straight drinks – and crooked friends.

The meal was adequately prepared and served, and Gargan assured his hostess it was top-notch: 'Best dinner I've had in years.' He did not mention that one did not combine a béarnaise sauce on meat with sour cream on potatoes; that would have spoiled his carefully crafted public image of a lonely bachelor weary of steamed hotel food.

They finished the wine – and Gargan was properly appreciative of that. They had dessert and coffee, then moved to comfortable chairs for a Rémy and a few amaretti. They waited until the chef and serving maid had departed before they got down to business.

James Gargan had learned a long time ago that in any confrontation, absolute honesty was a powerful weapon. It threw your opponent off-balance. They expected chicanery and you hit them with the truth. They rarely recovered.

'Connie – ' he said. 'May I call you Connie?' Then, without waiting for permission, he continued: 'Connie, I want to form a partnership with you. That tip on the Lexington, Kentucky, action by the WDC – you gave it to Kealy, and he passed it along to me. It worked out just fine, and I want to thank you. I also want to cut Kealy out of this arrangement. I figure you've got a snitch in WDC headquarters, and I want to take advantage of that. Without using Kealy as a middleman.'

She stared, unblinking. 'You don't fool around, do you,

Mr Gargan.'

'Jim,' he said. 'No, I don't fool around. I just think it makes more sense if you and I deal one-on-one.'

'What's in it for me?'

'The wholehearted cooperation of the Department,' he said earnestly, leaning toward her. 'I'd just as soon put Molly Turner and the WDC out of business. Wouldn't you?'

Constance Underwood took a deep breath. She was wearing a black silk Kamali jumpsuit cinched with a haute couture version of a motorcyclist's belt: wide black leather decorated with metal studs. She saw his eyes flick to her bosom and note that she wasn't wearing a bra. She could stagger her opponents, too.

She stood and paced back and forth, conscious of his gaze following her. No celibate bachelor here, she thought; I can take him.

'The wholehearted cooperation of the Department,' she repeated. 'That's so much bullshit. I'm sure you meant it kindly, Jim, but it means nothing. Senator Dundee is on the front line, zinging Molly Turner every chance he gets. He acts; you react. I'd be a fool to give up dealing with Kealy and the senator; they're fighting my war.'

He wasn't dismayed by her rejection; he had prepared a fallback position.

'All right,' he said equably. 'What you say makes sense. But how about this – a way to make the best of all possible worlds: You continue to give your tips to Kealy, and you score Brownie points with the senator. At the same time you pass those tips directly to me, which gives you a gold star after your name at the Department.'

'What's the matter?' she challenged. 'Don't you trust Kealy?'

'I don't trust anyone, Connie.'

'Does that include me?'

'Of course,' he said with a tight smile. 'You don't trust me, do you?'

'Not completely,' she acknowledged.

'Good,' he said. 'Keep it that way.'

She continued her pacing, holding her elbows, head lowered. He let her mull his proposition for a few moments. Then:

'Connie,' he said quietly, 'right now you need all the friends you can get. If Virginia Terwilliger pushes through her reorganization plan, you're going to be out on your ass.'

She stopped pacing, shocked. She looked at him in astonishment. 'You know Virginia?'

'Never met the lady.'

'Then how do you know what she's up to?'

'Connie, it's my business to know. It's my job.'

'Exactly what *is* your job?'

'I work out of a division that rides herd on every crackpot group in the country. The Ku Klux Klan, Nazi Party, Posse Comitatus, the Commies, and all the nutty little militant gangs that like to throw bombs.'

'I suppose you've planted informers with all of them.'

'Of course,' he said cheerfully. 'It's the only way to get things done.'

'Then why do you need my tips on the WDC? Don't you have a snitch in there?'

'Did have,' he admitted, 'but it was terminated. And I figure it would be easier to use your informer than to try to put one of ours in place.'

'Well,' she said, 'at least you're honest.'

She sat down on the couch, a little closer to him than necessary, and took a sip of cognac. She stared straight ahead, pondering. He waited patiently.

'Tell me,' she said reflectively, 'what usually happens to all these violent groups you monitor?'

'Usually they self-destruct. Few of them last more than five years. Mostly they destroy themselves in one of two ways: First, they pull wilder and wilder capers to get more

254

money. Inevitably we catch up with them; they're lousy crooks. Second, there's a falling-out amongst the leaders. These people are on very big ego trips. They've all read how Hitler got started. So there's a lot of competition and squabbling at the top. Bull sessions lead to arguments which lead to confrontations, usually with casualties. Then we begin to get disillusioned defectors, and we squeeze out the evidence and testimony to put the whole gang out of business.

'What do you think will happen to the Women's Defense Corps?'

He shrugged. 'Right now Molly Turner seems to have the whole thing under firm control. I can't see anyone challenging her. So I have to guess she'll be forced into wilder and wilder actions just to prove she's doing something. Eventually she'll go too far. They always do. Who's your snitch at her headquarters?'

The sudden question startled her. She turned sideways to stare at him. 'You don't expect me to tell you that, do you, Jim?'

'I thought you might. But it doesn't make any difference – as long as she's close to Turner.'

'She is.'

The thought occurred to him that it might be Molly Turner's sister. Maybe those anonymous letters were getting to her after all. But he mentioned none of this to Underwood.

'Well, Connie,' he said genially, 'what's it to be? Do you want to keep working only through Kealy or can you and I deal?'

'All right,' she said. 'I'll play both sides of the street.'

'Good. Believe me, your cooperation will be appreciated. The time may come when you'll need our help. We'll be there.'

'I'll remember that,' she said, 'and hold you to it.'

She leaned forward to set her empty brandy snifter on the cocktail table. He reached out and touched her breast

255

lightly through the black silk.

'Don't start something you can't finish,' she said sharply.

'I can finish,' he assured her.

APRIL 20, 1990

Beginning in 1988, an independent film producer, Make Out Productions, Inc., of Hollywood, California, began producing a series of R-rated movies for showing in theaters and on cable TV. They were also available in video cassettes.

The casts of these low-budget films were young unknowns, frequently teenagers, with little or no professional experience. The scripts, as Make Out executives candidly admitted, were trash: plots inexplicable and dialogue mawkish. Most of the movies were made on location; the company owned no studios.

All the productions concerned the activities of high school or college students. Amorous relations were emphasized with frontal nudity shown in the sex scenes. Coarse vulgarity was another element of Make Out films: food fights, mud wrestling, wet T-shirt contests, drunkenness, drug trips, and vomiting.

Generally the movies dealt with boys' efforts to seduce girls. The Make Out philosophy seemed to be that this animal yearning to 'score' made for hilarious cinematic entertainment. All the boys were randy, all the girls secretly complaisant, although they put up a maidenly pretense of protecting their virginity.

Such scenes as boys peering through keyholes and girls undressing before open windows were standard fare in the movies, which bore such titles as *The Campus Flasher*, *Jock Meets Jane*, *Julie and the Football Team*, and *One Sheet for Three*.

Film critics dubbed the productions 'lubricious nonsense,' but the movies were an enormous financial success

256

with their combination of youth, nudity, and sniggering double entendres. In 1989, Make Out Productions, Inc., grossed more than 200,000,000, most of that from an audience composed of youngsters between eight and eighteen.

The majority of adult moviegoers considered the films puerile garbage, to be treated with amused contempt. But feminists were outraged by what they felt was a misogynistic message in the movies: their incitement to rape, treatment of young girls as sex objects, exploitation of sexual aggression.

Church groups cooperated with women's organizations in an effort to put the producer out of business. Sermons were preached, letters were written to theater owners followed by picketing, protest demonstrations were held, a national boycott was organized – all to no avail; the films continued to be produced and continued to earn heavy profits.

Records of the Women's Defense Corps indicate that early in March 1990, Molly Turner selected Make Out Productions, Inc., as the next target for direct action.

At the time, two films were being shot, one in La Jolla, California (*Bikini Madness*), and the other near Plaquemines, Louisiana (*Teenaged Swamprats*). It was decided these two production sites would be hit and destroyed. At the same time, the headquarters building on Hollywood Boulevard would be bombed and demolished.

It is evident that this three-phase combat operation required sophisticated coordination. While the basic planning came from WDC headquarters in Canton, responsibility for the attacks was delegated to the California and Louisiana regiments.

Molly Turner sent Rod Harding and Todhunter Clark to Los Angeles as advisers. The bombing was a tricky job since the offices were not in a detached building, but part of a low-rise row of commercial establishments.

Brother Nabisco determined what would be needed to gut the building with minimum damage to adjoining structures. He and Rod worked closely with selected California WDC sisters, and the women did the actual emplacing and fusing of the bombs.

The attacks on the production sites at La Jolla and Plaquemines were planned as carefully. The assaults were to be launched on a Friday night when there would be few movie personnel present. The WDC sisters in the combat teams were ordered to wear black clothing and darken their faces.

It was also planned that on the night of the attacks, April 20, Molly Turner would be addressing a meeting of female convicts in an upstate New York prison. Ann Harding, in Canton, was, in effect, commander of the entire operation, with authority to cancel the action if things turned sour.

The incendiary bombs at the Hollywood Boulevard headquarters building were emplaced during the day by WDC sisters posing as would-be actresses. The high explosives were concealed in lavatories, air-conditioner ducts, and broom closets. They were equipped with electronic remote-control devices so they could be detonated from outside the building.

These bombs were set off at midnight, California time. The resulting explosion totally demolished the building, including a film vault in which the negative of a completed movie was stored. Firemen summoned to the scene were able to keep the conflagration from spreading to adjoining structures. But all Make Out Productions, Inc., records were destroyed.

It had been hoped this act of deliberate arson could be accomplished without casualties – but it was not to be. Examination of the ruins several hours later revealed the bodies of a man and a woman. Subsequent newspaper reports of the incident hinted that an executive and his secretary had been having an affair and using his office as

258

a rendezvous.

In addition, a passerby, a tourist from Sioux Falls, South Dakota, was fatally injured in the blast.

The attack on the La Jolla production site also began at midnight. The single security guard was taken prisoner at gunpoint, bound and gagged. The WDC combat team formed a perimeter guard while demolition experts went to work.

Cameras and sound recording equipment were pounded to wreckage with sledgehammers. Trailers, mobile homes, generators, floodlights, and sets were destroyed with fragmentation and incendiary grenades. It took less than a half-hour for all the equipment to be reduced to rubble.

No casualties resulted from this action.

In Plaquemines, Louisiana, the attack was scheduled to begin at 2:00 AM, but didn't start until almost forty minutes later because some of the troops became temporarily lost during the advance. The colonel of the Louisiana regiment waited until all her forces were in position before signaling the assault.

Most of the cast and technicians working on *Teenaged Swamprats* had driven to Baton Rouge to spend the evening, but there were at least a dozen at the production site, some sleeping, some partying in one of the trailers.

The sudden appearance of the WDC sisters, wearing dark clothing, faces blackened, was initially treated as a joke by the personnel. But the display of a wide variety of weapons, and the discharge of several of them into the air, proved the seriousness of their situation.

The captives were herded, under guard, off the premises, and demolition of equipment and sets began. It seemed the action would be completed successfully without casualties.

But then, while the destruction was proceeding, a van arrived bearing three cameramen, three sound technicians, two grips, and an assistant director, all of whom had spent the evening carousing in Baton Rouge. Later reports

259

indicated that several of the men were intoxicated.

The van was halted by armed WDC sisters, and the passengers ordered to get out and put their hands over their heads. They began to exit from the van. The second man out, Frank K. Hilliard, the head grip, from Van Nuys, California, suddenly whirled on the nearest WDC sister and attempted to wrest the M-16 from her grasp. She fired and he was killed instantly.

This was the sole casualty of the Plaquemines engagement. The complete destruction of property was completed without further incident. The attacking force then withdrew after blowing up all the vehicles at the site to forestall pursuit.

Despite the deaths at the Hollywood Boulevard headquarters building and in Louisiana, the WDC action of April 20 was deemed a success. There was no positive identification of the perpetrators and no arrests were made.

Following its usual custom, the Women's Defense Corps made no claims of 'credit' for the raids. But the media and the American public had no doubts as to their responsibility. Yet Make Out Productions, Inc., was held in such contempt by most adults – and particularly by fundamentalist church groups – that there was general approbation rather than outrage at what had happened, despite the casualties.

Six weeks after the events described above, Make Out Productions, Inc., filed for bankruptcy under Chapter Seven.

MAY 29, 1990

They stared at each other, and they both knew they both knew.

'He's screwing her, isn't he?' Ann Harding said.

'Oh, Miz Ann,' Todhunter Clark said, lowering his eyes, 'it's none of my business. I can't get involved in this thing.'

'It *is* your business,' she said fiercely. 'You *are* involved. I've been getting these letters . . .'

He looked up. 'What letters?'

'Anonymous letters. Spelling it out. Times and places. All the sickening details.'

'Just someone looking to make trouble. Forget it.'

She looked at him scornfully. 'You've never lied to me, Tod. Don't start now. Well, she'll never take him away from me. Never.'

Brother Nabisco was seated on the floor, pushing toy cars around with little Jeff. They had built a bridge of books and magazines, and the boy was maneuvering his favorite wooden car over the bridge and around imaginary curves.

Since the attempted assassination of Molly in December, the WDC had tightened security precautions. An armed guard was stationed at Canton headquarters twenty-four hours a day. Neither Molly nor Ann appeared in public without bodyguards. Clark had been delegated the task of protecting Jefferson Turner Harding – a job they both enjoyed.

It was a little after noon, bright sunlight streaming through curtained windows that had been equipped with inside steel stutters, now open and latched back. Ann had come home to spend an hour with her son and make certain he ate his lunch.

Rod had taken an early morning flight from Charleston to Washington to deliver a bag of personal mail to Molly and check on security precautions at her apartment and the WDC offices. Ann could guess what his frequent trips to the capital included, but she could not bring herself to forbid him to go. She was not ready for a confrontation – not yet.

'I talked to Lucille this morning,' Clark said. 'I called her from your phone here. I hope that's all right.'

'Of course.'

'She said she's finished checking out all her crew who

knew about that action at the drill field. She swears they're all clean. She says the mole must be over here. I told her we hadn't finished looking.'

Since the aborted attack at the Lexington, Kentucky, park, strict need-to-know rules had been circulated to all WDC sisters. Only those closely involved were informed of a planned action before it went down. For instance, not even public affairs officer Yvonne Popkin was told of the Make Out raids until they were over.

'You know, Miz Ann,' Clark said, 'the snitch might have been Lois Campbell, and with her gone, we'll have no more trouble.'

Ann Harding didn't answer. She sat stiffly in an upholstered chair, gripping the arms. She watched her son. How he moved, how he smiled. She saw her husband in him – and herself.

'I don't know what I'm going to do,' she said dully.

Brother Nabisco sighed. 'I don't really think I'm the one to talk to about this, Miz Ann.'

'Who *can* I talk to about it?' she demanded. 'My mother? My in-laws? They wouldn't understand, and it would just upset them. You're my friend, aren't you?'

'Oh yes,' he said, almost sadly, 'I'm your friend. There just isn't anything I wouldn't do for you and Jeffski here.'

'Then tell me – what do you think I should do?'

'Well . . .' he said cautiously, 'I hate to give advice to people on how to live their lives. Have I made such a big, crashing success of mine? But I do think you might give it some time. You know, a lot of troubles just go away by theirselves without a body doing a thing to nudge them along.'

'You're saying Rod and Molly might just get tired of each other and break up?'

He shrugged. 'It could happen, you know. It's worth waiting awhile to see.'

'Then what am I supposed to do – welcome him back

262

with open arms?'

'You love him, don't you?'

'Yes,' she said in a low voice. 'I love him. And this is what I get for it.'

'Well, Miz Ann, people are people, and if you're looking for perfection, you're not going to find it in this world.'

'My own sister,' she said bitterly. 'You know, I always looked up to her. I thought she was smarter and harder and braver than me. I really worshiped her. She could do no wrong. But these last few years have taught me a lot. I can do things, too. I mean, I'm practically *running* this outfit. And I've learned to give speeches. I was beginning to think of us as equals, and now this comes along, and I start thinking, well, if she can take my man away from me, then she's got more on the ball than I have.'

'Shee-it!' he said disgustedly. 'What kind of talk is that? You got more than she'll ever have. Why, you're *twice* the woman she is, Miz Ann.'

'You really think so, Tod?'

'I *know* so. You got more natural good-looks and kindness. Molly, she's a wild one – that's for sure. Galloping here, there, and everywhere, and stirring people up. She's good at that – no doubt about it. But when it comes to the nitty-gritty, the *work*, sitting at a desk and getting things done, and making sure everything goes smooth, she's nowhere to be found. Miz Ann, this outfit would be nothing without you, and that's the truth.'

She rose from her chair, swooped, plucked Jeff from the floor, and hugged him in her arms, covering his face with kisses. He squirmed.

'Here's the truth!' she cried joyously. 'Here's the only truth that counts.'

'Oh yes,' Clark said, smiling.

She rubbed noses with her son. 'No one is ever going to take you away from me,' she told him. 'No one. Ever. I'll kill anyone who tries.'

Brother Nabisco nodded. He could understand that.

JUNE 11, 1990

Dundee sat alone in his private office in the Hart Senate
Office Building. The door was locked. The senator had
taken off jacket and shoes and loosened his tie. He had
instructed his staff: no interruptions and hold all calls.

The time had come, Dundee acknowledged, to decide
if he was serious about making a run for the roses. It was
only mid-1990, but presidential campaigns had evolved
into two-year affairs, and if he really had that famous 'fire
in his belly,' now was the time to make his move.

As he judged the situation, he had two big problems.
The first, most important, was money. He thought he
might make a strong run for the nomination for 25 million.
If he was nominated, he'd need at least another 75 million
for the campaign – but he'd cross that bridge when he
came to it. The funds provided by his special friends had
been just seed money – sufficient to start the Draft Dundee
movement. Now he needed the promise of big bucks if he
was to declare that he was a candidate.

So money was the big hurdle. If Dundee couldn't raise
the shekels, he wouldn't have to worry about his second
problem: the campaign staff.

He had known from the start that Ruth Blohm was
okay for the preliminary sparring, but she had neither
the expertise nor the experience to manage a national
campaign. But he'd want Ruth to stay on. Her ideas about
'political engineering' might just turn out to be sound. And
she was a hard worker; Dundee liked that.

Thomas J. Kealy was another who just didn't have
the clout to wagon-boss a nomination campaign for the
presidency. He was smart, personable, and knew how to
keep his mouth shut. But Tom just wasn't a political
animal.

Dundee had promised Kealy a key role in the campaign, and he intended to keep that promise. But Tom didn't have what it took to be top honcho. Maybe chief of personal assistants – something like that: an important title that didn't mean a goddamn thing.

The senator took his feet off the desk, found a sheet of paper, and began to scrawl notes on what kind of a campaign staff he'd need. A real Hitler in command. Political advisers. Liaison men to labor, business, minority groups. Plenty of media experts. Pollsters. Maybe his own TV crew.

Dundee figured he'd need a staff of at least 100, not counting outside consultants. If he wanted good people, that meant a horrendous payroll. Which brought him right back to his first problem – where was the money coming from?

He had a lot of personal chits he could call in, of course. And he could count on individual contributions from people who approved of his stand on Molly Turner and the WDC. The PACs were good for hefty donations. But all that didn't amount to a bucket of warm piss. To attract the millions he needed, he required the covert support of, say, a dozen men around the country who pushed buttons.

The senator sat and brooded. Was it worth the trouble? The stress, physical exhaustion, insults in the media and maybe physical assaults on the street? Was it worth all that grinning, working the fence, kissing smelly babies and ugly women, eating slop, and never getting enough sleep?

The senator was fond of quoting backwoods aphorisms like 'Fish or cut bait' and 'If you can't stand the heat, get out of the kitchen.' The one he uttered aloud at this point in his ruminations was 'Shit or get off the pot.' And, comforted by that, he pulled the phone close and began making calls to men who might be persuaded to bankroll his try for the big enchilada.

During the next few days he was able to get through to most of the men on his list. Few people, no matter how powerful or wealthy, failed to return the call of a US senator. Naturally, Dundee did not make a pitch for funds over the phone. He said merely that there was a matter of some importance he'd like to discuss with the listener at a personal meeting.

They all made the same reply: they would check their schedule and get back to the senator as soon as possible to arrange a mutually satisfactory date. He heard nothing more for a week, but that didn't worry him; he knew what was going on. All these men knew each other. They knew what he wanted all right, and the senator reckoned they would select one man to listen to his sales talk and report to the others with a recommendation: go or no-go. Sure enough, H. Fairchild Curtiss finally called. He was chairman of the board of a New York bank holding company – not the largest in the country but well up there.

Curtiss asked in his toneless voice if the senator could manage to meet him at the Imperial, Curtiss' private club in Manhattan. Dundee recognized the ploy: you come to us; we don't go to you. He told Curtiss he'd be delighted.

On June 11, he flew up to New York, accompanied only by his bodyguard. While Jake Spencer leafed through a copy of *Penthouse* on the plane, Dundee planned his appeal to H. Fairchild Curtiss. There was no use trying to con him; Curtiss and his pals could give lessons to carny pitchmen.

There was a stretch limousine waiting for them at La Guardia. It had a completely equipped bar, and Dundee and Spencer had a couple of belts on the drive into Manhattan. When the limo pulled up before the bronze doors of the Imperial Club, the senator told Jake to stay in the car; if he wasn't safe inside the Imperial, then the President wasn't safe inside the White House.

He was escorted up a flying staircase by a flunky wearing a tailcoat. He was ushered into a rich, gloomy chamber with stained glass windows. H. Fairchild Curtiss came out of the tinted shadows and offered a white paw. Dundee pressed it delicately, and the two men murmured small talk until the servant tiptoed from the room, closing the heavy oak door softly behind him.

Curtiss politely offered a drink, a cigar, or both. Dundee just as politely declined. They then lowered themselves into deep leather club chairs set at an angle to each other. They both crossed their knees. They both made temples of their fingers. They regarded each other with wary interest.

'For your information, Senator,' the banker said with a wintry smile, 'this room is quite secure. We have it inspected frequently. Now then – what can we do for you?'

Dundee plunged right in, stating flatly that he wanted to become an active candidate for his party's nomination for president. He had come to solicit funds to make that candidacy viable.

He started to review his career as a senator, but Curtiss held up a pale hand.

'We are familiar with your record,' he said with his chilly smile.

He was, Dundee decided, a cold fish. An absolute neuter. Politicians might be stupid, venal, drunks – whatever. But, by God, they were human. This guy in his Savile Row suit had no personality at all. He was not a person; he was a thing.

Speaking quietly but firmly, Dundee outlined the same platform he had presented to his buddies at the motel in Silver Spring – his Bottom Line political philosophy. He wanted to put the country on a paying basis. Abolish corporate and capital gains taxes. Subsidies for foreign investments. Increase import taxes. Make the State Department concentrate on economic expansion. Turn over many government functions to private enterprise.

The banker heard him out without interrupting. When he was finished, Curtiss said only, 'What about this woman? This Molly Turner.'

Dundee explained that his vendetta against the WDC had been designed to gain publicity.

267

'It has succeeded beyond my wildest expectations,' he said. 'And, as I'm sure you recognize, sir, I will have to temper my attack if I am to attract the votes I need to be nominated and elected. But I do believe that the WDC under Molly Turner is a clear danger to everything this nation stands for. I honestly and sincerely believe that.'

A slight shade of color, the palest pink, crept into H. Fairchild Curtiss' cheeks.

'They're trying to get in,' he said in a strangled voice.

Dundee stared at him, bewildered. 'Who?' he said. 'Into what?'

'The goddamn women,' the banker said, displaying passion for the first time. 'Into this club. The Imperial. Can you imagine? An exclusive club for gentlemen only. Has been for more than a hundred years. Cannot private citizens associate with their own kind?'

'Of course,' Senator Dundee said.

'The women say no. They say the Imperial and clubs like it are where business contacts are made and high-level political arrangements arrived at. They say many members have their initiation fees and dues paid by their companies, which in turn deduct such fees and dues as legitimate business expenses. Well then, these women claim, such clubs, enjoying a Federal tax benefit, must open their membership to everyone. Everyone! Can you imagine such a state of affairs?'

'Disgusting,' Dundee said.

'The bitches!' Curtiss said savagely.

There seemed little more to be discussed. A few minutes later, the banker rose, offered his frigid hand a second time, and promised that he would inform Dundee within a week whether or not 'his group' would support the senator's campaign.

Now occurred a coincidence which was considered of little significance at the time, but which was to have a meaningful effect on the fortunes of many – and even on the history of the United States of America.

Just one day after Dundee's meeting with H. Fairchild Curtiss, the New York State regiment of the Women's Defense Corps invaded the Imperial Club. The sisters did not wear their uniforms, but were all elegantly dressed.

They moved purposefully into the dining room, bar, reading room, library, and even the directors' room. Club officials asked them to leave, but they would not. The police were then summoned. Most of the sisters had to be carried out bodily from the club. Television cameras and newspaper photographers recorded the scene.

The sisters were charged with illegal trespass and released on their own recognizance. (All charges were later dropped.) Two days after that, a different group of WDC members repeated the invasion. By this time, the Imperial Club had become the butt of derisive jokes in the press and on TV.

When the colonels of the New York regiment stated publicly that the invasions would continue indefinitely, directors of the Imperial Club sought a meeting with the announced intention of discussing conditions under which women would be admitted to membership.

And a day after that, H. Fairchild Curtiss phoned Senator Lemuel K. Dundee.

'It's go,' he said crisply.

JULY 27, 1990

'You're making a good buck,' Rod Harding said, looking around the cramped Chinatown apartment. 'You could afford something better than this grungy joint.'

'I'm hardly ever here,' Molly Turner said, shrugging. 'I'm on the road so much. This is just a place to flop.'

'Our own little love nest, complete with cockroaches and a rusty tub.'

'You complaining, lover?'

'Not me,' he said. 'Never complain and never explain:

269

that's my motto.'

'How's everyone in Canton? Ann?'

'She's fine.'

'And the boy?'

'Shooting up like a weed. Seems like he outgrows his clothes and shoes every week. Now Todhunter Clark is calling him King. King Harding. How about that? Clark really loves that kid.'

She didn't answer. He knew how she disliked Brother Nabisco and said no more about it. He spilled a shopping bag of mail onto her desk.

'Here's your goodies,' he said. 'The University of California at Berkeley wants you for a series of three lectures.'

'That's nice. Will they pay?'

'Sure. Expenses and a fee. And Virginia Terwilliger came to Canton and had a long talk with Ann. All afternoon, in fact.'

'What did they talk about?'

'How should I know? I wasn't there. You'll find a long, confidential memo from Ann about it. It's sealed; I don't know what's in it.'

'Come on, Rod; Ann doesn't hold out on you. What did she and Terwilliger talk about?'

'Read Ann's memo,' he said shortly, taking off his shirt. 'We've got about three hours. Four, tops. Then I've got to start back.'

'If four hours is what you'll give me,' she said, 'four hours is what I get. You're the boss.'

'Since when?' he said.

They lay naked in bed.

'You don't like me much, do you?' she said.

'What are you talking about?' he said. 'Like you? I love you.'

'Love? Maybe. Your idea of love. But you don't like me.'

'All right,' he said. 'You're just too intense.'

'What's wrong?' she jeered. 'You're not man enough to

270

handle me?'

He turned his head to stare at her. 'What kind of sexist bullshit is that?'

'You're right,' she said contritely. 'I'm sorry. But don't try to change me into something I'm not. You knew what I was when we started this.'

'Yeah,' he said, 'I knew: a pain in the ass.'

They made love with anger and hostility. Finished, they pulled away abruptly.

'Jesus!' she gasped. 'Get us a cold drink.'

'You get it,' he said.

She considered that a moment, then rose from the bed, padded into the kitchenette, and opened two beers.

'Thank you very much,' he said.

'You're quite welcome.'

'All I'm saying,' he continued, 'is that you can be a ranting, raving hotrod in your work. That's okay; I know how much it means to you. But when it comes to us, you and me, can't you, for God's sake, relax? I'm not your enemy.'

'Yes, you are,' she said in a low voice. 'In a way.'

'What the hell is that supposed to mean?'

'I don't understand it myself. But I know that deep down I want to punish you. You really need a woman like Ann.'

'Oh sure. That's why I'm fucking *you*.'

'There you go: you're fucking me. Did it ever occur to your caveman brain that I may be screwing *you*?'

'All right,' he said, 'we're fucking each other. Does that satisfy you?'

'Not yet,' she said. 'One more time.'

They laughed so much they slopped their drinks.

'Seriously, Moll,' he said, 'I wish to hell you'd try to unwind a little with me. You don't always have to come on so strong. I'm not out to demolish you. I really am your friend.'

She didn't answer, but got out of bed, searched around for a pack of cigarettes. She lighted one, then sat in a

271

scruffy wing chair with a bare leg swinging over one of the arms. He sat up in bed, back against the headboard, and watched her.

'I've been with men before you,' she said, staring at the cracked ceiling. 'Not a lot, but some. Then I met Norma Jane Laughlin. God, did that woman open my mind. It was like being let out of prison. I was sore about all the years I had wasted. You're the only man I've banged since Norma Jane died – in case you're interested. You love me in your way – you say, and I believe you. And I love you in mine. That's okay. We can get along. But no way, *no* way, am I going back to the way I was before Norma Jane. I'm sorry for you if you find me too intense, too wound-up. But that's the way I am. Take it or leave it.'

'I'll take it,' he said promptly. 'Now get back in the sack.'

'Not yet. Now that we're letting our hair down, let's go all the way. You're not really gung-ho for the WDC and what I believe in – are you?'

'Sure I am. I'm a feminist. Not as nutty about it as you are – but then who the hell is? But I do believe in what you're fighting for.'

'I'm not so sure,' she said, staring at him. 'Sometimes I think you don't believe in anything. Sometimes I think the WDC is just fun and games to you. You're like a mercenary. You and Clark.'

He thought about that for a moment. 'There is some truth there,' he admitted grudgingly. 'I can't claim to get as angry as a woman about rapists or pornography. But I'm not in this just for the money and the laughs. It's just that I've seen so much shit in the army, in Nam, and then as a cop, that I turned off. Nothing made sense. Then you came along with this crazy crusade of yours, and you were willing to put your ass on the line, and I liked that. So I decided to go along for the ride. Sure, I'm part mercenary. But also, I get a kick out of associating with people who really believe. Maybe some of it will rub off on me. I know

272

that's all mixed up, but that's the way I feel.'

'You don't think we're going to win, do you?'

'Oh, you're going to win,' he said. 'But not all you want. That's not the way things go. You'll get some, maybe most. But there are a lot of things you're not going to get.'

'Like what?'

'Like changing the way men think about women. Like changing the way women think about themselves. Maybe human nature can change, but it'll take a hundred years.'

'A journey of a hundred miles begins with a single step.'

'And a screw in time saves nine,' he said. 'Now will you get back in bed?'

'Okay,' she said.

He brushed his blunt fingers over her bony body. 'Skinnier than ever,' he said. 'It's like going to bed with a Boy Scout.'

'Maybe you like that.'

'Maybe I do. Be Prepared, kiddo.'

They made love slowly, intently, staring into each other's eyes.

Later, when he was dressing, she said, 'I wish you'd get rid of Todhunter Clark.'

'Why?'

'I don't like him.'

'He is doing a great job.'

'I know that, but I don't like him. He looks at me like he knows something about me I don't know.'

'Now you're being silly.'

'Rod, you think he knows about us?'

He bent over to tie his shoes. 'How would he know that?' he asked, voice muffled.

'Maybe you told him.'

He raised his head to stare at her. 'Oh sure. And I also put a notice in the *Canton Courier*.'

'Men like to brag about their so-called conquests; I know that. Maybe the two of you got beered-up one night and you told him.'

'Moll, will you stop it? Will you just, for God's sake, stop it?'

'Well, I don't like him. Get rid of him.'

'How the hell am I supposed to do that?'

'Just fire him. If you haven't got the balls for it, I'll do it.'

He groaned. 'Jesus, you're something, you are. Look, he's got the hots for Lucille Jackson over in Lexington. Suppose we keep him on the payroll, but transfer him to the Kentucky regiment as military adviser or something like that. Will that satisfy you?'

'Well . . .' she said, 'all right. As long as I don't have to see his wise-ass grin around Canton.'

'I'll talk to Ann about it when I get back,' he promised.

'Tell her I feel strongly about this.'

'I'll tell her.'

Dressed, he came over to sit on the edge of the bed. He bent forward to kiss her hard breasts. He straightened up, took her face between his palms for a moment.

'You okay, Moll?'

'I'm okay. I've got to go up to Michigan next week for a regimental review. But I'll be back here next Thursday. You'll come over.

'Well, uh, Thursday is my mom's birthday, and Ann is planning a party. I can't miss it. Tell you what: Why don't you stop off in Canton on your way back from Michigan. Come to the party. And maybe you and I can grab a couple of hours together out at the safe house.'

'I hate this sneaking around,' she said.

'So do I. You got a better solution?'

'Yes, I do,' she said, 'but you don't want to hear it.'

He stared at her. 'That's right; I don't want to hear it. Look, Moll, any time you want to call it quits, just say the word and I'll be long gone. I'm not leaning on you.'

'You bastard. You know I can't do that.'

'Then accept the situation and quit bitching about it.'

274

'What I really should do,' she said, turning her face away from him, 'is tell you to go take a flying fuck at a rolling doughnut. But I can't do it.'

He moved her head around until she was looking at him again.

'Is it so bad?' he said gently. 'Is it so awful to need and want a man?'

'Not any man,' she said. 'You.'

'You better find someone else,' he said harshly. 'I told you from the first: Ann is my wife and Jeff is my son, and that's the way it's going to be.'

'Okay, okay,' she said. 'You don't have to keep repeating it; I've got the picture.'

'Good,' he said. 'Now I've got to get moving. Knock us a kiss.'

They embraced. She held him tightly, so tightly that her body trembled. But she would not weep.

Because of space limitations, this brief history of the Women's Defense Corps during the 1980 – 1990s has concentrated on the nationwide actions that kept the WDC in the headlines and on TV screens for a decade.

But there were continual minor campaigns during this period that aroused scant attention. More importantly, the activism of WDC sisters resulted in a revolution in the way women reacted to what they perceived as harassment, injustice, and discrimination against their sex. They were no longer willing to work through courts and legislatures to have those wrongs redressed.

– In Land's End, California, a man found guilty of beating his wife to death with a baseball bat was sentenced to a year in a 'work program' because, the presiding male judge declared, the victim had 'provoked' the attack. WDC sisters kidnapped both murderer and judge. The former was beaten to death with a baseball bat, the latter tarred, feathered, and then released on the courthouse steps.

– *In Riverdale, Arkansas, a banker accused of child molestation was set free, although he had a record of thirty-four similar arrests. A WDC campaign, including publicity and a boycott, resulted in the closing of his bank and investigation by Federal authorities. His home was burned to the ground and his private plane destroyed.*

– *In River Bend, Florida, a group of construction workers who had been harassing female passersby with obscene shouts and gestures was assaulted by a platoon of WDC sisters armed with ax handles, tire irons, and chains. Six of the construction workers required hospitalization. The harassment ceased.*

These, and many other incidents of a similar nature, resulted in the angry denunciation of Molly Turner by men and women who condemned the 'aggressiveness' of the WDC sisters.

The controversy grew more impassioned but, in mid-1990, no one denied that Molly Turner's fierce advocacy of the dignity of women was changing the way men felt about women and the way women felt about themselves.

AUGUST 3, 1990

The annual convention of the National Women's Union was held at the Washington, DC, Convention Center from July 30 through August 4. It was an especially ran. unctious meeting, sparked by Virginia Terwilliger, who in her keynote speech boldly proposed that the National Women's Union merge 'completely and whole-heartedly' with the Women's Defense Corps, adopting the name, aims, and militant tactics of that organization.

'The result,' she declared, 'will be the largest association of determined women in the world!'

Her proposal set off a rancorous debate, not only on the convention floor, but in hotel suites and informal caucuses of state delegations. The argument continued all week, garnering heavy media coverage. Reporters were quick to point out that Molly Turner refused to express an opinion on the proposed merger and said only that she would abide by the decision of the convention delegates.

Virginia Terwilliger introduced a motion that the joining of the NWU and WDC be left to the judgment of the Executive Board. After heavy politicking for several months, she felt confident that she controlled a majority of the Board. But there was a core of veteran NWU members she had not reckoned with, and by mid-week it became apparent that her motion would be defeated on a floor vote.

Of course, Constance Underwood was not idle during all this. She skillfully rallied her own troops, and if she could not succeed in tabling the proposal indefinitely, she was able to fend off the attack of the pro-Terwilliger forces.

By Thursday, August 2, the opposing groups had hammered out a rough compromise that was to be presented to the entire convention for approval at the final session on Saturday evening, August 4.

The agreement called for a special board.to be elected to review and consider the entire problem and present their nonbinding recommendation to the 1991 convention. This board would consist of two NWU state chapter presidents, two WDC state regimental colonels, and three members of the Executive Board.

At 5:00 PM, on the evening of August 3, Constance Underwood was hostess at a cocktail party at the Four Seasons Hotel in Georgetown. The more than 100 guests included NWU staffers, politicians, NWU patrons, members of the media, business executives, and several ambassadors' wives.

Molly Turner and Ann Harding were invited, but neither attended, although both were in Washington for the convention. Virginia Terwilliger was present but seemed to avoid the hostess. Connie, strikingly dressed in a scarlet chiffon cocktail dress by Yves Saint Laurent, moved easily through the crush, exchanging kisses with men and women and greeting most of her guests by their first names.

By 7:00 PM, the crowd had thinned out, and Connie prepared to dash home, change her dress, and get to the Convention Center for the evening session. She was approached by a large, hulking man who, she was certain, she had never seen before and who had not been invited to her party. She did not like his smile.

'Miss Underwood?' he said.

'Yes,' she said. 'Who are you?'

'Doesn't matter,' he said with his smarmy grin. 'Could we have a few words together? In private.'

'I think not,' she said coldly. 'I'm pressed for time. If this concerns NWU business, write a letter to headquarters. It will be answered, I assure you.'

'You assure me,' he repeated. 'I like that. No, this doesn't concern NWU business. It concerns you and Billy McCrea. Remember him?'

She was not a timid woman, and gave no sign of her agitation. 'Billy McCrea?' she said. 'I know no one by that name.'

'You're good,' he said admiringly, 'but it won't wash. Billy McCrea – the beautiful, brainless boy you were paying for fun and games. Come on, lady, let's talk about him – or you'll be in the headlines tomorrow: NWU PREXY LINKED TO ADDICT SUICIDE. How does that grab you?'

She thought swiftly, looking around at her departing guests. 'There are a few people I have to say goodbye to. Then I'll be able to give you a few minutes.'

'Suits me,' he said, shrugging.

Ten minutes later they faced each other in a small anteroom.

'Now then,' she said, 'what's this all about?'

'Billy McCrea,' he said. 'Remember? I admit the kid was a dumbo, but he wasn't quite as stupid as you figured. He kept a notebook which ended up in my possession. I was leafing through it the other day, and there you are,

278

plain as day. Your name, address, phone number, the dates you met him, how much you paid. And some personal stuff I won't mention because I'm a gentleman.'

'Oh sure,' she said. 'I can tell that by looking at your tie with the gravy spots.'

'I like bitches,' he said pleasantly. 'I enjoy cutting them down to size. Y'see, Miss Underwood, my wife needs an operation. Her plumbing. It'll cost ten thousand, and I haven't got it. But you have. And I have Billy McCrea's little black book.'

'I'll think about it,' she said tonelessly. 'What's your name? How do I get in touch with you?'

'You don't,' he said, smirking. 'I get in touch with you. No rush.'

'Then your wife's plumbing can wait?'

'Not indefinitely,' he said. 'Sooner or later I'll need the ten big ones. I'll give you a call.'

She waited until he left, then found a public phone and called the unlisted number James Gargan had given her.

'Jim, I've got to see you tonight,' she said. 'Late. Say one o'clock at my place.'

'Trouble?' he said, picking up on the tone of her voice.

'I think so. I need your advice.'

'All right. One o'clock. I'll be there.'

'I love you,' she said.

She did what she had to do: rushed home, changed, cabbed to the convention. She presented a sure, confident manner, beat down some motions and amendments she didn't like. She smiled pleasantly at Molly Turner and Ann Harding – embraced them, in fact – and was back at her Watergate apartment in time to shower before Gargan arrived.

When he entered, she put her arms about his neck, pulled him to her frantically. She kissed him, thrusting a long tongue deep into his mouth. He moved back, held her, looked at her.

279

'Is this the trouble you mentioned?' he said.

'No,' she said with a nervous laugh. She sat close to him on the couch and as she crossed her legs her terry cloth robe fell open. He stroked her smooth knee and thigh while he listened to her.

'All right,' he said when she had finished. 'Billy McCrea was the addict who committed suicide – right? I remember reading about him.'

'He wasn't an addict; I'll swear to that. Billy was clean.'

'Then you knew him?'

She was silent.

'Connie, if you want me to help, you'll have to tell me everything about this.'

'Yes, I knew him.'

'Had sex with him?'

'Yes.'

'Paid him for it?'

'Some small loans,' she said defensively. 'On occasion. He didn't have a lot of money. He was a sweet boy. Not too smart, but sweet.'

'Okay, now let's talk about the man at the hotel. You never saw him before?'

'No. Not that I remember.'

'What did he look like?'

'Big. Stooped. Heavy through the neck and shoulders. A drunk's face – all blood vessels. A lumpy nose. And the most obscene smile I've ever seen.'

'I get the picture,' Gargan said. 'How did you leave it? Are you supposed to contact him?'

'No. He didn't give me his name, address, or phone number. He said he'd call me. He acted like there was no rush.'

'Good. If he calls, stall him. Tell him you're still thinking it over. Tell him you're trying to raise the cash. Tell him anything – but put him off as long as you can.'

'You can help, Jim?'

'I think so. Sounds like a cheap blackmailer to me. You

pay him ten grand and that's just the first installment. He'll bleed you dry. You really think Billy McCrea kept a notebook?'

'I didn't even know he could write.'

'Well, don't worry about it, hon. I'll contact some local cops who might be able to make the guy from your description. We'll nail him.'

'Oh Jesus, Jim, I hope so. You know what a bind I'm in at the NWU right now. That kind of scandal I don't need.'

'Not to worry, kiddo,' he said, touching her cheek. 'Leave it all to Daddy Jim; I'll take care of it.'

'What would I do without you?'

'See Tom Kealy more often,' he said with an innocent smile.

'Oh him,' she said. 'You know, he really is a wimp.'

'Keep seeing him,' he advised. 'You need that contact with Dundee.'

'He likes to wear my underwear.'

'Dundee?'

'Silly,' she said, laughing. 'Kealy.'

'I don't want to wear your underwear,' Gargan said. 'I don't even want you to wear it.'

'I know. At the moment I'm not.'

'Good,' he said. 'Saves time. Shall we?'

'Of course,' she said. 'We deserve it. Oh God, what a sweetheart you are!'

SEPTEMBER 8, 1990

Molly Turner spent a week in Denver, where she testified at the trial of three WDC sisters charged with attempted arson in the bombing of a video shop that sold pornographic tapes. All three were convicted, given stiff fines, suspended sentences, and put on probation for two years.

Turner flew back to Canton in a vicious mood. The conviction was a defeat, but what rankled even more

281

was that the bombing had been amateurish. The three convicted sisters had received little instruction and no practice in the use of explosives. Molly had delivered a harsh reprimand to the Colorado WDC colonel.

There were more problems awaiting her in Canton. The monthly remittance from NWU headquarters was late again. The colonel of the Alabama regiment and two of her aides had been arrested during an attempted holdup of a 7-Eleven store. The weapons they were carrying had been supplied by the WDC.

And Senator Dundee had made a virulent personal attack on Molly Turner during a TV talk show, calling her 'a disgrace to American womanhood' and 'the greatest danger to the achievement of female equality in our history.'

But what riled Molly Turner the most was that Rod Harding was absent on a gun-running trip from Miami, while Todhunter Clark was much in evidence, still serving as personal bodyguard to Jefferson Turner Harding.

'I told Rod to get rid of that guy,' Molly said brusquely to her sister. 'Didn't he tell you?'

'He told me,' Ann said quietly, 'and I said I'd discuss it with you.'

'Well, I want him out of here. Send him to Lexington or any other place where I don't have to look at his sappy face. But I want him gone.'

'We'll talk about it later,' Ann said.

They worked together at the warehouse, going over invitations, correspondence, vouchers, bank balances, personnel changes. By 6:00 PM, on September 8, the staffers had departed, the outside armed guards had come on duty.

'Have you heard from Terwilliger?' Molly asked.

'She called from Detroit. She claims we've got three definite votes on the special board. She thinks our best chance is to swing the president of the Michigan chapter – a woman named Stacy. But in return for her vote, Stacy wants the right to replace the Michigan colonel. Terwilliger said to ask you.'

'Screw it,' Molly said wrathfully. 'I picked the Michigan colonel personally. She's a good soldier and I'm not going to dump her just to get Stacy's vote.'

'Molly, will you loosen up? Sometimes you've got to give a little to get what you want. Go along with Stacy on this, and the special board will recommend merger. Then, Térwilliger swears, you'll be president of the whole shooting match. After that, you can find an important job for the Michigan colonel you dumped, and everyone will be happy. That's the way things get done.'

'It's not the way *I* do things,' Molly said definitely. 'I don't betray sisters just for my own benefit.'

Ann didn't answer immediately, but began shuffling papers with hands that trembled slightly.

'I'll ask Terwilliger to see you in Washington,' she said. 'Maybe she can talk some sense into you. She's been working hard on this thing, and she deserves to be listened to.'

'All right,' Molly said reluctantly, 'I'll listen.'

'Now about Todhunter Clark,' Ann said, looking directly at her sister. 'I want him here. I don't know why you dislike him so – but that's your problem. I trust him, and he's marvelous with Jeff. He absolutely adores the boy. And Jeff adores him. I see no reason to get rid of him on your say-so. He's done a fine job for the Corps.'

'I just don't like him,' Molly said angrily. 'He goes, and that's that.'

'If he goes, then I go.'

'What?' Molly cried. 'What the hell are you talking about?'

'You heard me. If you get rid of Tod, then you get rid of me, too. I'm deadly serious about this.'

'Jesus Christ, I'm not firing the guy! Just passing him along to the Kentucky regiment. He and Lucille Jackson have something going, haven't they? He'll love Lexington.'

'I want him here.'

'You want, you want . . . Since when have you been calling the shots?'

283

Since I realized how much I contribute to this organization. As much as you do – and maybe more. On some things I'll take orders from you. On this business of Tod, I won't.'

'This is an army, kiddo; you knew that when you signed on. I appointed you second in command, and –'

'And who the hell appointed *you*?' Ann said hotly. 'If you had died when Lois Campbell was killed, you think the WDC would have folded? No way! It will survive without you, without me, without any individual. So don't give me any of the Nazi crap: "I am the Führer, and you *will* obey orders." As far as I'm concerned, you and I are equals. I have as much say as you do. And I say Todhunter Clark stays.'

'You really believe that?' Molly said, almost spluttering in her fury. 'You really think you or anyone else could run the Corps? Let me tell you something – I *am* the WDC. Without me it would just be another sewing circle – and don't you ever forget it. You sit here behind your desk, give orders to your fat typists, and think you're on the front line. Christ! The WDC is *my* idea, *my* creation, *my* baby.'

'My, my, my – that's just like you. Well, I've told you the way *I* feel. If Tod goes, I go.'

They were silent then, glaring at each other. Finally Molly drew a deep breath. 'Got anything to drink around here?' she said roughly.

'No,' Ann said. 'Yvonne Popkin is on the sauce again, and I won't allow any booze in the office.'

'Shit,' Molly said disgustedly. 'Then give me a cigarette, for God's sake.'

They sat there, puffing jerkily on their cigarettes, not looking at each other.

'All right,' Molly said finally, 'Clark can stay – if it means that much to you. I admit I may be a little paranoid about him. There are people *you* hate, aren't there?'

Then Ann Harding looked at her sister. 'Oh sure,' she said.

284

'Well, just keep him out of my way – that's all I ask. Now about your importance around here . . . I've never denied that you run the joint. I could never do it all by myself. I want you here; I wouldn't trust anyone else. After all, you *are* my sister. My true sister.'

'Then you've got to give me authority to do the job. You command the regiments, you plan the actions, you serve as the number one spokeswoman for the WDC. As far as I'm concerned, you're chairwoman of the board. But if I'm going to be chief executive officer, I've got to be delegated the authority I need. That includes hiring and firing, handling the money, making certain you've got the tools and financial resources to do your job.'

'Well . . . sure, I can see that.'

'And leaning on you when you should be leaned on. That's part of it, too. Molly, let's face it: you're a lousy politician. You pop off to the media without considering how your words will sound.'

'I say what I think and what I feel.'

'Sure you do. All I'm asking is that you think before you blow your stack in public. Think of how it's going to sound, and whether what you say will make us more friends or more enemies.'

Molly Turner stared broodingly at the floor. 'I just can't play games like that. I can't – what's that word? Dissemble. I can't put on an act. You know that.'

'Uh-huh,' Ann Harding said.

'Besides,' Molly said, looking up, 'it's been working, hasn't it? Membership is up. Contributions are up. We're on our way to taking over the NWU. Everyone in the country knows who we are, and we get those hundreds of letters saying, "God bless you." So we must be doing something right. Look, kiddo, don't ask me to change who I am. I just can't do it. Okay?'

'Okay, Molly. You can be yourself if you let me be myself.'

285

'Of course. I never want to change you, sweetie. God, I'm glad we had this talk. Clears the air. Now I know my little sister has grown up.'

'I've had to, after what has happened.'

'I still love you, baby. You know that, don't you?'

'I know. And I love you.'

'So the important things haven't changed, have they?'

Ann Harding smiled, and her sister embraced her, kissed her cheek, stroked her long, chestnut hair.

SEPTEMBER 25, 1990

Lemuel Dundee had been in national politics for more than twenty years and was no stranger to the perils and problems of campaigning. But even he was confused and awed by the complexities of organizing a campaign for his party's presidential nomination.

As he told his wife, he was beginning to understand what Ruth Blohm meant when she spoke of 'political engineering.' The nuts and bolts of a presidential campaign proved so complicated, so *endless*, that he saw at once he could never keep on top of it all, but would need an expert, dependable staff to whom he could delegate authority.

In the latter half of 1990, he began to assemble such a staff: political advisers, media advisers, financial advisers, speechwriters, polling consultants, even his own makeup man for TV appearances, and an advance crew to precede him on tours to arrange schedules, transportation, and security, and to ensure close co-operation with local politicos, Draft Dundee groups, and claques of sympathizers.

He complained to Tom Kealy that he had little time to think about the issues. Kealy, who had been fretting because he seemed to be losing his position as Dundee's top aide, immediately volunteered to form a group that would devote its time solely to composing position papers and selecting vote-getting issues for submission to Dundee for his approval.

The senator liked the idea and told him to go ahead. This issue group, known to other staffers as 'Kealy's think tank,' soon numbered more than twenty: academics, news analysts, economists, scientists, sociologists, and one poet. They worked out of a single cramped office, spending most of their time in bull sessions, the air furry with cigar smoke.

Meanwhile, Ruth Blohm was absent from Washington, helping Lyle Hayden test in-depth analysis of voting blocs to influence the governor's race in Dundee's home state.

Late in August, Dundee summoned his senior staffers – twelve men and women he called his 'Dirty Dozen' – to a crowded conference in his Capitol hideaway. He told his startled aides that he intended to make a public announcement of his candidacy as soon as possible.

They had a hundred reasons why it should not be done: the election was two years away, he would become the front-runner and an inevitable target, the voters would get bored with him, he'd peak too soon, etc., etc. But he was obdurate, and finally set the date of September 25 (his wife's birthday – a nice, sentimental touch) for his formal announcement.

Unbeknown to his aides, Dundee had been urged to announce his candidacy immediately by an emissary from H. Fairchild Curtiss. The moneymen felt an early declaration date would spur the contribution drive, increase Dundee's public exposure and, by building momentum, would make him unstoppable by convention time. The senator acceded to their wishes; he had no choice.

During the next few weeks, there was a mad scramble among staffers to devise the most effective setting for the senator's declaration and to write him a speech that would earn generous time on the evening TV news programs.

After much debate, it was decided to ignore the formal trappings of power and go the 'jes plain folks' route. Dundee would announce on the front lawn of his Spring Valley home, surrounded by his wife, children, and grand-

287

children, a rented Labrador retriever at his feet. The senator would be wearing a worn cardigan sweater, hand-operated lawnmower in the background.

Media experts rushed to complete the details, anxiously consulting the National Weather Service and praying the Great Day would not be rained out. It wasn't. It was, in fact, clear, sunny, mild. 'Dundee weather,' campaign workers chortled to every reporter they could buttonhole.

The mikes and public address system were set up and tested. TV vans with their crews and cameras showed up on schedule – and promptly blocked traffic. A crowd of curious neighbors gathered to lend the proper hometown touch. And enough reporters (including a representative from the *NWU Call*) were on hand to make Dundee's announcement a media event.

His wife, held firmly erect between two sons, beamed boozily behind the senator as he spoke. He started by expressing 'heart-felt' gratitude to her, his family, friends, Abraham Lincoln, Franklin D. Roosevelt, and John F. Kennedy – all his idols, mentors, and inspiration.

Then, speaking without notes (he had memorized Simon Christie's final version of the speech), the senator announced his intention of actively seeking his party's nomination to be President of the United States of America.

'If I did not believe I am uniquely qualified to lead this great nation during the challenging years that lie ahead, I would not be standing here before you today. I love this country too much to see it shackled, as it has been so often in the past, by inexperienced, incompetent, or indecisive leaders.'

The senator also included the following:

'We must get America moving again.'

'Never negotiate from fear, but never fear to negotiate.'

'A job for everyone willing to work . . .'

'World peace and domestic tranquility are my two main concerns.'

'Education is the bulwark of liberty.'

288

'We are entering an age that will test our intelligence, our resolve, and our willingness to sacrifice for the future.'

'Home . . . family . . . our children and our children's children . . . Old Glory – and I am not ashamed to use that term . . . Freedom . . . Independence . . . Equality . . . regardless of sex, age, race, or creed . . .'

'Jesus Christ!' the *NWU Call* reporter muttered. 'He's got everything in there but Mom's Apple Pie.'

But it was a good speech: short, forcibly delivered, and throbbing with sincerity. When he concluded, to generous applause, he turned and kissed his wife, children, grandchildren and, by mistake, an attractive anchorwoman for NBC News who happened to be standing nearby.

His staff was delighted with the way it had gone, and their euphoria was not diminished by the subsequent commentaries of political analysts. Dundee's announcement was labeled 'Imagery at its best' and 'Political theater at its most effective.' Columnists conceded the senator had a good chance of capturing his party's nomination, and remarked on his courage and confidence in declaring so early in the campaign.

The crowd on Dundee's front lawn drifted away. The TV vans packed up and departed. Finally, only the excited staffers were left, enjoying drinks and a buffet set out for them in the senator's dining room.

Jake Spencer, a double bourbon in hand, plucked at Tom Kealy's sleeve. 'Got a minute?' he asked hoarsely with his loppy grin.

'Can't it wait, Jake?' Kealy said, still enjoying the elation of the senator's successful presentation.

'I don't think it better,' Spencer said, now gripping Kealy's arm. 'Let's you and me go someplace private.'

He practically dragged Kealy out back, to a tiled patio where summer lawn furniture had been stacked.

'What's all this about?' Kealy demanded, angry at being absent from the celebration.

Spencer let him wait while he pulled a cigar from an

inner jacket pocket, stripped the cellophane, bit off the tip and spat it away. He lighted up and blew a plume of smoke over Kealy's head.

'Billy McCrea,' he said. 'Ever hear of him?'

Kealy was gripping a tall gin and tonic; the ice rattled against the glass.

'Billy McCrea?' he said. 'No. Who is he?'

'Was,' Jake Spencer said. 'A drug addict who took a long dive off his fire escape about a year ago.'

'Oh . . . yes . . . I remember. I read something about it.'

'But you didn't know him?'

'Of course not.'

Spencer sighed. 'Well, Tommy, you know in my line of work I've got to deal with a lot of nogoodniks. I mean real cruds. I don't like it – but what can I do? A couple of days ago one of these scumbags comes to me and says he's got hold of Billy McCrea's little black book. How he got it, I don't know. Maybe he was the kid's dealer – who knows? Anyway, he claims you're in the book. Your name, address, private phone number, the dates you met with Billy McCrea and how much you paid him.'

'That's impossible!' Kealy cried desperately.

'Yeah, well, that's what I told him. But then he showed me the photocopies of the pages where you're listed. To tell you the truth, Tommy, it looks legit to me.'

Kealy drained his drink, turned his back, walked a few steps away.

'So now,' Jake Spencer said in a louder voice, 'this bum is trying a shakedown, pure and simple. He doesn't want to contact you directly and asked me to act as a go-between.'

'How much does he want?' Thomas J. Kealy said in a strangled voice.

'Ten thousand.'

'First installment,' Kealy said bitterly.

'No, no,' Spencer said earnestly. 'He swears it's a one-shot deal. You get the pages from McCrea's notebook and

290

the photocopies he showed me, and that's that. You pay him, he delivers, and then he gets out of town. You never hear from him again.'

'Jake,' Kealy said, almost choking, 'I don't know about people like this. I mean, they're outside my experience. But you – you know how to deal with them. I mean, you have the experience – correct? Couldn't you . . . ?'

'Couldn't I what?'

'Oh Jesus, I don't know. Scare him off. Threaten him. Something like that.'

'Tommy,' Jake said, seriously and judiciously, 'maybe there was a time I could have done that. But now I have a responsible position – personal bodyguard to a US senator who is running to be President. I couldn't do anything that might spoil his chances – you know? And neither should you – if you get my meaning.'

Kealy considered that a moment. 'Then you think I should pay off?'

'Yes,' Jake said sadly, 'I really think you should. I don't see where you have any choice.'

'How much time do I have?'

'I can stall this guy for a while,' Spencer said, 'but not for too long. Think it over.'

Kealy nodded vigorously. 'I will. I'll think it over.'

The next two days were the worst in the short, happy life of Thomas J. Kealy. He had been buoyed by the success of Dundee's announcement – to which his group had made a considerable contribution. But now he had this blackmail threat. And, in addition, Constance Underwood seemed to be losing interest in their trysts – which, as far as Kealy was concerned, were essential therapy to keep him in fighting trim.

His wife noted his depression. 'Oh thweety,' Dori said sympathetically, 'you're working *tho* hard.'

Finally, with some self-distrust, Kealy acknowledged he was out of his depth and better seek expert advice. So he mentioned casually to Dundee that his brain trust was formulating a position paper on law and order and wanted to solicit input from the Justice Department. Did the senator know anyone over there who would be cooperative and discreet?

'Sure,' Dundee said immediately. 'Give Jim Gargan a call. Mention my name. You can trust him.'

Kealy finally got through to Gargan, who sounded intelligent and understanding on the phone. Kealy, somewhat nervously, suggested a private meeting on a bench in Lafayette Park, the same bench on which he had hired Jake Spencer so many months ago.

James Gargan didn't seem to find the invitation outlandish. He acted as if meeting senators' top aides on park benches was the most natural thing in the world.

'Noon tomorrow?' he said. 'I'll be there.'

'It's about – ' Kealy started.

'That's all right, Mr Kealy,' Gargan said. 'Don't say any more on the phone, especially about the senator.'

'Oh . . .' Kealy said confusedly. 'Yes. That's right. But, uh, this has nothing to do with the senator or his campaign. It's, ah, a personal matter.'

'I'll be there,' Gargan repeated, and hung up.

It was a nice, crisp day, and both men were carrying topcoats over their arms when they met. They lighted cigarettes, chatted of this and that, and stared at the White House, where the President and the foreign minister from Burundi were exchanging compliments before a battery of microphones on the lawn.

'Well now . . .' James Gargan said.

Thomas Kealy blurted out the whole story: Jake Spencer, Billy McCrea, the attempted shakedown by an unidentified 'crud' with Jake acting as go-between.

'I don't know what to do,' Kealy concluded miserably. 'I acted like a fool – I admit it. But if this gets out, my career will be ruined and the senator's campaign will be hurt. It's not the money; I can afford that. But I don't believe what Jake says about this guy leaving town. I think

292

this thing will hang over my head forever, and I just – '

Gargan interrupted by putting his hand lightly on Kealy's arm.

'Not to worry,' he said in the kindliest way imaginable. 'I'll take care of it.'

'Thank you, sir,' Kealy said humbly.

OCTOBER 3, 1990

In its April 1990 issue, *Modern American Trends*, a scholarly journal, published an article by Professor T. Henry Fellows that aroused a great deal of interest and comment. Fellows, a sociohistorian, drew a parallel between the American Civil War and the rise and success of the Women's Defense Corps. Disparate as these two events may seem, the writer argued that they had much in common in their strategy and tactics, and in the social changes that resulted.

Fellows pointed out that the Civil War began in what was still an age of chivalry. Military officers of both sides had studied Napoleonic battles and believed in the 'gentlemanly' conduct of war under which the rights of noncombatants were generally respected, and soldiers sought only to kill, wound, or capture other soldiers.

So it was in America in 1861. By 1865, following the sledge-hammer campaigns of General Grant and General Sherman's destructive march to the sea, the entire nature of the struggle had changed; the world became conscious of the concept of 'total war,' although that term was not yet in general usage.

Similarly, Professor Fellows stated, the feminist movement had been in a chivalrous mode prior to the time Molly Turner and the Women's Defense Corps appeared on the scene. Now, for the first time, a large, organized group of dissatisfied women turned to direct, violent action to achieve their goals. Win or lose, Fellows wrote, their strategy of total war would have a profound effect on American life and especially on the interrelationship of men and women.

Professor Fellows' startling thesis was still being debated when, in the fall of 1990, an event occurred that gave credence to his views.

For a number of years, the Willoughby Togs knitting mill in New Bedford, Massachusetts, had been the scene of a bitter struggle between the owners and employees over the issues of wages, working conditions, and unionization. More than 80 percent of the workers were women, and they were paid an hourly wage far below union scale.

There had been several strikes that failed because the mill was located in a depressed area, and strikebreakers were easy to hire. The struggle, marked by deep animosity on both sides, was finally taken to the courts, where the hearings, trials, and appeals dragged on and on.

Meanwhile, the mill owners, perhaps foreseeing their eventual defeat, began construction of a new mill near Claxton, Mississippi, claiming the New Bedford factory was obsolete and could no longer be operated profitably. Opponents claimed the company was fleeing south to take advantage of a large pool of unemployed, nonunion labor.

Molly Turner and the Women's Defense Corps apparently had been aware of the Willoughby Togs problem for some time, but did not become actively involved until the spring of 1990. Correspondence shows that Ann Harding was in touch with the colonels of the Massachusetts and Mississippi regiments regarding the new factory being erected near Claxton.

Research of the WDC files reveals that Rod Harding and Todhunter Clark made several trips to the Claxton area, during which they instructed and advised local WDC sisters on a project designed to destroy the new knitting mill as soon as it was completed.

It now seems evident that Todhunter Clark designed the

entire demolition package. He put together bundles of plastic explosives to be detonated by remote control from a radio transmitter a half-mile away. The bombs were to be placed so that the heavy walls of the new mill would fall inward, collapsing the roof and crushing the expensive looms that had just been installed.

It was determined that the security guard consisted of one night watchman who sat in a sentry box near the locked gate. Once an hour he patrolled the interior of the chainlink fence surrounding the mill, accompanied by an attack dog, a Doberman pinscher.

At approximately 1:00 AM, on the morning of October 3, a WDC sister, selected for her histrionic ability, came screaming to the guard hut of the new factory. She was disheveled, blouse torn, fake bloodstains on her face and bared breast.

She babbled a tale of forcible rape, and the solicitous watchman unlocked the gate to offer assistance. Whereupon she drew a handgun and relieved the watchman of his weapon. Other WDC sisters appeared, and the Doberman was shot with a tranquilizing dart gun.

The bombs were in position within thirty minutes. The combat team then departed, taking with them the bound and gagged watchman and the comatose attack dog. At precisely 2:00 AM. Brother Nabisco flipped the switches of his radio transmitter, and the new knitting mill collapsed into a pile of rubble.

The blast, of course, alerted the entire community. But other than a number of broken windows and shattered water, gas, and telephone lines, damage was not extensive. There were no casualties. The watchman and his revived dog were released an hour later, five miles out on a country road.

Following its usual customs, the WDC made no claims of 'credit' for this action, but the public assumed the Corps had been responsible. Certainly James Gargan had no doubts. He had a thick dossier on Todhunter Clark (as he

295

did on Rod Harding) and knew that Clark had the expertise to engineer such a sophisticated job of demolition.

Proving it, of course, was something else again.

After the destruction of their new mill, Willoughby Togs eventually settled with employees of their New Bedford factory, allowing a strong union led by women.

In a follow-up to his April monograph, Professor T. Henry Fellows wrote a letter to the Readers' Column of the December 1990 issue of *Modern American Trends*. He cited the bombing and destruction of the Claxton mill as proof of his thesis that Molly Turner and the WDC had brought the philosophy of total war to the feminist movement.

'In view of such passionate resolve,' Professor Fellows wrote, 'I predict the WDC will triumph just as Grant and Sherman won – unless authorities have an equal iron will to apply repressive and violent countermeasures. Such a course, I fear, would rend the fabric of American society. We are, in fact, in the midst of an extreme sociological revolution. How we handle it will be a measure of what kind of a nation we are.'

OCTOBER 18, 1990

To a journalist attempting to present a balanced account of the Women's Defense Corps, one of the most puzzling aspects was the relationship between Rod Harding and Todhunter Clark. These two were the only males to occupy positions of authority and responsibility in a movement that was almost wholly female.

At first glance it would appear the two had much in common. Both were approximately the same age, both ex-soldiers who had served in Vietnam, both street-smart, cynical, and knowing. And both apparently had that particular type of courage that springs from recklessness rather than deep devotion to a cause.

Curiously, it seems clear that Rod Harding was the more nihilistic of the two. Assuming the pains of growing up black in white America, one would suppose that Todhunter Clark had more cause for misanthropy. But the evidence proves he had a muffled hope, a buried streak of romanticism, that was to have a profound effect on the WDC and those involved in it.

On October 3, the two men were at the farm near Canton, West Virginia, discussing the progress of the search for the informer who had frustrated the action in Lexington, Kentucky, a year previously.

'Well now,' Brother Nabisco said, popping the tab on a Coors, 'we're getting down to the nitty-gritty. Only about four or five left to check out, and they're all upper-crust people.'

'You think I did it?' Harding said.

'Naw,' Clark said, grinning. 'I don't think that. You think I did it?'

'Shit, no,' Harding said. 'And Ann didn't, and Molly didn't. Scratch the four of us. Who does that leave?'

'Lucille Jackson swears her crew is clean, so the leak must be over here. There's Lois Campbell, the lady who got wasted, and Yvonne Popkin, and Florrie Pendergast – she handled logistics – and one or two others who were in on the planning and knew the date and time.'

'All right,' Harding said, sighing. 'Maybe it was Campbell, and we don't have a problem anymore. But just in case, we better check out the others.'

'Can't be too careful,' Clark said casually.

'Yeah, that's right.'

The two men stared at each other.

'You know,' Harding said with a frozen smile, 'Ann saved your black ass.'

'No, I didn't know,' Brother Nabisco said. 'How did she do that?'

'Molly wanted you out, but Ann wouldn't hear of it. I didn't get the details, but knowing Ann, I'd guess she stood up for you. Probably said if you go, she goes.'

'Well, I do appreciate that, I assure you,' Clark said. 'I like this job.'

'That Claxton thing . . .' Harding said. 'It was a beaut.'

'I had fun,' Clark acknowledged. 'Boom!'

Harding looked at him narrowly. 'Just don't get the idea that you're indispensable around here.'

'Now, massa, why should I get an idea like that?'

'You're a snotty bastard – you know that? Ann went to bat for you this time. And for your information, I did too. But try to keep out of Molly's way. She knows what she wants, and she won't stop till she gets it.'

Clark looked at him with a corner of his mouth lifted. 'You'd know more about that than me.'

Rod Harding came up off the cot, took two steps, and swung a clenched fist at Clark's face. The next moment the two men were rolling on the dusty floorboards, grappling.

'Nigger bastard!'

'Honky asshole!'

They wrestled, unable to strike effective blows. But both knew all the tricks of street fighting.

Finally, Clark broke a choke hold, rolled free, and got to his feet, swaying. 'What the fuck is this?' he said, rubbing his throat. 'All we're doing is getting dirty and bloodied. You want to go down the cellar, get us a couple of cannons, and go outside and start popping away at each other?'

'You want to?' Harding said, climbing stiffly to his feet. 'I'm game.'

'Someday maybe,' Brother Nabisco said. 'Not today.'

'Whenever you're ready,' Harding said. 'Meanwhile, I don't think you and I better go on actions together. I don't want to spend all my time watching my back.'

'No need for that,' Clark said coldly. 'That ain't my style. You'll know when it's coming.'

They straightened the room in silence, picked up the spilled beer cans. They cleaned themselves up as best

298

they could, and opened fresh beers. They sat drinking, glowering at each other.

'If you ever,' Harding said, 'and I mean *ever*, make another wiseass remark about Molly and me, I'll blow your fucking head off. And I mean that. The same holds true if I find you so much as hinting to Ann or anyone else.'

Clark turned away disgustedly. 'You shithead,' he said. 'She already knows.'

'Knows?' Harding said, astonished. 'Ann? How the hell could she know?'

'She's been getting letters. Unsigned letters. Right from the start. Places, times – the whole bit.'

'Son of a bitch!' the other man said bitterly. 'That's the law doing that, trying to throw a monkey wrench in the WDC. Or maybe someone on Dundee's staff. He's capable of dirty tricks like that.'

'Yeah, well, don't give me that bullshit about blowing my head off if I so much as hint, because your sweet woman knows you're cheating on her.'

Rod Harding sat hunched over, head drooping. 'Oh Jesus,' he said dully, 'what the hell am I going to do?'

'You know what to do,' Brother Nabisco said. 'Stop it. Or you're going to lose the finest wife and greatest son a man ever had.'

'I'll tell you the truth,' Harding said in a low voice. 'Molly is in my blood. She's like a fire.'

Todhunter Clark put the tips of his forefingers together, and the tips of his thumbs, and held up the open, spade-shaped oval for the other man to see.

'That's all it is,' he said.

Harding shook his head. 'That's what I thought,' he said, 'at first. Now I'm not so sure.'

NOVEMBER 5, 1990

Samuel Briskin, the campaign manager for the governor

running for re-election in Senator Dundee's home state, was an old-line politician, complete with cigar and flowered tie. He did not take kindly to the governor's orders to cooperate with Ruth Blohm and Lyle Hayden in their experiment in political engineering.

'Jee-*zuz*!' he said to Governor Phillip K. Halvorsen. 'I was stuffing ballot boxes when those kids were at the teat. What the hell can they tell me about campaigning?'

'Go along with them, Sam,' the governor counseled. 'The senator is picking up half the tab, and no one says we have to follow their advice.'

So Briskin and his staff worked grudgingly with Blohm and Hayden. They selected three areas that were crucial to Halvorsen's re-election bid: an inner-city ward, a populous rural county, and a relatively new suburban development. Hayden and his crew went to work.

In the rural areas, the governor had been speechifying on the need for higher commodity prices and low-interest farm loans. Hayden's profile showed that the main hidden interest of the farmers was what they perceived as a lack of respect from the state government and a resentment that they were discriminated against in favor of city dwellers.

In the inner-city ward, the in-depth analysis revealed that, while the campaigning governor had come out foursquare for busing, the main concern of the voters was not better schools, but a pervasive fear of crime and a desire for better police protection and harsher punishment for convicted criminals.

In the suburban area, despite the high educational level of the residents, there was found deep, hidden racial prejudice. The suburbanites wanted assurance that the state government was aware of their desire to protect the value of their newly purchased property and willing to cooperate on revised zoning laws to keep out the 'wrong people.'

And all three areas found Halvorsen something of a fuddy-duddy, with an old-fashioned haircut, three-piece suits of ancient cut, and an annoying habit of sucking his teeth.

'Governor, it's all bullshit,' Briskin declared. 'You stick to your image, your schedule, and the issues we've outlined for you. You're a shoo-in.'

But Halvorsen had studied the most recent polls and knew he was far from being a shoo-in. In fact, he confided to his wife, if he couldn't turn things around in the last weeks of -campaigning, he might be a shoo-out.

So, after reading and rereading Hayden's voluminous analyses, he decided to go for broke. He had his hair darkened, styled, and blow-dried; he took a two-day crash course from a professional to correct his more annoying speech habits; and he bought a new wardrobe of Italian-cut suits in light colors.

Then he set his writers to work and returned to the three decisive voting areas with speeches tailored to the needs, dreams, fantasies, and prejudices of those blocs.

On November 5, Dundee and his top campaign staff gathered in the living room of the senator's Spring Valley home to watch the election results. Ruth Blohm was not present. She, Lyle Hayden, and Ruth's father were in the Blohms' home in Arlington.

They had dined well on an enormous bowl of linguine with clam sauce to which Ruth had added shrimp and chunks of lobster tails. That, a salad, and a jug of California chablis had fortified them as they watched the Blohms' old, flickering television set.

After dinner, Eric Blohm and Hayden settled down over the chessboard while Ruth stayed glued to the TV, switching channels to seek the most recent results and predictions.

'Turn that damned thing down,' her father called grumpily. 'How do you expect a man to think?'

'Listen, Father, my job and my whole career are hanging on what happens tonight. Lyle, aren't you excited?'

He stroked his blond beard, smiling. 'More curious than

excited. I know we're going to win. The unknown is by how much.'

'I wish I had your confidence,' she said worriedly. 'As far as I'm concerned, it's all up for grabs.'

Halvorsen's was the only race she was interested in, and she kept a running tally with hastily scrawled notes on a scratchpad. Early results showed the governor and his opponent running neck-and-neck, with the three voting areas Hayden had analyzed not yet reporting.

It was shortly after midnight that the first break came: the inner-city ward went for Halvorsen by a sizable majority. Ruth Blohm greeted the news with a whoop of delight.

'One down and two to go,' she crowed. 'We're winning! Why didn't I buy a bottle of champagne to celebrate.'

'There's some cherry brandy in the cupboard,' her father remarked mildly. 'Break it out.'

By 1:30 AM, it was all over. Halvorsen had taken 58 percent of the popular vote. The three decisive voting blocs had provided his margin of victory. His opponent had conceded.

Ruth threw her arms about her father's neck and kissed his wrinkled cheek. Then she kissed Lyle Hayden on the lips. Then she kissed both men again. Then she insisted they all have more cherry brandy.

They were all laughing when the phone rang.

'Now who the hell is that?' Eric Blohm said. 'At this hour.'

Ruth picked up the phone.

'Miss Blohm?' someone asked.

'Yes.'

'Senator Dundee calling. Just a moment, please.'

She heard that plummy voice: 'Ruth?'

'Yes, Senator.'

'Congratulations, my dear. It was beautiful and I love you.'

'Thank you, sir.'

'And give my thanks to Hayden. The two of you did a

marvelous job. I just talked to Governor Halvorsen, and he specifically asked that I extend his heartfelt gratitude to both of you.'

'Thank you again.'

'Ruth, I'd like you in my office the first thing tomorrow morning. We've got to discuss how this political engineering can be applied to the ninety-two campaign.'

'I'll be there, Senator.'

An hour later she was driving Lyle back to the airport, both of them exuberant and guessing how much the Dundee campaign chest might cough up for in-depth analysis in the race for the nomination.

'Millions,' Ruth said gaily. 'Oh, Lyle, I'm so sorry you have to get on a plane at this hour.'

'I'm not,' he said. 'I'll go back to Atlanta in the morning. I've already checked into a motel.'

She gave a great hoot of laughter and put a warm hand on his thigh.

'You beautiful man,' she said. 'You think of everything.'

He picked up her hand, kissed her palm.

'What will your father say?' he asked.

'He'll say, "Hurray!"' she told him.

DECEMBER 19, 1990

James Gargan had an unusual job. He was never given orders – and rarely suggestions. He was brought into small, private conferences at which policy decisions were handed him. How he carried out those decisions was his responsibility.

Nothing was ever put in writing. They kept him on a long leash. If he succeeded, fine. They didn't want to know how he did it. He was rewarded with praise, raises, promotions. If he failed, he was out there by himself with not a friend in the world. That was okay; he accepted it.

At one of the cloistered meetings – at which he was

303

given the directive to do everything possible to further the nomination and eventual election of Senator Dundee – Gargan entered the paneled room to a greeting by one of the mandarins.

'Ah,' he said, 'the iceman cometh.'

The name stuck. James Gargan: the Iceman. He accepted that, too. Was rather pleased by it, in fact. It meant he would not let emotions get in the way of doing a job.

Dundee was not his only assignment, of course; he was playing in a dozen poker games. But the Dundee scenario tickled him – all those passions, conflicts, hostilities. He spent hours lounging in his hotel suite, working out the permutations and combinations.

Finally he called Jake Spencer at night.

'Jake?' he said. 'Gargan here.'

'Jimbo!' Spencer said boisterously. 'How's by you?'

'Can't complain,' Gargan said. 'I hear your boy is doing okay.'

'I think the old fart is going to make it. God knows he's got the bucks, and he doesn't mind spreading it around.'

'Lucky you. Jake, something's come up I want your take on. Can we meet?'

'Sure, Jimbo. Where and when?'

'That park up near Friendship Heights. The boat dock where we met before.'

'Suits me.'

'Tomorrow at midnight?'

'Okay. I'll have his nibs safely tucked in bed by then.'

They sat on opposite sides of a wooden picnic table. Both men were wearing hats and overcoats. A raw, damp night with a cutting wind. The half-moon kept ducking behind clouds. Gargan had brought along a plastic flask filled with Jim Beam, and they both had a belt.

'So, Jimbo?' Jake Spencer said. 'What's up – besides your cock?'

'Jake, how long have we known each other?'

'Oh God, twenty years at least. What's this going to be – one of those old boys' "Remember when" sessions?'

'Not exactly,' James Gargan said, leaning back on his bench and taking a Smith & Wesson .44 Magnum from his overcoat pocket. He held it negligently, but the muzzle was pointed at the other man.

'What the hell,' Jake Spencer said.

'Don't try to take me, Jake,' Gargan said gently. 'Please don't. At this range I could plink your eyes out and you know it.'

'Jimbo,' Spencer said, still calm, 'what's this all about?'

'Take a look around.'

Spencer looked slowly, swiveling his heavy shoulders. He saw at least three men standing in the moon shadows of trees and the boat dock shanty. They all wore overcoats, hands in their pockets.

'Who're they?' he said bitterly. 'The garbage crew?'

'Something like that,' Gargan acknowledged. 'Don't lean forward, Jake. And keep your hands where I can see them.'

'But why?' Spencer said. 'You owe me that. *Why*?'

Gargan sighed. 'I had a sweet game plan all worked out. Everything was coming up roses. And then you have to go and get greedy. Your weakness, Jake. You wasted Billy McCrea – *you*, not any hired caveman – and grabbed his appointment book, and now you're leaning on Constance Underwood and Thomas Kealy. You're screwing me up, Jake. Those people are important to me. I can't let it happen.'

'Oh . . .' Spencer said. 'That. Well . . . okay, maybe I went for some bucks. So what? I'll forget it and turn the little black book over to you, and that's the end of that.'

'We already have the book, Jake. Picked it up tonight.'

'Jimbo,' the other man said, moving his neck nervously inside his collar, 'can't you give me a break? Twenty years, Jimbo. That's how long we've been friends.'

305

'Friends?' Gargan said. 'You haven't got any friends, Jake. Not me, not anyone else.'

'Jesus Christ!' Spencer cried. 'Are you going to pop me right here?'

Gargan shook his head. 'Ah Jake, you really haven't been keeping up, have you? We don't pop people any more. We've learned from the Argentines. People just disappear. One day they're here, the next day they're gone.'

'My family will ask questions – you'll see.'

'What family, Jake? You've got a brother in San Diego who hates your guts. He hasn't talked to you for years. He couldn't care less about you.'

'The senator,' Spencer said desperately. 'And his staff. They'll wonder what happened to me. They'll ask questions.'

'Maybe,' Gargan said equably. 'For a day or two. The local cops will go through the motions. Then they'll bury your disappearance in the file for more important cases. I can work it. You know how these things go, Jake. A short paragraph in the papers: "Senator's Bodyguard Missing." It'll all be over in a week. No one will remember.'

'I can't believe this,' Jake Spencer said in a clotted voice. 'I can't believe you're going to burn me.'

'Oh, Jake, Jake,' James Gargan said sadly, 'we're just going to relocate you, that's all.'

He gestured, and the big men moved out of the shadows.

'I never did like the name Jimbo,' the Iceman said.

Early in 1991, the Justice Department prepared a statistical analysis of direct actions 'proved or reputed' to be the responsibility of the Women's Defense Corps. Although intended only for internal distribution and classified 'Secret,' the analysis, with minor deletions, has been obtained under the Freedom of Information Act.

It reviews 264 separate incidents occurring in 1990. Four-

teen fatalities resulted, of which six were WDC sisters. There were 153 injuries reported, 79 of which were suffered by WDC members.

The analysis of the 264 actions includes 19 bombings, 24 cases of arson and attempted arson, 2 alleged assassinations, 1 kidnapping, 44 incidents of assault and battery, and 114 reports of destruction of private property. The remainder of the actions were classified as illegal trespass, harassment, malicious mischief, etc.

The most significant section of the analysis deals with the targets of the WDC activities. By far the largest percentage were accused or convicted rapists. The second largest classification was wife beaters. The third, child molesters. These three categories accounted for 87 percent of the cases included in the Justice Department report.

The analysis shows a surprisingly low number of prosecutions and convictions of Women's Defense Corps members involved in the 264 direct actions. Indictments were sought in 19 cases and obtained in only 12. Nine court cases resulted, and guilty verdicts obtained against four WDC sisters. Fines and probation were the heaviest sentences.

There is little doubt that the Department of Justice, while closely monitoring the activities of the WDC, was reluctant to go to trial in defense of rapists, wife beaters, and child molesters.

Justice might be – or should be – blind, but prosecutors had little appetite for testing that principle in the courts. In effect, the American public was expressing its approval of vigilante justice insofar as the actions of the WDC were concerned. By careful selection of targets, Molly Turner was able to disarm her critics and turn condemnation to praise.

At the same time, Senator Dundee, in his campaign speeches, was winning applause for his 'law and order' theme, pleading for a return to the traditional method of seeking justice through courts and legislatures.

More than one political analyst of the period commented

on this dichotomy in the attitude of the American public. Sympathy for Molly Turner and the WDC existed along with a yearning for more peaceable methods of redressing the wrongs committed against women.

This conflict sharpened as the 1992 presidential campaign accelerated, and more and more voters came to the realization that they couldn't have it both ways.

JANUARY 3, 1991

The contradiction in the voters' attitude toward Molly Turner and the Women's Defense Corps described above was a cause of much debate and not a little frustration among the principal advisers on Lemuel Dundee's campaign staff.

The senator made his position plain. He had derived 'a lot of mileage' from his anti-WDC crusade, and he was not about to give it up until it was proved to him that it was definitely hurting his chances to win the nomination.

'Look,' he told his aides. 'The guys I'm up against have no color, no excitement, no charisma. Let's face it: on the big issues – the economy, nuclear disarmament, the environment, and all that shit – we're all talking alike. The only thing I've got that they haven't is my strong opposition to Molly Turner. What we've got to decide is if it's doing me more good than harm.'

'Senator,' Tom Kealy said earnestly, 'the most recent polls aren't encouraging. Women are generally siding with the WDC.'

'Not entirely,' speechwriter Simon Christie objected. 'You're doing fine in the Midwest and Sun Belt – the conservative states. So California and New York are pro – WDC. They're not the whole country.'

'But they represent a helluva lot of electoral votes,' Dundee said grumpily. 'And you know the convention will go with the guy who looks to have the best chance of winning.'

'Senator,' Ruth Blohm said, 'I think we should start looking beyond the convention. What we need is a computer analysis of the states you'll have to carry. How many liberal states can we lose and still win? What I'm suggesting is that instead of spreading you thin, we target those states where your anti – WDC campaign is going over big, and see if they'll give you the majority you need.'

'It's a good idea,' the senator agreed. 'But while we're getting that, I think we better give more thought to getting into the preliminary straw polls. Florida is next month, and Minnesota a few weeks later. Then comes New Hampshire. I think we better meet this issue head-on and find out exactly where we stand. What do you think?'

The discussion continued for more than an hour. Then Dundee called a halt and chased everyone out. But he grabbed Ruth Blohm and asked her to remain a few minutes.

'Baby,' he said, 'after what you and Hayden did for Governor Halvorsen, I've got a lot of trust in you. I want the two of you to go through voting records and pick out, say, a half-dozen crucial voting districts that'll mean life or death. Can you do that?'

'Of course, Senator,' she said cheerfully. 'The TV networks do it all the time to make their preliminary predictions. I'm not suggesting we accept their choices; we can select our own counties or wards. I gather you'll want in-depth analysis?'

'Maybe,' he said cautiously. 'We'll cross that bridge when we come to it. For the time being, I just want you to pick a – uh, what do you call it?'

'A representational sample?'

'Yeah, like that. A few districts that'll give us the answers we need. Can you do it?'

'Sure. Get on it right away.'

After she departed, Dundee loosened his tie, opened

his collar, shucked off his shoes. He told his secretary to hold all calls and locked his office door.

The problem, he acknowledged, was that he was caught between a rock and a hard place. His heavy financial backers – and particularly H. Fairchild Curtiss – were virulently anti – WDC. If he moderated his opposition to Molly Turner, the money tap would be turned off. They'd rather see him defeated than have him end his jeremiads against the WDC.

Senator Lemuel K. Dundee wasn't about to be defeated.

He phoned James Gargan on a direct line that didn't go through his office switchboard. Gargan came on almost instantly.

'Yes, Senator,' he said pleasantly. 'How are you today?'

'Okay,' Dundee said shortly. 'Is this line clean?'

'No problem, sir,' Gargan said, switching on his tape recorder.

'Jim, this WDC thing – you still think the whole thing will self – destruct?'

'I do,' James Gargan said confidently. 'It's an aberration. Like the Black Panthers. And the Weathermen. Who remembers them now? Senator, all these outfits are *people*. And people have wants and needs and ambitions. After a while the cause gets lost in the human shuffle.'

'I hope you're right.'

'All I can go on is past experience. Believe me, they devour each other. The same thing will happen to the WDC. You'll see.'

'When?'

'Sooner than you expect.'

'Before the election?'

Gargan didn't answer immediately. Then:

'Yes, sir,' he said. 'Before the election.'

Senator Dundee hung up, feeling a lot better. He decided at that moment to keep pounding away at Molly Turner and the WDC. It was not right that the American traditions of justice and peaceable means of redressing wrongs should be flouted.

Also, H. Fairchild Curtiss would be happy.

'You bastard!' Lemuel Dundee cried joyously. But whether he was addressing Molly Turner, Curtiss, or himself, no one could have said.

FEBRUARY 16, 1991

The storm came shrieking out of the west. It was a killer, slamming the mid-Atlantic states with freezing winds and snow that drifted to five-foot depths. Temperatures plunged to zero.

Molly Turner had driven over from Washington, DC, on Friday afternoon. On Saturday morning she made it to the Hardings' home to spend a few hours. By that afternoon she realized she'd never make it back to Hillcrest Avenue; drifts were piling up and lightning kept splitting the dirty sky.

'Don't even try it,' Rod Harding advised. 'They won't start plowing until the snow stops. You and Ann can have the bedroom. I'll take the couch. Okay, Ann?'

'Of course,' she said.

'We've got enough food for a couple of days,' Rod said. 'How we doing on Jeff's milk, hon?'

'There's plenty,' Ann said. 'And a can of condensed milk if push comes to shove. We've got enough food in the freezer to see us through. If the power goes off, we'll just put it all on the back porch.'

So they settled in, trying to ignore the rattling of windows, the occasional drumrolls of hail. They were snug, sitting around the kitchen table, drinking beer and munching pretzels. Now and then Ann looked into the living room, where Jeff was busy with crayons and a coloring book his aunt had brought him.

'So?' Molly said. 'What's going on around here?'

'Rod and Todhunter Clark finished the security checks,'

311

her sister said. 'You tell her, Rod.'

He shook his head. 'Not a lot to tell. Molly, we did everyone connected with that screwed-up Lexington action. Everyone's clean.'

'Bullshit!' she said. 'Someone tipped off the cops.'

'It could have been Lois Campbell,' Ann said quietly. 'It's the only answer. Since she died, we haven't had any serious leaks.'

'What about Popkin?' Molly demanded. 'When I left her in DC, she was drunk as a skunk. Did you check her out?'

'We checked everyone,' Rod assured her. 'We fed a phony action to Popkin, with no result. We told her there was a raid planned on an armory in Clarksburg, and then we staked out the place. The law didn't show up.'

'Damn it,' Molly said, gnawing at the hard skin around her thumbnail. 'I still think we got a mole. I hope it's not a nigger in the woodpile.'

'Don't start that again,' Ann said stonily.

'Where is he, by the way?'

'Over in Lexington,' Rod said. 'Courting Lucille Jackson. He was due back last night, but called and said he was snowed in. He'll make it when he can.'

Molly rose and began to stalk about the kitchen. The Hardings sat calmly, watching her pace.

She seemed as taut as a stretched wire. Touch her and she'd thrum. The skin on her face had tightened over hawk nose and hard cheekbones. Her helmet of blond curls was shorter than ever – a skullcap. The darting eyes burned, and her gestures had become more abrupt, hands trembling with tension.

'Take it easy, Molly,' Rod said casually. 'You look like you're going to levitate.'

'You know that business in Michigan?' she demanded. 'The conjugal rights case?'

They nodded; the papers and TV news programs had been giving it a big play.

It had happened in Corinth, Michigan, on January 14. A young (twenty-six) married woman, Carol Poague, childless, had stabbed her husband, Edward, to death with a heavy carving knife. Immediately after the murder, Carol called the police and surrendered.

She admitted the killing. She stated that her husband had wanted sex that night, but she had worked eight hours in the kitchen of a local restaurant and 'was not in the mood.' He insisted; she refused.

He had struck her once in the face with his clenched fist. It was, she acknowledged, the first time he had ever hit her. She had fled to the kitchen. He pursued. She plucked the knife from a magnetic rack on the wall. She warned him not to approach closer. When he did, she said, she stabbed him once. The blade penetrated his heart, severed an artery, and he died almost instantly.

This sad domestic squabble might have caused little comment outside of Corinth. But Carol Poague was a member of the Women's Defense Corps. She was determined to base her defense on the principle of 'mutual consent' for married couples rather than 'conjugal rights' for the husband only.

'What was I?' she asked during a television interview. 'A chattel? What is any wife? A piece of the husband's property like his tractor mower or golf clubs? Conjugal rights should include the right to say no. I prefer the term "mutual consent." I tried to make Edward understand that, but he couldn't. He thought conjugal rights means sex on demand. Well, it doesn't.'

The Women's Defense Corps established a special fund to pay for the defense of Carol Poague. She insisted her case be argued on the principle she had already stated: mutual consent in marriage versus the traditional view of conjugal rights.

The trial was scheduled to start on March 18, 1991. It had already attracted worldwide attention, and the small courthouse in Corinth was flooded with requests for press passes from foreign journalists.

'I went up to Corinth last week,' Molly Turner said, still pacing in jerky strides. 'First I talked to our lawyers. They said the prosecutor is going for a guilty verdict on a second-degree murder charge. The lawyers think he has a good chance of getting it. Corinth is a small, conservative town – mostly farmers and shop-keepers. Also, Edward Poague was a local boy, while Carol is from Detroit.'

'That's not going to help,' Rod Harding said.

'Tell me about it,' Molly said bitterly. 'Anyway, the lawyers believe they can plea-bargain the charge down to manslaughter if Carol will plead guilty. She'd probably get three to five. They wanted me to talk to her about it. I wasn't happy about that, but I figured she should have the option. She said no, no, and no. God, that is one strong woman. I love her! She's going to fight it out on her terms, win or lose.'

'If she loses,' Ann said, 'how much can she get?'

'Up to twenty years.'

Ann was silent.

'So I went back to our attorneys,' Molly said, 'and told them no soap, they'd have to do the best they could with the defense Carol wants.'

She sat down again, put her forearms on the kitchen table. She did not raise her head when she spoke.

'Ann, you talk to Virginia Terwilliger lately?'

'Two or three times a week,' Ann said.

'She tell you that we met in DC?'

'No, she didn't tell me that. Probably thought you'd fill me in.'

'Well, we met a couple of weeks ago. She made her case for a complete merger of the NWU and the WDC. She practically guaranteed I could be president. But the whole thing hinges on the recommendation of the special board. And apparently *that* depends on the vote of Stacy, the Michigan NWU chapter president. But like you said, in return for her vote, Stacy wants the right to can the

314

colonel of the Michigan WDC regiment and put in her own favorite.'

'I didn't know anything about this,' Rod Harding protested.

'That's right,' Molly said. 'I'm repeating it now for your benefit. Anyway, Ann, since we talked about it in September, I've been giving it a lot of heavy thought, and I've decided I just can't do it.'

'Oh Jesus!' Ann said, sighing.

Then Molly raised her head to look directly at her sister. 'Listen, hon, that Michigan colonel – Grace Peddleton is her name – is one great soldier. She's got guts from here to there, does everything I've asked her to do – and more. Her sisters love her. I'm not about to kick her out for the sake of my political future.'

Ann slapped the tabletop sharply with an open palm. The crack made the other two jump.

'Goddamn it!' she said furiously. 'What's wrong with you? I told you that to get along you have to go along.'

'Who the hell are you to tell me what to do?' Molly screamed at her.

Rod Harding, spectator at a tennis match, swiveled his head from side to side as each woman yelled. He made no effort to stop the quarrel.

'I just want you to use your brain!' Ann shouted. 'Like I said, you fire Grace Peddleton, and we get the largest women's organization in the country with you as president. *Then* you find a good job for Grace. Doesn't that make sense?'

'I won't do it,' Molly said hotly. 'No one gets fired for my sake. That's not the way I am. I'd rather let the whole thing go down the drain than do that to Grace.'

Harding stood, walked slowly into the living room, picked up Jeff, and carried him back into the kitchen. It worked; the women calmed.

Rod sat down again, his son on his lap. He gave the boy a pretzel, and they all smiled to see him gnaw on it.

315

'Well, anyway,' Molly Turner said, 'I told Virginia Terwilliger that no way was I going to fire Grace Peddleton. She can be the Michigan colonel as long as she wants.'

'And what did Terwilliger say to that?' Rod asked curiously. 'A lot, I bet.'

'You better believe it,' Molly said. 'She cussed me out something fierce. She called me a hard-nosed bastard. Which I am – I admit it. But when she saw I wouldn't budge, she said she'd try to figure out how to swing another vote on the special board.'

'And that's how you left it?' Ann demanded.

Molly nodded. Then, Jeff squirming on his father's lap, they all moved into the living room, where the boy resumed scribbling in his coloring book. The adults lounged, hearing the storm pounding away outside.

'After I left Corinth – ' Molly Turner said, '– that was on Wednesday – I went down to Detroit and spent all afternoon with Grace Peddleton. We talked about how we could grab Carol Poague before her trial ends and get her out of there.'

'Oh my God,' Rod said. 'You're nuts! Security at that Corinth courthouse will be six deep in cops.'

'We're going to do it,' Molly said defiantly. 'Screw the security. There is no way they will be expecting a raid. Grace and I think we can pull it off.'

'What makes you think Carol will cooperate?' Ann asked. 'You said she's a strong woman who wants to see this thing through on her terms. She's not going to go along with you.'

'We'll make her. Just grab her and hustle her out. That beautiful woman is not going to do any fucking twenty years.'

'Watch your language,' Ann said sharply. 'Jeff picks up words so quickly.

'Suppose you get her out,' Rod said. 'Then what? Where does she go? They'll pick her up in a week.'

'It'll need a lot of planning,' Molly acknowledged. 'A

complete change of identity. New name, new identification, new appearance. Then we'll get her to a different state – or out of the country, if that's what she wants.'

'It's insanc,' Ann said. 'Tell her, Rod.'

'You tell her,' he said. 'She's your sister.'

'It can be done,' Molly insisted. 'I know it can. Listen, Corinth is a one-horse town. Maybe four or five cops, with some sheriff's deputies and state troopers brought in for crowd control during the trial. Right now, Carol is being held in the clink. It's a tincan jail across the street from the courthouse. She'll be escorted across the street every day before the court session and escorted back to jail when it's over. Plenty of chances to grab her outside the courthouse.'

Rod Harding began to get interested. 'She's not being held in a cell inside the courthouse?'

'I just told you. She's in a two-by-four jail across the street.'

'Rod . . .' Ann said warningly.

Molly stared at her. 'I'll tell you something, sister mine,' she said. 'With or without your help, or Rod's help, or anyone else's help, this thing is going down. Grace Peddleton is all for it. She'll bring enough sisters up to Corinth from the Detroit area. No one will recognize them. Grace is eager and anxious to command. So it's going to be done. Are you with me or against me?' she said harshly.

Husband and wife looked at each other. If a signal passed between them, Molly Turner didn't see it.

'It's going to take some long and careful planning,' Rod Harding said cautiously.

'Then we better get started right now,' Molly said. 'I brought along a map of the town.'

The three of them sat close on the couch, the map of Corinth spread over their laps. They began to plot the rescue of Carol Poague.

MARCH 24, 1991

Thomas J. Kealy was in a manic mood. Now he knew how to dress for a Sunday at Connie Underwood's country home. He wore his shabbiest sport jacket – the one with suede elbow patches – khaki slacks, a heavy turtleneck sweater. A soiled trenchcoat was tossed rakishly over his shoulders like a cape. His horn-rims were tucked carefully out of sight.

Even her driving didn't bother him anymore.

'Do with me what you will!' he shouted happily.

She glanced briefly at him, then back at the road. She took a curve at much too high a speed, felt a skid start on a patch of melting snow, corrected for it expertly, and roared into a straight-away. She drove as she did everything else: grim, purposeful, not to be denied.

The man who looked after her property had brought in firewood and stacked the refrigerator. Kealy lugged in a case of assorted wines and liquors to replenish her stock, and Connie carried a box of new tapes for her cassette player.

They started a fire to take the chill off the big room, and opened a bottle of '81 Mondavi white. They lounged on the thick pile carpeting in front of the fireplace.

'That trial in Michigan . . .' she said. 'The conjugal rights case . . . Have you been following it?'

'Of course. Who hasn't?'

She looked at him curiously. 'What do you think?' she asked.

'Oh, she's guilty – no doubt about that. She admits it. Her defense is ridiculous. If they turn her loose, it'll be open season on every husband in the country. But she'll be convicted.'

'Uh-huh,' Constance Underwood said. 'That's what Molly Turner figures. That's why she and her cutthroats

318

are going to free Carol Poague. They're going to grab her between the jail and the courthouse and get her out of the country.'

'What?' He sat up so suddenly that he slopped wine onto his sweater. 'Are you sure of that?'

'I'm sure.'

'Jesus Christ! I've got to make a phone call.'

'You can't,' she said. 'The phone hasn't been connected yet. Besides, there's no rush. It's not scheduled until next month. You can call Gargan tomorrow.'

'My God,' he said, settling back, 'kidnapping a prisoner – what a crazy thing to do.'

'Molly Turner is a crazy woman.'

'She really thinks she can pull it off?'

'She wouldn't be trying if she didn't.'

'Connie, who told you about this?'

She looked at him coldly. 'You have no need to know.'

'Okay, okay,' he said hastily. 'I just don't want to give Gargan a bum tip.'

She couldn't have cared less; she had already told James Gargan about it. He had thanked her politely and said he'd handle it.

Mesmerized by the flickering fire, they sipped their white wine and talked casually of this and that. After a while, she put her glass aside, lay supine, and let him play with her. He was so grateful, he almost wept.

She felt his fingers and mouth on her body and was mildly stirred. Just mildly. Compared to Gargan, Tom Kealy was a soufflé, a mousse. Gargan was steak tartare.

'I'm hungry,' she said finally. 'Let's have dinner.'

They roasted two Rock Cornish hens in the microwave, mixed a big bowl of Caesar salad, and opened a bottle of '89 Beaujolais. Kealy set the table. Underwood told him he was a genius at folding napkins. He made them look like miniature cocked hats.

They cleaned up after dinner, and Kealy suggested they take the remainder of the wine into the sauna and 'do

319

things.' But Constance shook her head.

'Sit down,' she commanded. 'There's something I've got to tell you.'

They sat in facing blond wood armchairs with white sailcloth cushions.

'I've got to stop seeing you,' she said abruptly.

'What?'

'This is the last time we can be alone together,' she said stonily.

'But why?' he cried.

'Tom, you're a married man. And you work for a politician everyone perceives as being antifeminist.'

'He's not!'

'That's the way people see him,' she went on relentlessly. 'All that could add up to a lot of trouble for me if it ever gets out.'

'How could it get out? We've been very discreet.'

'In Washington?' she said. 'That's a laugh. I'm fighting for my life in the NWU-WDC thing. We're coming up to the July convention. I can't risk anything that might endanger my chances. If Molly Turner ever found out I was fucking Senator Dundee's personal aide – his *married* personal aide – she'd mash me like a steamroller.'

'But I love you,' he said piteously.

'That's nice,' she said. 'And I like you – I really do. But you represent a danger to all my plans. You can see that, can't you?'

In truth, he bored her. Since becoming intimate with James Gargan, she had no need for Kealy or any other man. Gargan was all she needed. And he was a bachelor. And he was wonderfully potent. And he never came crawling on hands and knees to snuffle beneath her skirt.

'Oh my God,' Thomas Kealy said, groaning. 'What am I going to do?'

'Go back to your wife,' she advised.

He begged, he pleaded, he even shed a few genuine tears. He beseeched her to make their separation tempor-

320

ary, their affair to resume after she won a victory at the NWU convention. But she was adamant.

'Then I'll have to be more careful than ever,' she said. 'No, Tom, this has got to be a clean break. I'll work out some safe way of getting tips on the WDC to you by phone, but I can't see you anymore.'

He sat there, staring at the cold, imperious woman who had made all his fantasies come true. Never to wear her kimono again! And never, he knew, never in a million years could he persuade his wife to spank him.

'Oh, Tommy,' she'd say, 'you're tho thilly.'

In a fit of anguish, he flopped to his knees before Constance Underwood's chair, hugged her legs, attempted to nuzzle her, his face wet with a new freshet of tears. But she pushed him away and stood up.

'You're so silly,' she said.

APRIL 17, 1991

The trial of Carol Poague, which most of the residents of Corinth, Michigan, had expected to last no more than a week, had dragged on for a month.

A patient judge had allowed defense attorneys to present a parade of witnesses – historians, sociologists, psychologists – to tell the jury (eight men, four women) that the traditional concept of conjugal rights was outmoded and likely to result in psychic harm and emotional trauma for the wife.

The jury – mostly middle-aged, middle-class – listened politely to the erudite scholars, but there was no evidence they were being swayed by what they heard. Betting among reporters covering the trial was 20 to 1 for a guilty verdict. The odds rose to 50 to 1 when Carol Poague took the stand and calmly admitted the slaying.

Molly Turner and her entourage, including Rod Harding and Todhunter Clark, arrived in Michigan on April 11.

They stayed at the Co-Zee Motel near Southfield. In the week following, they held several meetings with Grace Peddleton and her lieutenants. Tactics were finalized, personnel and weapons selected, transportation arranged.

The action was definitely scheduled for the afternoon of April 18, following court recess for the day.

Peddleton requested she be allowed to command the attack in person. Molly Turner agreed, but insisted on being present in Corinth during the action. She assured the colonel that all on-the-scene decisions would be solely Peddleton's responsibility. Turner's role would be that of an observer, evaluating her troops' combat efficiency.

The final planning conference ended at approximately 5:00 PM, on April 17. Shortly thereafter, Todhunter Clark left for Corinth, accompanied by a black WDC sister. He was driving a battered Chevy van crammed with weapons, grenades, explosives, and other paraphernalia that would be needed the following day.

Molly Turner, Rod Harding, Yvonne Popkin, and Grace Peddleton had dinner at a restaurant adjoining the Co-Zee Motel. They ate barbecued ribs, baked potatoes, French-fried onion rings. Then they separated.

Turner and Harding returned to the motel, to the room he was sharing with Todhunter Clark. Rod had a pint of sour mash bourbon, and went down to the end of the hall for a plastic tub of ice cubes. They each had one mild drink. A half-hour later they were in bed.

'Rod, I've got the jitters,' she confessed. 'About tomorrow.'

'Sure you do, Moll,' he said. 'So do I, so does Tod, so does Grace, so does everyone else. It's natural. Hon, we've done everything we can possibly do. The plan is a good one. All we need now is luck.'

'I wish I could command,' she said broodingly. 'But Grace wanted the chance to show what she could do. It's her territory; I couldn't say no.'

'Don't worry about it,' he advised. 'You've got to learn

322

to delegate authority. Grace strikes me as being a very competent woman. She'll do fine; you'll see.'

'Maybe we should have another drink.'

'No,' he said. 'You're going to need a clear head tomorrow.'

'Just a weak one. A lot of ice, a lot of water.'

'Okay,' he said. 'Just one more.'

He got out of bed to mix fresh drinks. When he leaned over to hand her the glass, she reached out to fondle him.

'Here, here,' he said. 'None of that.'

'So beautiful,' she breathed. 'So beautiful.'

'Sip your drink,' he told her. 'Relax.'

'I can't. I'm wound up tighter than a tick. Rod, I'm tired. I don't mean sleepy. I just mean bone-weary.'

'You're entitled. You've been going at it for four years.'

'I feel drained. I've come to the point where I have to psych myself up to talk to the sisters. It used to come so easy. Now I have to make the effort.'

'Physical exhaustion,' he said. 'When this Corinth thing is over, you should take a month off. Go to some hot place and just lie on the sand.'

'You think that's what it is – physical exhaustion? I hope you're right. I can cope with that. But goddamn it, I'm beginning to doubt. Rod, am I doing any *good*? Am I really changing things?'

'You're doing good,' he said. 'You're changing things.'

'Oh God, I hope so. But I don't know . . . Sometimes, late at night, when I can't sleep, I think about retiring. You know, I'm not too old to be a mother.'

'Of course you're not.'

'It's an awful temptation, Rod. A real home, a good man, kids. Sleeping in the same bed year after year after year. No more motels. No more speeches and meetings and interviews and actions.'

'You could combine both,' he pointed out. 'Be a wife and have a career. Grace Peddleton is married and has two kids.'

'She can do it,' Molly Turner said, 'but I couldn't. I have to do things one hundred percent. Either what I'm doing now, or give it up and concentrate all my energies on being the best wife and mother the world has ever seen. That's the way I am.'

'I know,' he said tenderly.

He began to love her, with his fingers, his palms, his lips, his tongue.

'Ah Jesus,' she said, sighing. 'That's what I need. Don't stop.'

She came alive beneath his hands, flushed, flesh hot with a skim of sweat. He worked on her lanky body until she gasped.

'Come on. Come *on*!'

He rolled atop her.

'Am I too heavy on you, Moll?'

She shook her head, eyes closed. 'Sweet. So sweet.'

He penetrated and began to move.

'Holy Christ!' she cried, lips drawn back from her teeth in a passionate grimace.

'Lover!' she said. 'Lover!'

'Lover,' he repeated. 'Lover.'

He thought she wept, but couldn't be sure. Finished, she would not release him, but hugged him tightly with her whippy arms. His face was buried in her neck and shoulder; he nipped gently at her soft skin.

'Lover,' she said again. 'Lover, don't go away from me. Not yet. Stay right where you are.'

He stayed, for a while, then slowly withdrew. He propped himself up on his palms and looked down at her.

'Moll,' he said, 'were you serious about settling down?'

'Hell, no,' she said. 'Who needs that crap?'

APRIL 18, 1991

Broadway, the main street of Corinth, Michigan, sloped

324

gently downward from north to south. At the top of the rise was Bill's Gas Station and Garage. The midsection was the business district, including courthouse, civic center, and jail. At the southern end was a large one-story structure that had originally housed a supermarket. It had gone out of business during the 1981 – 83 recession and was still unoccupied.

Todhunter Clark had selected this building for the scene of a diversion to draw police officers away from the courthouse area.

'No one's going to get hurt,' he had promised after his initial reconnaissance. 'It's just a big old empty shed. I can give you lotsa noise, lotsa smoke, but no real damage. I won't even take the walls down. But the blast will bring everyone running. Instant chaos.'

Clark's crew put the explosives in place early on the morning of April 18. As usual, he planned to detonate the charges by radio transmitter. The signal to press the button would be a walkie-talkie report from a WDC sister who would attend the trial and alert him when court adjourned for the day.

The explosion would be the go-ahead for Grace Peddleton and her combat team. They would be in cars parked nearby, and would also infiltrate the small crowd that gathered daily outside the courthouse to watch Carol Poague brought out in manacles and marched across the street to the jail.

The moment Clark set off the diversionary blast, Peddleton and her soldiers would uncover weapons carried in purses and shopping bags. They would then take up positions and prepare to free the prisoner when she appeared.

Escape routes had been carefully plotted on back roads to avoid roadblocks that would undoubtedly be set up on the main arteries. The attack force would grab Poague, hustle her into a car, and be out of town before authorities, stunned by Brother Nabisco's explosion, could react.

That was the plan.

Grace Peddleton's team came into town early in the afternoon, singly and in twos and threes, driving a variety of nondescript vehicles. The troops were divided into three squads, assigned to crowd control, perimeter defense, and the actual attack to liberate the accused woman.

Molly Turner and Rod Harding arrived in Corinth shortly after 2:00 PM. He was driving their rented Ford Ranger pickup. Turner was wearing a 'disguise' she sometimes used when present at an action: a long, black nylon wig, wide-brimmed fedora pulled low, dark sunglasses.

Harding had previously scouted the area, and had selected Bill's Gas Station as the best vantage point from which he and Molly could observe the attack. He pulled into the station, gassed-up the Ranger at a self-service pump, then drove to the edge of the concrete apron and parked. He and Molly sat in the truck, ostensibly consulting an unfolded road map.

At 3:19 PM, the gas station was rocked by a tremendous explosion. Windows rattled, cans of oil came tumbling from a display rack.

'Beautiful,' Harding said softly.

He and Molly got out of the truck and joined a group of mechanics and customers who were staring southward where a heavy cloud of greasy black smoke was ballooning up into the sky.

'Jesus Christ!' someone said in awe. 'That looks to be the old market. I'm going down to take a look.'

The observers ran for their cars and gunned out of the gas station. Turner and Harding stayed where they were. He reached into the pickup, brought out a small pair of binoculars, handed them to Molly. She took off her sunglasses, began to focus on the courthouse area.

The moment Todhunter Clark's charges had gone off, he and his assistants immediately headed out of town. He drove the van at a sedate speed along a predetermined route to Southfield that bypassed the main roads.

Following the explosion, Grace Peddleton's soldiers deployed around the courthouse portico. Most of the spectators on Broadway, and those pouring from the courthouse, began running southward to the scene of the blast.

Carol Poague appeared in the courthouse doorway.

'Now!' Peddleton shouted to her troops.

But as the accused woman exited, it became apparent that she was not only handcuffed, but had been fitted with ankle shackles connected by a short length of chain. And instead of her customary guard of two Corinth policemen, she was surrounded by at least six cops.

At the same moment, sharpshooters rose from concealed positions on the roofs of the courthouse, civic center, and jail. They aimed rifles, shotguns, and automatic weapons at the WDC sisters below.

Someone roared through a bullhorn: 'I call upon you to – '

Afterward, it was never definitely determined who had fired the first shot. But when one gun went off, a general fusillade from the uniformed officers followed.

'Hold your fire!' the bullhorn screamed. 'Hold your fire!'

But it continued for almost a minute. Grace Peddleton and three of her soldiers were killed instantly. Two Corinth policemen were slain. The wounded lay in widening pools of blood on the courthouse steps. Some of the WDC troops made it to their cars and escaped. Most did not.

When the firing started, Molly Turner watched through binoculars for a moment, then turned a white face to Rod Harding.

'Trapped,' she said in a scratchy voice.

He took the glasses from her and looked long and hard, scanning the street and the rooftops.

'A setup,' he said harshly. 'We were suckered.'

'I've got to get down there,' Molly Turner said, and started away.

'And commit suicide?' Harding cried. 'There's not a god-damned thing you can do. It's over. We lost.'

He grabbed her arm in a tight grip. She fought him, but

couldn't counter his strength. He got her back into the truck, slid behind the wheel, and headed out of town.

She huddled back in her corner, weeping. 'Oh Jesus,' she kept repeating. 'Oh Jesus.'

He didn't speak, but drove grimly, keeping an eye on the rear-view mirror and watching the road far ahead for barricades.

'Some of them must have been killed,' Molly Turner said dully. 'Maybe a lot of them. All that firing . . .'

'That's what happens when you play with guns,' Harding said. 'Who knew about this besides Peddleton's group? Who knew the exact time and date?'

'Me, you, Ann, Clark, Yvonne Popkin, a few others.'

'Why Popkin?'

'She had to get the statements and news releases ready. Not claiming responsibility, but expressing sympathy for Poague. Put the radio on.'

'Not yet,' he said. 'Who hired Popkin originally?'

'I did. Or Ann did. I don't remember. The NWU told us we needed a press officer.'

'The NWU recommended her?'

'I guess so.'

He said no more, but switched on the radio. They didn't hear the first report until ten minutes later. Then the country music was interrupted for a 'special news break.' The announcer said the death toll now stood at eight, with three of the wounded in critical condition. He called it the 'Corinth Massacre.'

They got back to the Co-Zee Motel a little before 6:30 PM. Todhunter Clark was there, drinking straight bourbon and watching TV. He looked up as they came in.

'I'm packed,' he said. 'I think we best get out of town.'

'I do, too,' Harding said. 'But not from Detroit. They may have the airport covered. We'll drive to Toledo and fly out of there. What's the latest?'

'Ten dead,' Brother Nabisco said stonily. 'Seven of ours, three of theirs. Fourteen wounded. And another eleven of ours arrested. Grace Peddleton bought it.'

Harding poured bourbon into a plastic cup and handed it to Molly Turner. She held it in a trembling hand. He let her take one gulp, then took the cup back and finished the whiskey.

'Where's Yvonne Popkin?' he asked Clark.

'In her room. She's smashed. Trying to pack, but mostly crying.'

Harding looked at Molly Turner. 'Tod and I can handle it,' he said.

'No,' she said fiercely, 'I'll do it myself. Alone.'

Popkin was sitting on the edge of her bed, hunched over, holding her face. Stringy hair made a tent. An empty bottle of vodka was nestled into one of the pillows.

Molly Turner took two steps into the room, grabbed a fistful of that dry, lifeless hair, and jerked her head back. She saw a face wet with tears, gaunt with drink.

'Who did you tell?' Turner demanded.

'What?' Popkin said, looking up dazedly, trying to focus.

'Who did you tell?'

'I didn't – '

Molly Turner slapped her with an open palm, putting arm and shoulder into the blow. Popkin's head jerked to one side, cheek reddening.

'Who did you tell?'

'I don't – '

Slap!

'Who did you tell?'

'Why are you – '

Slap!

'Who did you tell?'

'I swear I – '

Slap!

'I'm going to keep hitting you,' Turner said coldly. 'And hitting and hitting. If you pass out on me, I'll bring you to and keep on hitting you. I'll knock your fucking head off, you stupid cunt. Now . . . who did you tell?'

329

'I didn't think she would – '

'Who?'

'Underwood,' Popkin said, sobbing. 'Connie Underwood. Molly, I needed the job. And she wanted to know what was going on. I didn't tell her everything – I swear I didn't: I drink too much. I realize I have a problem. Sometimes I forget things. I didn't see what was so wrong – she's on our side, isn't she? Some things I told her – not many – and some things I forgot. She's one of the family, isn't she? A sister.'

'Did you tell her about Corinth? The date and time?'

Yvonne Popkin raised a wet face, nodded miserably. She began to rock back and forth, making a low, keening sound.

Molly Turner clenched a hard fist and drove it into the woman's face. Something cracked. Popkin fell back onto the bed, mouth open, eyes glazed.

'You're coming with us,' Turner said, rubbing her knuckles. 'You can drink yourself to death for all I care, but you're not going anywhere without permission. Do you understand what I'm saying?'

Popkin managed a nod, holding her bleeding face in cupped palms.

'Now get yourself cleaned up,' Molly said, 'you piece of shit.'

She marched from the room.

MAY 24, 1991

'I was always a vagabond,' Todhunter Clark said, laughing, stroking little Jeff's fine, wheaten hair. 'Here, there, and everywhere. This place, all you folks, are giving me something. Like a foundation. You know? Now there's Lucille Jackson, a fine lady. She's been making noises like she wants to get hitched.'

Ann Harding, pacing back and forth in the living room,

330

holding her elbows, paused to look at him.

'Can't blame her for that,' she said.

'Oh no, Miz Ann, no blame at all.'

'How do you feel about it, Tod?'

'Well, I'm betwixt and between. Five years ago I'd have shouted and been on my way. So long, honey! But now I'm not so sure. I'm getting a little long in the tooth, you know. The beard is getting whiter.'

'Beard,' Jeff said.

'That's right, King,' Brother Nabisco said, thrusting his goatee at the boy, putting his hand on it. 'This here is a beard. You're going to have one someday – if you like. So I'm coming around to Lucille's way of thinking.'

Ann resumed her pacing. A rainy afternoon, windows fogged, a drumroll outside. And inside, a silence that clotted the air and heavied their talk. It became hushed, intimate.

'What are you and Rod up to?' she asked suddenly. 'And Molly?'

'This and that,' he said casually.

'You're all spending a lot of time in Washington.'

'Well . . . yeah. Things to do. The convention coming up and all.'

'Tod, what *is* it?'

He raised his head to look at her. 'I think you better ask Molly, Miz Ann. It's not my place to say.'

'That Corinth thing . . .' she said. 'A disaster. I was against it from the start. But Molly insisted. All those sisters killed. I can't get it out of my mind.'

'It happens. It could have been a winner, but it went the other way. Everyone saw the risk. It's like a war; you got to take your losses. Never heard of a war without losses. Ours, theirs, everyone's.'

'You were at the motel? The one where Rod and Molly stayed?'

'That's right. Rod and I, we shared a room.'

'When did you go up to Corinth?'

'On the day before. In the evening. I drove a van up with all the stuff.'

'Then you weren't at the motel the night before?'

He hung his head, shaking it slowly. 'I don't like this, Miz Ann. I don't like this third degree.'

'You're right, Tod,' she said swiftly, 'and I'm sorry. It's no concern of yours.'

He said nothing.

'I got another one of those letters,' she said with a tinny laugh. 'Rod and Molly in the Co-Zee Motel on the night of April seventeenth. The time, the room number – everything.'

'I wasn't there,' he said in a low voice. 'I don't know nothing about it.'

She sat down in an armchair facing him. Sat with crossed legs, folded arms, huddled in on herself.

'Tod,' she said, 'tell me what to do.'

'Oh no,' he said, 'I can't do that. No one can. It's your life. You got to live it.'

'Advice,' she begged. 'I'm not saying I'll do what you tell me. I just want advice.'

He shrugged. 'I'm not so great in the advice department. Last time we spoke of this, I said to let it go, maybe it'll just fall apart by itself.'

'But it hasn't, has it?'

He didn't reply.

'All right, Tod, I'll make up my own mind. I'll decide what to do. But can I count on you?'

'You know you can, Miz Ann.'

'It's for me, Tod,' she said fiercely, 'and for Jeff. Don't say I can count on you if you don't mean it.'

'I mean it, I swear.'

'No matter what?'

They stared at each other a long moment.

'Beard,' Jeff said.

'No matter what,' Todhunter Clark said in a cracked voice.

332

'I'm going to off that bitch,' Molly Turner said.

Her quiet tone and expressionless features shocked Rod Harding more than any ranting and raving. He wondered if her passion for the cause had turned to something twisted and psychotic.

'Molly,' he said, just as quietly, 'you can't do that.'

He explained, as reasonably and logically as he could, that killing Constance Underwood would accomplish nothing. The risks were tremendous. The possible dangers to Turner, her career, the WDC, were incalculable.

'You're going to be president of the combined NWU-WDC,' he told her. 'With Grace Peddleton dead, Stacy can appoint her own WDC colonel in Michigan. That means Virginia Terwilliger will get Stacy's vote on the special board. Molly, you're a shoo-in. There's no need to chill Underwood.'

'I'm going to kill her,' Turner repeated adamantly. 'The only thing you've got to decide is whether or not you're going to help me. Either way, that is one dead lady.'

Rod Harding thought about it for several minutes. Then:

'Okay,' he said finally, 'I'll help you – on three conditions. One: Ann is to know nothing about this – absolutely nothing. Two: Todhunter Clark has to be brought in to help me. I know you hate his guts, but it's going to be a tough job setting her up, and I can't do it alone. Three: You're going to have to pop her yourself. Tod and I aren't going to do the job for you.'

'Agreed,' Molly Turner said, still with that icy calm that made him wonder.

This murmured conversation took place on the flight back to Canton after the Corinth Massacre. In the following week, Harding and Clark moved to Washington, DC,

into a fleabag hotel in Chinatown, not far from Molly
Turner's apartment. They began their surveillance of Constance Underwood.

Harding explained to Brother Nabisco what they were
going to do: establish the woman's time-habit pattern. 'If
we tail her for, say, a month or so, the chances are pretty
good that we'll be able to predict where she'll be and what
she'll be doing at any time of the day or night.'

'Crazy,' Todhunter Clark said, shaking his head. 'You
cops know everything.'

They alternated eight-hour shifts, and for almost two
months they followed Constance Underwood and made
copious notes. They asked casual questions of doormen,
cabdrivers, waiters, servants. They amassed a great deal
of information about their target.

They zeroed in on her Watergate apartment, learned
about the bright red Jaguar roadster and the summer home
near Plum Point. As the weather grew warmer, she began
spending every weekend out there, usually joined by a
burly man they never did identify.

'Fuzz,' Todhunter Clark guessed.

'You're so right,' Rod Harding said, laughing. 'The guy's
got cop written all over him.'

By early June they had their time-habit chart as complete
as they were ever going to get it. They met with Molly to
go over what they had learned.

'Have you changed your mind?' Harding asked.

'No,' she said coldly.

So they worked it out. The best place to make the hit,
they decided, would be at the country house.

'Does she drive out with the guy?' Molly asked.

'Nope,' Clark said, 'never. She goes out early Saturday
morning, opens the place up. He drives out by himself,
gets there about noon. He leaves by himself on Sunday
evening. A few hours later she drives back to Washington
in her red Jag. By herself. They're careful.'

'Discreet,' Harding said. 'Very discreet people. I'd love

to know who he is, but Tod and I were too busy to tail him.'

'That's all right,' Molly Turner said. 'We've got enough. We'll take her at the summer place. What's it like?'

Harding explained. A dirt road leading through woods from the paved road. An ivy-covered chainlink fence around the property. Locked gate. Then, inside, the A-frame redwood cabin, glassed front and rear. No drapes. Sundeck and a small swimming pool, now filled. Nearest neighbors a half-mile away.

'That gate . . .' Molly asked. 'Does she lock it again after she's inside?'

'Negative,' Clark said. 'She leaves it open so her guy can get in.'

'Much traffic on the paved road?'

'Moderate on weekends,' Harding said.

'And on the dirt road?'

'Zilch,' Brother Nabisco said. 'Maybe one or two cars an hour. Not many houses back there.'

'The glass . . . ' Molly said. 'You can see right into the place?'

'Affirmative,' Harding said. 'I took a look through binoculars. But there's got to be a bathroom and probably a bedroom. What you see through the glass walls are the big living room and kitchen.'

Molly Turner pondered all that, pulling softly at her lower lip.

'The gate's unlocked?' she said. 'So I can just walk right in. Up to the front door. Is that glass, too?'

Harding nodded.

'Then I'll just knock or ring the bell.'

'You figure she'll let you in?' Todhunter Clark asked.

Molly Turner looked at him with stony eyes. 'Why not?' she said. 'We're friends, aren't we?'

On the sunny morning of June 15, when Constance Underwood set out for Plum Point in her Jaguar, she was followed by Molly Turner, Rod Harding, and Todhunter Clark in Molly's black Volkswagen Rabbit. Clark was

335

driving, but he soon lost the speeding Jag.

'That crazy lady,' he complained. 'She drives like a maniac.'

'Don't sweat it,' Harding said. 'We know where she's going.'

When they arrived at the dirt road, Clark pulled onto the verge and parked. Molly and Rod climbed out. He had a walkie-talkie in a musette bag.

'Check with you from the gate,' he said to Brother Nabisco.

'Sure, old buddy,' Clark said. 'If I get rousted by the troopers, I'll drive a ways and then come back. So if you can't raise me, don't get antsy. I'll be here when it's time to dee-part.'

He settled negligently behind the wheel of the parked VW. Molly and Rod began strolling down the dirt road, making no effort at concealment.

'It's about a five-minute walk,' he said. 'Maybe a little more.'

'No strain,' she said. 'Nice day.'

'Moll,' he said, 'you're sure you can do this?'

'I can do it.'

'Follow our plan exactly. It'll go like silk; you'll see.'

When they got to Underwood's property, the gate was unlocked and open. The Jaguar was parked inside. They stood under the trees on the far side of the road.

'Great place,' Molly said, inspecting the cabin. 'Wouldn't mind owning it myself.'

'Uh-huh,' Harding said. 'You see the pool – over to the side?'

'I see it.'

'About thirty feet from the door to the pool. Can you make it?'

'Easy.'

Harding took out his walkie-talkie. After some squawky static, he succeeded in getting through to Clark on the paved road.

'We're here,' he reported. 'All clear?'

'Fine,' Clark said. 'No problems.'

Rod turned to Molly. 'It's all yours. Just remember everything I told you.'

'I'll remember,' she said, pressing her shoulder bag tightly against her side.

'Give us a kiss,' he said, smiling.

She went up on tiptoes and kissed his mouth. He drew away and touched her face.

'Luck,' he said lightly.

She turned, crossed the road, walked through the open gate up to the house. When she got to the glass front door, she stood a moment, peering inside. She saw Constance Underwood fussing around the refrigerator. She also saw an interior door which, she guessed, led to the bedroom and bathroom.

She rang the bell, saw Underwood start and turn. She came slowly across the big room and stared at Turner through the thick glass door. Molly smiled and waggled her fingers. Constance gave her a stiff smile in return, then unlocked the door and pulled it open.

'Molly!' she said. 'Whatever are you doing here?'

'I was in the neighborhood, and thought I'd stop by for a minute and say hello. May I come in?'

'Well . . .' Underwood said reluctantly, 'just for a minute. I'm expecting company soon, and I have a million things to do.'

Molly entered. Underwood closed the door. When she turned, her guest was facing her, a revolver in her hand. Connie looked at the gun, then raised her gaze slowly to meet Turner's eyes.

'What . . . ?' she said, her voice steady. 'What on earth is going on? Molly, what *is* this?'

'You fucker,' Molly Turner said. 'You killed my sisters.'

'What in God's name are you talking about? Now put that gun away and let's discuss this.'

'You're dead,' Turner said. 'I want you to know that

337

now. When I leave here, you'll be gone.'

She moved back two paces and stood solidly, feet apart, the revolver unwavering in her fist, muzzle pointed at Underwood's chest.

'Molly, please tell me what this is all about. Surely I have the right to – '

'The only right you have is to die. I know about Yvonne Popkin and you telling the cops about Corinth.'

'Molly, I swear I – '

'Seven sisters dead,' Turner said. 'And the wounded and those in jail. All because of you.'

Underwood didn't try to explain or to plead. 'You're a maniac,' she said in a raspy voice. 'An utter, complete maniac.'

'That's right. That's me: a maniac. And the only thing that'll cure me is spitting on your corpse. Now you move very slowly toward that door over there. I'll be behind you. Try anything and I'll blow your fucking head off right here.'

In the bedroom, shielded from view from the road, Molly stepped up close behind Underwood and slammed the revolver against the side of her head with all her strength. Constance gave one small groan and collapsed.

Molly put the gun back into her shoulder bag. She bent over the unconscious woman, pulled the long hair apart to see if the scalp was split. She saw no blood. Then, pulling, tugging, hauling, she undressed Underwood completely. She folded the clothes neatly and laid them on the bed.

She went back into the living room to open the front door. Then back to the bedroom to turn Constance Underwood onto her back, grasp the naked body under the armpits, and drag her out of the bedroom, across the living room, out the door, down to the filled pool. Into the warm, bland sunshine.

On the edge of the pool, at the deep end, Molly Turner released the body, straightened up, and took a deep breath. She stretched, flexing the muscles of her shoulders and arms. She didn't look across the road where Rod Harding stood and watched.

Then Turner went down on her hands and knees, and rolled Constance Underwood into the pool, close to the short diving board. Leaning over, she clutched Connie's long black hair, yanked her head under the water and held it there. Bubbles came popping up.

She raised the head, looked at the slack face. Then she pushed Underwood beneath the water again for another two or three minutes. She released the body. It floated free, facedown, hair splaying out like a spider's web.

Molly Turner stood and waved to Rod. He spoke into his walkie-talkie, then came slowly across the road, through the gate, to the pool. He glanced briefly at the naked corpse, bobbing gently.

'You okay?' he asked.

She nodded.

'Any problems?'

'No.'

'Where did you take her?'

'In the bedroom.'

'Blood?'

'I didn't see any,' Turner said.

'What did you touch?'

'Only the knob on the inside of the front door.'

'Wait here,' he said.

He went into the house, into the bedroom. Constance Underwood's clothing was neatly folded on the bed. No blood on the rug, no signs of a struggle. He went out through the living room, using his handkerchief to wipe clean the inner brass knob of the front door. He left the door slightly a jar, then rejoined Molly at the pool. He looked again at the naked corpse, now slowly sinking.

'Accidental death by drowning,' he said with a bleak smile. 'She hit her head on the diving board or the bottom of the pool. It'll work. Now let's get out of here.'

They walked casually down the dirt road. Todhunter Clark was standing by the Volkswagen Rabbit, smoking a small cigar.

'Hey there,' he said. 'Everything copasetic?'

'Just right,' Rod Harding said.

They were five minutes on the road back to Washington when they passed a car driven by James Gargan going the other way. But they didn't know that, and neither did Gargan.

In Molly Turner's apartment, they had a beer and stared at each other.

'Well, you did it,' Harding said to Molly. 'Satisfied?'

'I wish I could kill her again,' she said.

Any historian attempting to write an account of the Women's Defense Corps – however brief and incomplete – cannot neglect a phenomenon that accompanied the movement, although it had limited sociological significance.

I refer to a number of all-male groups and organizations, most of them short-lived, formed in opposition to the stated aims and purposes of the WDC. These included:

The Men's Defense Corps
The Macho League of America
The All-Man Society
Men for America
Males Against Militancy (MAM)

These and similar groups, of extremely small membership, had as their avowed goal the continued 'superiority' of American men. Several attempted organization of armed paramilitary forces similar to the WDC sisters, but there is no evidence that any of these masculine associations took part in militant actions in direct opposition to the WDC.

One organization engendered by the growth and success of the Women's Defense Corps was the Society of Intersexual Relations. This was a legitimate and scholarly association of sociologists, psychologists, and sexologists formed to estimate the WDC's influence on American society.

Two Society members have written and published books of more than passing interest on the Women's Defense Corps. They are: The WDC: Role-Reversal in American Men and Women, *by J. Cynthia Alcott (Burnett Publishing Co., 349 pp., 15.95) and* The WDC: A Political Revolution, *by Dr Simon Hertz (Foley & Smith, Inc., 426 pp., 18.95).*

Both books are recommended to serious readers.

JULY 10-13, 1991

The annual convention of the National Women's Union was held in the Americana Hotel in New York City, where the organization had been born in 1982. The yearly meeting, usually festive and sometimes rambunctious, opened on a subdued note because of Constance Underwood's recent death by drowning.

In her place, Ann Harding delivered the keynote address. If Ann lacked Molly's fiery rhetoric, she had a sincere, quietly impassioned manner on the podium. Her audience listened attentively in silence, but gave her a standing ovation when she had concluded.

Without mentioning the strains and conflicts between the NWU and the WDC, Ann pleaded for a true sisterhood of all women. Trivial matters of procedure and tactics, she said, should not be allowed to impede progress toward the goal of genuine equality.

The convention then began a program of debating and voting on a series of resolutions, most of which were devoted to economic aims – to bringing women's income into parity with that of men.

Meanwhile, a great deal of behind-the-scenes politicking was going on. Virginia Terwilliger worked mightily to keep

her adherents on the special board in line. She thought she
had a majority of votes recommending a complete NWU
– WDC merger, but she was leaving nothing to chance.

She delivered the same entreaty to all the members of
the board, supporters and opponents alike:

'Listen,' she'd say. 'The WDC is only doing what the
NWU was set up to do in 1982. Look over our original
Declaration of Liberation. You'll see that the WDC is
following that blueprint – nothing more, nothing less. Sure,
the NWU could have done it by ourselves, but somewhere
along the line we got too old, too tired, too lazy. Then along
came Molly Turner. She has revitalized this organization,
made it search its soul and return to the reasons why it
was founded. I tell you that we need this woman – and her
sister, Ann. Without them we're dead!'

Her impassioned appeal did the trick, even convincing
the older conservatives who had expressed dismay at the
violence of the WDC's vigilante justice.

On Friday night, July 12, following the convention's
evening session, the special board met in a locked room.
At that time, a complete merger of the NWU and WDC
was approved by two votes. It was recommended that the
combined organization be called the Women's Defense
Corps.

Finally, it was agreed that the special board's recommendation be presented to the full convention as a unanimous
decision.

'Bingo!' Virginia Terwilliger shouted exultantly.

She stage-managed the final session of the convention
on Saturday evening, July 13, with great skill and political
acumen. Opening ceremonies included ballad singers from
Augusta, Georgia, a two-minute TV film clip of the Corinth Massacre, showing the bodies of WDC sisters lying
dead in their blood, and a moving prayer for 'our sorrowing
sisters everywhere.'

Then the chairwoman of the special board took the
microphone to announce the unanimous recommendation

of the board for 'complete and total merger.' The convention exploded with cheers, shouts, applause, and impromptu demonstrations.

Molly Turner was then nominated for the presidency of the new Women's Defense Corps. The reaction of the delegates was so wildly enthusiastic that it became evident that no other candidates had a chance. Molly was elected by acclamation, and ten minutes later took her place at the rostrum and faced a cheering audience.

Nothing in her appearance suggested triumph or even satisfaction. She was wearing a plain shirtwaist dress that came perilously close to being dowdy. She was unsmiling, and her gaunt face was free of makeup. She made no effort to quell the crowd's excitement, but stood silently until, finally, the noise died down. Then she leaned forward to speak into the microphone.

'I want you all to stand,' she said quietly. 'Everyone on your feet. And I want you to take the hands of your sisters to your right and left.'

She waited then, watching sternly as the delegates rose and joined hands.

'Please,' Molly Turner said, 'remain standing while I tell you what is in my heart.

'You have just seen a film of our dead sisters in Corinth. Many of them I knew personally. But I swear to you that *all* of them died bravely, willingly, and even gladly for the sake of what we all believe. I swear to you that their sacrifice shall never be forgotten, and their brutal murders shall not diminish our resolve.

'In fact, their deaths can only strengthen our determination to go forward with renewed vigor. We have come a long way; we have a longer way to go. Now we are all linked: one organization, one sisterhood, one soul. I swear to you and I swear to the world that we will go on fighting as long as one sister is alive to carry on the battle.

'And it is a battle. No, it is a war! Oh yes, there will be casualties; every war has casualties. But they will never

343

deter us from our righteous cause. If I must die in this war, I swear to you I will die happily for the sake of the emancipation of women everywhere.

'Hold the hands of your sisters tightly! Swear with me that not even the threat of death will dismay you or make you falter on the road we have chosen. We are all sisters. Remember that! We shall go forward until we triumph. Nothing can stop us. Nothing! And if sacrifice is demanded, we shall die with the knowledge that our cause can never die.

'Sisters! I swear to you here and now that I pledge every ounce of my strength and my blood to our new sisterhood. I swear to you that I shall never stop fighting. Never! And I swear that I love you all, for you are in me and I am in you. Will you take the vow of sisterhood with me? Now? Will you swear, as I have, to sacrifice all you hold dear for the sake of what we believe? If you are willing, raise your joined hands and tell me that you so swear.'

It was a very emotional moment, and even later, shown on television, the scene had the power to move viewers – some to tears. For all over the convention floor, standing women raised their linked hands and cried, 'I swear, I swear!'

The TV cameras caught shots of weeping women, of women surrendering to what was almost a religious ecstasy, of sisters angry and determined, screaming their vows with hysterical fervor.

Molly Turner descended from the podium and began to embrace delegates in the front rows. The crowd surged forward and ushers fought to keep order. All over the hall sisters embraced with tears and kisses.

On the dais Virginia Terwilliger sat stolidly, observing this flood of sentiment without expression. Friends came to pat her shoulder and congratulate her on her victory, but she shrugged them off and watched the adulation of Molly Turner.

There was an excessive tone to all this that disturbed

344

her. It smacked too much of revivalist meetings, political frenzy, and demented crowds shouting, 'Sieg heil!' A supremely rational woman herself, she found this emotional outpouring vaguely distasteful.

And, pondering its implications, it frightened her.

AUGUST 26, 1991

Senator Lemuel K. Dundee had never fully anticipated the complexities, frustrations, and pressures of a presidential campaign.

Despite the administrative efforts of Thomas Kealy and other aides, there were a great number of important decisions only Dundee could make, and it seemed there just weren't enough hours in the day to get the job done.

It was a frenetic hodgepodge of tugs, hauls, pushes, and shoves. Senator Dundee felt himself split and splintered, and if he was hitting the bottle more than he ever had, it was understandable; sometimes a man had to relax – just take off his shoes, loosen his tie, put his feet up, and try to figure out where he was going next.

The Corinth Massacre had been a big plus – a lot of crazy ladies trying to free a woman on trial for murder. The hell with the moral and philosophical issues posed by Carol Poague, said the senator; what it came down to was a violent effort to subvert justice. Insurrection was not too strong a word for it. Rebellion was another.

Senator Dundee used both words in speeches hurriedly prepared by his staff of writers. He called the Corinth Massacre 'a blot on American history,' and audiences listened in respectful silence when he told them that the law – courts, judges, juries, legislatures – was the only barrier we had against brute force and jungle justice.

His strong condemnation of the WDC increased his ratings in the polls by almost 8 points. But it proved to be a brief improvement.

After the death of Constance Underwood, Tom Kealy reported there would be no more inside tips on WDC activities. Even worse, the merger of the NWU and WDC, with Molly Turner as president, presented Dundee with a greatly strengthened enemy. His ratings in the polls began a downward slide.

'Not amongst men,' Kealy assured him. 'You're holding with men. But the women are deserting you.'

'Son of a bitch!' Dundee said bitterly. 'Are they all going to start carrying guns and shooting up courthouses? Ruth, do you believe those polls?'

'I never have put too much faith in them, Senator,' she said promptly. 'But in this case, I don't think you should ignore the numbers. Especially after that emotional "I swear" speech Molly Turner gave at the convention; they're still talking about that. Oh, the gender gap is there – no doubt about it. And it's growing. A lot of women saw those dead WDC sisters on television, and they felt horror and sympathy. The only way they can express their outrage is by opposing you; you're the most visible symbol of the anti – WDC feeling in the country. You're getting a reputation as a woman-hater. I know it's untrue and unfair, but there it is, and you've got to face it.'

'But goddamn it, I *love* women!' he protested. 'I'm just out to protect our traditional American values of justice and the rule of law. Ahh, screw it! Ruth, have you and Hayden done anything about picking those key areas for in-depth analysis?'

'We've got them selected, sir. Now we have to figure out a reasonable sample for each locality. Then Lyle will write a computer program for weighting of the interview results. It's going to take time.'

'So all we have at the moment are the polls?'

'That's correct, Senator.'

Dundee was silent, looking down and twiddling his thumbs. Finally he spoke to all his assembled campaign aides.

346

'I gather,' he said, sighing, 'you all feel I should moderate my attacks on the WDC?'

Heads nodded.

'Discretion is the better part of valor,' someone said.

'Thank you very much,' the senator said with heavy irony. 'And a turd in the hand is worth two in the bush. Well, I'll think about it. Thank you all for your help. I'll let you know in a day or two which way we're going to jump.'

The moment his office was empty, he called H. Fairchild Curtiss on his outside line. He made an appointment to meet with the banker on the morning of August 26, a Monday. At the Imperial Club.

On the flight up to New York – with a new bodyguard hired after Jake Spencer disappeared – Dundee came to the conclusion that Curtiss needed him as much as Dundee needed the banker and his heavy-money pals.

Who else were the well-heeled going to back? The other declared candidates in Dundee's party were a bunch of putzes. One Washington columnist had called them the Seven Dwarfs: Dopey, Dopey, Dopey, Dopey, Dopey, Dopey, and Dopey. And the incumbent President they were running against was a disaster: a rummy who fucked secretaries in the White House elevator – everyone knew that.

So H. Fairchild Curtiss and his buddies had no one to turn to but Lemuel K. Dundee. The realization that he was in the catbird seat made the senator feel a lot better, and on the limousine ride in from LaGuardia he treated himself to a wee bit of the old nasty, with soda, reflecting that it was a few minutes after noon, and that made it all right.

He met with Curtiss in that same somber chamber that reminded Dundee of a funeral parlor. And the banker had all the genuine warmth, charm, and charisma of a mortician.

This time, the senator resolved, he wasn't going to kiss

ass. So the moment the two men had exchanged amenities and took facing armchairs, Dundee rose to his feet again and spoke while standing. That put him on a higher, dominant level. Politicians learned tricks like that.

He laid it on the line to Curtiss. Generally, he said, his campaign was going well. His staff was organized and efficient. He had won the two straw polls he had entered. His indignant reaction to the Corinth Massacre had increased his national exposure. He had established functioning campaign organizations in every state.

'The only fly in the ointment,' he said, fixing the banker with an honest, sincere stare, 'is these goddamned polls.'

He explained that the polls showed he was leading all the competitors in his own party and ahead of the incumbent President who had already announced his intention of running again. That is, Dundee was top runner in the *totals* of those polled, but he was sadly deficient when it came to a female-male breakdown.

'I don't see the problem,' Curtiss said fretfully. 'If you have a higher percentage, why should you care whether your votes come from men or women?'

Dundee explained that in politics it was not wise to take anything for granted. The defection of women, if allowed to continue, might well wipe out his total advantage.

'There's a definite gender gap,' he said. 'I can't deny it. The ladies think I'm a woman-hater. That's not a matter of fact, but a matter of perception – which is more important than reality. My opposition to Molly Turner and the WDC has run up a big score for me with male voters. But it has also alienated a hell of a lot of gals in this country. If they keep on deserting me in droves, I could be in deep trouble.'

'So?' the banker asked. 'What do you suggest?'

'Sir,' the senator said, 'there's more than one way to skin a cat, and you can catch more flies with honey than you can with vinegar. My staff urgently recommends – and I concur – that I moderate my attacks on the WDC. I don't mean to cut them out completely, but just soften the tone.'

'I don't like that,' Curtiss said stiffly.

'It will have three advantages,' Dundee went on, ignoring the objection. 'One: It will win back or at least mollify some of those female voters who see me as a woman-hater. Two: It will stop all this bullshit that's been written about me as a one-issue candidate. And three: It will give me more time to speechify about the economy, foreign affairs, the environment, and so forth. To present myself as a thoughtful, reasoning candidate capable of handling *all* the problems of the presidency – not just this foo-faraw that Molly Turner has stirred up.'

Curtiss looked at him coldly. '*I* think you underestimate the potential for lasting damage that this woman represents. To my way of thinking, she is an enemy of everything this nation stands for. Did you hear her speech at the convention? That was nothing more or less than a declaration of war. I tell you that Molly Turner and the WDC threaten the very foundation of American society. And incidentally, my wife feels the same way I do. The only reason my associates and I agreed to back your candidacy was that you were willing to oppose this woman and her morally reprehensible program. Now you are suggesting that you soften your opposition – or perhaps even drop the issue entirely, for all I know. Is that your intention?'

'Curtiss,' Senator Dundee said harshly, 'you and your old buddies have bet a lot of money on me. Hard cash. Are you willing to see it all go down the drain just for the sake of your own prejudices? Because that's exactly what's going to happen if I keep knifing the WDC. I'm going to get so far out on a limb that I'll never get back. The women will saw it off, thumbing their noses at me, you, and your friends. If you want to lose and boast, "Well, we stuck to our principles," that's up to you. But if you want me to have a chance of winning, you'll have to let me do it my way.'

The banker was silent.

'You and your guys,' Dundee went on, getting angry now, 'you sit in your stainless steel executive suites, and you don't really – with all due respect – know what the fuck is going on in this country. I tell you that if I keep up my anti – WDC campaign, I'm going to lose to some shmuck who doesn't owe you a thing. Would you like that? Listen, the first duty of every politician is to get elected – to whatever. He promises the moon to get into office. Once he's in, he can do anything he goddamn well pleases – as long as he doesn't get caught.'

'Are you suggesting,' Curtiss said, 'that you trim your sails to the wind and then, once elected, you'll put Molly Turner and the WDC behind bars, where they belong?'

'That's exactly what I'm suggesting,' Lemuel Dundee said, thinking this guy wasn't so smart after all; he bought campaign promises like every other dummy. 'We've got to get our priorities straight. First: get me elected. Second: put the blocks to Molly Turner and the WDC'

H. Fairchild Curtiss sighed. 'Senator, you are a vulgar opportunist. Whatever happened to men of wit, sophistication, and refinement in American politics?'

'They never got elected,' Dundee said, 'because they didn't represent the voters.'

'I'm afraid you're right,' the banker said, rubbing his forehead tiredly. 'Very well, do it your way. Do what you must to get elected. In that happy event, I should warn you, my associates and I intend to demand payment.'

'Of course,' the senator said. 'What else?'

SEPTEMBER 6, 1991

The following letter, bearing the above date, was written by Virginia Terwilliger in Baltimore, Maryland, to Ann Harding in Canton, West Virginia. It is published here with the express permission of both women.

350

Dearest Ann,

I had planned to make a special trip to Canton to have a nice long talk with you about several things that have been on my mind since the convention. But then, two weeks ago, I did something exceedingly stupid – I slipped getting into the bathtub, came down hard on my tailbone, and broke my left leg. It took two strong paramedics and my poor hubby to get me out of the tub!

So now I'm hobbling around on crutches, loaded down with an enormous cast. Naturally my trip to Canton will have to wait awhile, but the things that concern me can't wait – so I decided to write and tell you how I feel.

First of all, Ann, I hope you, your handsome husband, and darling Jeff are in good health and enjoying this glorious weather we've been having. Under separate cover, I am sending Jeff a picture book about dinosaurs (nonsexist!). All kids love dinosaurs – at least mine did.

Now to get down to business. Ann, I hope you will treat the contents of this letter as strictly confidential. I know you are a discreet woman, and you have never betrayed my trust in the past – which gives me the courage to write you so openly and honestly now.

To start with, I was shocked by the way Molly looked at the convention. She is so thin, so drawn. She never was a fleshy woman, of course, but now she's just skin and bones. She's not ill, is she?

And there is now an almost feverish intensity about her that disturbs me. I know how passionately she believes in our cause, but her zeal seems to have developed hysterical overtones. We are all enthusiastic about the WDC and its future, but surely cool heads are as important as warm hearts.

I know Molly's 'I swear' speech created a sensation at the convention and later in the media. I wish I could join in the general approval – but I cannot. That speech had a frenzied tone that dismayed me. Yes, we want our sisters to be ardent in their beliefs. But we also want

351

them to be *thinking* women who use their brains to arrive at conclusions. I felt that Molly's performance came dangerously close to demagoguery.

Since the convention, I have learned that Molly has recruited a private staff at WDC headquarters in Washington. The other employees, holdovers from Constance Underwood's NWU staff, call the newcomers 'Molly's Mafia.' Did you know that?

There are four or five of these young firebrands close to Molly, and apparently they are very tough ladies indeed. Or at least they dress tough. Guns in their shoulder bags. Cartridge belts. Combat boots. One wears camouflage jeans. All they need are hand grenades hanging from their belts to look like Central American terrorists.

Now Ann, you know that is not the image we want the WDC to project. I worked hard to make Molly president of a united organization. We succeeded. Now I am having, if not second thoughts, then some vague misgivings that the new WDC may be getting off on the wrong foot. And you know me – I speak my mind, no matter what. Which is why I am writing you this letter.

Darling, I am not trying to put Molly down or deny the enormous contribution she has made to our movement. She never was disciplined; we all knew it. But now Molly is president of the largest women's organization in the country. I was hoping her new position would calm her down a bit. You know – give her a little more dignity, turn her into the serious executive.

But it hasn't worked out that way. I have learned that since Corinth, Molly has insisted on leading every large-scale combat action herself. I don't mean she insists on command; she just wants to *be* there. She lets local officers direct the sisters, but there's our Molly – right up front with her private gang.

Ann, I have read a great deal of political history. I know that to succeed, revolutions need men and women just like Molly – idealists who'll charge loaded cannon because they feel so deeply, they're so committed. But then, when the revolution is won, those same hotheads don't know what to do with the victory. They can't plan and organize a new society, they can't administer, they can't manage.

I'm not saying our revolution is won. Far from it! But different times require different tactics, even though the strategic aims remain the same. I'm suggesting that Molly has made her point. *Our* point. Perhaps it's time to soften our rhetoric, find other, less violent methods of achieving our goals.

I'm telling you how I feel in hopes that it may start you thinking about new ways to advance our cause that will never again result in TV films of WDC sisters lying dead in the street.

Ann, as soon as I can throw away these damned crutches, I'm going down to DC and tell Molly what I've written here. I know exactly what her reaction will be: she'll tell me to get lost – if she phrases it that politely!

Meanwhile, dear, we have a huge organization to run. With the enthusiastic concurrence of the Executive Board, I would like you to become, in effect, the Chief Executive Officer of the WDC. Molly is obviously incapable or unwilling to give the job the time and attention it demands. Molly would remain as president, but the day-to-day management of the WDC would be your responsibility. There would be a generous raise in your salary, of course.

It will mean your moving to Washington, DC, I fear. Before you say no, please give this request some very heavy thought. Ann, I know your capabilities – as do all the members of the Executive Board. You are a brainy, steady, sensible lady, and exactly the woman we want to build the WDC into a political force to be respected and reckoned with.

One final note that I hesitate to mention but feel I should before you hear it from some less sympathetic source. There are very ugly rumors afloat concerning Molly and your husband, Rod. Naturally, I don't believe them for a moment, but wanted you to know so that you will be better prepared to counter such vicious gossip in the event it becomes public.

Darling, you know how many enemies the WDC has. They would like nothing better than to discredit our cause by publication of such filthy slander. Unfortunately, we all live in glass houses, and our private lives are really not private at all – but reflections on the WDC. And the good of the WDC must come before everything else.

Ann, I will phone you in a week or two. Please think carefully about becoming our CEO and moving to Washington. One big advantage is that it will bring us closer together! With much love, and best wishes for you and yours – and be careful getting into the bathtub!

Affectionately,
Ginny

SEPTEMBER 30, 1991

Essentially, James Gargan was a cop – and a good one. He believed in the two basic principles of police work: anyone is capable of anything, and things are rarely what they seem.

On June 15, when he had found Constance Underwood's body in her swimming pool, he had known almost at once that it was murder – and an amateurish job at that. It didn't take him long to find the heel furrows in the carpet and grass where she had been dragged to the pool. Inspection revealed the brass knob of the front door had been wiped clean.

The convincer was that pile of clothing neatly folded on

354

the bed. Connie wouldn't do that; she stepped out of her clothes and left them on the floor. Or flung them here, there, everywhere. She was used to having a maid pick up after her. Never in a million years would she strip for skinny-dipping and arrange her discarded clothing in such a precise stack.

So James Gargan got into his car and drove home, leaving it to the local cops to call it an accidental drowning. He figured the WDC had uncovered Underwood's snitch and had taken revenge for the Corinth Massacre. He reckoned Rod Harding and Todhunter Clark had done the actual killing.

He never considered that Molly Turner might have done it. It was, perhaps, a typically male reaction – and very uncoplike. But then he still did not appreciate the nature of the woman.

His first problem was to replace Underwood's informer – whoever she may have been – in the upper echelons of the WDC. Gargan could try to infiltrate a newcomer, but it might take months before his mole was in a position to deliver useful intelligence.

A faster method, Gargan decided, was to select someone already close to Molly and turn her. A secretary maybe, or an aide, a confidante. Perhaps someone who handled communications and correspondence.

By late August 1991, he had an informer in place. She was a rough young bimbo named Clarice Dale, one of 'Molly's Mafia.' She had a black lover who dealt coke, and it was easy for Gargan to set up a frame. Clarice Dale turned to keep her stud out of the slammer. It was that simple.

When Gargan heard Molly Turner's 'I swear' speech on television and watched the emotional reaction of the convention delegates, he knew Senator Dundee was going to need all the help he could get. But before Gargan committed more of the Department's time and energies, he thought he better make certain he had the senator's executive assistant in his hip pocket.

So he called Thomas J. Kealy and suggested a meeting. Kealy didn't sound too enthusiastic, but finally invited Gargan for a drink at his Georgetown apartment. They met at 9:30 PM, on the evening of September 30.

Kealy was sipping white wine. The only hard stuff he had in the house was bourbon, a brand Gargan had never heard of before. But he accepted a shot, water on the side, just to be polite. It turned out to be dreadful stuff with a fusel oil flavor and smell.

The two men sat in facing armchairs, and Gargan could see that Kealy was trying hard not to appear nervous. But he crossed and recrossed his knees three times in as many minutes, and held his wineglass in both hands to conceal a tremor.

'Say,' Kealy said. 'That was a terrible thing about Constance Underwood, wasn't it?'

'A tragedy,' Gargan said somberly.

'I happen to know she was a good swimmer, but the papers said she had a big lump on her head. The police think she hit her skull on the diving board or the bottom of the pool.'

'Yes, I read that.'

'She was a lovely woman,' Kealy said sorrowfully. 'I really miss her.'

Gargan nodded.

'Anyway,' Kealy continued, 'with her gone, I guess we won't be getting any more inside tips from the WDC. The senator wasn't too happy about that. There's no way you could get someone inside the WDC, is there?'

'Oh no,' James Gargan said quickly, 'I don't think we'd even want to try. Too risky – after all the scandals of the J. Edgar era.'

'I guess so,' Kealy said dolefully. 'Still, the WDC represents a threat to law and order – don't you agree?'

'Possibly. But we can't make preemptive arrests, you know. Kealy, is it my imagination or has the senator

356

softened his attacks on the WDC in the last month or so?'

'Well . . .' the aide said, twisting uncomfortably in his chair, 'I don't think he's changed his mind about the WDC. It's just that he wants to concentrate on other areas – the economy, foreign affairs, and so forth.'

'Oh – *that's* what it is . . . I've been reading so much about the gender gap in his polls, I thought he might be having second thoughts about dumping on the WDC.'

Kealy lurched to his feet. 'I'm going to have another wine. Can I freshen your drink?'

'No, thanks. I'll stick with this one.'

'By the way,' Kealy said, coming back with a filled glass, 'I don't think I ever thanked you for getting Jake Spencer off my back. I really appreciate it.'

'Glad to be of help.'

'Whatever happened to him?'

'He relocated,' Gargan said.

'There wasn't another guy involved, was there?' Kealy asked in a low voice, looking into his wine. 'It was Jake pulling the blackmail on his own, by himself.'

'That's right. It was all Jake.'

'I should have known he was capable of something like that.' He looked up suddenly at Gargan. 'But he really did have Billy McCrea's notebook?'

The other man nodded.

'Where is it now – the notebook?'

'I have it,' Gargan said quietly.

Kealy gulped down his wine, ran to fill his glass again. Gargan waited patiently until Kealy was back in his chair again, knees crossed, dangling leg jerking up and down. Then Gargan leaned forward, forearms on thighs, and spoke earnestly.

'Mr Kealy,' he said, 'just between you and me, the only interest the Department has in this matter is to see Senator Dundee elected President of the United States. This personal affair of yours is of no interest to us whatsoever except as it affects the senator's chances of getting elected.

357

I assure you that you can depend on our complete discretion.'

'But the notebook . . . ?'

'In our Top Secret file. Very few people have access. Only the most trustworthy.'

'I still don't see why you didn't destroy it.'

'Mr Kealy,' Gargan said virtuously, 'it's illegal to destroy records that may become part of a criminal investigation.'

The two men stared at each other.

'I guarantee that you have nothing to fear,' Gargan continued. 'The notebook will remain buried. All we ask in return is a little cooperation.'

'What kind of cooperation?' Kealy asked suspiciously.

'You're as close to the senator as anyone on his staff. You know who he sees and what he's thinking. You're smart enough to identify possible trouble areas – like his alkie wife. And if the senator is elected – as we all devoutly hope – I'm certain he'll reward your years of loyal service with a responsible job on his White House staff. You deserve it. Now here's what we'd like you to do . . .'

James Gargan spelled it out in detail. He would be Thomas J. Kealy's sole contact with the Department. Kealy would report once a week, or more often in case of an emergency.

'Verbally,' Gargan warned. 'You and me, face-to-face. Nothing in writing, nothing on the phone. This apartment is as good a place to meet as any.'

What was expected from the senator's aide was simply information: people Dundee met, talked to, corresponded with. His schedule. Names of staff personnel. Their histories, personal habits. Any overseas contacts the senator might have. His plans for the future. Whose opinions he sought on domestic issues and foreign affairs.

'Just information,' Gargan said sincerely, still leaning forward. 'Just facts. We're not asking you to do anything illegal. Certainly nothing you feel may jeopardize the senator's career. Or President Dundee's chances for a successful administration. We simply want to know what's going on. We're behind Dundee – one hundred percent. And it's possible that what you report will enable us to prevent him from making horrible mistakes – like putting his trust in people we know from our files are strictly bad news. Mr Kealy, this is the greatest favor you could do for the senator. You're protecting him . . .'

He went on and on in the same vein, and before he left he had Senator Dundee's executive assistant signed, sealed, and delivered.

The next day he played the tapes recorded by the tap in Kealy's apartment. His superiors listened intently, smiled, patted Gargan's shoulder, and assured him that he had done a splendid job.

OCTOBER 16, 1991

When Laura Templeton, former president of the National Women's Union, died in July 1990, it was revealed that she had bequeathed half of her estate to the Women's Defense Corps. The bequest included Templeton's home in Spring Valley – by coincidence, not more than a half-mile from the residence of Senator Lemuel K. Dundee.

Following the election of Molly Turner as president of the new WDC, she was offered the use of the Templeton home as her private domicile in Washington. But after an inspection, she turned it down.

'Too much flowered chintz,' she said. 'I wouldn't be comfortable. I'll stay in Chinatown.'

Then, after a week's consideration, Ann Harding decided to accept the offer of the Executive Board, and become Chief Executive Officer of the WDC, and transfer to Washington. She was offered the use of the Templeton home and, with Molly's approval, agreed to move in.

Ann's decision was based on several factors. She recognized the truth of what Virginia Terwilliger had written in her long letter: the WDC needed a strong managerial hand at the helm while Molly and her Mafia were gallivanting around the country.

And by being in nominal command of WDC headquarters, Ann would have a better opportunity to forestall or temper Molly's more outlandish plans.

'Also,' she remarked offhandedly to Todhunter Clark, 'Molly is living in Washington, and Rod seems to be spending a lot of time there. Maybe it will help some if Jeff and I are there in our own home.'

'Can't hurt,' he replied stolidly.

The Hardings' Canton home was rented to the sister who would be in charge of the Canton WDC operations, and Ann prepared for the move to Spring Valley. She packed clothing, personal belongings, confidential files, Jeff's toys, and Rod's gun collection. And the thick sheaf of anonymous letters that Ann had saved and kept locked in a portable strongbox.

Rod rented a truck, and Brother Nabisco volunteered to help with the packing and unpacking. It was agreed that he would continue to reside in Canton, keeping an eye on the safe house and serving as a twice-a-week courier, carrying documents between the Canton data-processing center and WDC headquarters in Washington.

The only hitch in their travel plans was caused by Jefferson Turner Harding. Rod and Todhunter Clark had intended to drive the rented truck, with Ann and Jeff following in the Harding family car. But Jeff, after seeing the bright red truck, insisted on riding in the cab.

So it was decided that Clark would drive the truck with Jeff alongside him, armed with his toy six-shooters. Rod and Ann would follow in the Buick Regal.

It was a brisk, snappy morning, air sharp and sky polished. The roads were dry and traffic mercifully light. They made good time, even with several stops for Jeff, whose appetite for Big Macs and french fries seemed insatiable.

Ann Harding wanted to drive the first half, and Rod made no objection. He lounged in the passenger seat, smoking a pipe, with his window down a few inches to let the smoke escape.

'Rod,' his wife said, 'do you think we're doing the right thing?'

'Whatever you want, hon,' he said placably. 'It's a nice house, nice neighborhood, and the money's good. Can't beat that.'

'And we'll be able to see more of each other,' she said, staring down the highway.

'That's right,' he said equably.

His calm angered her.

'Did I show you a long letter I got from Virginia Terwilliger? About a month ago?'

'Why no, hon. I don't recall seeing anything like that.'

'She's worried about Molly. Says she's been acting crazy. Ginny is afraid about what her wildness might do to the WDC.'

He looked out at the landscape flashing by. 'There wouldn't *be* any WDC if it wasn't for Molly.'

'Ginny admits that. But she says Molly has made her revolution; now maybe it's time to start trying other methods. No more guns. No more violence.'

'Don't try telling Molly that.'

'I didn't, but Ginny did. She got the reaction she expected: Molly told her to stuff it. She's going along just the way she always has, and if the Executive Board doesn't like it, she'll pull out and start her own army.'

'Yeah, that sounds like Molly. She's got a mind of her own – as you well know.'

'Rod, how do you feel about it? I know how much Molly has accomplished, but after the Corinth Massacre, I've started thinking there has to be a better way of getting things done.'

He propped his cold pipe on the dashboard. 'Honey, I hate to get involved in these philosophical debates. You

361

and Molly started the WDC. You *own* the goddamned thing and can do anything you like with it. Me, I'm just a hired hand. I take my orders from you and Moll.'

Short silence.

'Since when have you been calling her "Moll"?' she asked stiffly.

He turned his head to look at her. She was beautiful, even with set face and pressed lips. A lovely, full-bodied, striking woman. Long chestnut hair falling in a wild tangle to her shoulders. She stirred him, and he didn't want to let her go.

'Ann,' he said quietly, 'I've been calling your sister "Moll" for some time now. She doesn't seem to object. Do *you* object?'

'Call her what you like,' she said sharply. 'Makes no never-mind to me.'

They drove on without speaking, keeping the red truck in view. Rod reclaimed his pipe, knocked the dottle into the ashtray, began to refill it from an oilskin pouch.

'You agree with Terwilliger?' he asked her finally. 'You think what Molly's doing is bad for the WDC?'

'You know these young hotshots she's been traveling with? The ones who dress like terrorists?'

'Yeah,' he said, grinning, 'I've seen them. Molly's Mafia – that's what they're called. They're just acting out parts, hon. I can't see where they're doing so much harm.'

'They're not exactly the public image the WDC wants to project.'

'"Image,"' he repeated. '"Project." You're beginning to talk like a real politician.'

'Because the WDC *is* politics,' she said hotly. 'I know you think politicians are a bunch of clowns, but I'm going to have to work with them and talk their language if I expect to get anything done. And to save Molly's ass if she gets us into another Corinth Massacre. Can't you calm her down? She'll listen to you, won't she?'

'About as much as she'll listen to you or anyone else.'

362

'Oh?' Ann said. 'I thought she'd do anything you wanted.'

He whipped his head sideways to stare at her. 'Now just what in hell is that supposed to mean?'

'Just what I said. You're close to her – traveling with her and all. She trusts you, doesn't she?'

'Maybe,' he said cautiously. 'But no way can I get her to do anything against her nature.'

'No,' Ann said sadly. 'I guess not.'

'Jesus Christ!' he exploded. 'What *is* all this shit? We're talking in riddles. What exactly do you want me to do? Spell it out.'

'Just try to get her to act like a human being. Like a sister,' she added in a low voice.

'You mean try to make a pussycat out of a tiger?'

'Just remind her of her responsibilities.'

'Listen, hon – Molly's only responsibility is to her cause. Everything else comes in second-best, way back.'

'Yes,' his wife said sorrowfully. 'I'm afraid you're right.'

'She's a special woman,' he said. 'You know that. Like a wild mustang. Maybe you can break her to bridle and bit – but then she wouldn't be Molly, would she?'

'I guess not.'

'You and the WDC have got to take her as she is – or kick her out. You're never going to change her. She's got a fire.'

'And you admire that – her fire?'

'Well . . . sure. There aren't many people in this world as sure as she is.'

'Rod,' Ann said unexpectedly, 'is everything all right between us?'

'Of course,' he said immediately, and heard the banjo sound of his own voice.

NOVEMBER 29, 1991

From all available evidence, it is apparent that the first

open conflict between sisters Ann Harding and Molly Turner occurred about a month after Ann moved to Washington, DC, and assumed de facto command of the Women's Defense Corps headquarters.

Their disagreement started with the publication by the WDC Research Department of a statistical analysis showing that less than 50 percent of divorced mothers were receiving child support payments to which they were legally entitled.

Ann Harding, after studying the depressing statistics, suggested that the combined NWU – WDC had the resources to act, in effect, as a collection agency and bring pressures to bear on delinquent fathers.

With chapters in every state, city, and town, the organization was in a position to seek out men who had reneged on their legal responsibilities and force them to pay up.

Ann wrote a long memo on how this might be done. She planned a national computerized list of offenders: name, last known address, physical description, job classification, etc. The file would be used in the initial task of locating the deadbeats.

Once found, they would be subjected to the moral suasion of specially trained teams of WDC sisters. If that failed, a gradually intensifying program would include publicity, picketing of their homes, letters to their employers, threats of arrest and/or garnisheeing of their salaries, and other forms of harassment until they were shamed into contributing to the support of the children they had fathered.

Molly wholeheartedly endorsed Ann's plan, but she made no secret of her contempt for the methods suggested to wring payment from the offending fathers.

'If they don't pay up,' she said wrathfully, 'we're going to kick the shit out of them.'

Ann pointed out that physical violence would be counterproductive. It would be poor public relations for the WDC. And a badly injured father who couldn't work would hardly be in a position to make the child support payments required of him.

But Molly was adamant. 'We've got to scare these assholes,' she said. 'Fear is the only thing that's going to make them shell out. Once they hear about a couple of yo-yos getting their lumps, they'll come up with the cash – you'll see.'

Their argument was loud and rancorous. Both were strong-minded women, and each wanted her way. Their disagreement became so disruptive to the normal functioning of WDC headquarters that finally Virginia Terwilliger was called in to arbitrate.

She listened to each sister separately and was shocked by their bitterness. It seemed to Terwilliger that this was a debate about tactics – important certainly, but not a subject to inspire the venom that both women displayed.

She could only conclude that their quarrel over the ADM (Aid for Divorced Mothers) program was a public confrontation that concealed a much deeper, private animosity. With sadness, she guessed the cause of their enmity.

After listening to both sisters' arguments, Terwilliger decreed that Ann's methods were to be given every chance to succeed. Only when her program failed could Molly and her troops resort to the threat of violence to make the delinquent father pay his debts. And Ginny emphasized the word *threat*.

'In no case,' she told Molly sternly, 'should your storm troopers actually assault these guys. We don't want any more arrests or lawsuits.'

Ann Harding organized the ADM program with her usual managerial skill. A nationwide file of debtors was set up and continually enlarged as the program became known. As Ann pointed out, the ADM was almost self-supporting since it won so many new members for the Women's Defense Corps.

It also attracted very heavy media attention. Ann appeared on several TV news and talk shows, explaining the disgrace of divorced fathers who refused to pay the child support for which they were legally responsible.

Initial results were encouraging. About 70 percent of the delinquent fathers located began to pay their debts soon after they were contacted. Another 25 percent were able to prove they were unable to pay because of unemployment or illness.

There remained a hard core of recalcitrants who simply refused payment of any amount. And they obstinately challenged ADM representatives to make them pay. These cases were turned over to Molly Turner and her soldiers.

Molly devised her own program to bring these holdouts to heel. One of the most effective methods, they discovered, was to make threats against the man's automobile – and, if that didn't work, actually smashing windshields, ice-picking tires, and attacking the bodywork with baseball bats and ax handles.

Telephone harassment was also used, and annoyance at the man's place of employment, embarrassment on the street or in restaurants, informing the target's friends of his delinquency.

These crude methods proved effective. Surprisingly, they also earned the amused admiration of most of the American public, men and women both. No one could sympathize with a father who refused to provide for his children if he was able to, and the coarse tactics of Molly's Mafia seemed to be in the American tradition of frontier justice.

Until late in November . . .

Two years previously, F. Robert McIlhenny, a divorced father then residing in Peoria, Illinois, had moved to Levitt, Arkansas. In legal papers – now a matter of public record – he described his reason for the move as 'Business matters; more opportunities.'

But there can be little doubt that a primary motive for his sudden relocation was to avoid payment of $1000 per month in child support to his divorced wife, Dawn McIlhenny. This amount had been agreed upon by both parties in a divorce suit brought by the aggrieved wife, claiming infidelity, desertion, and physical and emotional abuse.

As usual, the main victims in this nasty domestic squabble were the children: Evan, five; Alice, three; and Albert, two.

In Arkansas, McIlhenny, apparently a knowledgeable and skilled salesman of commercial real estate, soon succeeded in creating a new, prosperous life for himself, including a three-bedroom home, a Porsche, and a young girlfriend for whom he purchased a lake-front condominium.

After all legal expedients had failed or were long delayed, Dawn McIlhenny appealed to the WDC for aid. Investigators of the ADM located the skipped father by his job classification: they checked applications for a realtor's license in all fifty states, and found McIlhenny living the good life in Levitt, Arkansas.

From all accounts, the fugitive was a crass, stubborn man intent only on his own ease and pleasures. He obstinately ignored or rebuffed all attempts by the ADM team to compel him to pay child support to which he was legally committed. Molly Turner's crew was then called in.

By this time, McIlhenny was self-employed, and there was little that could be done to embarrass him at his place of business. He laughed at threats from Molly's Mafia. But meanwhile he equipped his home and garage with an expensive security system, began carrying a handgun, and made no secret of the small arsenal he kept at his bedside, including a rifle and shotgun.

On November 25, WDC soldiers attempted an early morning penetration of McIlhenny's two-car garage, apparently with the intention of demolishing his Porsche and his second car, a classic 1958 Mercedes 300SL Gullwing.

Alerted by his newly installed alarm system, McIlhenny

appeared on the scene clad in pajamas and armed with his High Standard Model 8111 pump action riot shotgun. He fired three rounds at the invaders, wounding four WDC sisters, one of whom subsequently lost her left arm. The assault party scattered without returning fire. In fact, there is no evidence that they were armed.

The wounded sisters filed no charges against McIlhenny, nor did he sign a complaint against the WDC. There was a lull of three days during which McIlhenny boasted in several public places that he had defeated the WDC. He even granted an interview to the *Levitt Clarion* in which he urged other divorced fathers to 'stand up for their rights.'

At approximately 8:54 PM, on the night of November 29, F. Robert McIlhenny was killed instantly by a burst of automatic rifle fire through the picture window of his home. Neighbors found him lying in a welter of blood, shards of glass, and water and flopping fish from his shattered aquarium.

After an intensive investigation, Levitt law enforcement officials admitted they had insufficient evidence to justify an arrest. The murder of McIlhenny was given wide media coverage, and the consensus of the public was that the WDC had been responsible for the crime.

At the time it occurred, Molly Turner was in Salt Lake City, addressing a symposium of university students on the general topic of 'Women – the Next Fifty Years.' She was accompanied by her secretary, a new press officer, and two bodyguards. After hearing of the shooting, she released a short statement to the media deploring 'this unnecessary tragedy.'

James Gargan, in Washington, made only perfunctory efforts to aid in the investigation of McIlhenny's assassination. He feared that his informant on Molly's staff, Clarice Dale, might have been closely involved in the killing – may, indeed, have pulled the trigger herself. Gargan wanted to do nothing to endanger the security of his mole.

It is now evident that the brutal murder of F. Robert McIlhenny greatly exacerbated the hostility between Ann Harding and Molly Turner. The day after the shooting, Ann issued strict orders to ADM investigators that no more names and addresses of delinquent divorced fathers were to be given to Molly or any member of her personal staff.

Shortly after this ugly incident, Dawn McIlhenny applied for public assistance.

DECEMBER 23, 1991

Some find faith in love, and some in fury. Molly Turner's sure belief sprang from anger, hurt, and revenge for betrayal. Her passion was an assertion of herself – and of all women. She saw the world divided, not between the haves and have-nots, but between the ares and are-nots.

Her spiky temper would not permit compromise. If Ann Harding wanted to launch a political campaign for a Federal law decreeing capital punishment of all convicted rapists, Molly wanted to execute every rapist personally. She would not temporize, nor sacrifice, today's vengeance for tomorrow's justice.

Her passion fed itself. But instead of enlarging, it imploded and condensed, becoming something hard, impervious, and without mercy. Just as her body thinned, her fervor concentrated, too – a thing of flint and steel. Nothing, no one, could touch her core.

She had a saint's capacity for self-sacrifice and the hubris of a sinner. Her certitude allowed no doubt. The universe circled her alone, and she could move stars. There were other people, she knew, with wants, needs, loves, and hates. But none was as strong as she.

As the Christmas season approached, Ann Harding made plans to return her family to Canton for a week. She wanted Jefferson Turner Harding to spend some time with his grandparents, and she wanted to inspect the workings of the WDC's data-processing center in the warehouse on River Street.

Rod was willing, Jeff was excited and, unexpectedly, Molly Turner announced that she, too, would return home for the holidays.

'A couple of days around Christmas,' she told Ann. 'I haven't seen Mother in months.'

So the entire clan was reunited in Canton on Sunday, December 22. There was a big dinner in Mrs Josephine Turner's Hillcrest Avenue home. Todhunter Clark, Lucille Jackson, and three members of Molly's personal staff were also invited.

The evening went off well, everyone sharing a buffet of baked ham, yams, and three-bean salad. There were two pies and two cakes for dessert. And a container of Heavenly Hash for Jeff – an ice cream he dearly loved.

Later, they sat around and talked. There was an open fire in the grate, and Brother Nabisco taught Jeff how to toast marshmallows. The others had drinks and coffee and idly discussed the 1992 election. Most agreed that Senator Dundee had the best chance to beat the incumbent.

'Over my dead body,' Molly Turner said.

On December 23, Ann told her husband that she would spend most of the day at the WDC warehouse. She left the Harding home at approximately 9:30 AM. Since Rod had announced his intention of going out to the safe house to take an inventory of weapons and equipment, Jeff was left in care of his grandparents, Luke and Cecily Harding – which pleased them mightily.

At around noon on that Monday, Molly Turner joined Rod at the safe house. He had started the kerosene heater, but the leaky shack was still cold enough to make them huddle under scratchy old army blankets on the cot.

'Long time, Moll,' he said.

'Yes,' she said, shivering. 'Too long. Did you really take inventory?'

'I really did. We're getting low. I think Tod or I or maybe both of us better make another gun run to Miami.'

'Ann refuses to spend any more money for guns. But that's all right; you go ahead. I've been padding my expense account and getting kickbacks from my staff. I've got the money.'

He pulled away to stare at her. 'Jesus, Moll, you're sure you know what you're doing?'

'Don't worry it. And don't get so far away. Warm me up.'

He gathered her in. He couldn't understand it, couldn't understand himself. It was still sexual, but it had gone beyond that. It was, he thought, her affirmation. Himself so detached, cynical, uncommitted, he grasped her close as if her belief might rub off on him. It wasn't her feminism he wanted to share – all faiths are the same – but he was drawn by that singing heart that cried, 'I can change the world!'

If she was right – if her life was right – then he was wrong, and his life was wrong. My God, what if it all turned out to be Yes instead of No? He groaned and put lips and tongue to her poor little pancake breasts.

'What's wrong, honey?' she asked.

'You've got the balls, Moll,' he said with a cheap laugh. 'Not me.'

'Don't say that. It's not true. I couldn't have done anything without you.'

'Don't crap me,' he said. 'You never have; don't start now. If it wasn't me, it would have been someone else – right?'

Silence. Then:

'But it *is* you,' she said. 'You make me happy. Isn't that enough?'

'Sure,' he said, touching her cheek. 'It's enough. Absolutely.'

He bent to kiss her flesh – and tasted bone. She was a bundle of sticks, and he feared she might snap.

371

In that beaten shanty, they shouted their pain and pleasure. Her face changed; he did not recognize her; she was another woman. A death's-head grin and eyes that blazed. She did something inside her, gripping him.

Then, when they had cried out their bliss, she would not release him, but anchored him with arms and legs.

'Don't go away,' she commanded. 'Not yet.'

So they lay entwined. He reached out an arm to pluck blankets from the dusty floor and flick them atop their cot.

'Ah Jesus,' she said. 'So good. I forgot.'

'Forgot what?'

'Everything. You, me, the world. Including sister Ann.'

'That bothers you?'

She shook her head. 'It's not important. I thought about it and decided it's not important. I'm not going to take you away from her. I wouldn't want to even if I could – which I can't. You're never going to leave her; I know that. It's okay. I just want a few minutes of your time.'

He sighed and she took his face between her palms. 'That bothers you?'

'It doesn't bother me because I think you're lying. To me or to yourself or to both of us.'

'Think what you like,' she said, shrugging. 'That's the way it is. Anytime you want to stop, just say so.'

'You know I can't.'

'Hooked, are you?' she jeered. 'On a bag of bones?'

'That's right; I'm hooked. Addicted.'

'Oh, sweetheart,' she said, kissing him frantically. 'What a couple of sad sacks we are.'

Still she would not allow him to roll free, but kept him atop her, pressing him close. She ran splintery fingers up and down his strong shoulders and back, his buttocks.

'Bodies,' she said dreamily. 'How wonderful. When are you going to make the gun run?'

'What?' he said. 'You switched gears on me.'

'When are you going to Miami?'

'I don't know. Is there a rush?'

372

'Can you get some of that plastic explosive? The stuff that looks like chewed bubble gum and sticks to everything.'

'I guess so,' he said cautiously. 'Why? What do you need that for?'

'Carol Poague got ten to fifteen in Corinth. She'll be up for parole in seven, but no way is she going to rot in jail for seven years. Right now she's in Jackson. I'm going to break her out of there.'

He closed his eyes. 'You're going to get yourself zapped,' he said.

'So?'

He wanted to say, 'What's *with* you?' But he knew what was with her.

'All right,' he said finally. 'I'll get you the stuff.'

'Will you and Tod help me?'

'I can't speak for him. It's his decision. But I'll help you.'

'I can bring it off,' she said fiercely. 'I know I can.'

He didn't think so, but he was past caring. It would be, he thought, a kind of expiation for him. A statement. Kilroy was here. He laughed then, thinking she might be insane, and he just as loony.

'What are you laughing at?' she demanded.

He told her.

'You think this is a sane world?' she said. 'The only way to beat it is to be the maddest of the mad.'

'You're succeeding,' he assured her.

They were in a good humor as they dressed, teasing and chivying each other and laughing. Working together, there seemed nothing they might not do.

Rod Harding turned off the heater and, zipped into their down parkas, they came out onto the porch. He snapped the big padlock on the front door. They stood there a moment before they went to their cars.

Off in the woods, stamping her feet to keep warm, Clarice Dale saw them exit from the safe house. She ripped off her gloves and fumbled with the camera and telephoto lens that one of James Gargan's men had taught her to operate.

She crouched behind the thick trunk of a leafless oak and snapped away. She thought she got some good shots of the embraces, the pattings, the fondlings, the kisses.

Ann Harding took over as Chief Executive Officer of the Women's Defense Corps with her customary vigor and efficiency. She brought to the leadership of the WDC a professionalism it had heretofore lacked.

One of her first projects was to improve WDC relations with Congress, the White House, and those government agencies involved with issues that concerned the WDC. She set up a Political Department whose efforts were almost wholly devoted to lobbying for legislation favored by the WDC.

She enlarged the WDC legal staff. She forged closer bonds with other special interest groups. She started a drive to bring younger women – especially college students – into the WDC, and to give them a voice in WDC affairs.

She learned how to use the print and broadcast media to further the aims of the WDC. She changed The Call *to a slick-paper monthly magazine available to non-WDC members by subscription and newsstand sale. She led a national campaign to establish Women's Day as a national holiday.*

Perhaps the most significant and far-reaching program she sponsored was to make the Women's Defense Corps into a worldwide organization. A plan was devised to charter WDC chapters in every foreign nation. If sufficient success was achieved, Ann intended to hold the first International WDC Convention in Washington, D. C, in 1995.

Virginia Terwilliger observed all this purposeful activity with admiration and approval. She was convinced that the WDC was moving into a new phase, with less emphasis on

*the revolutionary fervor of Molly Turner, and a greater
concentration on the sturdy pragmatism of Ann Harding.*

*It seemed to Ginny that Molly was becoming archaic.
Her charisma was still valuable to the WDC, no doubt of
that, but it was now Ann who appeared on TV talk shows,
spoke eloquently of the goals of women in print interviews,
and made headlines with a constant stream of new ideas to
solve old problems.*

*Just as Ann Harding gained power and popularity during
the early months of 1992, so did the presidential campaign
of Senator Lemuel K. Dundee. As his strength grew –
evidenced in national polls – contributions increased. He
began to count delegates to his party's national convention,
scheduled to be held in Miami on July 20, 1992.*

*It all looked good, and his staff counseled him to watch
his speech and actions carefully, lest a single gaffe suddenly
reduce his chances for the nomination and, eventually, the
election.*

*But when the shock came, it was not of Dundee's
making . . .*

JANUARY 6, 1992

Ann Harding presented a calm, steadfast manner to the
world. If she was in emotional turmoil, no one would
know. Not her husband, her son, her co-workers, the
public. And certainly not Molly Turner.

On January 6, Todhunter Clark came over from Canton
toting two big canvas sacks of mail, reports, bank and
accountant's statements, periodicals, etc. Ann heard him
joshing the secretaries and staff in WDC headquarters and
waited patiently in her office, knowing he'd stop by.

As usual, his first question to her was, 'How's the King?'

'Jeff's fine,' she said, smiling. 'He's going to school now,
Tod. Pre-kindergarten.'

'No kidding? How's he like it?'

'He loves it,' she said, laughing. 'Got in a fight his first day and made the other boy cry.'

'That's my King,' Brother Nabisco said, grinning. 'He was a buster from the word go. Here – I bought him a present.'

He fished a long wooden whistle from his jacket pocket. It had holes for fingering, like a flute, and was painted with woodland animals.

'It's from Germany,' Clark said. 'Jeff'll probably send you right up the wall blowing on it, but maybe he can learn to toot a tune.'

'Thank you, Tod. I'm sure he'll love it. Close the door, will you, and sit down for a minute.'

He closed the office door, then took the armchair along-side her desk.

Ann picked up her phone. 'Patty,' she said, 'hold my calls, will you? Thanks.' She turned to Clark. 'How's Lucille?' she asked.

'Bright-eyed and bushy-tailed, thank you.'

'Getting married, Tod?'

'Thinking on it, Miz Ann.'

'Don't think too long,' she warned, 'or some other man will grab her off. She's not going to wait forever.'

'Her very words,' he said mournfully, and they both laughed.

'Tod,' she said, 'you going to Michigan with Molly? On that prison break she's planning.'

He didn't answer immediately. She looked up and found him staring at her.

'I didn't guess you knew about that, Miz Ann.'

'Of course I know about it,' she said sharply. 'Rod's down in Miami right now, getting the stuff. He had to tell me. Are you in on it?'

'No,' he said. 'Oh, I'll help them fix up the van they're going to use to take the stuff to Michigan. I'll work on the fuses and timers and all. But no, I'm not really in on it. I mean, I'm not going to Jackson with them.'

'Why not?'

'I figure it for a meat grinder. I've been in meat grinders before, and maybe if this thing had gone down a year ago or so, I'd have gone along. But since I been seeing Lucille Jackson, I've had this terrible desire to keep my black ass in one – piece. Miz Ann, I wish you could talk Molly out of it.'

'Molly and I arcn't talking much these days.'

'Well, she sure as hell ain't talking to *me*. Then talk your husband out of it.'

'Don't think I didn't try,' she said bitterly. 'Goddamn it!' she cried, slapping her palm on the desk top. 'She's going to ruin everything I've been working for. I've been trying to prove we're peaceful, reasonable women ready to work with anyone who can help us, and she'll make us look like a bunch of raving maniacs running around with guns and dynamite and killing innocent people. Tod, can this thing possibly work?'

'Don't see how, Miz Ann. It's Loony Tunes time.'

She rose and began to stalk about the office, gripping her elbows.

'It'll take us years to recover,' Ann said. 'If we ever do.'

'You tell Rod all this?'

'I told him,' she said furiously. 'For all the good it did. He said he promised her, and he wouldn't go back on his word. She'll get him killed.'

'Could happen,' Clark said calmly. 'Herself, too.'

Suddenly he saw that she was weeping.

'Miz Ann . . .' he said helplessly.

'Sorry,' she said huskily, wiping her cheeks with the backs of her hands, 'but this thing has been driving me crazy. I don't know, Tod – he must love her.'

'Oh, I wouldn't – '

'Look at this,' she said, yanking open the top drawer of her desk and reaching to the back. 'Those letters I told you about – I've been getting them regularly. And then, a week ago, these came.'

She handed him an envelope. Addressed in a woman's hand-writing. Postmarked Washington, DC. He opened it. Six photographs. Molly Turner and Rod Harding embracing on the porch of the safe house in Canton. Clear, sharp photographs.

And a little note attached: *MERRY CHRISTMAS*!

'Jesus Christ!' Brother Nabisco said disgustedly. 'Someone's got a sick mind.'

'But they're true, aren't they?' she demanded. 'The person who sent them might be sick, but the photos don't lie, you can't deny that.'

'Miz Ann, it could just be like a friendly kiss for the holidays, and they . . .' His voice trailed away.

She sat behind her desk again, leaned forward, face hidden in her palms. Her voice was muffled; he could hardly hear her.

'It's bad,' she said brokenly. 'Really bad. She's hurting the WDC. She's ruining me – my marriage. She's taking my husband away from me. What am I going to do? Divorce him? Take Jeff and go? Where? And what will the scandal do to the WDC? I've worked so hard all my life trying to be a good wife, a good mother. And then the WDC. I've given it everything I've got. I've never hurt anyone. Now it's all going down the drain because of her. Is that fair? God forgive me, but sometimes I wish she was dead. I hate to say that, but it's the truth. She's making my life a disaster.'

Then . . .

'I don't know what all this is going to do to little Jeff,' she added.

Clark leaned over and touched her shoulder. She took a tissue from a side drawer and wiped her eyes.

'Oh God,' she said dully, 'what am I going to do?'

He stood up, walked to the door.

'Well, Miz Ann,' he said slowly, 'there are ways, and there are ways. Let me think on this awhile. And give my love to little Jeff – y 'hear?'

378

He left, closing the door behind him.

Ann Harding stared at the closed door with stony eyes.

FEBRUARY 12, 1992

So confident was Senator Dundee of his eventual election to the presidency that he organized a special task force to plan his administration. Thomas J. Kealy was assigned the task of recruiting a committee of prestigious volunteers who would make recommendations on the domestic and foreign policies, the strategy and tactics of the Dundee White House.

But first, Kealy decided, the newly formed brain trust would do well to come up with a list of potential vice-presidential candidates. They would, of necessity, be experienced men of good reputation, be attractive campaigners, and capable of extending Dundee's appeal. That meant no one too handsome, too intelligent, or possessed of superior oratorical skills or charisma.

Eventually a list of twenty-five possible running mates was presented to Dundee. He went through it rapidly, striking out names with a Magic Marker pen.

'Not him; he's too sappy . . . The mob owns that guy . . . He's been divorced twice . . . That one is too poor . . . His wife's got a boyfriend on the side . . . This guy has sold his soul to the banks . . .'

And so on and so on. In the end, the list was whittled down to six names. The senator thought any one of them would add strength to the ticket without eclipsing the First Banana. They were all capable men – but not *too* capable.

'Now what I want you to do,' he told Kealy, 'is to make one copy of this short list and get it to Jimmy Gargan at Justice. Ask him, as a personal favor to me, to run a check on these guys. And tell him, for God's sake, to treat the list as super-top secret. The last thing in the world I want is for the *post* or *Times* to get hold of it. Then I'll have more enemies than a hound dog has fleas. Get the names to Gargan right away.'

'Will do,' Tom Kealy said, having taken to using that phrase so often that other staffers now referred to him as 'Will-do Kealy.'

The executive assistant had been meeting regularly with Gargan. He reported on the progress of Dundee's campaign, predicted future plans, revealed whom Dundee was consulting and the sources of his funding.

All this, to Kealy's way of thinking, was innocent stuff, most of it a matter of public record. But Gargan seemed satisfied with what he heard and rarely leaned on Kealy for more confidential revelations. One of the times he pressed was when Kealy mentioned H. Fairchild Curtiss, the banker. Gargan wanted to know all about his relationship with the senator.

On the matter of checking potential vice-presidential choices, Kealy saw no reason for a private tête-à-tête. Instead, he invited Gargan to lunch at Mel Krupin's on Connecticut Avenue. Because Kealy was known there, he was given a status table near the stairway.

Gargan arrived a few minutes later. The two men had Bloody Marys and munched new pickles and peppers while they decided on their lunch. Kealy selected the pickled herring appetizer; Gargan chose the chopped liver. Then they both ordered chicken soup, steak tartare, baked potatoes, and the house salad. And another round of Bloody Marys.

As soon as they were seated, Kealy got down to business, leaning over the table and speaking in a low voice. Gargan had to bend forward to hear him over the noise of the lunchtime crowd. The executive assistant explained what the senator wanted.

'No problem,' Gargan said. 'You've got the list with you?'

Kealy nodded.

'Pass it to me under the table,' Gargan ordered. 'From

380

where I sit, I can see three reporters I recognize and probably a lot more I don't.'

Kealy handed over the envelope beneath the tablecloth.

'Absolutely top secret,' he said earnestly.

'Of course,' Gargan said. 'What else?'

During the appetizers and soup, he pumped Kealy casually about the progress of Dundee's campaign. He seemed to listen absently, nodding his head now and then. But when the steak tartare was served, he said:

'You talk like everything's coming up roses. But the polls show your boss isn't doing so great with women.'

'Well . . . yeah,' Kealy said. 'But the male votes more than make up for the gender gap. The majority is still on our side. Of all registered voters, I mean.'

'Uh-huh,' Gargan said, and then was silent as they both dug into their food.

'Something wrong?' Kealy asked.

'No,' Gargan said. 'What could be wrong?'

'You seem quiet.'

'Just thinking. I've got something that could be a big plus for your boss. But it's high-level stuff, and I'm wondering if I should tell you or keep my mouth shut.'

'Tell me!' Kealy said eagerly. 'You said you wanted to see the senator make it.'

'Oh we do, we do. But this is dynamite.'

'What? What?'

Gargan waited a few more minutes, letting Kealy's impatience grow. Then:

'Well . . .' he said, 'okay. But this is for Dundee only. Not a word to anyone else. Understood?'

Kealy raised a palm. 'I swear.'

'Put your fucking hand down,' Gargan said savagely. 'You don't know who's watching us. Well, I think you should tell the senator to start sticking it to Molly Turner and the WDC in the next month or so. I mean really giving it to them. We happen to know that crazy lady is planning a big action. The only thing we don't know, at the moment,

381

is the exact date. But we'll learn that in time to call out the troops. A lot of people could get hurt.'

'Jesus,' Kealy breathed. 'How did you find out about it?'

'From a usually reliable source,' Gargan said primly. 'Look, there's no way this thing can succeed. It's going to be another Corinth Massacre – maybe worse. So I figure if the senator starts popping off again about violence being no solution to the problems of women, and then this bloody thing goes down, it'll prove how smart he is.'

'You're so right,' Kealy said. 'Can you tell me what it is?'

'No.'

'Okay, okay,' Kealy said hastily. 'But you don't know when it's coming off?'

'A month maybe,' Gargan said. 'Six weeks. We'll get the exact date a few days before it happens, but there will be plenty of time for Dundee to hammer away at Molly Turner and the WDC for fostering a climate of brutal violence. How does it sound to you?'

'It sounds just great,' Tom Kealy said enthusiastically.

'You think he'll go for it?'

'I know he will. I'll convince him. It's going to get him elected president. After another massacre, even the women who are against him are going to see that he's been right all along.'

The two men smiled. There was an almost sexual satisfaction in being kingmakers.

After they separated, James Gargan returned to his office and immediately dictated a long memo on the luncheon to prove to his bosses how skillfully he was engineering the election of Senator Lemuel K. Dundee.

It was the worst mistake he ever made in his life.

MARCH 19, 1992

Rod Harding led the way, driving alone in an unmarked van. Molly Turner, a hundred yards back, drove her Volkswagen Rabbit. Three members of her personal staff were with her, including Clarice Dale.

They intended to take their time, obeying all traffic laws and speed limits. When they arrived in Michigan, they'd plot the jailbreak with the state WDC regiment. They had already gotten word to Carol Poague, and she was eager to cooperate.

Harding and Todhunter Clark had worked on the vehicles for a week, while they were parked outside the Canton safe house. The van was fitted with two bunk beds. Beneath blankets and pad mattresses were compartments that held the *plastique*, automatic rifles, and ammunition.

Brother Nabisco rigged a number of bombs, some fitted with adjustable timers, some set to explode in five seconds, some on contact. The last were nestled in boxes of cotton batting. But even so, Clark advised Harding not to hit any deep potholes.

'Or they'll be scraping you off the trees,' he said.

'Thank you,' Rod said. 'I'm encouraged by your confidence.'

Clark did most of the work on Molly's VW, building compartments in the trunk and under the seats. She'd be carrying handguns, machine pistols, ammunition, and grenades.

'You got enough stuff in there to start a revolution,' he told her.

'I already have,' she said coldly.

The two vehicles left Canton about 9:00 AM, on the morning of March 19. Todhunter Clark stood outside the safe house, took off his fur hat, and waved goodbye.

There was a morning ground fog. But as the sun rose,

the mist burned away. The sky became pearlescent, the air as sharp as ether. The temperature rose to 48°F, and the road was dry.

They intended to take Route 50 to Chillicothe, and then turn north on 23 up into Michigan. Traffic was unexpectedly heavy, and several cars got between Rod's van and Molly's VW. But that didn't bother them; they had planned to stop at a roadside luncheonette and have a late breakfast.

They met at Rowina's Cafe, just west of Athens, Ohio. Rod and the four women sat at one table and had orange juice, eggs with bacon, home fries, toast and coffee. They joked and laughed. Later, a waitress remembered them as 'nice people.' She said they were good tippers.

Harding left first. A few minutes later the women departed. When they were on the road again, Rod's van was out of sight. But they were not concerned. They had planned to meet him again in Columbus and spend the night there.

It was then approximately 11:45 AM. On a clear stretch of road, about two miles east of McArthur, the right front and right rear wheels of the Volkswagen Rabbit exploded and flew off the axles. The car was then traveling at about 50 mph. It swerved to the right, lurched, and began to roll over. No one was wearing a seat belt. Molly Turner was smashed against the windshield. When it shattered, she was almost completely decapitated and died instantly.

Clarice Dale, in the front passenger's seat, also died during the rollover. Her skull was crushed against the right pillar, and she suffered fatal internal injuries.

The two women in the rear seat, investigators later said, apparently survived the rolling of the car. But when it came to rest on its roof, the VW burst into flame, a conflagration fed by burning fuel and the explosion of ammunition and grenades. The two women, unable to claw their way free, were incinerated.

Cars and trucks halted on the road; drivers and passengers rushed to help. But no one could get near the flaming wreck. And when the ammunition and grenades continued to detonate, the would-be Samaritans hastily backed away. A truck driver called for assistance on his CB radio.

Rod Harding, at the time of the crash, was east of Allensville. Because he was unable to spot Molly's VW in his rearview mirror, he had slowed down and switched to the righthand lane to give her a chance to catch up.

Shortly thereafter, two police cars, sirens screaming, sped past him, heading eastward. They were followed a few moments later by a fire rescue unit and an ambulance. Harding pulled onto the verge and stopped. He sat there for a few minutes, considering his options.

It was probably just a highway accident and had nothing to do with Molly. And even if her car was involved, she had given him strict orders: 'If anything happens to us, you just keep going. Understand? Get that stuff to Michigan.'

He hesitated, not knowing what to do. But fifteen minutes later, when her car still hadn't appeared, fear began bubbling in his stomach and he wondered where his loyalties lay.

'Son of a bitch!' he said bitterly, and with horn blaring, he swung the van into a careening U-turn, ignoring the fury of oncoming drivers. He sped eastward, his coldness growing as he failed to spot Molly's car.

The traffic slowed as he came to the scene of the wreck. Cops were trying to keep traffic moving, but everyone wanted to look. Harding looked, too. He saw the burned-out hulk of the VW, sloshed with foam. Firemen were working with pry bars to get the crumpled doors open. Rod knew they could take their time.

He stared, but kept the van moving. He wasn't going to Michigan. He didn't know where the hell he was going.

He was near Athens when he heard the first report on the van's radio. 'Four women dead,' the announcer said solemnly. 'Not yet identified.'

'And one dead man,' Rod Harding said aloud. 'Not yet identified.'

At about the time Harding was crossing the Ohio River back into West Virginia, James Gargan was at his desk in Washington, DC. He was working doggedly away at a stack of memos.

His aide came in with a ragged piece of tape torn from the AP ticker. He put it on Gargan's desk.

'Four women killed in a smashup in Ohio,' he reported tonelessly. 'The car was registered to Molly Turner.'

Gargan read the bulletin, feeling his stomach suddenly churn.

'All right,' he said. 'Get through to Columbus on this. I want everything – who the women were, where they were heading, how it happened. Tell them to get cracking, and give us a report every fifteen minutes even if they've got nothing new. I mean, convince them this is top priority.'

'You think it was an accident?' the aide said.

'Oh God,' Gargan groaned. 'I hope so.'

The aide looked at him sympathetically. He knew what was going on.

Gargan went back to his paperwork, but couldn't concentrate. After a while he gave up and just sat there, considering all the permutations and combinations. None were calculated to make him come up smelling like roses.

It grew worse as the afternoon dragged along. The two victims in the front of the burned-out VW were definitely identified as Molly Turner and Clarice Dale, Gargan's informant. No make yet on the other two.

Then the coup de grâce: It hadn't been a highway accident; both right front and right rear wheels had been blown off with explosive charges, detonated by a method still unknown. But it was clear that Molly Turner had been assassinated, along with Clarice Dale and the two other women. Clean sweep.

James Gargan rubbed his forehead and found he was sweating, though the office was cool. He pondered how best to handle this mess, and finally decided to bite the bullet. He called Senator Dundee. It took him almost five minutes to get through to the man some Washington correspondents were now calling 'Lucky Lem.' Some luck, Gargan thought grimly.

'Senator,' he said, as calmly as he could, 'it's very important that I see you as soon as possible. Privately.'

'Can't it wait?' Dundee said peevishly. 'I'm up to my ass in quorum calls.'

'Sir,' Gargan said, 'I really do think you should see me immediately. And alone. It's not something I can give you on the phone. It may have a serious effect on your campaign.'

'Oh-oh,' the senator said, 'I don't like the sound of that. All right, I'll meet you in the library of the Metropolitan Club in an hour.'

They sat close together on a leather couch. They spoke in low voices because there were several corpses buried in club chairs and reading Trollope.

Gargan told the senator of Molly Turner's death.

'I'm surprised you haven't heard of it, sir,' he said. 'It's been on radio. Network TV will have it tonight. And in the morning papers, of course.'

'It was an accident, wasn't it?' Dundee said anxiously. 'A highway crackup?'

'Well, ah, not exactly . . .' Gargan said, staring down at the way his hands were climbing over each other.

He then proceeded to spell it out.

'It was murder,' he concluded. 'Or execution or assassination – you name it.'

Dundee looked at him, face whitening. 'Couldn't you put a lid on it?' he asked hoarsely.

'Impossible,' Gargan said. 'It was a local thing. By the time I got the word, the cops were talking to reporters.

387

No way to cover it.'

They stared at each other. Gargan was the first to look away.

'There may be some backlash,' he said hesitantly.

'Backlash?' Dundee said in a loud voice that caused two of the skeletons in club chairs to look around angrily. The senator lowered his voice:

'I'll tell you what, you hog-sucking, crap-assed son of a bitch – you and that prat boy Tom Kealy have done me in.'

'Now look, Senator – '

'*You* look, you piece of shit. In my ignorance and innocence I believed what you and Kealy told me. Dump on Molly Turner, you said. She's going to be involved in a bloody slaughter, and I'll come out with a four-word speech: "I told you so," that'll make the great American public think I'm the smartest gink to come down the pike since Billy Seward bought Alaska for two cents an acre.

'So now some asshole kook knocks off Molly Turner after I've been putting the shaft to her – and guess who gets the blame? My rating with women right now is iffy. This thing will push me off the charts. Oh, no one will think I was personally involved in Turner's death, but I can see the statements now – "Senator Dundee created a climate of enmity and hostility that inevitably led to the cruel murder of this brave and noble woman." And so forth and so on. You and Kealy have crucified me.'

'Senator, there was no way I could have foreseen that –'

'That's your job, shithead – isn't it? To foresee? What the fuck do you think the government is paying you for – to wander around with your thumb up your ass? I can tell you right now, you cocksucking, motherfucking bastard, your days are numbered. Your bosses will be hearing from me, and you'll be hearing from them. If you're lucky, they may reassign you to guarding a Federal outhouse in Hernia, Wyoming. As for Kealy, maybe I'll let him clean out the spittoons I'm going to put in the Oval Office the moment I get there. You prick!'

The senator stood abruptly and stomped away. James Gargan sat there on the deep leather couch, clenching his hands to control the tremble. Curiously, his first reaction to Dundee's tirade was admiration. He thought this guy might not make a bad president after all.

Then, calming, he began to assess his own situation. He knew the senator would do exactly as he threatened: go straight to Gargan's superiors and demand his head. And he knew his bosses would cave; Dundee had too much clout to ignore. The best Gargan could hope for was a pissy-assed field assignment, far from DC.

Over the years, he had collected a private file of his own: documents, photos, letters, tape recordings – all kept in a safe deposit box in Raleigh, North Carolina. Maybe, James Gargan thought, it was time for him to resign from the government, collect his pension, and go into business for himself.

Just like Jake Spencer . . .

APRIL 11, 1992

In the month following the assassination of Molly Turner, the backlash was even worse than Dundee had anticipated. The senator was convinced that most of his bad publicity was being orchestrated by Ann Harding and the Executive Board of the Women's Defense Corps.

First of all, there was an elaborate funeral in Canton, West Virginia, that received wide media coverage. The WDC called for a National Day of Mourning, with two minutes of silence at noon when Molly Turner's coffin was being lowered into a grave at Canton's Calvary Cemetery.

But it didn't stop with Molly's burial. Senator Dundee was excoriated for weeks in speeches, newspaper columns, and editorials. As he had predicted, he was not accused of personal complicity in Molly Turner's murder, but his blatant antifeminist stance was blamed for inflaming rabid masculinists and inspiring the brutal execution of Molly and her three aides.

Lemuel K. Dundee might have been many things, but he was not a man who crumpled under pressure. He called his staff together and announced a 'damage control' program designed to restore him as front-runner before his party's fast-approaching nominating convention.

It has been estimated that almost two million dollars were spent in Dundee's efforts to regain his election momentum. The money went for radio and TV commercials, mailings, billboards, ten-minute audio cassettes, newspaper advertising, polls, five-minute videotapes, and all the other techniques of modern campaigning.

This media blitz continued through the first week of April 1992, with campaign staffers working horrendous hours and the senator himself keeping to a killing schedule of speeches, interviews, and personal appearances.

'Don't apologize,' he had decreed from the start. 'We're going to stonewall this.'

And so he did, stating that although he deplored Molly Turner's murder, as did every law-abiding American, he still believed her methods were wrong.

'The end does not justify the means,' he trumpeted.

Dundee worked hard, and his staff worked hard. Their almost continuous polling indicated they were achieving some results – but not enough. Approval by men of the senator's candidacy was holding reasonably firm, but his rating among registered female voters was still abysmally low. As one TV commentator remarked, 'Senator Dundee's gender gap has become a gender canyon.'

On April 11, a Saturday, a conference was held in Dundee's Spring Valley home. Staffers present included Ruth Blohm, media director Orrin Fischbein, chief speechwriter Simon Christie, Lyle Hayden, and other top advisers. It is of minor historical interest to note that Thomas

J. Kealy was not invited to attend this important meeting.

Polling consultant Robert T. Adler made the initial presentation, using flipover charts mounted on an easel. In varicolored columns and graphs, they showed the changes in Dundee's popularity from the day following Molly Turner's death to the most recent poll.

'The bad news is obvious,' Adler said grimly. 'The falloff in females is close to ten percent. What's worse, we've had an almost seven percent desertion by blacks and Hispanics. What I find particularly aggravating is that these declines show no signs of tapering off. Senator, if this hemorrhaging continues, you're in real trouble.'

'Shit,' the senator said dejectedly. 'You know the state delegations watch the polls as closely as we do. They all want to go with the winner. If they decide I haven't got a chance in November, they sure as hell aren't going to give me a chance in July, in Miami. Ruth, have you got anything?'

'More bad news,' Blohm said. 'Do you want to hear it?'

'Sure,' Dundee said resignedly. 'Pile it on.'

'Lyle,' she said, 'why don't you spell it out?'

Hayden rose and began speaking in soft tones, occasionally touching his silky blond beard.

'We did our first in-depth analysis of the key voting districts two weeks after the death of Molly Turner. As far as female voters are concerned, our analysis substantiates the polling results. Women see you as a woman-hater, or at least indifferent to women's problems and aspirations. They react with anger and, in some cases, hatred.'

'That's nice to know,' Dundee said.

'According to our analysis, at the present moment you are going to lose the women's vote by an even larger margin than the polls indicate. Now we come to our analysis of male voters. Here is where we differ from the polling results. Our investigation indicates that men, while they might claim to support you in public – including their statements to pollsters – actually have a hidden admiration of and sympathy for Molly Turner and what she did.'

'The hell you say!' the senator cried.

'It was as much a surprise to us as it is to you,' Hayden continued in his quiet voice. 'But the evidence is overwhelming. In public, men project the usual macho image and express contempt for the WDC. But privately – and quite possibly in the voting booth – they have a grudging respect for these women. The reasons are varied and complex. But generally, I would say, Molly Turner was absolutely right in her NWU convention speech of 1987. She stated then that this is essentially a violence-prone society with a strong tradition of pioneer and frontier justice. Meekness and a nonviolent approach to the solution of problems are seen as a sign of weakness. So she sought justice at the muzzle of a gun. And we have found that a preponderant majority of American males agree with that philosophy. The only way to handle bullies is to stand up to them. Life is one long shoot-out at the OK. Corral. Senator, in all seriousness I must warn you to expect a grave erosion of male support once they get in the privacy of the voting booth and can express their hidden feelings, prejudices, and desires without having to maintain a macho, anti-woman image.'

There was silence when Hayden finished. Most of the campaign staffers looked down at their hands, not wanting to observe Senator Dundee's reaction to this devastating report.

'So I can't count on the men?' he asked Hayden with a short laugh. 'Is that what you're telling me?'

'Yes, sir. I realize it's a hard concept to accept, but I stand by it.'

'I do, too,' Ruth Blohm spoke up. 'I've gone over Lyle's work a dozen times, Senator. The evidence is there. It shows most men subconsciously respect and admire Molly Turner. There she is with her six-guns blazing, going up against the bad guys. They can relate to that.'

'All right,' Dundee said. 'Assuming you're right, what

392

do we do now? How do we turn this thing around? Anyone got any ideas?'

They looked at each other.

'Senator,' Orrin Fischbein said finally, 'I don't see where we have any option other than to continue what we have been doing – spending every cent available on a media campaign that'll swamp the country. Good advertising and good PR will make the difference in the long run.'

'As Lord Keynes remarked,' Lyle Hayden murmured quietly, 'in the long run we're all dead.'

'Throw more money at the problem?' Dundee demanded of Fischbein. 'I've been a gambler all my life, and I can tell you that desperate money never wins. But I honest-to-God don't know what else to do.'

For almost two hours they discussed advertising, commercials, themes for speeches, interviews. Everyone talked, everyone took notes, and, in the corner of the living room, Martha Dundee played backgammon against herself, sipped bourbon, and listened to the world go by.

At last the senator rose to his feet. The mood was depressed, almost somber. What had held such bright promise a month ago now seemed a lost cause.

Ruth Blohm hung back, letting the others, including Lyle Hayden, precede her out the front door. When she was alone with Dundee and his wife, she said to him:

'Senator, can you give me a few minutes?'

'Sure,' he said, trying to smile. 'As soon as I have a drink to unwind. You want something?'

'No, thank you. But you go ahead.'

She waited patiently while he took off his jacket, loosened his tie, unbuttoned his collar. Then he kicked off his shoes and, in stockinged feet, padded over to pour himself a tumbler of bourbon from his wife's bottle.

He came back to slump in an armchair.

'Now then, little girl,' he said. 'What's on your mind?'

'The media blizzard isn't going to work,' she said flatly. 'You know it and I know it. You asked if anyone knows

393

how we can turn this thing around. I know – but you're not going to like it.'

He stared at her. 'Try me,' he said.

'Since Molly Turner's death, her sister, Ann Harding, has been acting president of the WDC. You go to her and cut a deal. Get her to agree to run as your vice president. The two of you go to the Miami convention as a team: our next president and vice president.'

'Jesus Christ!' Dundee shouted.

'It'll work,' Ruth Blohm went on earnestly. 'Having her as your running mate gets you off the hook for her sister's murder. And I guarantee it'll swing the women's vote back in your column. Senator, the convention will love it and the voting public will love it. It can't miss. If you can work a deal with Ann Harding, you're home free.'

'Wow,' he said thoughtfully. 'That's something. What an idea.'

'I've checked up on the lady,' Blohm continued. 'She's attractive. She's the all-American mother with a handsome husband, an ex-cop, and a cute little boy. And she's intelligent, shrewd, and knows how to roll a log. A very efficient public speaker. Photogenic. She and the WDC swing a lot of clout. She's the answer to your problems, sir.'

'You think she'll go for it?'

'I have no idea. That's up to you – what kind of a salesman you are. From what I hear about the lady, if she goes for it, she'll drive a hard bargain. The final decision will be yours.'

He looked at her closely. 'Was this your idea, Ruth?'

'Not entirely. Lyle Hayden and I worked it out together.'

He nodded. 'Hayden is one smart feller.'

'I know,' she said, grinning. 'I'm going to marry him – but he doesn't know it yet.'

The senator's grin was as genuine as hers. 'God bless you both,' he said.

Martha Dundee looked up from her backgammon

394

board, smiling brightly.

'Well, Ruth,' he said slowly, 'you've given me a hell of a lot to think about. I've got to ponder this mightily and touch many, many bases before I come to a decision. Meanwhile, you keep this idea under your hat. I'll let you know the moment I decide which way to jump.'

She stood, gathered up her coat. 'Senator, I hope the more you think about it, the better it will seem to you. If you can work it, it'll be the biggest rabbit ever pulled out of a political hat. 'Bye now.'

When the door closed behind her, Dundee turned to his wife.

'What do you think?' he asked.

She glanced up. 'Do you really want to be president?'

'Is the Pope a Catholic?'

'Then do what she says.'

MAY 29, 1992

'I think I'll take a run over to Canton, hon,' Rod Harding said casually to his wife. 'Visit with the folks awhile. And maybe Tod and I better clean out the cellar of the safe house. There's not much left down there, but what there is, we'll give to Lucille Jackson's regiment or just dump in the river.'

'That's a good idea,' Ann said absently. 'Get rid of everything. We have no need for that stuff anymore.'

So Rod called Brother Nabisco and arranged to meet him at the deserted farm at noon on May 29. But Harding drove over the day before. He stopped in Winchester, Virginia, at a store that sold old tools and army surplus. He bought a worn, zippered sleeping bag and a rusty, long-handled spade.

He slept the night of May 28 at his parents' home in Canton, West Virginia. They spent the evening visiting and looking at the albums of family photographs Luke and

Cecily Harding cherished. A Harding had died at Shiloh, and another had made and lost a fortune in the Yukon. Rod had brought along the latest color pictures of Jefferson Turner Harding for the collection.

He was out at the safe house by 9:00 AM the next morning, and went to work. It was balmy enough to shuck his nylon jacket and shirt. He labored away bared to the waist, but even so he sweated and was happy he had thought to bring along a cold sixpack of Coors.

He cleaned out the cellar and threw all the remaining handguns, ammunition, and explosives into the river. Then he made other preparations. He was finished by 11:30, and by the time Todhunter Clark arrived, Rod had his shirt back on and was sitting quietly on the cot, sipping a beer, looking at the leaky walls of the shack and watching the mad motes dance in the sunlight.

'Hey, man,' Clark said. 'How you doing?'

'Can't complain,' Harding said. 'You?'

'Just fine. What a smart day!'

'Isn't it though. How about a cold brew?'

'A splendid idea,' Brother Nabisco said, popping a can. 'How's the wifey?'

'Doing great. And Jeff is getting bigger every day.'

'Oh yeah,' Clark said, smiling. 'The King is going to be a giant.'

'He already eats like one.'

'Uh-huh. I've got to get over to see him one of these days. Bring him a spiffy little model car I bought for him.'

Rod Harding slid a Smith & Wesson .357 Magnum from under the pillow on the cot. He gripped it firmly in both hands, pointing the muzzle at Clark.

Brother Nabisco, standing, looked down at the gun, then looked up slowly to meet Rod's eyes.

'Oh man,' he said. 'That's heavy.'

'Why did you do it?' Harding asked in a dead voice.

'Do what? What you talking about?'

'It was you,' Harding said. 'Had your MO written all over

396

it. I figure you rigged directional charges to blow the wheels. You wouldn't have used a clock timer because her car might have been parked when it blew. So maybe it was rigged to the odometer or driveshaft to make sure the car was in motion. But I don't think so. I think it was remote control. I think you followed us in your heap up into Ohio. And when you got her in a good place, you pressed the button.'

'You're crazy.'

Clark took one small shuffling step toward Rod.

'Don't do that,' Harding said. 'Don't try to take me. You may be fast, but this little hunk is faster. Come on, Tod, tell me . . . Why did you do it?'

'I didn't do nothing. Besides, what's the big commotion about? She wasn't nothing to you.'

Harding was silent.

'A piece on the side maybe,' Clark said. 'But it wasn't like you was in love with her or anything like that.'

'I don't know what love is,' Harding said. 'A tight scrotum or a tight heart – I don't know, I swear to God I don't – and never will, I expect. But Molly was my woman. I mean we were close. And you wasted her. I can't let you do that, Tod. Not if I want to live with myself.'

'She was nothing to you, man!' Clark cried. 'Nothing!'

'No,' Harding said somberly, 'you're wrong. She was something to me. I can't say exactly what it was. Not in words, I can't. But she made me feel that maybe there's more than turds and vomit in the world. But that's neither here nor there. The important fact is that I had a thing going with her, and you knew it, and you blew her away. It's been eating at me. You shouldn't have done that, Tod. I always treated you okay, didn't I? You had no call to put her down.'

'I swear I didn't,' Brother Nabisco said, taking another small, shuffling step toward the man with the gun.

'I told you not to do that,' Harding said sharply. 'I'm going to pop you, but I'm going to make it as clean as I 'can. You rush me, and I'll hurt you bad.'

'You haven't got the balls for it,' Clark said scornfully.

'Wanna bet? Why did you do it, Tod? For Ann and Jeff? Was that it?'

'I just didn't like the bitch,' Clark said, shrugging. 'She hated me, and I hated her. It was just one of those things.'

'You're a freak,' Harding said. 'A fucking freak. You know that? Nam turned your brains to shit.'

'Yours, too.'

'Maybe. Maybe it did. But Molly Turner was important to me and you fragged her. If I let that go by without doing anything about it, then I really am nothing. You can understand that, can't you?'

'Cut the crap,' Todhunter Clark said, 'and do what you have to do.'

So Rod Harding shot him twice in the chest. The blasts knocked Clark off his feet, slammed him back and down. He slid into a corner of the shack, rolled, kicked twice and was still. Rod, who knew how hard it was to kill a man, leaned over and fired a third bullet into the back of his neck.

He pulled the worn sleeping bag from under the cot, got the corpse into it, and zipped it up. He dragged the bundle out into the sunshine, through the scrabbly woods to the deep pit he had dug that morning. He dumped the body and filled in the grave.

Finished, he roughed the earth, scattered some dead branches around. Then he threw the shovel and the murder weapon into the river. He went back into the shack and poured kerosene onto the small bloodstains on the wooden floor.

It was a sloppy job and he knew it. But he didn't care. He just didn't care. There were two beers left, and he drank those before he drove Brother Nabisco's clunker deep into the woods and left it there to rust. Then he got into his own car and started home to the nation's capital.

JUNE 16, 1992

Senator Dundee hadn't been lying when he told Ruth Blohm there were 'many, many bases' he had to touch before deciding whether or not to ask Ann Harding to be his running mate.

They included the old cronies who had provided seed money for his campaign. Political leaders with clout in several pivotal states. Chiefs of PACs who might come up with funds. A few important lobbyists. And one or two sympathetic journalists.

For more than a month Dundee sought their counsel. They were all men, and they all could be trusted to keep their yaps shut. The last thing in the world he wanted was a leak to the media.

The reaction, to the senator's amazement, was generally in favor of trying to work a deal with Ann Harding. But Dundee shouldn't have been surprised; the men he consulted were supreme pragmatists.

They knew very well that Dundee was in trouble, and without a dramatic change-around, his campaign was going down the drain. The feminist cause had nothing to do with it. All successful politicians are Faustian. So they urged Dundee to embrace the devil.

There was not unanimous approval. Many of the older, conservative pols threatened violent opposition if he ran on a manwoman ticket. The most outraged was H. Fairchild Curtiss. The senator was forced to listen to a ten-minute lecture in the Imperial Club.

He endured Curtiss' jeremiad in silence. It was then that he came to his final decision – on no other grounds than what this bastardly banker wanted was bad for the senator, bad for the party, and bad for the country – in that order. When Curtiss ran out of gas, Dundee rose to his feet.

'Sir,' he said, 'with all due respect, you're full of shit. I

399

don't know what world you live in, but it's not my world or the world I see around me. You can chop down the money tree; that's your prerogative. If you want to see all the bucks you and your asshole buddies have given me go down the crapper, that's your choice. But if you want to go with a winner, and enjoy all the goodies I can toss your way once I'm in the White House, you'll swallow all your prejudices and stick with me on this. I'm going to grab the brass ring, and if you're not on the merry-go-round with me, fuck you, H. Fairchild Curtiss.'

It was, he later told his wife proudly, 'my finest hour.'

He found out from Ruth Blohm that Ann Harding lived little more than a half-mile away in Spring Valley. He had a secretary call Ann at WDC headquarters, then switch the call to his private line.

'Mrs Harding?'

'Yes.'

'This is Senator Lemuel K. Dundee. How are you today, ma'am?'

'Very well, thank you.'

'Mrs Harding, we've never met, but I understand we're practically next-door neighbors. I have a matter of some importance I'd like to discuss with you, and I wondered if I might prevail upon you to visit me and my bride at our home.'

Her response was smooth and immediate.

'That's very kind of you, Senator. But I have a young son I like to spend as much time with as possible. I'd be happy to welcome you to *my* home.'

Dundee grinned at the phone. The woman was a born politician: He wants something; let him come to me.

'Why, I'd surely appreciate that, Mrs Harding,' he said in his most sincere, cow-flop accent. 'I've heard so much about you and admired the really fine talks you've given on the TV, I felt I wanted to meet you in person. We might do some good for each other.'

She ignored that. 'Tuesday evening at nine o'clock,' she

400

said crisply. 'Will that be satisfactory?'

'Just grand.'

'You have my home address?'

'I surely do, Mrs Harding, and I thank you for your kindness.'

They met on June 16. Ann sent Rod and Jeff to the movies, promising to tell her husband all about it later. She wore a severe tailored suit of pin-striped flannel, with a ruffled blouse. No makeup and no jewelry.

He was more dignified and impressive than she had expected. And handsomer. His thick white hair was artfully coiffed. He was dressed conservatively in a three-piece suit of raw black silk, and wore a small, polka-dotted bowtie that gave him an almost professorial air.

'Senator,' she said, after they had exchanged greetings and he was seated, 'may I get you a drink?'

'Thank you, no,' he said with a forgiving smile. 'I rarely partake.'

Bull*shit*! she thought.

'First of all, Mrs Harding, I must tell you what a pleasure it is to meet you in person. I've been a fan of yours for some time. I consider you one of the most effective public-speakers in the country.'

'Oh?' she said, annoyed because his flattery was getting to her. 'From a man of your experience, that means something. Was there any one speech you particularly liked?'

'Your address to the NWU convention last year,' he said glibly. 'I thought that was splendid.'

She realized this son of a bitch had done his homework.

'You're very kind,' she murmured.

'And second,' he went on, 'I want to express to you my heartfelt condolences on the untimely death of your sister. The loss of Molly Turner was a tragedy for the entire nation.'

Ann nodded, turning her wedding band on her finger.

'I'm a plain-speaking man, Mrs Harding,' Dundee said, leaning forward earnestly. 'I just don't believe in beating

401

around the bush. So I've got to say that you and I have been savaging each other something fierce, and I can't see where it's been benefiting either of us.'

'We have differing opinions, Senator. On some very important issues.'

He sat back. 'No, ma'am. There I think you're wrong. I believe in women's rights with all my heart and all my soul. My differences with your sister concerned the most effective way of getting those rights. Mrs Harding, it's been said that politics is the art of the possible. I'm a child of the Senate, and I know very well how slow, bumbling, and frustrating the political system can be. I also know it's the best way yet devised to get things done and bring about needed changes in our society if we want to avoid anarchy. Don't you agree?'

'To some extent,' she said cautiously. 'I agree that legislative methods to redress wrongs are to be preferred. But when justice is not forthcoming, pressures must be brought to bear. Our leaders must be shown that women's wants are unmet and women's anger is deep. That is why my sister adopted militant tactics.'

'And do you approve of those violent methods, Mrs Harding?'

'It's a question of timing,' she argued. 'I think my sister was exactly right in pursuing the course she did at the time she did. She succeeded in raising the consciousness of the nation. But I think she made her point, and it is now time for the WDC and other women's organizations to switch to more traditional methods of achieving what we seek.'

'I am happy to hear you say that. You are a very perceptive woman, and I agree with you completely.'

The senator paused, linked his fingers, looked down at them. Then he raised his eyes slowly to stare at Ann Harding.

'As you know, I am an active candidate for my party's nomination for President of the United States. Mrs Harding, I would like you to join my crusade and run with me

402

as the vicepresidential candidate.'

Ann blinked once, but her expression didn't change. There was silence a moment. Then:

'I sincerely believe,' Dundee continued, 'that together we will stand an excellent chance of winning the nomination in July and going on to take the November election.'

'I think,' Ann said, 'this may be a good time for a drink. Do you concur, Senator?'

'A small libation would not be inopportune,' he said in such a wry manner, mocking his own orotundity, that she found herself laughing.

'Bourbon?' she asked.

'However did you know?'

She brought him a healthy belt of sour mash with water on the side. A vodka on rocks for her. They raised their glasses to each other in a silent toast, and sipped.

'Mighty fine,' he said. 'Mrs Harding, I'm going to be absolutely honest with you. I have – '

'Wait, wait,' she said, holding up a palm. 'My mother taught me that when a man says, "I'm going to be absolutely honest with you," it's time to hang on to your wallet.'

'Well . . . yeah,' he said, grinning. 'I didn't figure your momma raised you to be an idiot. Okay, let me speak my piece, and you separate the wheat from the chaff. Right now I've got adequate funding. I can go down to that Miami convention, open me a big hospitality suite, sweeten up the reporters, and charm the pants off every delegate in sight – you should excuse the expression. And it's not going to do me a damned-all bit of good.'

She sat back, relaxed. 'You're in deep trouble,' she said. 'You're going to lose the women's vote. The state delegations know that. They want to go with a winner. You'll never get the nomination.'

'I'm a betting man,' he said. 'There's a slim chance I can pull it off by myself, but I don't like the odds. If I had you on my team, I'd clobber them. That's the long and short of it.'

'I can't deliver the women's vote,' she said. 'You know that. There are millions of female voters with millions of opinions.'

'Of course I know that. But with you on my side, enough women will swing to make the difference between winning and losing. Men, too. The nomination is the first hurdle. Once we're over that, we can concentrate on the November election. I'm convinced that you and I can go all the way.'

'In other words,' she said, 'you want me to pull your chestnuts from the fire.'

He looked at her, took a gulp of his bourbon. 'Yes,' he said. 'Look,' he went on, 'I didn't expect you'd consider this because you like the way I part my hair or because I'm such a swell guy. I want you to think of this as an opportunity. Think of what you could do for women's rights as vice president. That's something, isn't it? Isn't it worth the gamble? What's the worst thing that could happen? We'll be defeated. But a woman will have run for the office of vice president. The best thing is that you and I will end up running the country.'

They stared at each other a moment.

'You're a good salesman, Senator,' she said.

'Every politician is,' he said. 'And do you think I'd ask for your help if I thought you were a dummy who didn't have the potential to do a good job? I've been following your career. I know you can make a hell of a record in the history books.'

She pondered a moment. 'You've talked this over with your, ah, moneymen and party leaders?'

He nodded. 'I have, and they'll go along.'

'They've got no choice,' she said.

'The more you talk,' he said, 'the more I admire you. You're absolutely right; they've got no choice.'

She drew a deep breath. 'I'm not going to give you an answer this minute.'

'Of course not. Didn't expect you to.'

'There are people I have to speak to, too.'

404

'Sure. I understand that. But you're not turning me down this minute either.'

'Nooo,' she said slowly, 'I'm not doing that. But if I decide to save your ass, Senator, you're going to have to pay for it.'

He tilted back his head and laughed heartily. 'Oh God,' he spluttered. 'You and I would make a great team. We think alike.'

'Well . . .' she said, 'we'll see. I'll get back to you as soon as I can.'

'The sooner the better,' he said.'The convention opens on July twentieth. And if you're going to come in, the announcement will have to be made at least two weeks before that for maximum media effect.'

'I understand. And thank you for the offer.'

'My honor, ma'am,' he said. He finished his drink, put the glass aside. He rose and made a courtly little bow. 'Whatever you decide, I want to tell you it's been a down-right pleasure talking to you.'

'Thank you,' she said faintly.

The moment he was out of the house, she called Virginia Terwilliger in Baltimore.

'Ginny?' she said.'Can you come down to DC tomorrow morning? Something important we've got to talk about.'

Terwilliger picked up on the urgency in her voice. 'Bad news?' she asked anxiously.

'No,' Ann Harding said.'Good. I think.'

JULY 5, 1992

Ann Harding went through the same 'touching the bases' process as the senator. She consulted with Virginia Terwilliger and every other member of the WDC Executive Board. She sought the counsel of state chapter presidents and the chief executive officers of other women's organizations. She spoke with congresswomen, business execu-

405

tives, magazine editors, and feminist writers.

The main opposition came from colonels of WDC regiments and the cadre of militant sisters whose loyalty remained with Molly Turner. 'No compromise with the enemy' seemed to be their rallying cry, and they were vociferous in their total rejection of any deal with Dundee, no matter how advantageous it might prove to be to the WDC.

Ann Harding listened to everyone. When she came to her decision, it happened suddenly, after a conversation with one individual – just as Lemuel Dundee had made up his mind after his squabble with H. Fairchild Curtiss.

In her swing around the country, Ann visited Agatha Rockridge, the 'grand old lady' of the WDC and president of the South Dakota chapter. She was an elderly woman, tall, drawn, with a face like a walnut and hands that had done everything. But her hard, sparkling sapphire eyes looked closely at the world and judged.

Ann explained Dundee's offer, and the choice she now faced.

'I'm sure I can get something from him,' she said. 'He's hurting and needs the women's vote. I won't get everything we want, I suppose – maybe half a loaf. How do you feel about it, Agatha?'

'Half a loaf?' the older woman said, smiling. 'Oh honey, that's the story of every woman's life. You take half a loaf or even one-tenth of a loaf. You keep doing that and sooner or later you've got yourself a nice piece of bread.'

That's when Ann Harding made up her mind. She returned to Washington, DC, and met with Virginia Terwilliger in an all-day argumentative, sometimes rancorous conference. They finally agreed on a two-page letter of intent to be signed by Senator Dundee. The 'contract' including the following:

– Any vacancies that occurred on the Supreme Court during Dundee's tenure of office were to be filled by women.

– Women would be awarded a minimum of three cabinet posts.

– At least 50 percent of the White House staff would be women, including positions of executive authority. One woman would be a member of the President's close personal staff.

– The number of female ambassadors would be increased until women numbered at least 50 percent of US overseas representatives.

– A woman would be appointed to the Joint Chiefs of Staff.

– A woman would be nominated to head the Federal Reserve Bank.

'I don't think he'll go for all that,' Ann Harding said doubtfully.

'Of course he won't,' Terwilliger said.'But don't just stamp your foot and pout. Fight him. Get as much as you can.'

'I know,' Ann said, sighing.'Half a loaf . . .'

She called the senator's office and set up an appointment. This time she agreed to meet him at his home.

Rod Harding sat on the edge of the bed, smoking a pipe. The bathroom door opened; his wife came out in a billow of steam. A big towel was knotted about her. She gave him a brief smile.

She sat at the vanity, took off her shower cap, began to unpin her hair. Her movements loosened the towel. It fell away, and he saw her strong back. She began to brush her hair.

He set his pipe aside, went over and put his hands on the muscles between her neck and shoulders. He squeezed softly.

'My God, hon,' he said.'You're all tightened up. Hard as a rock.'

He began to massage her shoulders, kneading the flesh gently.

'That feels good,' she said. 'Don't stop.'

'I didn't intend to,' he said, leaning forward to sniff her powdery scent. 'How you doing on time?'

'It's set for nine o'clock.'

'You're in good shape,' he assured her. 'Want me to drive you over?'

'No,' she said, 'I'll go alone. I don't know how long I'll be there, and I don't want you to wait or have to call you to pick me up. And if the whole thing falls through, I don't want to have to ask him to drive me home.'

'It won't fall through. I guarantee it. He needs you more than you need him. Just keep remembering that.'

She leaned forward to peer in the mirror as she applied her makeup. He ran his fingertips across her bent back.

'You're getting me all excited,' she said.

'Me, too,' he said throatily. 'Hurry home.'

She started on her eye shadow.

'Anyone hear from Todhunter Clark?' she asked.

'Not a word,' he said casually, moving away from her.

'I don't understand it. Him going off like that. Not even saying goodbye to Jeff. Lucille Jackson can't understand it either.'

'Well, honey, he always was a footloose kind of guy. And a real violence freak. When Molly was killed, I think he realized there was no need here anymore for his particular talents. So he took off.'

'I suppose,' she said, sighing. 'Still . . .'

'You got more to worry about than Brother Nabisco,' he said, returning to kiss the back of her neck.

'I know. Now leave me alone so I can get dressed.'

He went back to the bed and relighted his pipe. He watched his wife dress, admiring her lovely, solid body and the way she moved. When she put on her bra, she leaned forward to cup her heavy breasts. He stared; he couldn't get enough of her.

'Do me a favor, Rod?'

'Sure, hon.'

'I want to rehearse this thing. You make believe you're Senator Dundee. I've just shown you that letter of intent I want you to sign. Now you pretend you're him. Okay? You read the letter. Then what do you say?'

'Mrs Harding, you really want me to sign this piece of shit?'

'If you want to get nominated and elected, Senator.'

'But this is ridiculous. If it ever gets out, I'm finished.'

'It won't get out. It's a single letter – no copies. You sign it and I keep it. If you stick to your promises, no one will ever know.'

'I can't go along with all this, and you know it. A woman on the Joint Chiefs of Staff? That's impossible.'

'Why impossible? There are some very qualified women in the armed forces.'

They continued this play as Ann dressed, with Rod acting the role of an indignant, irascible Senator Dundee, fighting to dilute the demands of the agreement he was being asked to sign. Ann replied, sometimes pausing to make her answers milder or stronger as she had second thoughts.

She was putting on a choker of small cultured pearls when she said:

'All right, hon, I think I've got it straight now. I'll be firm, but not stubborn. I'll give in when I have to, but not before.'

'You give a little, you get a little,' he said. 'What's with the fancy getup?'

She had donned a sleeveless sheath of black silk crepe, cut low enough to show cleavage. Gunmetal pantyhose made her legs seem slimmer. She had gone heavy on the makeup and perfume.

'The first time I met him I wore a tailored suit. All business. The lady executive. I think he was impressed. But I've been doing some research on the bum in the past few weeks. He's got the reputation of being a boozer and a womanizer. I'm hoping this outfit may fuddle his brains just enough so he gives me more than he intended to.'

'You'll scam the pants off him,' her husband said, smiling.

She stood before him. 'Do I look all right?'

He stood close to her and gripped her bare arms lightly. He stared into her eyes.

'You're beautiful,' he said. 'Just fantastic.'

'Everything's fine with us now, isn't it, Rod?'

'Couldn't be finer.' He leaned forward to kiss the tip of her nose.

She pulled away, then moved about the bedroom, picking up her purse and gloves. She checked to make certain she had the letter of intent.

'Sweetheart, I'm scared,' she said.

'Nah. You've never been scared in your life. You're a very gutsy lady.'

'Not scared about this meeting with Dundee. But what if he goes all the way and gets elected, and I end up vice president. That's what scares me. What the hell do I know about national politics and foreign affairs?'

'You'll learn,' he told her.

She considered that a moment. 'You're right. I always have been a quick study. Well . . . wish me luck.'

He came close to her again. They embraced tightly.

'I wish you all the luck in the world,' he whispered.

'You think I'm doing the right thing, Rod?'

'Of course you are.'

'The first woman vice president – that'd be something, wouldn't it?'

'Oh, honey,' he said with a wolfish grin, touching her cheek. 'Being vice president could just be the start. Dundee's not going to be President forever.'

She stared at him thoughtfully. 'Uh-huh,' she said, nodding. 'Why, he might not even live out his first term. You never know.'

410

THE CASE OF LUCY B.

by Lawrence Sanders

The three families were not unusual by the standards of Florida's Gold Coast. Affluently sun-warmed in their luxury beach-side homes, tanned and healthy as 100% pure fruit juice, they competed in conspicuous informality, drinking and partying together, changing partners.

The men lived in a world of smart business deals – deals that were only wrong if they didn't work out. Even if the business was pornography and behind it lurked the ice-smooth killers of organised crime.

The women, lithe and predatory, indulged their appetites for men, possessions and influence.

They all knew *they* were smart enough to keep ahead of the game and that *they* would never be among the losers in life.

Until things started to go wrong. Badly wrong. Until, blow by blow, they came to realise that they themselves, and even their children, could be the victims of their own casual conceit and greed. That the sun-and-surf surface of their world could collapse into quicksands of sudden violence and slow despair.

NEW ENGLISH LIBRARY

THE SEDUCTION OF PETER S.

by Lawrence Sanders

Peter S. was not corrupt from birth.

Childhood, adolescence, early manhood, he'd made the usual compromises, was never some pure and spotless moral paragon. But he'd been a pretty reasonable human being.

The corruption came later.

Too long in New York, struggling too long as an out-of-work actor, he was past the point where he could afford to be fussy. The job on offer would pay and pay well. He'd been trained as a performer and one performance is much like another. Like a moral tranquilliser, a little luxury would soothe away all doubts.

So the corruption began and grew, eating away at him. Others noticed. Outraged, his girlfriend rejected him. Friends edged away. The professionally, criminally corrupt began to gather round him. The Mob was interested . . .

NEW ENGLISH LIBRARY

THE YOUNG LIONS

by Irwin Shaw

Hailed as 'the outstanding novel to come out of World War II', *The Young Lions* begins during the troubled peace of 1938, and follows the fortunes of three very different men through the six tumultuous years to come.

Noah Akerman, trying to prove his manhood in a world gone mad, clutches at a forbidden woman and a destiny he dare not imagine.

Michael Whitacre, desperately trying to retrieve his self-respect, squanders his talents in a world of glitter and glamour.

A born hero, Christian Diestl is handsome, fearless, and never takes no for an answer.

'The finest of all the novels of the last war . . . unlike Norman Mailer, Irwin Shaw does not reduce his soldiers to the sub-human level; all the time we see them dually, both as fighting men, and ordinary citizens. We recognise them. We know their faces.'

Daily Telegraph

'Packed with incident, with credible versions of Berlin as the bombs fall and the morale crumbles, of desert warfare brilliantly illuminated, of simple love . . . of social history and human courage . . . Engrossing and heartening.'

Tribune

'Brilliant: Leaves the reader with a deeper understanding of the present world. No novel can be asked to accomplish more.'

New York Times

NEW ENGLISH LIBRARY

THE BETSY

by Harold Robbins

The first major novel of the car industry.

Love, hate, sex, ambition – the ingredients of a fabulous novel from the world's most widely read author.

THE BETSY tells an unforgettable story of the lives and loves, the men and women, behind an automobile conglomerate and its make-or-break attempt to create a totally new car.

'Harold Robbins, perhaps the biggest bestseller of them all, has lost nothing of his touch in his new novel. It's full of power, sex, action, vintage Robbins'

Sunday Mirror

NEW ENGLISH LIBRARY

LAWRENCE SANDERS

THE CASE OF LUCY B.   £2.50

THE SEDUCTION OF PETER S.   £2.50

THE PASSION OF MOLLY T.   £2.25

All these books are available at your local bookshop or newsagent, or can be ordered direct from the publisher. Just tick the titles you want and fill in the form below.

Prices and availability subject to change without notice.

NEL BOOKS, P.O. Box 11, Falmouth, Cornwall.

Please send cheque or postal order, and allow the following for postage and packing:

U.K. – 55p for one book, plus 22p for the second book, and 14p for each additional book ordered up to a £1.75 maximum.

B.F.P.O. and EIRE – 55p for the first book, plus 22p for the second book, and 14p per copy for the next 7 books, 8p per book thereafter.

OTHER OVERSEAS CUSTOMERS – £1.00 for the first book, plus 25p per copy for each additional book.

Name ....

Address ....

....